Collateral Risk

by

Gwenan Haines

Collateral Risk

Cover Art by *Kim Mendoza*

The Wild Rose Press, Inc.
PO Box 708
Adams Basin, NY 14410-0708
Visit us at www.thewildrosepress.com

Publishing History
First Crimson Rose Edition, 2017
Print ISBN 978-1-5092-1728-1
Digital ISBN 978-1-5092-1729-8

Published in the United States of America

Mia slipped her phone into her pants pocket and walked toward them, her face drawn. Nick wondered if her friend had been upset about Mia's oversight with the parrots but dismissed the idea. No, there was something else.

He stood unmoving, unsure whether he should wait and try to find out what was bothering her or excuse himself so she could talk to her mother. She reached them before he'd decided, which he supposed was its own decision.

"Mom, I've got to go. I'm sorry."

Angela reached out and caught her daughter in a tight embrace. "What is it, honey?" she asked, studying her daughter's face. "What's happened?"

"It's Mike."

Apparently Angela's expression was as blank as his own. Hadn't she mentioned a Mike before? She had said she was trying to get in touch with him and he'd felt a stab of jealousy. Yeah, it was definitely coming back to him.

"My partner at the Institute. We had…kind of a falling out over the weekend. He didn't show up for work today and I started worrying but I kept telling myself I was being paranoid."

"Did something happen to him?" Angela asked. "Is he sick?"

Mia shook her head. "Not sick. Dead."

Praise for Gwenan Haines

"As a reader, I want my senses to sizzle with spine quivering suspense, intrigue, romance and a ghost or two every once in a while. Ms. Haines is a writer with the flair and grace to give the imagination of the grown and sexy brain sensors a jump start."

~*Blackraven's Reviews*

~*~

"I for one will be reading everything from Gwenan Haines, now that I have discovered her."

~*S.J. Dagg*

~*~

"Haines is a fantastic writer."

~*Diana, The Offbeat Vagabond*

~*~

"Author Gwenan Haines was a new-to-me author, and oh wow, am I ever glad I found her."

~*Romance with a Bite*

Dedication

For my mother

Prologue

Bucharest, Romania

Thank God for soundproof rooms.

Otherwise, he'd definitely be hearing from the neighbors. Not that he didn't like heavy metal music. He couldn't remember how many classes he'd spent zoned out to the sound of Metallica back in high school, slumped in the back row with a single earphone surreptitiously inserted. Or maybe not so surreptitiously. Half the teachers in East Boston High had been so stressed out they didn't give a damn whether the fringe students, as he liked to think of himself, were learning anything or not. They just wanted to get through another day with their psyches still intact.

He could say the same for Gregori Chudnovsky, though the outcome wasn't looking so good for the middle-aged Ukrainian with the platinum blond comb-over. For one thing, it was pretty clear Chudnovsky didn't appreciate heavy metal, even after forty-eight hours of sensory deprivation. At least not Dope's "Take Your Best Shot," which he'd blasted into the interrogation room at full volume for the past six hours. To spice things up he'd interspersed it with unannounced bouts of the Meow Mix jingle. By his count, the jingle must've played maybe a hundred times

1

or so.

Not that he was counting, or even listening at all. Luckily for him, he'd been trained to block all that out. From the looks of it, Chudnovsky had missed that seminar at terrorist camp. He lay handcuffed to the metal cot in the windowless room, his eyes flicking to the locked door, then to the burnt umber walls, then back to the door again. Every few minutes he would strain against the handcuffs and fall back on the metal springs, his shirt wet with perspiration.

Such a shame.

The CIA agent hit mute on the iPad and smiled. "I hate to interrupt your auditory pleasure, but I thought maybe we could have a little chat."

"Go fuck yourself."

"It certainly does make it easier, you being familiar with the language and all."

"Fuck you. That's all you're gonna get outa me." Chudnovsky spat the words, then added a final epithet for good measure. "Asshole."

He hit the play button and cranked the speaker volume to its highest level. "Hard to get." He opened the door and stood on the threshold, a smile quirking his lips. "I like that."

Two hours later, he returned to find Chudnovsky lying motionless on the cot with his eyes closed. A ripple of panic surged through him until he saw the Ukrainian's chest rise. He crossed to the iPod and hit stop. The Meow Mix jingle ended in mid-meow. For a full five minutes he didn't speak, aware that silence could be even more unsettling than a barrage of cat sounds.

He pulled a metal chair away from the wall and sat

facing Chudnovsky, who had opened his eyes and was staring at the ceiling. "It's gonna get a lot worse than this if you don't tell me what the hell was going on up there."

"How should I know? People get sick, they die. It's an act of nature and that's all. You want to make it something more, go ahead."

"Three hundred twenty-eight dead in two weeks. An entire village of people whose organs suddenly started shutting down, whose eyes turned blood red and whose minds ended up as Silly String. In Siberia, I might add. One of the most isolated villages you could ever imagine. That's not an act of nature. Somebody made that happen."

Chudnovsky made a clicking sound with his tongue. "Some kind of flu."

"How it did get there?" He leaned forward so that his arms were draped over the back of the chair, his hands clasped a little too tightly. "And why did somebody put it there in the first place—that's the question that's really got me curious. Why the hell would somebody decide to kill off a bunch of old Russians in the most gruesome, most painful way possible?"

Chudnovsky laughed. "Wouldn't you like to know."

He shot up out of the chair and hurled it across the room. Before the Ukrainian stopped laughing, he threw a dark sack over Chudnovsky's head and smacked him hard across the temple with his Glock. "Yeah, as a matter of fact I would. And you're gonna tell me."

Silence.

He waited. He could wait a long time if he had to.

God knows he'd waited long enough in prisons before, when he was on the other side of the questioning. But just to speed things up, he hit Chudnovsky in the temple again.

Chudnovsky moaned but didn't say anything. Clearly, this wasn't his first interrogation. The guy was holding up better than he would've expected. And he was losing patience. He leaned over Chudnovsky and punched him hard in the gut, forcing his back into the metal springs on the cot.

Another moan.

A drop of blood splashed onto the floor. He punched the Ukrainian again, harder this time. He stood over the hooded man, fighting to catch his breath. The side of the sack was a darker shade of black where the gun had made contact with Chudnovsky's temple.

"Why did they die?"

"I don't know." The muffled voice didn't waver.

Another blow to the side of the head. "Why did they die?"

"I already told you I don't know."

Another blow. "I'm getting tired of asking nicely."

"It was a test." Chudnovsky's voice was so soft beneath the sack he almost didn't realize the man had spoken.

He leaned down over the Ukrainian, who stank of sweat and blood and urine. "What kind of test?"

No answer. The Ukrainian was breathing hard, his head thrashing from side to side.

"What kind of test?" He was screaming, his face inches away from the sack. His voice sounded distant to him, unlike his own. As if someone else were asking the questions. For the first time since he'd brought in the Ukrainian, he felt afraid.

He couldn't afford to fuck up, not again. Was anybody watching?

Nobody was watching. There were no windows, no cameras. The Agency had learned *something* from Abu Graib. It was only the two of them. Still, he felt uneasy. Since information about black sites had hit the press, everybody was pussy-footing around like a bunch of sissies. But they were happy enough when he got them what they wanted.

Except for the last time. They hadn't been happy then.

Well, that was only bad judgment on his part. A stupid mistake. It wouldn't happen again. He'd get their information and everything would be okay. Venter would start using him again, liked he used to.

"Please let me go." Chudnovsky choked out the words. "My arm hurts."

"Your arm hurts," he said sarcastically. "Gee, I'm sorry. Everybody in Krasnoyarsk dies in agony, and you've got a sore arm. How sad."

"I don't know anything."

"You sure about that?"

Pause.

He could almost see the Ukrainian's mind working, trying to find a way out, like a rat in a maze. "They wanted to see if it worked." Chudnovsky broke off and sucked in a sharp breath.

"To see if what worked? Some kind of drug? A virus or some kind of chemical?"

From inside the sack, Chudnovsky's breath came in labored gasps. His throat made little whistling sounds every time he inhaled. "I can't breathe."

"It's just anxiety." The agent wasn't sure if the gurgling was laughter or vomit. *Better not be vomit.* He suppressed a tic of panic. "Tell me what I want to know, and the hood comes off. It all stops."

The gasps were getting louder. "Fuck…you."

He was on him then. His hand balled itself into a fist and went straight for Chudnovsky's face, breaking the nose on impact. The whistling sound was loud now, too loud, but he couldn't stop his fist.

"Tell me what it was!" he shouted. "Tell me where they got it!"

"A…failed…test."

"What do you mean a failed test," he cried, grabbing the hood and pulling Chudnovsky close to his face. "Everybody in a village dies and that's a failure?"

"The children…" The wheezing was slower now, more drawn out and shallow. "The children…survived."

"You are one sad, sorry piece of shit," he said, his voice falling to a whisper. "You know that." He let go of the hood, and the Ukrainian fell back onto the metal springs, still gasping for air. The fist that he knew belonged to him smashed into Chudnovsky's cloaked face at the place where his nose had been.

The Ukrainian's body convulsed and went slack. He stood frozen above him, his hand poised in mid-air. He didn't know what to do. Start CPR? Wait? Run out into the corridor and call for help?

No, he couldn't call for help. If he did that…

He pulled off the sack and placed his hands on Chudnovsky's chest. The guy's face was an ominous shade of blue beneath the blood and bruises. He leaned down and blew air into the Ukrainian's lips. At the taste

6

of blood and vomit, his stomach turned. He didn't stop though. He kept pumping.

Ten minutes later he stopped. Chudnovsky lay still on the cot, his swollen face a mess of color. The Ukrainian wasn't coming back. He needed to tell somebody. He needed to wash the filth off his own face and arms.

He walked over to the chair and righted it. He sat down with his arms crossed over the back and rested his chin on his arms. He didn't want to think.

Twenty minutes later, the steel door swung open and Venter strode toward Chudnovsky's body. "What the hell's been going on in here?" He didn't as much as look in the agent's direction. Venter lifted the Ukrainian's wrist and felt for a pulse.

"He's dead," the agent said.

Venter glanced over his shoulder at him. "Thanks for letting me know."

He didn't smile. His mind searched for the right words, the words that would explain everything and make Venter understand. The words that would make it all right.

Venter turned and removed the glove that had touched the terrorist then threw it in the trash can next to the door. "Our best shot at finding out what happened, and you killed him."

"It was an accident," he said, trying to keep his voice level. "He wasn't cooperating."

The CIA station chief's expression was unreadable. "This isn't the first time you've fucked up."

"That was—" His voice trailed off.

"What?" Venter asked mildly. "An accident too?"

"A mistake," he said. "It won't happen again."

"You're right," Venter said. "It won't happen again. I want you on the next plane out of here. You can report for debriefing when you get to D.C. Keep your mouth shut, and there shouldn't be any problems."

"You're putting me on leave?"

A beat.

Venter's ice-blue eyes met his. "On permanent leave."

"You're firing me?"

"There's no shame in it. You've done good work. But it's time for you to get into something else. Start a security firm, work as a contractor, there's lots of opportunities for somebody with your...experience. I can't count on you like I used to. And I can't have any more corpses on my hands. We're not in Post 9/11 anymore. I've got people breathing down my neck if some ISIS suicide bomber gets a scratch on his big toe."

Venter's gaze went to the darkened window, as if he could see past it onto the ordinary street outside. Unlike most black sites, the Bucharest building was located in the middle of the city. It didn't look like a CIA interrogation site, it looked like a run-down DMV office.

"Krasnoyarsk was only the beginning. That's what Chudnovsky said," he told his former boss, hating the desperation in his voice. "I need to be in on this. I think they're planning something in the U.S. Something big."

"He said that?"

"No."

Another beat.

"But he would have if—"

"—if he'd lived," Venter finished for him.

8

He nodded. What else was there to do?

"And now we'll never know the rest," Venter said.

"Not from Chudnovsky. But there are others."

Venter pressed his lips together. The two of them stood there a few more seconds, the dead body between them. Finally, Venter stuck out his hand. "I'm sorry to see you go. Good—"

The CIA station chief never got the chance to finish.

The agent turned away, slamming the door behind him. As he walked down the corridor and out into the frigid air, he repeated Chudnovsky's words as if they were some kind of terrorist mantra. *Only a test only a test only a test.* Shoving his hands into his coat pockets, he headed toward the heart of the city.

It wasn't too late. He would know the rest.

Chapter 1

One year later

"Dammit!"

Mia Lindgren winced as the bagel knife sliced her fingertip. She wrapped the cut in a napkin and hurried over to the sink, turning on the tap and thrusting her pointer finger into the stream of cool water. Morning sunlight poured through the kitchen windows, warming her face and reminding her how late she already was. After a minute or so, she pulled her finger out of the water and inspected it. The cut was about a quarter of an inch long, not very deep. Nothing to get worked up about.

She crossed from the kitchen to the bathroom and opened the medicine cabinet, wondering if she would ever be able to cut herself and not freak out. For the past year she'd slipped into panic mode whenever she got so much as a paper cut. She could only imagine what would happen if she ended up with a scraped knee. All that exposed skin would leave her sleepless for a week.

You were the one who signed up for this.

She loved her work, but she still questioned her choice even though three years had passed since she first crossed the threshold of the Institute for Research of Infectious Diseases in Somersville, Maryland. Her friends, her mother, her stepsister, and just about everybody else she knew told her she was crazy to work there. She could still hear Ashley's horrified tone on the other end of the line when she'd called Burnleigh Hall to tell her half-sister the news.

"So you *want* to work with Ebola?" Ashley had asked, forgetting to season her tone with the usual dose of teenage cynicism. "Like, on purpose?"

Mia grinned at the memory as she dabbed antibiotic ointment onto the cut and covered it with a Band-Aid. Not exactly germ-proof, but it would do the trick. Anyway, it wasn't as if she didn't have a hermetically sealed Hazmat suit between her and the deadly viruses she studied. That should do a lot more than a Band-Aid in terms of keeping her alive. If anything, the Institute went overboard when it came to safety measures. There was nothing to worry about.

Other than being late. She glanced at the clock then headed back toward the kitchen and deposited her less-than-hygienic bagel into the trash can.

8:03 a.m., three minutes behind schedule.

Enough time to grab a granola bar and feed Dante, but that was about it. She could forget about applying any make-up, though that was a ritual she could easily dispense with. No need to look pretty while analyzing a new smallpox strain. She regretted that she wouldn't have time to look in on Nailini's parrots like she'd promised.

But Mia didn't have a choice. Otherwise Mike would be stuck waiting around for her in Biolevel-4, and he was already pretty upset with her. Nothing like leaving a guy stranded in a biohazard zone of the highest order to get him even more worked up than he already was.

Not that she could blame him.

The Iambs canister in the pantry was half empty. Mia made a mental note to stock up while emptying two and two-thirds scoopfuls of dog food into Dante's bowl and setting it down on the kitchen floor.

"Come and get it," she called out just as her red-and-white Siberian husky appeared in the doorway and bounded over to his food. Luckily he wasn't scheduled for doggie daycare that morning because if he had been no way would she make it on time, parrots or no parrots.

She just hoped last night's run had been enough to tire Dante out. At least a little. One thing Mia had learned since Nailini had convinced her to adopt the abandoned husky from her animal clinic was that for a husky a five-mile run was about as taxing as a stroll to the end of the driveway would be for other dogs.

Dante was definitely not other dogs. She had the decimated throw pillows to prove it. He was cute though, she had to give him that. Even if he had eaten her pricey whitening toothpaste the week before.

In the entryway, Dante's crate gleamed invitingly. She walked past it and grabbed her keys off the hook next to the door. Much as she knew the benefits of crating, she could never bear to leave him in it for an entire day. At nearly a hundred pounds, he was too powerful and too full of energy for her to do that to him. And she couldn't afford daycare five days a week, at least not yet.

She stood in the entryway, eyeing the three survivor pillows lined up at perfectly spaced intervals across the living room couch. It struck her that her choice of a pet was just as nonsensical as her choice of profession. What did a hyper-organized geek want with a dog whose sole purpose in life seemed to be wreaking havoc on her home? And how could somebody who thrived on control deal with pathogens that created chaos wherever they turned up?

Or maybe her choices weren't that unlikely, after all. Because it didn't matter how much time passed. She would always be that same little girl, trying to clean up the mess she'd made—the mess no amount of cleaning would ever fix.

Mia locked the front door and hurried down the steps of her rambling Victorian house. *Something else to fix*, she thought, forcing her mind to turn back from the destination it was heading toward. After nearly two decades of denial she'd gotten good at steering clear of the past—maybe too good.

As if on cue, her smartphone buzzed with a message from her mother.

Eleven days and counting! Can't wait to see you tonight!

She climbed into her Subaru Outback and turned on the ignition, texting back a quick reply in the affirmative. The last thing she wanted to do after a full day of working with Ebola was drive another two hours, especially under the circumstances. But she knew it would crush her mother if she didn't show. Mia owed her that much support, at least. Still, she couldn't help wishing Ashley or even her stepfather would be there. But Ashley was at Burnleigh Hall for summer school and Leonard Ward was overseas on yet another business deal. If he made it to see her mother once it would be a miracle.

Not that Mia had been a regular visitor. There was something about those kinds of places that gave her the creeps. What did it say about her, that she'd rather spend three hours autopsying a dead monkey than visit her own mother?

That you're not good at showing affection? How about just "emotions"? Kind of a blanket term, but anything narrower wouldn't really fit the bill.

Well, that was who she was and there was nothing she could do about it. She'd been distant for twenty-nine years so there was no point in changing things up now.

Which, come to think of it, may have been the reason she agreed to visit in the first place. Spending the evening with her mother gave her an excuse to avoid Mike. Of course, Mia wasn't sure he even wanted to spend time with her after what happened on Saturday. For the past month, they had spent more than a little free time together and Mike wanted it to continue.

No, not just continue. He wanted things to escalate. He wanted Mia to shift into full-throttle girlfriend mode.

The only problem was she had no intention of doing any such thing. Over the weekend after they'd spent the afternoon sailing the Chesapeake on his boat, she'd been ready to call it a day. But Mike persuaded her to catch a bite to eat and she reluctantly agreed. When they pulled into a tiny romantic place overlooking the water she had to suppress the urge to get up and run screaming for the nearest exit. She'd been blindsided and she knew it.

The worst part was that it hadn't been unbearable,

as some of her dates had been. As a team member at the Institute, Mike was one of the few people who understood her passion for deadly diseases. He got it, which was more than she could say for most of the men she'd dated over the past couple of years. There would always be a certain point during dinner when the guy would lean forward and ask what she did for a living. Followed by an unmistakable, highly predictable, highly negative, reaction. Some of them moved their hands away from hers, some actually pushed back their chairs as if she might have a few stray Ebola cells lodged under her fingernails.

Mike wasn't like that. He loved his work as much as she did, maybe even more. So when he leaned across the driver's seat on the way home from the restaurant and tried to kiss her it had been more than a little awkward.

She had winced.

It would have been bad enough if she hadn't responded but to pull away as if he were as deadly as the viruses they worked with—she had no idea how to fix things. On Sunday night she'd pulled out her cell phone at least a dozen times, only to put it back again.

What was there to say? That she felt bad he didn't seem to be taking too kindly to her *friend-zoning* him, as Ashley would say. Somehow she didn't think that would help. So she did nothing, only kept checking her cell for messages from a guy she genuinely did care about.

Just not enough.

Mia hit the accelerator as the trees blurred by, wondering if life would ever slow down. The summer was at its peak and the cloudless sky above her burned blue. Part of her longed to drive right past Somersville and spend the day walking along the shores of the Chesapeake Bay, safe from deadly pathogens and unruly emotions.

She knew she wouldn't do it and the irony of it was the deadly pathogens didn't scare her as much as the prospect of having to navigate human interactions. In less than twenty-three minutes she would walk out of her chemical decon shower, strip off her clothes and don a Hazmat suit. After that, she'd spend the next eight hours working alongside a man who probably wasn't speaking to her in a lab filled with viruses that threatened life on earth.

****

"My name is Angela Ward and I'm an alcoholic."

"Hi, Angela," everyone answered in what passed for a unified response. Angela Ward, a fifty-something blonde with perfect, unlined skin, folded her hands in her lap and graced the members of Nick Doyle's therapy group at Seahaven Rehabilitation Facility with a blindingly white smile.

It wasn't just her looks that caught everyone's attention. There was something else, a kind of Marilyn Monroe quality about her. *Charisma.* Or maybe magnetism, if there was a difference. Whatever it was, Angela's breathy voice had all eleven group therapy members sitting up in their lounge chairs.

Not everyone, Nick thought, glancing at the women in the group. Callie Jackson, an overweight chef who owned a multi-million-dollar chain of restaurants, was watching Angela with narrowed eyes, like a cat ready to pounce. Nargeeta Singh's gaze was equally distant, equally critical.

Clearly, they were immune to Angela's brand of charisma.

As for the rest of the group, mostly men, he couldn't say the same thing. Even Justin Sands of the screamo band *Shellshock* was sitting a bit straighter, his eyes fixed on Angela's ample breasts. The kid couldn't have been more than twenty-one or twenty-two and yet there he was, ready to be led to the slaughter like a lamb. Or maybe more like a tamed python with a drinking issue and a heroin problem. But ready all the same.

Hell, she could have passed for a woman in her mid-forties. Maybe even mid-*thirties. Talk about well preserved.* If he hadn't spent the better part of the past fourteen days listening to people tell the most depressing stories he'd ever heard, he would have listened as Angela Ward began explaining how she'd become a drinker. Part of him was curious to hear how a woman who obviously put that much stock in her appearance ended up as an in-patient at Seahaven. Alcohol didn't deal kindly with skin and it wasn't exactly a weight-loss tool either. Tough to maintain the cougar look when you were downing a bottle of vodka every night, though if you read the tabloids there wasn't any shortage of movie-star drunks.

Of course, vodka was his drink of choice, not hers. He had no idea what poison she'd picked. Whatever she drank and how much of it she imbibed, it was enough to land her a thirty-day tour of duty at one of the East coast's most exclusive detox centers.

It still floored him that he'd ended up there, though he couldn't say whether it was the FBI's insistence on sending him or the fact that he'd agreed that surprised him most. Well, it was more than half over. Sixteen more days and he'd be free.

Free to do what?

Absolutely nothing.

That at least was one question he could answer. Ever since his arrival at Seahaven he'd been accosted by questions—from other patients, his psychiatrist and even Father Donelan, the former Irish priest who founded the place back in the seventies.

Most of them he couldn't respond to, but for different reasons. He couldn't get into the details of his job at the FBI because counter-terrorism wasn't the kind of thing most people struggling to believe in a rosy future wanted to talk about. Not to mention that he hadn't met anybody yet with any level of security clearance, never mind his level. Granted, there did seem to be more than a few military types at the facility but as if by some unspoken agreement they steered clear of each other. Then there was the not-so-small fact that he was on leave for the next two months.

Mandatory leave.

If anything made him want to clam up about work it was that. His psychiatrist didn't want to talk shop but Nick still couldn't come up with anything useful. *Do you feel you're falling into the same mindset your father did? What effect did his alcoholism have on you as a child? Is your drinking a way to escape from the pressures of a job you only went into because your father worked for the Bureau?*

It was too much. Too much to think about and too much to handle emotionally, not when Rosa hadn't even been gone two years.

If she were still alive his former wife would have

spent all her time at Seahaven bonding with the other patients and the staff. By the time they checked out, she'd have had a list of names and email addresses long enough to put him to sleep.

Of course, if Rosa were still alive he wouldn't be there.

Maybe.

Fourteen days ago he would have agreed to that statement without question. That was the annoying thing about rehab, it made you doubt everything you thought you could count on. His marriage had been solid. Unlike his friends who went through divorces, or even the usual ups and downs that went with living with another human being, Nick never doubted Rosa would be his wife until Death drove them apart.

Which the son of a bitch had done without remorse exactly seven days after their tenth anniversary. Six months earlier, after they'd made love one night, she'd had a coughing fit. "That damn cold," she told him, "I just can't shake it." It had taken him a week of cajoling to get her to call the doctor. He'd been afraid from the start but for the wrong reasons. He'd feared pneumonia or even tuberculosis but never lung cancer. Rosa had never smoked and neither had he. As it turned out that fact—which he clung to even after the diagnosis—didn't matter. Seven days and six months later he stood over an open grave and watched his wife's coffin being lowered into the ground.

He started drinking the next night.

No, that wasn't right. He'd already been drinking. He drank for the duration of Rosa's cancer, to the point where some nights he was as out of it on alcohol as she was on morphine. If he were being honest, he would have to admit there had been nights before the cancer when he'd fallen insensible into their bed.

Fourteen days ago he would have said it was the stress of his job at the FBI.

Now he didn't know what to think.

Maybe that was a good thing. Still, he was getting tired of being around people so much. After so many months spent alone from the time work ended, he wasn't used to it.

Nick gave Angela an apologetic nod. He rose out of his chair and headed in the direction of the bathroom. She flashed him the same blinding smile and went on talking to the rest of the group.

He walked past the men's room and headed toward the main lobby, drawn by the sound of the television. Not that there would be anything good on. The only programs residents were allowed to watch were self-help shows and motivational speakers espousing the twelve-step method. Apparently Father Donelan was a great believer in leaving the outside world behind. Only when the mind was at peace could the alcoholic begin to process the issues he had refused to deal with prior to being admitted, according to the Seahaven brochure.

For some people that might be all right but for Nick it was another agony he had to endure. Bad enough he hadn't had a drop of booze in two weeks but to lose his access to news made him feel as if he were experiencing withdrawal from not one but two addictions. Seahaven did have wireless, but it was off limits for patients. He wondered how much trouble he'd get in if bribed one of the attendants to smuggle in a copy of *The New York Times*. Or even let him turn the flat-screen TV in the lobby to CNN for fifteen minutes.

Not gonna happen.

The attendants all seemed friendly but he suspected that beneath their placid expressions they were pretty tough. They certainly had the muscles to prove it. One night shortly after his arrival he'd seen two of them dragging in a college football player who definitely hadn't signed up of his own free will. The kid couldn't have weighed less than three-hundred pounds and his neck was massive. But the guards had carried him to his room as if he were some kind of anorexic model.

Maybe he'd go for a run. The place was pretty damn nice, he had to give it that. One hundred acres of manicured lawns sprinkled with distinguished stone buildings and flower gardens. If he hadn't known better, Seahaven could've passed for a college campus.

On the other side of the floor-to-ceiling windows, the rising moon cast bright shadows across the Chesapeake Bay. Everything looked suddenly beautiful, transformed by the unearthly light that fell across the grounds. He couldn't remember the last time he'd felt that way.

He was heading back toward his room for his sneakers when the most gorgeous woman he'd ever seen pushed through the double doors at the entrance. She breezed by him without so much as glancing in his direction and stopped at the check-in desk. Wisps of platinum hair escaped from a neat bun while she leaned forward to peer at the massive clerk's computer screen. She was quite tall but amply built, with skin so pale he wondered if she'd been sick recently.

Bad habit, that.

Not everybody's dying of cancer, Doyle.

"She said she'd meet me here at 9:00 and it's

already 9:17," the woman said, breathing hard. "She's hasn't been here already, has she?"

"Nope," the clerk behind the desk said. "Haven't seen her."

"She's expecting me."

"Mrs. Ward's probably just running a bit late, like yourself," he said, flashing her a smile of false placidity. "Why don't you have a seat? I'm sure she'll be right out."

The blonde looked at her watch and took a seat next to one of the floor-to-ceiling windows. She reached into her handbag and sent off a quick text, most likely to Angela Ward, who he guessed must be her mother.

She extracted what could only be a textbook, opening it to the place where a blue ribbon marked the page. Without so much as a glance at the seascape before her, she switched on the lamp next to her chair. In her right hand, she held an uncapped highlighter. Her smartphone lay a few inches away on an end table. With a final glance at the phone, she turned to her book and began reading.

Nick stood frozen in place. He wasn't sure if he was relieved she still hadn't noticed him or annoyed that she deemed him so insubstantial he didn't merit even a hello.

She probably doesn't hit on alcoholics. And she won't like it any better when the alcoholic hits on her.

He'd made up his mind to get back to his room and change to go running when she looked up from her book. "It's 9:23," she said to the clerk, her pale blue eyes troubled.

"I can see that," the clerk remarked, returning to

his game of computer Solitaire.

"It's been six minutes."

"Believe it or not, I can also do math."

"Make that seven," she said. "Seven minutes."

"My, my, how time flies." The clerk drawled out the words, clearly enjoying the effect he was having on the woman. Nick pictured Angela Ward sitting with her legs crossed at the ankles as the group hung on her every word. If his guess was correct, her daughter would be waiting there a lot longer than seven minutes.

"Can't you page her?"

"Sorry, but we don't page patients. If you're in a hurry, and you *obviously* are, I can call one of our attendants to go look for her. I already buzzed her room but she's not answering."

"Yes, please," she said. "Thank you."

The clerk picked up the phone and spoke into it a few moments before returning it to its cradle.

With a sigh of frustration, the woman returned to her book. Was it his imagination or was the hand holding the highlighter shaking ever so slightly?

"That's usually how it works." Nick crossed to where she was sitting. "Time. If you obsess over it, it only goes by more slowly."

She looked up at him as if he were from another planet. "Excuse me?"

"I was talking about time—lived time, that is—and about how mechanistic time is different than our perception of it. One of the ironies is that the faster we want it to pass the slower it will. Or at least that's how it will seem. Henri Bergson wrote about it back in the twenties in *Time and Free Will.*"

Her expression hadn't altered. "So you're telling

me I should shut up and wait?"

"Not at all," he said with what he hoped was an endearing grin. "Just a bit of advice from a guy who knows what it's like to obsess about time."

No response.

Well, so much for impressing the brainy chick. He held out his hand. "Nick Doyle."

She took it, though for all her impatience she didn't seem in any rush to make his acquaintance. "Dr. Mia Lindgren."

She set down the highlighter and gave him the once over. "Are you…a member of the staff here?"

"No. I'm a patient." He hoped he sounded a lot happier about that than he felt. "But by my count eleven minutes have expired since your arrival. So if you don't mind hanging out with a recovering drunk for another three to four minutes, I can take you to your mother."

Chapter 2

Mia walked alongside Nick Doyle as they navigated the labyrinthine corridors covered with expensive-looking paintings and oriental rugs. She scanned the ceiling for video cameras, wondering why the facility left such valuable objects out in the open. There had to be a least few addicts looking for the money for their next fix and from the looks of it, Seahaven's inventory could buy more than a few. Granted, the typical Seahaven resident wasn't a street junkie. She had no idea what Leonard Ward paid for her mother's month-long stay but she guessed it had to be a pretty big chunk of change. She remembered reading something about financial aid and work-study programs for qualifying applicants, but from the looks of it most of the guests weren't hurting for money.

Aside from a horrible rasping sound emanating from the Goodman Sun Room, the place seemed almost too perfect. *Like a gilded cage,* she thought, though from what her mother had told her patients could check themselves out at any time. And she knew she wasn't being fair. When she googled the facility shortly after her mother told her about it, she'd found mostly rave reviews. *Seahaven saved my life.* That comment, or comments like it, came up so often she couldn't help wondering just who was writing the reviews. Still, the place was beautiful and her mother had gone eleven days without a drink, which was a first.

"What's that awful sound?" she asked as they passed the sun room and entered a long, dimly lit hallway that looked very much like a hotel corridor at the Ritz Carlton.

"Shellshock," Nick explained. "Looks like group therapy's over. One of the patients belongs to the band. Every night the center holds a jam session after group shares that's open to all. Have you ever heard screamo music?"

"Not counting just now?" she asked. "No. And I hate to tell you but that's one hell of an oxymoron."

"I take it you're not a fan of Shellshock."

"Not if they're singing."

Nick laughed. "I have to say I agree with you. It's not exactly my taste either. Though I confess I do like some of the newer stuff that's out there."

"Not rap."

"Guilty as charged. Let me guess—strictly classical?"

Mia shot him a warning look. What was it about Nick that riled her? She'd only known him fifteen minutes and he acted as if he already had her pegged. She could almost imagine the invisible label he'd pinned to her blouse. *Snobby ice queen with a streak of OCD a mile wide.* Was it more irritating that he was right or that it seemed to amuse him so much? *Sixty percent right*, she amended firmly.

"Not just classical," she said. "I like the Beatles too."

"Well at least we've got one thing in common."

"Who knows, there might be something else."

"Reserving judgment is a matter of infinite hope."

She raised her brows. For somebody who came off as an ordinary guy, Nick Doyle certainly seemed to have a lot of reading under his belt. "F. Scott Fitzgerald," she said. "*The Great Gatsby.* One of my favorite books."

"Well, that makes two things. Luckily we're almost at the therapy room. One more common interest and I may propose."

"You wouldn't happen to have a secret passion for deadly pathogens, by any chance?"

"I can honestly say deadly pathogens don't interest me at all. The more distance I can put between me and the latest strain of Swine flu, the happier I am."

"Well, that's too bad. Because that happens to be my specialty."

"Swine flu?"

"Well, not swine flu specifically. Lately I've been focusing on Ebola."

"As in the virus that destroys your insides in a matter of days and leaves your brain in Zombie mode?"

A smile tugged at the corners of her mouth. "That's the one."

"Damn." Nick stopped in front of an unmarked glass door. "And it seemed so promising."

"Don't feel too bad." Her smile grew wider. "I get that a lot."

To her surprise, Nick looked relieved. "So you work for the CDC?"

"Close," Mia said. "The Institute for Research of Infectious Diseases. Otherwise known as IRID. It's a couple of hours south of here. Maybe you've heard of them."

"I've heard of them."

He didn't elaborate. No doubt he was as repulsed by the information as the other guys she'd dated. After the CDC, IRID was the largest research facility in the country that dealt with infectious diseases. Unlike the CDC, however, the Institute operated on a for-profit basis. Some of the top scientists in the world worked there, producing vaccines and other pharmaceuticals aimed at stopping the spread of seemingly unstoppable viruses and bacterial infections. Which sounded good on paper but didn't do much to endear her to good-looking men.

Not that she had any intention of endearing herself to Nick Doyle.

Mia sighed and turned toward the group therapy room. Through the glass, she could see her mother talking to an enthralled group of three men of varying ages. The remaining lounge chairs, pushed into an uneven circle, were empty. Angela looked away from the man sitting closest to her and motioned for Mia to join her.

Mia stood uncertainly with her hand on the doorknob. The last thing she wanted was to hear the same stories yet again.

Especially because she'd lived them.

Somehow they weren't as entertaining when you were a main character. Under normal circumstances Mia didn't give much thought to her childhood. Not that the first twelve years had been all that bad. Actually, they'd been the stuff of fairy tales. Doting father, cute little sister, stylish mom that everybody liked. Then came the kidnapping. And its aftermath.

"I think that's your cue," Nick said under his breath.

"Enter stage right," she whispered back, risking a sideways glance at him. There were smile lines around his mouth and tiny wrinkles around the corners of his eyes, but other than that Nick didn't seem all that old. Maybe a strand or two of gray in his dirty blond hair, but that was it. He wore a loose t-shirt and khakis but it was obvious the guy had the physique of a stunt man. Six-pack, broad shoulders, muscular arms and thighs. He could be a body double for somebody in Hollywood.

The eyes were a different story. One look into their dark blue depths and she felt like she was drowning. And not in a good way. Too much pain, too much sorrow. That's what she saw beneath the surface of Nick's unwavering gaze. After all she'd been through, how could she possibly be attracted to a man whose demons had gotten the best of him?

When he turned toward her she couldn't shake the feeling he knew what she'd been thinking. From the way he furrowed his brow, he didn't look too happy about it either.

The idea that he'd read her dismissal of him in her face troubled her. But on the other hand, it was probably for the best. Somehow she couldn't see him as the guy of kind who would stand for "friend zoning." Not that he was the kind of guy most women would want as a platonic acquaintance.

Most women would probably want to hop into bed with the guy at the first opportunity. Demons or no demons.

Not her. That was one thing she could be certain of. She wasn't about to make the same mistakes her mother had. After gesturing for Mia to enter the group

29

therapy room, Angela seemed to have forgotten about her daughter. Mia watched her mother reach out and lay a hand on the thigh of the eldest man in the group. Angela wasn't hitting on him, though Mia had no doubt the old man would take it that way. Or at least he'd hope she was hitting on him and would spend the remainder of his stay trailing after her like a lost puppy.

Mia knew her mother didn't mean to cause any pain. Most likely she truly felt bad for the man. But Angela couldn't stay anywhere for more than a day without cultivating admirers.

"You know," Nick said, "if you don't feel like group therapy, we could go grab a cup of coffee and be back here in fifteen minutes. I'd offer to buy you a drink but that's kind of off limits."

"Um, thanks for the offer but—"

Mia's cell phone buzzed. She looked down and saw the name that flashed across the screen. "*Oh, shit.*"

"Boyfriend?" Nick asked casually. Too casually.

"Worse. My best friend. Which ordinarily would be a good thing but I forgot to feed Hera and Zeus."

"As in the Greek gods?"

She nodded.

"I didn't realize they were on a schedule, being gods and all."

"They're parrots."

"Okay."

"Nailini—that's the friend—left this morning on a two-week expedition to the Bolivian rainforests. I'm supposed to be taking care of them until she gets back. But I cut myself this morning so I was late and then Mike didn't show up for work and he wasn't returning my calls and I had to go running with Dante because he

30

destroyed my survivor pillows so I swung by his place and then I was late to visit my mom and I forgot to feed the parrots."

The cell phone buzzed again.

After her rapid-fire fill-in Nick was staring at her as if maybe his previous assessment of her had been wrong. As if she were just a little bit nuts. What did she care if he had the wrong impression of her? It wasn't like she was interested in him.

"I think you'd better take that," he said. "Don't you?"

She shoved the phone into her pants pocket without looking at it. "I'm going to let it go to voicemail. Then I won't have to lie."

"If you take it you won't have to lie either. Just tell her you had some kind of crisis with the survivor pillows. I'm sure she'll understand."

"Very funny."

The phone buzzed a third time. Nick's eyes were on her, making her feel as if she were some kind of underhanded animal abuser.

Fine. She'd take the damn call. Removing the phone from her pocket, she flashed him an I'm-not-doing-this-just-because-you-told-me-to smile and crossed to the foyer at the end of the hallway.

****

Nick was in trouble and he knew it. What was even worse was that Mia Lindgren also knew it. How could he be absolutely infatuated with the woman and more or less despise her at the same time?

He didn't despise her. Quite the opposite. But he hated that ice-cold gaze of hers, the one that had sized him up and dismissed him in all of two minutes. Okay, not two. More like twenty. He glanced at the clock on the wall. Make that twenty-three.

Bad enough you're attracted to the woman. Don't start thinking like her too.

It wasn't his fault. He was vulnerable, for Christ's sake. Here he was trying for the first time in his life to deal with the issues that haunted him and he had to meet the most beautiful woman he'd ever seen.

No, not the most beautiful. Rosa had been just as beautiful, though in a different way. Rosa's dark hair and eyes gave her an exotic look, warm and just a little bit wild. She had always smelled of the kitchen, her golden skin tinged with a hint of cinnamon and nutmeg. When he held her in his arms it always felt like home.

Mia was a different story. Her beauty was marked by a kind of perfection. Her cheekbones were high, her nose slightly upturned, her lips full and bow-shaped. She struck him as some kind of Nordic goddess, to be worshipped from afar. And on top of it all she was probably six times smarter than he was. Not to mention distant. Oh, and she just happened to work with deadly viruses for a living.

Of all the women in the world for him to find attractive, did it have to be Mia Lindgren?

He didn't have a snowball's chance in hell of getting anywhere near the woman.

Which, now that he thought of it, was probably a good thing. According to Father Donelan, he was supposed to be cleansing his mind of all worldly concerns. Donelan hadn't come right out and said it but he was pretty sure that included sex.

Not that Mia Lindgren—make that *Doctor* Mia Lindgren—would ever have sex with him. That much was very, very clear. He'd seen it in her cool gaze. She was attracted to him or at least he thought she might be. Yet he could also sense in her a kind of revulsion when she looked at him.

Okay, maybe not *revulsion*, he thought. His mind searched for the correct word and couldn't find one. Even so, he'd felt her pulling away from him.

Could he blame her? What woman, never mind one who was drop-dead gorgeous, would want to get involved with a guy in rehab? Especially when her mother was staying at the same place for the same reason?

It would be completely crazy.

Aye, there's the rub. Just when he'd been ready to dismiss Mia as an impossible dream, she'd stepped down from her pedestal and shown him her human side. There was more to her than the statue he'd created in his head. When she panicked at the sound of her cell phone, she'd seemed warmer, even vulnerable and a little bit wacky.

Which had the unfortunate effect of making him want her even more.

On the other side of the glass, it looked like the follow-up therapy meeting was breaking up. Angela rose out of her chair and leaned on the eldest of the bunch as if she needed assistance, which he doubted. Her eyes darted to the empty space where Mia had been standing. He thought he detected a twinge of disappointment but it was hard to tell because the mask was back on before he'd even had time to realize it had slipped.

Mia's back was still turned when Angela emerged from the room with her newfound friend holding her elbow. A Texas-sized rock shone on her ring finger, but her companion didn't seem to notice. Either that or he didn't care. After a few murmured comments, he bowed and ambled down the corridor toward the private rooms.

Angela glanced at her daughter and then back at him, an unanswered question on her lips. "She had to take a call," Nick said. "I think it was an emergency."

"An emergency," Angela said quickly, a frisson of concern wrinkling her smooth brow. "What kind of an emergency?"

So much for placating the mother. "No, not an emergency. I just meant it was important. At least that's what she said. It was her friend from Bolivia. The one with the Greek parrots."

A look of confusion flickered across Angela's face. "Do you two know each other?"

"Uh, actually, no. We just met, Mrs. Ward. She was waiting for you in the lobby. I remembered your name from group and volunteered to take her to you."

Her gaze rested on his face a beat too long and he had the distinct impression she could be as analytical as her daughter. Unlike Mia, Angela Ward's appraisal didn't seem nearly as negative. Almost as if she were searching for ways he could be of use.

"Call me Angela." She grasped his hands in both of hers. "Thank you so much for bringing Mia to me. I completely lost track of the time."

Now *that* was one trait mother and daughter didn't have in common. "It happens. I've been losing track of whole days since I checked in."

"Not me." Angela's smile was so intense it startled him. "Eleven days counting today. Eleven days of sobriety after eighteen years on and off the wagon. This time it's the real deal though. I'm not going back. Not this time."

Nick nodded. He knew how she felt. He was proud of the progress he'd made in such a short time. Like Angela, he wanted to believe he'd be able to walk away from Seahaven and never need to have another drink. He just wasn't quite as confident as she was. Though there was something a little too forceful about her statement that made him skeptical. "That's great. I hope to say the same in a couple of weeks."

"Oh, here she comes," Angela said, her voice suddenly happy as a child's.

Almost as if the roles were reversed, Nick thought, struggling to keep his expression neutral.

Mia slipped her phone into her pants pocket and walked toward them, her face drawn. Nick wondered if her friend had been upset about Mia's oversight with the parrots but dismissed the idea. No, there was something else.

He stood unmoving, unsure whether he should wait and try to find out what was bothering her or excuse himself so she could talk to her mother. She reached them before he'd decided, which he supposed was its own decision.

"Mom, I've got to go. I'm sorry."

Angela reached out and caught her daughter in a tight embrace. "What is it, honey?" she asked, studying her daughter's face. "What's happened?"

"It's Mike."

Apparently Angela's expression was as blank as his own. Hadn't she mentioned a Mike before? She had said she was trying to get in touch with him and he'd felt a stab of jealousy. Yeah, it was definitely coming back to him.

"My partner at the Institute. We had...kind of a falling out over the weekend. He didn't show up for work today and I started worrying but I kept telling myself I was being paranoid."

"Did something happen to him?" Angela asked. "Is he sick?"

Mia shook her head. "Not sick. Dead."

Chapter 3

"Dead," Angela repeated. "How?"

"They're saying he drowned," Mia said flatly. "The second call wasn't my friend, it was the police. It was the first number on Mike's cell. They found his body floating in the Chesapeake Bay a couple of hours ago. Somebody noticed his boat drifting and called it in."

"Oh, honey, I'm so sorry." Angela took firm hold of Mia's arm and led her to a chair in the group therapy room. "You look like you need to sit down."

Mia didn't protest. "They want me to I.D. the—to I.D. him," she said, steering away from the word *corpse*. She wasn't ready to think of Mike that way, not yet. Maybe she wouldn't ever be ready. "I told them I'd be there as soon as I could."

"Why did you say 'they're saying he drowned'?" Nick asked.

Until he spoke, she hadn't realized he was still there. He stood a few feet away from the door as if he weren't sure if he should stay or not.

Well, that made two of them. She didn't want him or anybody else to see her this way. Every part of her felt exposed. It wasn't a feeling she liked.

Mia ran her fingertip along the arm of the lounge chair. "I don't know. I mean I guess it makes sense. Mike loved the water—he spent every free minute on his boat. We spent all day Saturday out on *Sorcerer II*.

And I know accidents happen—"

Nick took a few more steps into the room, his expression grim. "So what is it that's bothering you?"

"I don't know. If Mike were going to die anywhere, I guess it would be on the water. He was so passionate about sailing." She closed her eyes and tried to think. "Or maybe that's the reason I can't quite believe it. Mike had been sailing since he was a kid. He knew what he was doing. I find it hard to believe somebody so competent—so skilled—would have an accident. And the weather yesterday was perfect."

Angela was still standing over her, her hand on Mia's arm. "Not a cloud in the sky," she agreed.

Mia felt hemmed in, almost claustrophobic.

"You don't have to talk about it if you don't want to," her mother said. "It must be very painful for you."

It *was* painful. She had worked with Mike for the past three years, every day, side by side. And they had spent a fair amount of time together outside work, especially over the past few weeks. He was definitely one of the few people she could call a friend. Still, she hated that she'd allowed her emotions to get the better of her. After all, it wasn't like she hadn't lost people she cared about before. And death was inevitable, a part of the life cycle, the scientist in her insisted.

So why wasn't the rest of her listening?

"Do you know of anybody who would want to harm Mike?" Nick asked, disregarding her mother's remark. "Did he have any enemies?"

He sure asks a lot of questions for a rehab patient. She opened her eyes and found him staring at her intently. Studying her. For the first time in years she understood what it must be like to be on the other side of a friendship with her. It was a distinctly uncomfortable feeling to be put under a microscope.

"Nobody," she said, gently pulling her arm away from her mother's hand. "People at the Institute loved Mike. He got along with everybody, even our unit leader Trask, who can be a hard-ass to work for."

Everybody but you.

The words stung but she knew they weren't wholly accurate. Mike had been upset with her, no doubt about it. But after a few weeks, or even a few days, he would have put it behind him. Behind them. He would never have held her rejection of him against her.

Now he'd never have the chance to let bygones be bygones. He'd never have the chance to forgive her.

Just like the other time.

She forced herself to stop thinking, to focus only on her breath. Angela hadn't gotten the hint and was stroking her forearm.

"Can I ask you a question?" she asked Nick.

"Shoot," he said, folding his arms across his chest. "Though I can make a guess as to what you're going to ask."

"Okay, then, impress me. What am I going to ask?"

"You're going to ask if I'm a cop."

"Are you?"

"No," Nick said tersely. "I work for the FBI. Counter-terrorism. Though at the moment I don't even do that. I'm on leave. As you can see."

She waited a moment while she processed the information. She couldn't say it surprised her. He struck her as somebody with a military background, which wasn't too far off from the truth. Then there was the sadness and the pain. No, it didn't surprise her. But it did raise questions.

She set them aside. Much as part of her wanted to know more about Nick's background, she didn't have time to find out.

"I should go." Mia rose out of her chair. "I don't want to keep them waiting at the morgue."

"Are you sure?" Angela asked. "Another hour isn't going to make a difference. Even if you went tomorrow morning, I'm sure they wouldn't mind."

She knew her mother meant well, but the woman did have a way of making things seem even worse than they were. Not that that was possible in this case. "I already told them I was on my way. And I can't go tomorrow. I have to work."

Angela's eyebrows shot up. "Please tell me you're not actually considering going in to the Institute?"

"Of course I'm going in. Just because Mike's dead that doesn't mean I need a day off. It's not as if we're related or anything."

"He was your friend," her mother said, following Mia to the group therapy room door.

Mia clutched her handbag against her body. "He was. But I'll be better off at work than sitting around the house doing nothing."

"Maybe she's right." Nick took hold of Angela's arm and steered her toward the hallway opposite the one they'd come in. "Sometimes it's best to keep your mind off things."

He didn't know how right he was. Mia wondered about the way Nick had maneuvered her mother away from her, giving her the chance to find her own way out. Had he sensed Mia's reaction to her mother's attempts at comforting her?

Before she could make her exit, Nick pressed a business card into her hand. She stared down at the card then raised her eyes to him.

"Just in case you feel like talking," he said. "I'm not saying there's anything to your doubts. It's common in situations like this for people close to the, uh, deceased to question how they died. But if you think of anything else, feel free to give me a call. I've got plenty of time to listen."

It was nice of the guy to offer his services free of charge. Or was it just a subtle way of hitting on her? Either way, it didn't matter. He was right about what he'd said about people not wanting to accept it when loved ones died. She'd fallen into that trap once and she couldn't let it happen again. The sooner she accepted Mike's death, the sooner she could get on with her life. She stuffed the card into her purse and looked up at him.

"Maybe I will," she lied. "Thanks."

****

Mia had just pressed her fingertip to the sensor when she saw Chien Lu hailing her from the far end of the Institute corridor.

"Identification downloading," a synthesized voice informed her. "One moment please."

The light next to the door to the CC-5 suite flashed green and clicked. All she needed to do to avoid Chien was pretend she hadn't seen him and duck inside. She knew he couldn't follow her into the locker room, at least not until he could be sure she'd changed into her Hazmat suit.

Too late.

The light turned red just as Chien got close enough

so that there was no polite way to avoid talking to him. It wasn't that she didn't like her co-worker. Though she didn't know him well, the microbiologist always treated her with the utmost respect. As one of the few female researchers who worked in Biolevel 4—the section at the Institute that dealt with the deadliest pathogens— Mia had encountered more than her share of sexist comments. Chien's soft-spoken, probing questions were a refreshing change.

So why was she avoiding him?

But that wasn't really the right question. Why had she been avoiding everybody? Since Mike's funeral two days earlier Mia had virtually locked herself in the Ebola suite at the Institute, spending her days behind six-inch thick glass and locked doors. Her boss Dan Trask had already made a point to speak to her about it. He didn't like the idea of her working alone and if she were honest, she didn't either. It was too easy that way for something to go wrong. Trask had thrown out some names of researchers who were willing to transfer to the Ebola suite and she had summarily rejected all of them without even bothering to give Trask a reason. In the end, he'd reluctantly agreed to wait until Monday for her give him a name.

"Thank you for waiting," Chien said. "I hope I didn't delay you in anything important."

"Not at all." Mia did her best to ignore the burnt moist smell that pervaded the corridor. The giant autoclaves that sterilized their equipment didn't usually bother her but the scent was almost overpowering. Of course, she usually didn't linger outside the Ebola lab either. "I'm running some tests on a few blood samples Mike and I didn't get the chance to look at, nothing out of the ordinary."

"Monkey blood?"

"Human, actually. From a John Doe. The samples came in before—well, they came before the funeral but we never got a chance to look at them. The CDC sent them over to us for a second opinion. They think Doe might have died of Ebola, but they're not sure."

Mia was more anxious to begin testing than she let on. Whenever the CDC sent her a John Doe sample of a virus she always got excited. She was fascinated by the Unknowns, as they were called. She also wondered about the identity of the new corpse. Had he been a soldier? Diplomat? CIA agent? She had no way of knowing and afterward she never learned the identities of the men and women whose blood she'd analyzed. But that didn't stop her from making up all kinds of wild scenarios.

Chien Lu nodded ever so slightly. "May I offer my assistance? Caleb is out today and I have little to do. I would be happy to help you in any way I can."

Why did she get the impression he wasn't just talking about running blood tests?

Part of her wanted to say yes. It would be nice to have a second set of eyes, as well as another human being in the lab when she tried to put a name to the pathogen that killed her John Doe. And Chien's hands might look delicate but they were probably the steadiest in Biolevel 4, something she couldn't say about her own. Aside from her status as the lone female in BL-4, she had to overcome her reputation as someone who had nervous hands. Trask had suggested martial arts might help and she'd taken him up on it. Last month she'd successfully passed her brown belt test. She could kick three boards in half but her hands weren't noticeably better.

"Thanks, Chien." She pressed her fingertip to the sensor a second time. Too much time had passed and she had to reopen the door. "But I'd rather be alone today. I'm still…getting used to Mike not being around. It's going to take a little time. I hope you understand."

"Perfectly." Chien hesitated then seemed to make up his mind. "To lose someone we care about is perhaps the most difficult task we face as human beings. It's a task I haven't mastered yet either."

With a quick nod, he turned and walked rapidly down the hallway.

Mia stared after Chien's receding figure as the automated voice told her she was cleared. The door clicked open and she stepped into the locker room that marked the no-man's land between life and death. Chien's name had been on the list Trask had shown her. It had surprised her that Chien would be willing to abandon his work on H1N1 but on the other hand he'd been studying the virus for years. Maybe he was ready for a change.

Maybe she was too. Chien Lu would be a reliable partner and one who challenged her. He was married with a family, so there was no question of the same awkwardness that had happened with Mike repeating itself. And she couldn't go on working alone forever.

Or even past Monday.

Mia stripped down to her undergarments then removed those as well. She couldn't remember the last time she'd forgotten and worn jewelry to work, so she didn't need to worry about that. She pulled the plastic clip out of her hair and set that on the top shelf of her locker, next to her bra. Moments later she was passing through the tiled shower stall that glowed purple with ultraviolet light on her way to Biolevel 2, where she grabbed a surgical scrub suit and slipped it on, covering her hair and pulling on gloves. Her cut still hadn't healed so she was careful to inspect the gloves for holes. When she didn't find any she wrapped tape around the cuffs and attached it to the gloves, then taped her pant legs to the white socks she had just put on.

Her mind kept darting back to the cut. She knew she had to stop obsessing because if anything, that would make an accident far more likely. Before she could change her mind and go find Chien she stepped into the BL-3 room and then into the BL-4 area, which was little more than cinderblocks and a concrete floor. A blue biohazard space suit with her name written across the back in magic marker hung on one of the pegs. She grabbed it and stepped inside after inspecting it for tiny holes. It too looked fine.

She crossed to the staging area and hooked her suit up to one of the yellow hoses hanging from the ceiling. Her suit inflated and she quickly opened the incubator on the counter.

"Okay, Mr. Doe, let's see what you have to tell me."

Inside the incubator, several plastic flasks with screw tops stood in a rack. They glowed pink under the artificial laboratory light. Whoever sent the samples from the CDC had done a good job, a professional job. The layer of monkey cells awash in its nutrient bath contained tiny drops of blood from John Doe's body. If he had in fact died of Ebola the cells should have burst or shriveled up by now, especially since she hadn't gotten to the sample for days. Once she determined the blood sample did in fact contain the virus she could examine its structure under the electron microscope at the back of the room.

Doing her best to manage the heavy rubber gloves she wore over the surgical ones, Mia lifted the flask out of the incubator. Not for the first time she fought the urge to rip them off and use only her gloved hands. How much faster she would be able to work that way. Of course, to remove the damn things could well be a death sentence.

She placed the flask under the microscope closest to the incubator and turned her head back and forth until she found an angle that allowed her to see through the microscope eyepieces. The faceplate was another inconvenience, one that she longed to dispense with. Eventually, the glittering reddish gold fields of monkey cells appeared before her.

Every cell had exploded.

It was as if a tiny nuclear bomb had fallen onto the sample. Instead of cells she was looking at the remains of what she knew had been cohesive entities.

Well, it definitely wasn't malaria or anything else nonviral that sometimes produced similar symptoms. Whatever killed John Doe had to be viral. Nothing but a virus could have caused that kind of damage. But was it Ebola or something else? She felt a frisson of fear run through her, accompanied by the usual excitement. Despite the fact that the viruses she worked with could wipe out humanity, it still gave her a thrill to hunt down their identities. She felt like a detective tracking a killer. It was a heady sensation and she had to remind herself to be careful.

Mia carried the flask over to the Steriguard safety hood and stood beneath it a minute before unscrewing the flask then picking up a glass slide with a pair of tweezers. With her free hand she grasped a pipette and inserted its tip into the open flask. The hand holding the tweezers shook slightly and for a moment she thought she would drop the glass.

Broken slides were another no-no. Shards of glass could cut. Or leave a tiny perforation in a suit, in a place the researcher couldn't see it.

She deliberately slowed her breathing and set down the slide and the pipette. After a few minutes she felt steadier. She'd thought not having Mike there beside her wouldn't bother her but it did. If anything happened, there would be no one to help. No second set of eyes to notice perforations in her suit.

You'll be fine.

She wasn't sure about that but panicking wouldn't get her anywhere. And it wouldn't help whoever John Doe may have infected before he died. Mia lifted the slide again with the tweezers and pushed the button on the pipette. After the pipette sucked up the pinkish liquid she placed several drops of it on the slide and covered it with a second slide. Based on the state of the decimated monkey cells, she should have more than enough of the sample to see the virus they carried.

When she placed the slide into the electron microscope, she wasn't sure what to expect. Maybe the long worm-like filaments of Ebola, maybe something less exotic, like the tube-like structures that marked Marburg virus.

What appeared on the computer screen before her

was similar to those viruses but there were differences as well. Yes, the unknown virus had long filaments that were far larger than those found in the usual virus. But there were more filaments than usual, several more, and an icosahedral form bloomed from its center so that the virus looked a bit like an octopus.

Mia searched her memory for a virus that resembled the thing that floated before her. Nothing came to mind. Most viruses were round, or nearly round, in structure, and very small. Ebola's larger filaments were an anomaly in the viral universe, with the closest structure being the equally deadly Marburg virus. While virus X did resemble both viruses, it was clearly a different entity.

Her heartbeat sped up as she photographed the virus and dispensed with the slide. She hurried back to the incubator and examined the next two vials under the microscope. All of them were the same as the first. Every cell blown to shreds. Whatever the virus was it was a kind of Armageddon. There was nothing left in its path.

When she pulled out the final vial she expected more of the same. She almost hadn't bothered to examine it because Virus X was turning out to be remarkably consistent.

Or maybe not.

Not only were the monkey cells whole, but they were entirely undamaged. No fields of cellular debris. No shriveled or burst cells. Just a layer of reddish gold cells, perfectly formed, perfectly healthy.

Clearly, the last vial didn't contain the virus. Maybe the samples had been mixed up? That had to be it. Somehow a stray vial of blood had made its way into

John Doe's sample box. She didn't know where it had been shipped from but it was distinctly likely that whoever sent it had made a mistake, especially if the sample came from overseas.

As carefully as possible, Mia prepared another slide. Both hands were shaking and she swore, cursing her inability to separate her mind from her body. After what seemed like an eternity but was in reality only five minutes or so, she lifted the slide off the counter and crossed to the electron microscope. She placed the slide into the microscope and waited.

An octopus floated on the screen before her, its filaments undulating with life. Almost as if it were mocking her.

Well, that was odd. Really odd. As in getting-struck-by-lightning-twice-on-a-clear-day odd.

For the next half hour, Mia cleaned up and replaced the vials in the incubator. She then made notes about what she had seen. She documented everything, filling several sheets of the Teflon paper left out for her. She didn't understand any of it but she knew it mattered. She wanted to put a name to John Doe.

She had almost finished writing her last page of notes when her official "hot zone" pen gave out. With a sigh, she rose from her desk and lumbered over to Mike's work area. Even though she knew he wouldn't have cared if she stole a pen from his drawer, she hesitated. Somehow the fact that he was dead made taking something from his work area seem invasive— an uncalled for intrusion.

But borrowing a pen from a dead man to make notes about a virus that acted unlike any virus she'd ever heard of didn't fall under "uncalled for." Mia pulled open the center drawer and grabbed one of the Bics that lay unopened over Mike's notes.

She stared down at the notes.

Mike never kept notes in his BL-4 desk. He always brought them back into the BL-2, where he decontaminated them in a chemical bath and did his work there.

Mia pressed her thick rubber fingers onto the edge of the Teflon and lifted the top page out of the drawer. She read the first sentence and stopped, then reread it a second time. *Whereas the first three samples revealed extensive damage to the kidney cell samples, the final vial gave evidence of no such damage.*

Mia scanned the rest of the page. Mike's notes were nearly identical to the ones she had just made, other than the fact that they were undated—another anomaly. Mike never made notes without meticulously documenting when and where he'd analyzed the samples. Before she knew what she was doing, she lifted the remainder of the notes out of the drawer and pressed them to her chest. She hurried out of the lab as quickly as she could.

Mike had already tested the virus. He hadn't told her or dated his notes. And he'd left them in BL-4 in an area where no one would see them.

Why?

She walked back over the incubator and lifted one of the plastic flasks out of its tray. There was no label. She set it down and lifted another. No label. Forcing herself to keep her hands steady, she went through the rest of the samples. None were marked.

What had given her the idea the samples were from the CDC?

Not what, who.

John had told her that. She remembered now. How when she'd seen them in the incubator a week earlier he'd rattled off some story about the CDC wanting a second opinion. How he'd steered her away from it and gotten her started on a new shipment from Zaire. "The CDC says these need to take priority," he'd said.

So certain. So believable.

He'd lied to her.

Why?

She kept circling the question without getting anywhere. Closing the incubator, she crossed toward the exit and opened the steel door that led back into Biolevel 3. As she stepped into the decon shower and let the stream of chemicals run over her suit, Mia tried to make sense of what she'd found. She didn't understand any of it, but she had a feeling she'd been right about Mike's death not being an accident.

Now she needed to find out why.

Chapter 4

One more mile.

Nick picked up his pace as he passed the main
building at Seahaven and turned the corner, heading
toward the gardens that ran along the edge of the
property. The size and luxury of the place still floored
him. A couple of nights ago he'd decided to try to run
the trails that ringed the Seahaven buildings, just to see
if he could. He'd snagged a brochure from the lobby
and tried to estimate the distance but his guess hadn't
been close. He figured it was maybe five miles from
start to finish. Make that twelve. A bone-aching,
muscle-punishing twelve.

It nearly killed him but he made it. The second
time wasn't any worse than the first either. If he kept it
up maybe he could run the Boston Marathon that
spring. Finishing that marathon had always been on his
bucket list, especially after it had been bombed in 2013.
But he'd never had the discipline to train for it and the
year before he'd been too drunk to care one way or
another.

For the first time since Rosa's death he felt good
physically. His mental state was a different matter but
every day was getting just a little bit easier. He hadn't
been a heavy enough drinker to go through real
withdrawal but the changes within him were still
profound. When he first checked into Seahaven, the

craving for a drink had been palpable. Even after the first week he had to stop himself from walking out the front doors and driving to a local bar.

But by day twenty-one, he wasn't craving a drink anymore. Whenever he pictured himself passed out on the couch while Netflix flickered across his TV screen, he wanted never to touch the stuff again.

How the hell did Father Donelan manage it? He'd never expected to change in just four weeks (or three, but who was counting?). He'd sat through the orientation video and chalked it up as some kind of marketing gimmick, just another way to make a buck for an old priest. But the guy was obviously doing something right.

Nick sprinted past the gazebo and turned onto an adjoining path only to run smack into the priest. Donelan wheeled back, flailing his arms to keep his balance, much to the amusement of the young girl standing next to him. Angela Ward also seemed to find the incident highly entertaining.

Just his luck.

Bad enough to lay flat the man who probably had saved his life. Even worse to do it in front of the mother of the woman he was crushing on. Granted, he hadn't heard a word from Mia since he'd given her his business card and told her to call him. *Saw right through that ruse.*

It wasn't as if he hadn't wanted to be of assistance. He had. And though the cause of death struck him as pretty straightforward, one thing he'd learned over the years was that sometimes the people closest to the deceased had better instincts than the investigators. But even if she did think of something, what could he do besides listen?

"God, I'm sorry," Nick said, pulling out his earplugs and rushing to steady Donelan. "I probably shouldn't run with these things in but it's a habit I can't kick."

Even worse. He wanted to smack himself across the forehead. Not only did he seem oblivious, but he had to remind everybody he had an addictive personality. At least he was in good company as far as that went.

"Don't apologize to God, brother." Donelan's eyes crinkled at the corners. "Direct your apology to the wronged party, if you please."

"Sorry, *Father*," Nick amended. "That corner does come up kind of fast."

The broad-shouldered man smiled from ear to ear. Aside from the luxury of the place and the competency of the staff, Nick could understand why Seahaven had been such a success. There was something imminently likeable about the former alcoholic priest. Though he'd lived in the United States since he was nine, he'd never shaken his Irish accent and the aura of his homeland still hung over him. Gray streaks ran through his flaming red hair, which fell away from his broad face in thick waves. As a young man he must have made all his female parishioners' heads turn. Even in his sixties, he caught the attention of more than a few inpatients.

Nick turned his gaze toward Angela, who was watching Donelan closely. Had the priest turned her head as well? Or maybe he was simply the one man in the place she couldn't mesmerize and she liked a challenge. He'd missed that night's group therapy session but he was sure it had gone the pretty much the same way the others had. No matter who was talking, Angela always seemed to be the center of the circle. He didn't even think it was intentional. It just happened. When Angela Ward spoke, people listened.

Donelan placed his arm around the shoulders of the young girl beside him. "I'd like you to meet somebody very special," he said. "This is Ariana Macchia. She'll be staying with us a few weeks while her mom gets better."

"Hi," Nick said. "I think you'll like it here."

"Ariana's a very brave girl," Angela chimed in, smiling brightly. "Aren't you, dear?"

Ariana nodded. By Nick's estimate she couldn't have been more than six or seven years old. Six years old and here she was stuck at Seahaven for the next month. For Ariana's sake, he hoped her mom would take the program seriously. There was something fragile about the girl, almost ghostly. Her dark pixie-cut hair shone in the fading light, making her skin seem almost translucent. She was small and her bones looked as if they would snap in a strong wind.

Donelan cast a warning glance in Angela's direction. Apparently she got the hint. "Thank you so much for letting me walk back to Hope House with you and Father Donelan. It was a pleasure to make your acquaintance," she said, then turned toward Nick. "Maybe Mr. Doyle will be so kind as to walk me back to my room."

He could have sworn Donelan's mouth twitched as Angela took firm hold of his arm and pointed him down the trail that lead to the main building. "Nice to meet you, Ariana," he said. "Maybe we'll cross paths again."

"Maybe," the little girl said, a tinge of uncertainty

in her voice.

Neither of them spoke until they'd walked twenty feet or so. Nick wondered why on earth Angela wanted him to accompany her. He couldn't smell very nice. And after that first night the two of them had barely spoken two words to each other. Even in group therapy, they managed to avoid each other's gaze. It was odd, now that he thought about it. He supposed she disliked him. Or maybe it was the other way around.

"Poor thing," Angela said, clicking her tongue. "Dad took off when she was three years old and the mom's a hard-core heroin addict. She probably shouldn't be here at all, but this is one of the only places that lets parents bring their kids."

"She looks like she needs to spend some time outdoors," Nick said.

"She needs a lot more than that. Ian says they do quite a bit with the children. Puppet shows, kick ball, popcorn, and Disney movies at night. He said some of them like it so much they don't want to leave."

"Ian?" Nick tried and failed to keep the sarcasm out of his voice.

"Father Donelan," she said stiffly. "He's truly a great man. To build this place up from nothing took a lot of strength. And he got no help from the Church, I can tell you."

She could probably tell him a lot more than that. A bit ironic, really. Here he was a trained FBI agent and he knew next to nothing about Seahaven while Angela seemed to know everybody's business. *Like Rosa*, he thought, then dismissed the idea. Angela wasn't exactly making friends. She was...well, he wasn't sure what drove her to befriend people.

"So have you heard from Mia?" Angela asked. "About her friend who drowned?"

Nick tried to hide his surprise. He hadn't seen Mia since that first night but he assumed she'd been back to visit her mother and had chosen to avoid him. But from the sounds of it Angela hadn't heard from her daughter at all. For a moment, he experienced an odd sense of solidarity with the perfectly coiffed blonde.

"Not a word," he said.

"Me either," Angela volunteered as if she knew the question he'd stopped himself from asking. "Mia…is very dedicated to her work. You should know that about her."

"I'm afraid I don't see how that relates to me."

"Oh, I think you do."

What the hell was the woman talking about? Why should it matter to him if her daughter was a workaholic or whatever Angela seemed to be implying? Unless she'd somehow guessed he was attracted to her. Which, he supposed, hadn't been all that hard to figure out. He had never been very good at hiding his feelings.

Before he could formulate an answer that would make it clear he had no interest whatsoever in Mia, his smartphone buzzed. He pulled the phone out of the pocket on his running armband and stared. He didn't recognize the number, though he recognized the area code. Maryland. Just north of Baltimore.

He met Angela's cynical gaze. "Would you mind if I took this?"

"Be my guest."

He slid his finger over the screen and lifted the phone to his ear. "Doyle," he said in a clipped voice, hoping he sounded official. As official as a sweaty on-leave agent in a rehab facility could sound, anyway.

"Nick, it's Mia. Mia Lindgren. We met last week when I was visiting my mother."

"I remember," he said. "Uh, can you hang on a minute?"

"Sure," she said a little hesitantly.

"It's Mia," he mouthed to Angela.

"Speak of the devil," she whispered wryly. This time she was the one who didn't bother to hide her sarcasm. Clearly, she didn't buy his previous denial.

He couldn't blame her for being skeptical. It did seem unlikely that Mia would call him for the first time just at the moment he happened to be telling her mother they weren't in contact. "Can I, uh, catch up with you later?"

"Not a problem," Angela said. "Let me give you some privacy. I wouldn't want to interrupt."

He called out a goodbye but she was already out of earshot. Or at least she acted as if she were, walking quickly down the path without turning her head. He'd try to smooth mother hen's ruffled feathers later. Right now, he needed to take Mia's call. He stared at the phone in his hand, a wave of emotion surging through him. *Keep it business-like.* "What can I do for you?"

"I'm sorry to bother you, but I came across something at work today that made me even more certain Mike may not have drowned."

"What did you find?"

"To be honest, I'd rather not get into it over the phone. I was wondering if you might have any time to meet. I could drive out there tomorrow after work and get there around seven-ish," she said. "Of course, I'd need to see my mom first. I feel terrible but I've been so tied up at work I haven't been able to stop in again."

Funny, she hadn't even mentioned the funeral. *Mia is very dedicated to her work.* What would it be like to get involved with somebody so driven? Then again, he could say the same for himself. Even when he'd been married to Rosa he had seldom left the office before he'd put in a twelve-hour day. And that was erring on the conservative side. One of the things that bothered him most about Rosa's death was that he'd been the one to convince her to put off having a child. He'd robbed her of the experience of being a mother. Maybe things might have been different if he hadn't been so focused on his job. Still, what would it be like to date somebody exactly like him?

It would be a disaster.

He wasn't going to date Mia. He was going to help her. Or at least try to. "Tomorrow's fine. When you're through visiting with your mother just give me a ring. There's a cafeteria that stays open pretty late. And a kind of pseudo-Starbucks we could try if you like caffeine." He hesitated. "Or we could go someplace. I'm not a prisoner, after all. We can come and go as we like." *Though it's not encouraged.* Father Donelan's remark niggled his brain. Well, Father Donelan wasn't investigating a potential murder.

He isn't interested in a beautiful blonde either. Who the hell was he kidding?

"The cafeteria's fine," Mia said quickly. "I don't think it would be, uh, appropriate for us to leave."

Appropriate. Great. "Sure," he said. "And be sure not to bring any cakes with nail files in them or anything."

She laughed, but he got the impression she didn't

find his attempt at humor all that amusing. *Stop trying so hard.* He knew he was being way too obvious and wished he was better at playing it cool. "I promise not to tempt you to escape."

Now *that* was funny. "Till tomorrow," he said.

"Till tomorrow. Hopefully I'll have more to tell you by then.'

Nick wasn't sure what she meant but he didn't like it. "Look, I'm glad you found whatever it is you found. But until we have to chance to talk things over, I don't think it's a good idea to do any, uh, detective work."

"I know."

She didn't sound all that convincing. "For argument's sake, let's say you're right and your buddy didn't drown. If that's the case then you need to be careful. If you start poking around where you're not supposed to you're going to alert whoever may have been involved that they need to be careful." *And you might get hurt.*

Pause.

"I'll be careful."

Uh-huh. "Mia, I'm serious. We're not taking about a lab where you can control the environment. If I'm going to believe what you're telling me, then we're talking about a guy who was potentially murdered. There are too many unknowns for you to be taking risks."

"My whole life is one big risk. In case you don't remember, I work with deadly pathogens every day. I think I can handle a little b & e."

"What do you mean *b & e?*" Worse and worse. He had to hand it to her though, her use of the lingo was cute.

"I believe that stands for breaking and entering," she said tartly.

"I know what it stands for. But if for one moment you are even considering—"

"I said I'd be careful," she said, cutting him off. "See you tomorrow night."

The call ended.

He swore and shoved the phone back into his armband pocket. It didn't take a rocket scientist, or even a microbiologist, to figure out what her next move was. Mia was going to find a way into Mike Chandler's residence and she was going to do it soon. He just hoped she was right when she'd told him she could handle it.

****

Nick lay back on the bed with his legs stretched out. He was still sore as hell but the long shower had definitely helped. He glanced at the clock. 8:07 p.m. and he wasn't even close to being ready for bed. Not at all. The paperback thriller he'd been reading lay on the bedside table where he'd left it the night before. It was a good book, fast-paced and full of action, but he didn't feel like reading.

He knew damn well what he wanted to do. The only question was should he give in to his impulse or try to resist.

His mouth quirked. A month ago he would have been thinking the same thing about downing a liter of vodka. Now he was just trying to figure out whether or not to use the internet. There was no technology at all in the room, part of Donelan's prescription for recovery, and he hadn't brought his laptop with him for the same reason.

But he had the iPhone. And the employee password for Seahaven's wireless connection, which he had just happened to catch of glimpse of on his way past the check-in desk earlier that night.

He grabbed the phone off the nightstand, nearly knocking the thriller onto the floor in his haste to log on. So much for Donelan's prescription. Hell, a couple of hours on the web wouldn't kill him. If anything, it might help him find a killer.

It took him a few minutes to find Mike Chandler's obituary, as well as the article about his death that ran in the local paper. He clicked onto the link and read the story that appeared on his screen.

Microbiologist Drowns After Boating Mishap

A former scientist who worked with deadly pathogens died over the weekend in the Chesapeake Bay, according to authorities. Emergency responders found the body of Michael Paul Chandler III, thirty-eight, of Somersville, Maryland, about fifty yards from his sailboat, the Martinsville Sheriff's Office said today. Chandler was currently employed by the Institute for Research of Infectious Diseases.

The Martinsville Sheriff's Office was notified on Monday afternoon that a body was seen floating in the vicinity of Chandler's boat, The Sorcerer II, which had drifted close to shore and appeared to be empty at the time. According to the Sheriff's office a male body identified was pulled out of the water at 4:43 p.m. that day. The male, later identified as Chandler, was pronounced dead at the scene by the Martinsville County Medical Examiner. Witnesses interviewed on the scene did not recall seeing Chandler set sail that morning or over the weekend, though several town residents recollected him as a frequent visitor to the dock. "He was always out on his boat," said Carey Foster, owner of the nearby Blue Moon Diner. "He was very friendly, always stopping in for a bite to eat or just to say hello. I never would have guessed in a million years what he did for a living."

At the Institute, Chandler studied a variety of pathogens considered Class A bioterror agents. Prior to working at the Institute, he worked as a researcher at the United States Centers for Disease Control and Prevention in Atlanta, Georgia.

Nick bookmarked the story then typed "Michael Chandler" AND "microbiologist" into Google. The usual deluge of entries appeared and he began sorting through them as quickly as possible, which wasn't all that fast because the screen was so damn small.

An hour later he logged off and closed his eyes, leaning back against the wooden headboard.

What had he learned about Mike Chandler?

Quite a lot, actually.

He supposed it had to be a mark of age, that the amount of information about private citizens that was readily accessible to anyone who owned a computer still surprised him. In just over an hour he discovered that Chandler had grown in up in a wealthy Connecticut town and attended Phillips-Exeter Academy. Following graduation at the top of his class, he'd gone on to Harvard, where he enrolled in ROTC and rowed for the crew team all four years. He attended graduate school at Berkeley and earned his Ph.D. ahead of schedule, at which point he'd promptly accepted a job working for the CDC. In 2011, he left the CDC to work with the deadly pathogens at the Institute in Somersville.

Nobody had bothered to take down Chandler's Facebook page, which showed about two dozen profile pictures of the scientist on various boats over the years. In most of the recent photos Chandler appeared in the same sailboat, which he guessed was *The Sorcerer II* mentioned in the news article. There were also a number of article citations with cumbersome titles that may as well have been written in Hindi. Every now and then the word Ebola or Marburg would catch his attention, but just what the scientist had managed to find out about those diseases wasn't clear to him. Many of the Facebook shots showed him surrounded by friends and (he guessed) family, but as far as Nick could make out Chandler had never been married and didn't have children.

The fact that Chandler spent four years as a member of the Harvard crew team along with the guy's lifelong interest in sailing gave credence to Mia's theory. He didn't remember the weekend Chandler died as being anything besides sunny and brisk, but he googled the weather for the days in question anyway. According to weather.com the high for Friday through Monday had been a balmy seventy-one, with the low falling somewhere into the forties. No thunderstorms, no rain, not even a few hours of strong wind. It had been just like he remembered it—near perfect weather, especially if you happened to be a sailor.

It made sense that a guy like Chandler would have spent every free moment out on the water, especially during the summer. Mia told him the two of them spent Saturday out all day and had returned to the harbor late that afternoon. He might have decided he'd had enough and driven back to his place outside Somersville. It was just as likely he would've tried to get in another day outside.

And then there was the matter of the body.

That seemed to suggest the guy spent Sunday out on the bay. Maybe something had gone wrong. There were other factors besides weather that might result in a drowning. Technical problems. Or maybe it was something as mundane as a stupid human error. If Chandler had gone out on the water alone, he might have lost his balance and fallen into the water. Granted, it seemed unlikely but unlikely didn't mean impossible. Most so-called suspicious deaths turned out to be some variation on unlikely. People made mistakes all the time—and paid with their lives.

So why the hell did Mia question the story? Denial? Guilt over something, a fight maybe?

He didn't want to think about that, so he shoved the idea to the back of his mind. She said on the phone she'd found something new. What the hell was it? Whatever it was it had to have been pretty convincing for her to even consider breaking into his place. Nobody would be there, not after so many days had passed with nothing to disprove the obvious explanation. The sheriff's office would keep the case open for a while but Nick had a feeling they weren't devoting much manpower to it anymore.

Before he changed his mind he pulled up Dalton Ross's name and was calling the guy at home. Late at night. When he was supposed to be devoting all his energies to getting better. If it had been anybody else, Nick wouldn't have been so uneasy. But on the other hand there was nobody else at the FBI he could rely on like he could rely on Ross.

Funny, too, because he hadn't even known the guy all that long. He'd hired Ross as a transfer from the Chicago office two years earlier partly because he felt sorry for the guy. Back home, he'd had a cheating wife and a sleazy best friend. Now the guy ran his own unit and had married one of the most ethereal creatures he'd ever come across. He got the job and the girl, in the end. Meanwhile the guy who hired him was falling to pieces and fantasizing about a woman who barely acknowledged his existence.

"Hey," Nick said. "I didn't wake you, did I?"

"No," Dalton said. "We're up. Laura worked late so we just finished dinner."

"Is she there with you now?"

Pause. "Yeah. Is that a problem?"

Only if she hears what we're saying. Which she would. Hell, even if she didn't she would guess it anyways. It was a little bit creepy, the way Dalton's wife always seemed to know what everybody was thinking. Dalton had tried to tell him some weird story about her being psychic and having dreams but he'd stopped him before he had the chance to finish. Back then, the craziness of the real world had been about all he could handle.

Of course it had been Laura and one of her dreams that freaked his buddy out enough get a few people together to "talk" to him one night after work. They called it an intervention but it felt more like an ambush. Nick was furious at the time and he was embarrassed to say some of that had been directed toward Laura. Now he wanted to thank her for saving his life.

"No, it's not a problem," Nick said, trying to infuse his voice with false vigor. "It's just…well, I'm actually calling because I need a favor."

"What kind of favor?"

Nick could almost hear his buddy in counter-terrorism turning over the possibilities. He tried to think of a good way to phrase it, a way that would make it sound as if work were the furthest thing from his mind.

"Please tell me you haven't checked out. I swear to God Laura will kill you if you've gone AWOL. And then I'll kill you. Or at least bludgeon your corpse."

"I haven't gone AWOL."

"You're sure?"

"What the hell kind of question is that?" Nick didn't bother to hide his irritation. Yeah, he needed Dalton's help and yeah, the guy was his buddy, but did that give him the right to treat him like a five-year-old? He'd been the one to hire Dalton, for Christ's sake.

"Sorry," Dalton said. "I didn't mean it like it sounded. I know you're gonna make it."

So why do you sound like you're not one hundred percent sure of that? "There's a microbiologist who drowned out this way a few days ago. I doubt they've released the autopsy results yet, at least not publicly, and I need to see them."

"You need to see them." Not a question. More like a judgment.

"Do you think you could give the medical examiner's office a call and see if they'll fax over the findings to your office?"

"And I'm guessing you want me to scan them and then send them to via your personal email?"

"You guessed right."

A third pause, significantly longer than the first two. He could hear Dalton on the other end of the line.

A few seconds later, he covered the phone and said something Nick couldn't decipher.

"I suppose you're not gonna tell me why you want the results or tell me anything else any normal person would feel entitled to know before following up on this?"

"You're a regular psychic."

"Don't get cute."

"Sorry," he said. "Speaking of…cute…how is Laura?"

"She's fine. Would you like to say hello or do you prefer to avoid her because you know she'll give you an earful for trying to work when you're supposed to be getting well."

"I'm fine with avoidance. And I know she'll give you the earful, so that gives me some satisfaction."

On the other end of the connection, Dalton laughed quietly. "I'll make the call tomorrow and get you the stuff as soon as they get it over to me. Happy now?"

"Actually, I am. I know I acted like an ass that night and when I see Laura again I want to tell her she—"

"She knows. Trust me, she knows."

Nick hesitated. "She hasn't had any more, uh, dreams, has she?" He didn't believe in psychics but when Laura described her vision to him the night of his intervention it had seemed damn real. There had been things, more than a few, that nobody could have known. Fears he hadn't shared with anyone. Not even Rosa.

"No," Dalton said. "That's how she knows. About saving your life."

A surge of gratitude welled up inside him. All those years of denial and it took somebody's nightmare to convince him he needed to get help. Or scare him enough to get it. "Well, tell her thanks for me, okay?"

Nick powered down his phone and picked up the thriller off the nightstand. Now it really was late, especially considering the morning-to-night routine Donelan's itinerary recommended. None of the activities were mandatory but he'd tried to adhere to the schedule for the most part. Because whatever he might have to say about the priest's methods, he had to admit they worked. At least they seemed to for him.

Twenty-one days and counting, he thought, remembering the way Angela Ward insisted on announcing her tally to anyone who would listen. It was worse than listening to a thousand renditions of Ninety-nine bottles of beer on the wall.

He adjusted the reading lamp so that the light shone onto the bed and opened the book to where he'd left off. Tomorrow he would see Mia Lindgren and he hoped he might have some news for her as well.

"One more day," he said, wondering if it might just be possible Mia wanted to meet with him for other reasons besides Chandler's death. "Not that anybody's counting."

Chapter 5

It wasn't B & E.

As Mia inserted Mike's key into the front door of his condo she wondered what it was about Nick Doyle that made her want to impress him. If it hadn't been for the concern in his voice she might have backed out of her plan to search Mike's place. But Nick's skepticism had been too much to take. She was a trained scientist for God's sake. She'd been right about what she told him over the phone. If she could handle Ebola, she could manage to get in and out of a dead man's house after dark without being seen.

Especially if you have a key.

The white lie she'd told Nick niggled at her sense of protocol. She shouldn't have made it sound as if she were going to break the law. She'd actually used the term B & E.

He had practically goaded her into it. Not just into using the lingo but into visiting Mike's condo in the first place.

Um, no. The guy had done his best to talk her out of it.

The key clicked into place and she pushed the door open. She'd been inside Mike's place several times, so the shadows weren't unfamiliar, but that didn't make it any less creepy. She stepped inside and peered into the shadows. She didn't want to risk turning on a light. If

Mike's death really hadn't been an accident, it probably wasn't a good idea.

Or maybe she was just a paranoid freak who couldn't accept her partner was gone.

That was why she was here, wasn't it? If she searched the condo for evidence and came up with nothing, she'd accept that her theory was wrong. Just like she did back in the lab.

She pulled an LED flashlight out of her jacket and swept it across the living room. Someone, probably Mike's parents, had taken some of his things out of the place. She tried to remember if there had been curtains or shades that ran across the sliding glass doors along the far wall or if they had always been bare. Mike's parents had told her at the funeral that they planned to put the condo on the market as soon as possible. Maybe they'd already been there to clean up. And the police had searched the place the day after the drowning, though she had her doubts about how thoroughly they'd done it.

Everybody, including the police, seemed to buy into the idea that he'd drowned. A dead body washed ashore tended to be pretty convincing. Just not to her.

"Hello," she called out. "Is anybody there?"

No answer.

Not that she'd expected one.

Mia took several steps forward into the living room, unsure where she should start. She wasn't even sure what she was looking for, because she had no idea why someone would want to kill Mike in the first place. He'd always struck her as a genuinely nice guy. Harvard educated and rich with a pedigree to match. And Mike wasn't a snob either. He had a sense of fundamental decency and was the only guy she'd ever met who'd actually read his school's honor code. As for friends, he literally had dozens in cities across the country. Make that across the globe, she amended. Mia had her doubts about how many of them would stick around if he'd been poor but Mike's good nature made her wonder if she wasn't being overly cynical. He wasn't the kind of guy who had enemies—not to mention the sort of man most women would love to spend their lives with.

Stop.

Beating herself up about rejecting Mike wasn't going to get her anywhere. *And that nice, honorable guy lied to you.* No, not lied. He'd never outright deceived her. But he certainly hadn't mentioned he'd been working on some mystery virus without her either. In the two years she'd been working at IRID, Mike had never kept anything from her. They'd been partners and had shared everything, at least as far as work went.

At least that's what she'd believed.

A quick inspection of the living room didn't yield much. There was a smattering of DVDs and a bookshelf filled with popular novels and a few textbooks that looked as if they were left over from grad school. The framed photos scattered throughout the room were of his family and friends. Caught by the flashlight's beam, Mike's boyish grin leapt out at her from a shot taken that summer.

She knew because she'd taken it.

Stop it. His death isn't your fault.

Mia aimed the flashlight at the picture over the fireplace and breathed a sigh of relief. No boyish grin in this photo. Instead a large canvas showed the *Sorcerer*

II out on the open seas, sails billowing as it raced toward an unknown destination.

Mike's true love had never been a woman. *Sorcerer II*, not Mia, had captured his heart.

Crossing from the living room to the hallway that led to the bedroom, Mia stopped at the threshold. The door was ajar a couple of inches, enough to prevent her from seeing inside. It felt like a violation to enter, especially after their fight, but she wasn't going to learn anything standing there in the darkness.

Firmly placing a gloved hand on the knob, she pushed the door open and waited for her eyes to adjust to the gloom. The shades were drawn, making the room nearly pitch black. Mia shone the light onto a king-sized bed, a couple of night tables, a large closet and an old-fashioned roll-top desk.

A desk. That was promising.

She closed the door behind her and crossed toward it. It looked antique, and the cubby holes were filled with rolled papers, like something out of a Dickens novel. Mia leaned down and pulled out a piece of paper from one of the cubbies. The typeface was tiny and it took her a few seconds to make out the words running across the top of the page.

Residents of Siberian Village Found Dead

The World Health Organization is helping the Russian Ministry of Health investigate the cause of a mysterious illness that has killed nearly eighty percent of the 253 residents of a small village in Siberia.

A joint statement released Wednesday said 198 residents of Krasnoyarsk recently died from the disease. There have been no other cases reported in nearby villages or elsewhere in Siberia at this time.

"The Ministry and WHO are currently investigating the cases," Yuri Smirnov, the Russian minister of health, said in the statement, *"possible causes of the disease are being considered, but definite identification of the cause and source may take some time."*

Initial reports from the Russian government indicate that the unknown illness struck primarily adults, leaving children relatively unscathed. "The symptoms include a mixture of respiratory illnesses, fever and generalized neurological symptoms, including convulsions and hemorrhaging in most of the patients," Dr. Mikhail Vernadsky, a team leader of the WHO country office in Russia, said in an email to media.

Preliminary autopsy results indicate that most residents died within twenty-four hours upon becoming ill. "This can be a mixture of a number of known diseases—virological, bacterial or toxicological. While the labs are excluding the various pathogens, we are providing support to [the Ministry of Health] to make sure that an in-depth analysis of cases is done to identify possible causes or exposures which will give us a better picture. The investigation is ongoing."

According to Vernadsky, one reason the illness may not have spread beyond Krasnoyarsk is due to the village's extremely isolated location.

Mia scanned the print-out and saw that the article had appeared a year earlier. It looked as if it had been cut from an internet site and pasted into a Word file. At the bottom of the article she recognized Mike's neat letters. He'd made a notation in pencil, so lightly she could have easily missed it in the dim light. *What went wrong? Why didn't it kill the kids?*

Questions assaulted her brain but she shoved the article into her jacket pocket and continued the search. She could try to make sense of what she'd found later.

She knelt before the middle drawer and pulled.

Locked. Mia swore under her breath and cast her gaze around the room. There had to be a key. And she needed to find it. When it came to organization, Mike wasn't as meticulous as Mia. But there was usually a method to his madness.

Unless he didn't want anybody to find it. Which he probably didn't.

Think, Mia. She knew Mike better than almost anybody. Where would he keep a key?

Night table, dresser drawer, kitchen drawer. She ran through the possibilities, unsure where to start.

A noise from the front of the condo interrupted her thoughts.

She froze.

Trying to ignore the beating of her heart, she listened for a sign that somebody was inside the condo with her. All was silent.

Probably her imagination.

She wasn't that imaginative.

Or maybe Mike's parents stopped by to clean the place out.

The place was dark.

Or maybe it was the wind rattling the glass.

It wasn't windy.

Mia killed her flashlight. She struggled to identify the sound she'd heard. Not a window breaking. Not a key turning. Not footsteps.

More like a sliding glass door opening, ever so slowly.

Or closing.

She counted out another minute. And another.

One-hundred twenty seconds.

All was silent. If there was an intruder, he was patient.

Either that or he knows somebody's in here.

She hadn't brought a weapon.

She didn't own one. The only enemies she worried about were in the lab.

She waited a full two-hundred forty seconds before she got up and made her way toward the door, saying a silent prayer of thanks that she'd worn her running shoes. If she was being paranoid, better to find out for sure so she could get back to searching the place.

She counted out another sixty seconds. Her muscles were so taught she felt as if she'd snap in two if she had to wait much longer.

Footsteps. Moving toward her.

Mia inched backward, holding her breath. If she moved quickly she could reach the closet before the intruder entered the bedroom. Either that or she could wait and try to push her way past the guy.

Better go for the closet.

She fumbled to open the slatted doors as the footsteps grew closer but her hands were shaking. Shutting them behind her, she wedged herself behind a wool coat and some dress pants.

The bedroom door opened.

She tried not to breathe.

The intruder walked into the room and stopped. A few seconds later, the footsteps began again, moving from one side of the room to the other. *As if he's searching for something.*

It was only a matter of time until whoever it was reached the closet.

She should've made a run for it. She was a sitting duck in the closet.

Bad decision.

Not that she could do anything about it now. Mia peered into the dark in search of a weapon. If she could surprise the guy, she'd have a shot at getting out.

The best she could do was a hiking boot. She lifted it off the floor and held it with both hands. Another few minutes and the intruder would reach the closet. For once in her life, she resisted the impulse to count. Accuracy didn't seem all that important at the moment.

The footsteps stopped outside the closet doors. Mia tightened her hold on the boot. Maybe he'd leave. Maybe he'd turn around and walk out of the condo.

Right.

She saw it then. A wooden bat, resting against the wall, like a gift from God.

When the intruder flung the doors open, she didn't hesitate. She lunged for the bat, swung it hard and exploded out of the closet.

From the soft thud she knew she'd connected.

A surge of triumph shot through her.

"Jesus!"

The voice was familiar. Male. And far too sexy.

Mia dropped the bat and reached for her flashlight. "Nick?"

Nick stood a few feet away, rubbing his right arm. "You're stronger than you look."

She shone the light on his arm. An angry red spot had appeared just above the elbow. "Sorry."

"Would you mind aiming that somewhere else?"

"Are you okay?"

"Nothing's broken. Though tomorrow I'm going to have a hell of a bruise."

"You're not bleeding," she added helpfully, pointing the flashlight at the floor.

"No," he said, "I'm not."

He might not be bleeding, but he didn't look all that happy to see her either. "I'm really sorry."

"You already said that."

"I thought you were an intruder."

"I *am* an intruder. As are you."

He was right. Still, he'd almost scared her to death. "I know—but I told you I'd be here."

"So b & e's okay if it involves premeditation?"

"No," she admitted. "But—I mean—what are you doing here? Aren't you supposed to be at Seahaven?"

He made his way over to the desk chair and sat down. "I am supposed to be at Seahaven. But I had a conversation earlier tonight with a woman who told me she planned on breaking into a dead man's home. I guess you might say I got a little worried."

"Sorry."

"You know, your conversational skills seemed a lot better the first time I met you. Though you do seem a bit nicer."

She grinned. "I've been told I come across as a bit of a snob. I don't mean to."

"I know. I've never won any awards for friendliness either. Now let's get out of here, okay?"

Mia pulled the folded print-out out of her pocket and handed it to him, along with the flashlight. "We can't. At least not yet. I think this may be important. And I have a feeling there might be something in the

78

center drawer he didn't want anybody to see. It's locked. That's not like Mike."

Nick skimmed the article and raised his eyes to her. "You think this relates to his death? Wouldn't it be normal for him to have something like this here, considering his line of work?"

"I'm not sure. But it seems odd—the writing at the bottom."

"*Why didn't it kill the kids*," Nick said softly.

"And I haven't told you everything yet."

She waited for him to ask what she hadn't told him, but he said nothing. "A few more minutes can't make much difference. Let's see if we can get that drawer open." He handed the flashlight back to her. "Aim it at the lock."

He reached for two large paperclips in the tray on the desk. He unbent one and inserted it into the lock, using the second for leverage. A minute or so later he pulled the drawer open and peered inside.

Mia stood behind him, straining to see its contents. "Is that a planner?"

"Looks like it." He handed a small leather-bound book to her.

She shone the light on it and began flipping through the pages. Most of the entries looked straightforward. From what she could tell, the majority referred to harbors he'd sailed to with friends. Next to the times and locations, he'd written names of people who sounded vaguely familiar. Every couple of weeks, her own name showed up. From what she could remember, it seemed to gel with the times and dates they'd hung out. She turned to the days before his body surfaced and was disappointed to see nothing filled in.

"Find anything else?"

"Maybe." He lifted computer print-outs of three more articles out of the drawer and tucked them into her pocket. "How about you? Anything interesting in there?"

She tried to ignore the quickening of her pulse. Every time Nick got within a foot of her alarm bells went off. Something about the man unsettled her. Was she afraid of him—or was it desire she felt? Either way, it wasn't good. "Not that I can see. Nothing that jumps out at me, anyway."

She flipped ahead to the end of the month. Unlike the earlier pages, the planner was mostly blank. "Looks like he didn't have much coming up. Either that or he intended to become a recluse."

"Maybe he didn't fill it in."

"You don't know Mike."

A muscle worked in Nick's jaw. "And you did."

Something in his tone made her wonder just how well he thought she'd "known" Mike. She opened her mouth to correct him then changed her mind. Why should she care if Nick believed she'd been involved with Mike? It wasn't like there was anything between the two of *them*. She didn't know the first thing about Nick, really. *Except that he checked himself into Seahaven.*

Mia pushed the thought aside. Nick's personal life was none of her business. If he could help her figure out what happened to Mike, great. But anything beyond that was off limits.

"Mike was always out on his boat with somebody. He said he needed to be someplace outside after spending eight hours a day cooped up in a lab. And he wasn't exactly spontaneous. Whether it was work or his personal life, he liked to be in control."

Nick pressed his lips into a thin line. "Sounds like somebody I know."

"What's that supposed to mean?" Of course, she knew damn well what he meant. And what he was implying. *Fine. Let him draw his own conclusions.* If he thought she was a control freak there was nothing she could do about it. The worst part was he was right. She was a control freak. But she didn't like the idea of him putting her into a box. A very neat, very square box.

The sound of a key in the lock prevented him from answering.

"You heard that, right?" she whispered.

"The light."

Hands shaking, she managed to find the button on her flashlight and turn it off. The front door swung open as she shoved it into her jacket pocket.

"Let's go." Nick grasped her hand and pulled her toward a large window. Lifting the sash, he pulled back the shade and propelled her toward the opening. "See if you can squeeze through."

She didn't argue. Setting her foot between his clasped hands, she hoisted herself up and leaned forward to raise the screen. She'd gotten one leg through when the sound of footsteps echoed across the condo.

Hurry up.

She wasn't sure at first if Nick had spoken or her inner voice had suddenly gotten really loud. Scrambling over the sill she dropped to the ground and crouched next to the wall, hoping the visitor would stay in the living room.

Nick pushed himself through the window and fumbled to close the screen. "Come on," he said over his shoulder. "We need to get the hell out of here."

She struggled to keep up with him, staying close to the wall. Most of the units were dark, which wasn't surprising considering the late hour. When they reached the parking lot, Nick turned to face her.

"Drive back to your place and stay there. I'll be there as soon as I can."

Mia wasn't sure what disturbed her more—the fact that he knew where she lived or that he wasn't planning on leaving the complex. She glanced at the darkened condo. "Tell me you're not going back there."

"I won't be long. I just want to see if I can get a glimpse of whoever's inside. And when whoever's in there comes out, maybe I can get a plate number on the vehicle." The parking space in front of the condo was empty but whoever was inside could have used one of the other spaces, farther off.

"I don't think that's a good idea."

"Maybe not. But I can't think of a better one right now."

"Well, I can. Leave with me."

Nick shrugged and looked away. "You said you wanted to find out if your friend's death was something besides an accident, right? This is our best shot at doing that. Do you really want to pass that up?"

"Then I want to go with you." Actually, she wanted to put as much distance between Mike's condo and herself as possible. But he was there because of her— she couldn't just leave him.

"Thanks," he said, "but you'll only slow me down. It'll be safer for us both if you head back to your place."

"We left the window open. Whoever's in there will know somebody was in the condo."

"Probably. But there's nothing we can do about that now." He took firm hold of her shoulders. "Now go. The sooner you get out of here, the sooner I can do my job."

To her surprise she didn't wince at his touch. She'd always been wary of being touched, even when she was a kid, but the sensation of his hand on her skin didn't bother her. Unsettled her maybe. But not in the way it usually did.

"You seem to be pretty busy for a guy on leave."

"I needed a distraction."

"So that's what I am? A distraction?"

He nodded, his eyes on hers. "Rehab was getting boring."

She stifled a laugh. "Glad I could spice things up."

In the condo, a flicker of light appeared in one of the windows. "Looks like our visitor's on the move. Either that or he spotted that open window and got nervous."

Mia clasped her keys but didn't turn away. *The man is a trained FBI agent. He can take care of himself.* So what was she worried about?

"Don't stay too long, okay," she said.

"So you don't think I can fend for myself?"

"No, I do. It's just—" She broke off in mid-sentence. If she'd learned one thing over the past twenty-nine years it was that things could go wrong, no matter how many precautions you took. "Just be careful, okay?"

He studied her face. "Okay."

"Is that a promise?"

"That's a promise." Nick turned her around and pointed her in the direction of her Subaru. "Now get the hell out of here."

****

Even Dante was tired of it.

Mia stopped pacing and folded her arms across her waist. "Don't give me that look."

He laid his head on the carpet, but whether he understood her or not was open to debate. It was unnerving, how well her husky sensed her mood.

Not that it was all that tough to figure out. She'd been pacing for the past hour, her gaze darting to the door every few seconds. Hadn't he said he wouldn't be very long? *Promised* her he wouldn't be long?

He promised he'd be careful. Which, depending on how you looked at it, could mean just about anything. Which, apparently, it did.

Her gaze came to rest on the clock on the mantel above the fireplace. 3:23 a.m.

"One hundred and ninety-four minutes," she said aloud, not bothering to disguise her irritation.

Dante's ears pricked up.

"Make that one hundred and ninety-five." She looked away from the clock, only to find her eyes riveted to it a few seconds later. She knew she should be reading through the clippings she and Nick had found at Mike's condo instead of wasting time worrying. But they lay in a pile next to his planner on her kitchen table. Both unread.

"That's it." She strode across the room and turned the clock so it faced away from her. She stood back and inspected her handiwork. "Better. Much better."

Dante made no response. He'd obviously made up his mind that she was completely nuts. Which, she thought wryly, she probably was. Not to mention exhausted.

Something's wrong.

She should've stayed there with him. It seemed obvious now, but it was too late to do anything about it. Another mistake. Mia fought not to remember her first mistake, the one she'd been paying for her whole life.

Holly.

Even now the name caused her throat to constrict. She'd turned thirteen a few days earlier and had spent most of the time since begging her parents to let her take Holly to the park. She was a teenager, too old to be treated like a baby any longer. She babysat other kids so why not her own sister? Didn't they trust her?

They did. For one afternoon. And they regretted it the rest of their lives.

They shouldn't have trusted her. Because the truth was she hadn't wanted to take Holly to the park because she was sister of the year. She'd wanted to bring her there so she'd have an excuse to see Brett O'Malley.

Brett lived across the street from the park. He was always out on his front lawn, tossing around a football with his high school buddies or just goofing off with them. Every now and then, his girlfriend would come over and the two of them would disappear in his car.

Once in a while he'd even be out there all by himself.

Mia lived for those times.

Of course, the Haggerty High quarterback didn't know she existed. But that didn't stop her from walking by his house on her way to the Cumby's at the center of town. And it didn't stop her from concocting all kinds of fantasies, most of which involved him crossing the street to the park and striking up a conversation with her. As soon as the two of them made eye contact, the connection between them would be unbreakable. He'd ditch his girlfriend and ask Mia out and they'd live happily ever after.

At thirteen, Mia was too old for swing sets and slides. But Holly was only seven. She loved going to the park, loved hanging out with her big sister.

The day her mother finally caved was the happiest day of Mia's life. At least until 2:27 p.m., which was when she realized her sister was gone.

As it turned out the cliché was true. Because Mia hadn't turned away from Holly for more than few minutes. Just long enough to stutter an awkward response to Brett's question.

"You haven't seen Claire, have you? My mom said she thought she saw her walk over here a couple minutes ago."

"Uh, no," she'd stuttered. "I, um, haven't seen her."

"She's got long, dark hair. Kinda tall. Maybe you've seen her around."

She shook her head. "If she, uh, shows up, I'll, uh, tell her you're, uh, looking for her."

"Thanks."

Brett scanned the empty park and stood a minute before turning around and heading back toward his house. When she thought back over it, she remembered how his face had darkened then. Or was she changing the story to fit what happened. And why did she want to believe the high school senior had seen something?

He'd certainly never admitted to it, not when the police questioned people in the area or afterward, when the media circus died down and things got back to normal.

Normal wasn't quite the right word though, was it?

When Holly's body turned up a year later, miles from the site of the abduction, it was unrecognizable. Her mother had started drinking heavily by then. And her father was gone.

He'd sent postcards at first. Mia pinned them up on her bulletin board, tracing his route on the USA map tacked over her bookcase. But the postcards dwindled to one every six months or so. Then after a couple of years had passed they stopped completely.

She never heard from him again. But apparently her mother had. Because Angela Lindgren was already remarried.

Mia was old enough now—and had been through enough therapy as a child—to understand that none of it was her fault. She hadn't forgotten about Holly for very long. Whoever was going to take her had probably been watching her for weeks, at least that's what the police detectives told them. It wasn't her fault that her father saw Holly in her every time he looked into her face. It wasn't her fault that her sister's death, along with her father's desertion, devastated her mother and propelled her into alcoholism.

None of it was her fault.

She knew that. But she also knew that a single slip-up could cost a life. That carelessness when it came to details like time had irreversible consequences.

And she knew she had it in her to become the kind of person who fixed things, not the kind that destroyed them forever. A virus destroyed everything in its path, leaving nothing behind. But she had the ability and the motivation to disable even the deadliest pathogen.

Well, that was the idea anyway.

Mia eyed the Band-Aid on her finger and smiled wearily. Shaky hands. If only she could banish them the way she banished memories. Banished any emotion that threatened to disturb her carefully cultivated equilibrium.

So much for that.

Ignoring Dante's unblinking gaze, she crossed back to the mantel and turned the clock far enough around so she could see the numbers.

Two hundred and seven minutes.

"I'm going back."

Dante tilted his head.

"Don't try and talk me out of it either," she warned, grabbing her keys out of the tray next to the front door and slipping on her sneakers.

If her husky thought it odd she'd decided to walk him in the middle of night, he didn't protest. Springing to his feet, he trotted over to the door and pushed his nose toward the opening.

"You stay here. We don't need anybody else disappearing."

Her voice faltered on the last word. Even after so many years the pain was still there, just under the surface. She took a deep breath and edged past the dog, deliberately ignoring his dejected slump.

She was halfway down the walk when he stepped out of the shadows.

"Going somewhere?"

Chapter 6

Mia strode over to where he stood at the end of the walkway. "You've got to stop doing that."

"Doing what?" Nick couldn't resist. He knew she had a right to be annoyed—he'd been hours, far longer than he'd intended—but she was damn sexy when she got mad. The more he got to know her, the more he realized how thin the sheen of ice that she used to mask her emotions really was.

"You know perfectly well what."

"Humor me."

"For one thing, you've got to stop sneaking up on me when I least expect it. For another, if you say you're going to be back at my place soon then you should do it. Or at least let me know what's going on. I thought—"

He waited for her to finished but she'd apparently changed her mind about clueing him in. "I expected to leave Mike's place about an hour ago. But I couldn't get a decent look at whoever it was and I didn't want to risk such an obvious tail. And I did make you a promise."

She made a noise that sounded a bit like *hmmphh*. "C'mon then. We'd better go back inside before you collapse. I don't plan on dragging that body up the steps and depositing you on a bed."

Was she really upset with him or was it some kind

of defense? He wasn't sure and he was too damn tired to start analyzing Mia Lindgren. All he wanted was a couch and a glass of water.

Odd that a month ago he would've craved vodka, not water. He wondered if the effect was temporary or if it would last the rest of his life. Either way, he wasn't sure he cared. He was just glad his mind felt clear for the first time in months. Years, maybe.

He felt alive again. It was a painful feeling but a good one too. Like getting the sensation back after being left out in the cold for too long. He'd been numb for years—even before Rosa had gotten sick. But he hadn't been capable of admitting it.

As he trailed after Mia his eyes followed the movement of her hips. The glint of the streetlamp lit her pale hair and he realized with some surprise that he was responding to her as a man, not an FBI agent or even a friend.

He wanted her.

Which totally sucked.

No matter how much he wanted Mia he couldn't act on his feelings. For one thing, he wasn't ready. Hell, he wasn't even supposed to be at her house in the first place. He should be back at Seahaven, reading his thriller. Instead he was out in the middle of night, breaking into a dead man's condo and lusting after the guy's former girlfriend. Father Donelan would have his head for this.

He forced the thought out of his head. He'd deal with Donelan in the morning. For now, he had to get a handle on the raging lust coursing through his body.

"Christ."

Mia opened the door, just enough to give him a

prime view of her breasts. "Did you say something?"

"No," he said through gritted teeth. "I mean, uh, yeah, I did."

She raised an eyebrow. "Which is it?"

"I just, uh, wondered if I could have a glass of water?"

If she noticed his sudden inability to form a coherent sentence she didn't mention it. "Sure," she said, holding her hand out in front of her and kneeling. "Hang on a sec."

Before he had a chance to see what was coming, an enormous dog was on him. "Whoa, boy," he said, gently removing the dog's paws from his chest. "Calm down."

"Dante, down!" Mia flashed him an apologetic smile. "He won't hurt you. He just gets excited when he meets new people."

Excited wasn't exactly the word for it. Manic with a healthy dose of insane was more like it. Nick took hold of the husky's paws and held them.

"Are you planning on dancing with him?" Mia turned from the refrigerator, bottled water in hand. "Looks like you two are ready to tango."

Nick held on a few more seconds before letting go. The husky sat before him, eyeing him with respectful dislike. Clearly, he saw Nick as a rival. "Dogs don't like to stand on two legs for very long. It's a quick way to get him out of the habit. And of letting him know you're the alpha."

He knelt and scratched the husky behind the ears. The dog didn't resist but he wasn't letting down his guard either.

Mia walked over to him and gave him the water.

"Thanks for the tip," she said. "I guess I should take him to obedience school. I sort of inherited him and haven't had the chance to do much in the way of training."

"Huskies are tough to train. They're working dogs—smart and strong-willed, with tons of energy. And they're highly independent." Nick unscrewed the cap and took a swig.

She gave Dante an affectionate look. "They're definitely high maintenance."

"Kind of like you."

She gave him a sly look. "Lucky for you, you don't have to train me."

He laughed. "Now that's a feat I wouldn't attempt."

Nick drained the rest of his water. It quenched his thirst but hadn't done a thing to lessen his craving for Mia. Despite the late hour, he wasn't a bit tired. Which was a damn good thing, since he had a two-hour drive ahead of him. He wasn't sure if Father Donelan would notice his absence or not but he wanted to be there in the morning either way. Nick didn't think he'd let the FBI know about his temporary disappearance but didn't want to take any chances. He'd didn't want to spend any more time on leave than he had to.

So you can go back to burying yourself in work, like you always did.

So what if he did? His worked mattered. Even at his worst moments with the Bureau, he'd never doubted that, never lost faith. And if he'd paid a price for that it was his choice. His mistake. He'd take responsibility for the consequences. In the meantime, he had a job to do.

Like your father.

He gave Dante a final scratch behind the ear and crossed to the kitchen table. "Are these the clippings from your buddy's place?"

He could never manage to keep the jealousy out of his voice when he asked about Mike. Well, too bad. It wasn't as if he was going to act on his desires. He lifted one of the print-outs and scanned it. "Have you read this?"

"Not yet." Mia came up next to him and peered down at the print-out. "Controversial Scientist Creates Deadly New Flu Strain for Pandemic Research."

"Why would a guy—a really smart guy—develop a variation on the Spanish flu? One that people's immune systems can't fight? What happens when that virus gets out into the world?"

"Sounds a little like *Frankenstein*, doesn't it?"

"*A little*?" Nick set the print-out down and picked up the next one.

"Kawaoka's in the minority, but some scientists believe the best way to prevent a pandemic is to create viruses that help them study the genetic changes involved." She pointed to a section of the article. "Through selection of immune escape viruses in the laboratory under appropriate containment conditions, we were able to identify key regions that would enable the 2009 H1N1 virus to escape immunity."

Nick ran a hand through his hair. "I don't know what the hell that means."

"It means that by studying his new and improved version of Spanish influenza he might be able to figure out how to save people from a new and improved version of Swine flu. Viruses mutate. That's a given. If

H1N1 mutates into a more deadly form, it would take time to create an antidote. Kawaoka's trying to stay one step ahead of it."

He turned to face her. "Yeah, well, from what I remember a few million people died from the flu back in 1918."

"Not a few million. Twenty million. Twenty-one point five to be exact, or as least that's as close to an exact figure as we can get."

"What happens if somebody gets hold of one of Dr. Frankenstein's experiments?" he asked. "I might not know a hell of a lot about science, but I'm certain of one thing. There are no appropriate containment conditions. Terrorists find out about something like that and—"

"—and we're looking at the end of the world as we know it."

"Jesus."

Mia nodded. "As for the terrorists, they already know about Kakaowa's work. It was widely reported back in 2014."

"Jesus."

"From the look on your face, I take it the other articles are more or less the same."

"Pretty much." He thrust them toward her and sat down at the table. "The question is why did your—why did Mike—have these locked inside his desk?"

Mia finished reading the articles and took a chair opposite him. If it hadn't been for the fact they were talking about the end of the world, it would have been cozy, sitting there with her. Small problem.

"If he wasn't dead, I'd say it would be natural for him to have them. Working with this stuff is what we do. If he came across those articles, he'd keep them." She hesitated, averting her gaze. "I would too."

"Well, you're right about one thing, Bride of Frankenstein," he said. "The man's dead. And I'm guessing this has something to do with it."

"So you believe my theory—about him not really drowning."

"I'm starting to. I called to get the results of the autopsy and hopefully should have them in a day or two if nobody decides to stall."

"You think they're going to stall?"

"I don't know. We'll see. I'm supposed to be on leave, so it's possible the powers that be don't want me getting involved in something I shouldn't be."

They got that right. Under the yellow overhead light, Mia's hair fell down over her shoulders in pale waves. He'd never seen it down. He almost wished he hadn't.

She gave him a hard look. "Maybe you shouldn't. I mean, you're supposed to be getting better, aren't you? Healing. This can't be helping."

"It is helping," he said quietly. "You're helping."

She looked away. For several seconds, she didn't speak. "I don't think so," she said at last. "I've never helped anybody. Not even my own mother."

"Mia—"

"Stop, okay?" She held up a hand. "Just stop."

"Okay." He wanted to reach out and take her hand in his. No, he wanted to take her upstairs and show her how much she'd helped him heal, one long kiss at a time. But if he told her that he'd lose her. Whatever had happened to her in the past had scared the hell out of her. If he pushed too hard, he'd lose her.

And he wasn't going to get involved with her in the first place. Wasn't that what he kept telling himself?

"You still haven't told me what happened at Mike's." Mia arranged the articles in a neat pile and looked across the table at him. "Did you get anything else besides the plate number?"

The change of subject was a relief. Far better to talk about murder and deadly pathogens than feelings. From the look on her face, he knew she felt the same way. "No. I got as close to the condo as I could without risking being seen. Whoever it was didn't leave by the same way he got in. By the time I heard a car start on the other side of the lot it was too late to see anything. I was lucky I got the plate number. Stealthy little bastard."

"You should've called the police."

"Not necessarily. I'm not sure we want to tip our hand at this point. And it may have been somebody for something too—somebody who didn't have anything to do with Mike's death. It's possible somebody else who knew him has the same questions you do. You're not the only one who went out sailing with him. Whoever it was came in by the front door. Even if they picked the lock, it's a pretty bold move. Anyway, we'll know more in the morning when I call in the plate number."

"Unless the powers that don't want you to know," Mia pointed out.

"There are other ways to trace a license plate." He pressed his lips together. "If I have to, I'll use them."

"Even if it means getting in trouble with the FBI?"

"Yes."

Mia leaned forward across the table. From the far end of the kitchen, Dante lifted his head. Still protective. He didn't blame him. "Why are you doing this?"

Because you're beautiful and I can't stop thinking about you. Nick wondered how his ice princess would react to that statement. The truth was, he wasn't blowing off rehab just for Mia. The more he learned about Mike, the more he got a bad feeling about the guy.

He stood up from the table. "I know I shouldn't be the one pointing this out, but it's 4:12 a.m. Way past my curfew. If I don't head back to Seahaven, there's a good chance Donelan will notice I'm not there."

Mia stood up as well. "You didn't answer my question."

He hadn't and there was a reason for that. But if he were going to help her, she needed to know the truth. Or at least part of it. "I'm doing this because if your friend didn't drown—and if he kept those articles for anything other than professional curiosity—then we're looking at a potentially dangerous situation."

Her eyes darted away from him. "That seems like a stretch."

"Does it?"

She didn't answer.

"Come on, Mia, I know that brain of yours has already figured this out way before I did. You had it figured out as soon as you got that call, didn't you?"

No answer.

"What if Mike decided to pull his own version of Dr. Frankenstein?" Nick pressed. "What if the wrong people found out about his work and decided to take matters into their own hands?"

Mia frowned. "Mike wouldn't do that."

"I hope you're right."

"But you don't think so."

"Do you?"

"I don't know what to think," she said in exasperation.

Nick didn't say anything.

"What went wrong," she recited. "Why didn't it kill the kids?"

He still didn't answer.

"Why would he write that? I mean, okay, I get that he would want those articles. But why write *that*? Mike would never have written something like that. It sounds like—" Her voice trailed off.

"One step at a time. Tomorrow I'll call my friend over at the bureau and badger him until he gets me the autopsy just to shut me up. If Mike's death wasn't an accident there should be signs of a struggle. Scratches, blood under the fingernails, that kind of thing. Even a full day at sea won't get rid of that stuff. And I'm going to put a name to those plates. After that, we'll know more."

She sighed. "I still haven't told you the reason I called you at Seahaven. What I found. At the lab."

"What did you find?"

Mia ran her fingertip along the surface of the pile of articles. There was a Band-Aid over her left index finger. It struck him as cute but he knew it was anything but that. A cut like that could do a hell of a lot of damage, at least in her line of work. He ignored the twinge of worry that niggled his brain. There were safety measures. And the woman was a trained scientist. She knew what she was doing.

She looked up at him. "I found some notes Mike

made. He'd left them in the lab. Usually we work together—always—it's too dangerous not to. But he'd obviously been there on his own."

"What were the notes about?"

"They described some new samples he'd analyzed. They were still there at the lab—I'd just written a report that said almost the exact same thing as his. Two of the slides contained an unknown virus. It resembled Ebola but there were differences. The cells in the slides—they'd just—exploded. It was unlike any virus I've seen before. I tried to match it to a known pathogen afterward but I couldn't."

Was it sadness in those pale blue eyes—or fear? Maybe a little of both. "Where did the slides come from?"

She shook her head. "That's just it. Usually samples are clearly labeled. We never know the names of the subject they were taken from, but we know the date of arrival and the location they were sent from. That helps us with identification. But these were completely unmarked. There was nothing—no information. All I know is they came into the lab a little more than a week ago. There was a third slide too, with the same virus, but this one was unaffected. It was—perfect."

Nick tried to sort out what she was saying. "So, the third sample—why was it different?"

"That's just it—I don't know."

"Who else would have seen the samples or Mike's notes?"

"Nobody. We're the only ones authorized to enter that area. The door to the outer section of the lab is programmed to respond to our fingerprints. And to get to the inner section, you have to put on a space suit. It's not like somebody could sneak in there without being noticed."

"What about your boss? Higher ups?"

She hesitated. "Trask could get in, I suppose. And the people above him, too. There's a keypad below that's programmed to respond to certain codes, including ours. But there'd be a good chance they'd get caught. It takes an hour just to get ready to enter the unit."

"He could've made copies."

Mia said nothing.

It couldn't be easy, implicating your lab partner. Or your lover. "Thanks for telling me."

It was still dark outside. Beyond the warmth of her kitchen, blackness stretched out in every direction. He walked toward the door and gave a nod toward Dante. "Be good."

In the end, that's what it came down to. Being good. Such simple words. But so many people had trouble doing just that. If Mike had been following in Kawaoka's footsteps that would explain the clippings and the reason the virus hadn't been labeled.

How much would terrorists be willing to pay for a deadly virus with no cure?

The amount would be staggering. Beyond comprehension.

So would the aftermath.

Mia wanted answers but what if the answers were far worse than anything she could have anticipated?

She caught up to him in the entryway and laid a hand on his arm. "So you'll call tomorrow—once you get the results of the autopsy? And the trace?"

"I'll call tomorrow, either way." He kissed her lightly on the forehead and smoothed her hair with his hand. He shouldn't have done it but couldn't stop himself. "Don't worry."

She rose up on her toes and touched her lips to his. She backed away from him so quickly he could almost believe she hadn't done it. "Don't forget to take your own advice."

Taking his own advice.

He couldn't remember the last time he'd done that.

Chapter 7

Mia reached the entrance to her lab and kept on walking. Over the weekend she'd done nothing but agonize over Mike's death. *You mean analyze.* She still hadn't even cried about the loss. What she had done was spend hours sorting through the few facts she had.

Now she was going on two hours sleep and her brain wasn't working at top speed, so she wondered if her decision about a new partner was due to impaired judgment or sound reasoning. Either way, she wasn't going to change her mind.

Don't look back.

The door to Dan Trask's office was ajar. She hesitated at the sound of his voice. Obviously, he was on the phone and Trask didn't take kindly to being interrupted. On the other hand, she wanted to get this over with.

"…I already told you, that's not going to work," he was saying, his voice tense. "Not on this end, anyway."

Mia held her fist a few inches from the door. She wasn't eavesdropping. Okay, maybe just a little bit. She strained to hear her boss but he'd lowered his voice.

She knocked gently and waited.

The conversation stopped.

A few seconds later Dan pulled the door open and waved her inside, though he didn't look all that happy to see her. Come to think of it, he hadn't looked all that happy for quite a while. His military haircut was tinged with more gray than she remembered, which made him look older than his actual age. The gray flecks in his green eyes were more noticeable too. He looked as tired as Mia felt.

She sat down in the chair across from his desk.

"Listen, we can talk about this later, okay? Somebody just walked in."

An inaudible voice barked something into the phone.

"I've got to go."

Trask hung up the phone. "What can I do for you, Lindgren?"

It wasn't a question. He steepled his fingertips under his chin and waited.

"I made a decision. About who I want to work with." Mia waited for him to ask who she'd chosen but he remained silent. She pushed a strand of her hair behind her ear and pressed on. "I'd like to work with Chien Lu. He brought up working together the other day and after thinking it over, I think he'd be the best person to take Mike's spot. He's a solid researcher and he's worked with Ebola in the past."

Trask regarded her coolly. Still no response.

"And I like him." She sounded like a moonstruck school girl. But she couldn't take it back and qualifying her statement would only make it worse.

Still nothing.

"He's very qualified," she blurted out. Was the man making her squirm on purpose? Hadn't he told her yesterday she had to pick a new partner—virtually threatened to fire her if she didn't get him an answer by Monday?

Trask leaned back in his chair and gazed out the window. Beyond the Institute was nothing but fields. Nobody wanted to live next to a facility that specialized in infectious diseases. Which was fine with the administrators who ran the place. The fewer eyes around, the better.

"Is there someone else you've got in mind?" Mia asked finally, not bothering to hide her frustration. "You said last week—"

"I know what I said last week."

"Did you change your mind? Now you don't want me to work with anybody?"

"Don't be ridiculous. You know you can't work alone."

"Then what's the problem? Chien's a first-rate scientist."

"Chien's gone."

Mia stared at him. "What?"

"He's gone."

"What do you mean gone? Gone where? I just talked to him on Friday."

"So you said." He smiled but there was no humor in it. "Forgive me for not answering you sooner, but I'm still processing the whole thing myself. His wife called first thing. He never came home over the weekend. She thought maybe he'd shown up here this morning."

"Did he?"

"No."

"Are you sure?"

A muscle moved in Trask's jaw. "The surveillance videos show him leaving the facility around 5 p.m. on Friday. Just like he always does. I know you tend to be skeptical of others' competence, but I assure you that wherever the guy is, he's not here."

"What do the police say?"

"The police don't say anything, mainly because they don't know he's missing. His wife told me she hasn't called them. Said she's sure he'll turn up."

That delay seemed odd. Why hadn't the police already been called? Did his wife know more than she was telling? "And you're not—sure?"

He sighed. "I'm not sure of anything right now."

Do you think it's related to Mike's death? Mia stopped herself from asking the question. She'd known Trask for three years and he'd been her boss ever since she started at the Institute. He struck her as a decent guy and she'd always appreciated that he hadn't hit on her—something she couldn't say about all her former bosses. But she'd thought Mike was an open book and it turned out he'd been doing research without her knowledge. Whatever Mike's reasons were, she'd misjudged her partner. Maybe she'd misjudged her boss as well.

"What about his wife, doesn't she have any idea where he might have gone?"

"She says she doesn't."

"Was there…anybody else? Another woman?"

"Who knows. Maybe."

"Chien doesn't strike me as the cheating type."

"Me either. Though that doesn't mean much."

They sat in silence, neither of them sure what to say next. Or unwilling to say it. Did Trask know what Mike had been working on? Did Chien? Mia knew he always kept his office locked when he wasn't using it. And if there was a key, she had no idea where it would be. And she couldn't very well search it without being detected. The place was full of security cameras.

If Trask found her searching Chien's office—or even Mike's—he'd fire her on the spot. No questions asked. She couldn't risk that, no matter how much she wanted to find out what was inside. If she lost her position at the Institute she'd lose herself.

The cell phone in Mia's lab coat pocket vibrated but she ignored it. The last thing she wanted was to open a message from Nick under Trask's sharp gaze.

Trask reached for his coffee mug and took a sip. "Remind me never to drink the stuff from the cafeteria." He made a face.

Mia's phone buzzed again. If it was Nick he wouldn't text a second time unless it was important. She rose from her chair. "I should probably get to work."

He gave her a curt nod. If there was a hint of a smirk in his expression it was impossible to tell. The man was a stone wall.

"Of course." Trask stood up as well. "I've assigned Caleb Hastings to be your partner. When Chien gets back, you can work with him, as requested."

If he gets back. She forced her expression to mirror her boss's. There was nothing wrong with Hastings. His work was thorough and he wasn't inexperienced. Still, there was something abrasive about him—he always seemed a little oblivious to everybody else, the kind of guy who wouldn't stop asking tedious questions at staff meetings, even when they'd gone well over the allotted hour. Then there was the issue of him hitting on her. After the debacle with Mike, even the possibility made her nervous. Chien had been safe, but she wasn't sure about Caleb. Geeky guy, twenty-something, fresh out of grad school.

Maybe he had a girlfriend. And no matter what, it was better than working alone. She definitely didn't want to be on her own any longer, not when scientists seemed to be disappearing on a daily basis.

Trask's gray-green eyes bored into her. "Is that arrangement acceptable to you?"

It took a moment to compose her answer. It was unusual for Trask to ask how an employee felt about anything, never mind a personnel decision. The disappearances must be getting to him too. "Of course," she said a little too enthusiastically. "Absolutely."

"He's not my first choice due to the lack of experience, but we're a little shorthanded now. And it's only temporary."

"I understand."

When she reached the door Trask called out to her. "Yes?"

"I know it's unlikely, but if you happen to hear from Chien, you will let me know?"

"Of course," she repeated.

He turned back toward the desk and picked up the phone.

She stepped out into the corridor and headed toward her office. When she turned the corner at the end of the hallway, she pulled out her phone.

The messages weren't from Nick. Instead her mother's photo stared up her.

She clicked on the first message.

19 days and counting! Expected to see you here last night. Guess you had other plans...

The ellipses were a nice touch, Mia had to give her

that. She hated to admit it but her mother had a point. Mia had only visited once during her mother's entire stay. Her stepfather was still out of town and Ashley couldn't very well leave Burnleigh in the middle of summer school. And a visit to Seahaven would give her the chance to tell Nick about Chien's disappearance. It was important to keep him informed. A memory of the previous night's goodbye flickered across her brain and she ignored it. She'd simply been saying goodbye. The brush of her lips against his had meant nothing.

Mia hit the microphone and dictated a response.

"Be there tonight. I promise. Can't wait to see you."

It always struck her as strange, that her stepsister Ashley refused to call her friends but thought nothing of dictating text messages with them for hours at a time. But when it came to her mother, Mia understood. So much easier to keep her at a distance. So much easier not to talk. About rehab. About anything.

How many more years could she keep her mother at arm's length? If Angela was serious about giving up drinking—and she certainly seemed to be—their relationship would have to change. Would her mother finally confront her about what happened all those years ago?

Mia's cell phone buzzed. She clicked on the message and stared at it a few seconds.

Nick says hi. ;)

That answered one of her questions, anyway. Her mother hadn't changed.

If she didn't know her mother so well she'd think Angela was vying to get the two of them together. Which would be a bit too much interference but at least it would suggest her mother wanted Mia to meet someone. But her daughter's happiness had never been foremost on Angela Ward's list of priorities.

Her mother hadn't sent the message to hint at a potential romance with Nick. She'd sent it to remind Mia that Angela saw him every day, not just in passing on the occasional visit. In some strange way, she was *competing* with Mia. She'd never been sure if her mother was jealous or if she said the things she did out of resentment.

Mia looked up and saw Caleb Hastings heading toward her. With his nerdy glasses, overgrown curls and bowtie, he was a walking cliché of a geek. He was the youngest member of the unit and, if Mia admitted it, the most gifted after Chien. She didn't know him well—though that would certainly change—but didn't relish the idea of working with him.

If she were being honest, she'd have to admit she wouldn't relish the idea of working with anybody besides Mike. But that didn't give her the right to trash the guy before he started. She had to at least give him a chance.

Just not yet.

She deleted the message and deposited her phone into her lab coat pocket. Flashing her new partner a quick smile, she pressed her fingertip to the ID pad next to her door and slipped into her office, closing the door behind her. She knew she'd been rude and she regretted it, but she wasn't ready to deal with any more changes.

****

Nick stared down at the illegible scrawl that filled the first page of his notebook. He'd thought the autopsy results would clear things up but that wasn't the case.

Just the opposite, in fact.

Mike Chandler had indeed drowned. According to the coroner's report, death was due to "asphyxia as a result of aspiration of fluid into air passages, caused by submersion in water." The water samples taken from Chandler's lungs matched the samples taken from the Chesapeake Bay, so there was no question that Mia's partner died when he fell—or was pushed—into the ocean.

Beyond the certainty that Mike drowned, little else was clear. Granted, Nick had to base his analysis on what Dalton Ross had told him. Which was a problem in itself. Ross didn't want him getting involved in a murder case while he was supposed to be in rehab. On top of that, the local police weren't exactly cooperating. They hadn't released the autopsy to the FBI and didn't seem interested in doing so. Unless the FBI took over the case, which wasn't likely—not with everything else going on—there wasn't a whole hell of a lot Nick couldn't do about it. Luckily for Nick, Dalton Ross had called in a favor from somebody he knew on the force. Dalton still hadn't actually seen a copy of the autopsy but he'd gotten enough information to raise questions about what happened to Mike the day he died.

But that's all they were. Questions. Nothing definitive pointed to murder and the local police seemed happy enough to stick with their original conclusion. After drinking one too many on Sunday evening, Chandler fell off his boat and drowned. End of story.

Except it wasn't, at least in Nick's opinion. For one thing, there was trauma to the back of the head. The coroner and the police believed it had most likely been caused by a fall due to Chandler's inebriated state. The guy had been drunk—drunk as a skunk—and his corpse had the blood-alcohol level to prove it. It made sense. Just like the abrasions on the guy's body made sense. And the bruises.

The coroner's report stated that such extensive damage was not uncommon in victims drowned at sea. Before they washed ashore, corpses often collided with rocks and other debris, even boat propellers. Not to mention the fact that a dead body was prime fare for fish and crustaceans like lobster and crabs. According to the report, the circular lesions that covered Mike's bloated body were evidence that the majority of the injuries were post-mortem. As for the others, it was common for an avid sailor to sustain a few cuts and bruises. Went with the territory.

Nothing out of the ordinary. No reason to suspect murder.

That's what the coroner believed. And the police. And even Dalton Ross.

"Listen, buddy, I know you're probably bored out of your skull there," Dalton had said when he'd called Nick with the results. "I would be too. But don't get sidetracked when you're so close to the end. If the Bureau sees that you checked out early, you might end up on leave for a lot longer than two months."

"Who said anything about checking out?"

There was a pause on the other end of the line. "Laura did."

"Just because your wife had one of her dreams or visions or whatever she calls them, doesn't mean I'm about to go AWOL." He kept his voice steady. "I've made progress. I feel better than I have in years. And

111

I'm not just saying that to placate you."

"I don't doubt it."

"What else was in that dream?"

"It doesn't matter what was in the dream. Like you said, dreams can be wrong—even Laura's dreams. Just be careful, okay? Get through the rest of the program and get the hell out. We need you back here at the Bureau."

Nick realized he'd balled his hand into a fist. He wanted to punch a wall. He wasn't even sure why he was so angry. Maybe he hadn't made as much progress as he thought. "What about the trace?"

Dalton sighed. "You're not gonna let this go, are you?"

"Just tell me what you found. I don't have a lot of time. My group therapy session starts in an hour."

"Promise me one thing."

"What's that?"

"That whoever she is, you're not gonna fall in love with her."

"Please tell me you're bullshitting me right now." *Was that in the damn dream too?* He wanted to ask but remained silent. He wasn't going to give Dalton the satisfaction of knowing he'd rattled him.

"You've been through a hell of a lot over the past couple of years—the past *few* years, ever since Rosa got sick. I don't know what it feels like to lose the woman you love but I know if I lost Laura I'd be in a pretty rough place.

"Don't patronize me. Or psychoanalyze me." *I was the one who hired you. And as I recall you were the one in bad shape, not me.* Nick looked down at his fist and saw that the knuckles were white.

"Sorry. But I call 'em like I see 'em. I've been there."

"I know." He knew his anger was misplaced. Dalton wasn't just a guy he'd hired. He was his best friend, one of the few people he trusted. But that didn't give him the right to tell him what to do. "So what did you find? About the plates."

Dalton laughed softly. "You never give up, do you?"

"Not usually."

"It was a rental." He rattled off the name and location of the agency. "I called the manager and got him to tell me the name and address of the guy who rented it."

"And?"

"Guy's name is Brendon Thompson. I ran his name through the database. Nothing came up. Either the guy's clean or it's not his real name. The fact that he paid cash tends to make me think it's the latter."

"Did you get a description?"

"Nope. Manager didn't remember him."

"Okay, thanks, buddy."

"No problem. Oh, and if there's anything else you need, *don't call*."

"Thanks for the support."

Nick had spent the hour after their phone call staring at the notes he'd made during their conversation. If he studied them long enough, maybe he could tease out some kind of lead. But nothing came to mind. Had Mike Chandler been beaten, hit on the back of the head, and dumped into the Chesapeake Bay? If so, who had done it—and why? Had Chandler been peddling a deadly virus to somebody—somebody who didn't want him to talk?

Maybe Dalton's right. He didn't want to admit it but it was possible he'd bought into Mia's story because he'd wanted it to be true. No, he didn't want Chandler to have been murdered. But he'd been lonely for the past year. He'd been drinking far too much, so much that it landed him in rehab. Sure, he could tell himself the FBI was hyper-vigilant about that stuff— that he never really had a problem.

But if he did he'd be lying. He had tried to forget about his problems with alcohol. Suppose his interest in Chandler's death was just an excuse to get close to Mia.

Mia.

He'd kissed her forehead. Nothing more than that and he felt guilty, as if he were betraying Rosa somehow. It wasn't the kiss that fueled his guilt though. It was the emotion behind it. Mia made him feel alive.

She was so different from Rosa. Hell, she wasn't even his type. Methodical, distant, intellectual. A control freak. Sure, she was beautiful. But in all his life he'd never been attracted to anybody like Mia. Not even close.

But he couldn't get her out of his head.

Maybe he could bring it up in group therapy. He wondered how Angela Ward would react to *that* share.

He glanced at the digital clock next to the bed. If he didn't hurry up he'd be late to the session and he didn't want that. Donelan hadn't been happy about his departure the night before and he didn't want to antagonize the priest any further. Dalton hadn't been kidding about the FBI extending his leave. He'd seen that kind of thing happen before. And he got the idea it wouldn't take much to nudge them in that direction.

Nick did good work but he'd never played politics. He didn't have a lot of support from higher up.

He shoved his notebook into a drawer and headed out, locking the door behind him. The group therapy room was on the other side of the lobby so there was a fair chance he'd run into Mia on his way there. Angela had made a point of letting him know Mia was coming for a visit. She'd also made it clear she didn't want Nick butting in on their time together.

He didn't blame her. Much as he wanted a few moments alone with Mia, he had to respect her mother's wishes. And he could always call her later. A phone call would be best, anyway. No physical contact required. Quick and easy.

If he saw her in the lobby he'd give her a nod and keep walking. They were both adults, for Christ's sake.

Aside from the fact that you're acting like a lovesick school boy.

He picked up his pace, deliberately slowing it down again when he reached the lobby. He glanced at the place he'd first seen Mia but the chair was empty. As was the entire lobby. If Angela and Mia were together, they'd gone someplace else.

Ignoring the stab of disappointment that cut through him, he crossed to the other side and caught up with a few patients on their way to the meeting. Nargeeta Singh and the lead singer from Shellshock— Nick had forgotten the guy's name—were deep in conversation about the difference between Step Four and Five. He fell into step alongside them, hoping they wouldn't consult him on the matter.

He'd been there for three weeks and still hadn't bothered to read through the manual handed out to patients when they checked in. He knew there were twelve steps but, beyond that, he had no clue. It wasn't that he didn't believe in it. He just hadn't had the time or the interest to really learn the stuff.

Callie Jackson looked over at the three of them as they walked in. "Hey, Nargeeta. Hey, Justin." She let her gaze rest on him a few more seconds than she had on the other two. "Nick. What a surprise."

Was there a hint of sarcasm in her greeting? He supposed she didn't approve of him missing a few meetings. Well, it was voluntary. It wasn't as if they were required to go to group. Wasn't that what Seahaven was all about? Finding your own road to recovery?

Nick smiled. "Good to be here."

"I love your positivity." This time the sarcasm was hard to miss.

He wasn't surprised to find that Angela wasn't there. The other faces were mostly familiar, though a few of them were new. He sat down next to Justin, who was still talking to Nargeeta, though from the sounds of it their conversation had progressed from Step 5 to Screamo music.

Father Donelan appeared in the doorway just as the session was about to get underway. Donelan didn't usually attend the sessions, preferring to leave that to the counselors that worked under him. Nick wondered why the priest was there.

Donelan took a seat at the opposite end of the circle and rested his hands on his knees. "This meeting is now ready to convene," he began, launching into the script that opened every meeting. "Hello, and welcome to the Seahaven support group meeting. My name is

Father Donelan and it is my turn to lead the meeting tonight. Please join me for a moment of silence, after which we will recite the Serenity Prayer."

Unlike the others in the circle, Nick didn't lower his gaze. He wasn't traditionally religious, but he'd always found the serenity prayer calming. Not tonight. With Mia in the building, calm was the last thing he felt.

He remained silent as the rest of the group murmured in unison. "God, grant me the serenity to accept the things I cannot change, the courage to change the things I can, and the wisdom to know the difference. Living one day at a time, enjoying one moment at a time, accepting hardship as a pathway to peace; taking, as Jesus did, this sinful world as it is, not as I would have it; trusting that You will make all things right if I surrender to your will; so that I may be reasonably happy in this life and supremely happy with You forever in the next. Amen."

When the group finished reciting the prayer, Donelan picked up the narrative again. "This group is committed to creating a safe place for men and women to share their experience, strength and hope. This is not a therapy group, no one is here in a professional capacity. Our purpose is to grow spiritually—to grow in our relationship with God. We are not here to talk about others, to condemn, criticize, or judge anyone. Our desire is to improve the quality of our lives by looking honestly at who we are, by learning from listening to and sharing with each other, by placing ourselves in the care of our Higher Power, Jesus Christ, and by engaging in healthier behaviors."

Several members of the group nodded in

agreement. Nick liked the idea, but still didn't quite see the difference between therapy and group shares. He also didn't relish the thought of sitting through a meeting when Mia might walk by and see him. He wasn't ashamed of being there, but he felt vulnerable all the same. No way he could cut out early, not after last night's adventure.

Donelan's eyes were on him. "All right, we're ready for our first share."

Callie Jackson's hand shot up.

The priest hesitated only a moment. "All right, Callie, you have the floor."

"Hi, I'm Callie and I'm an alcoholic and a food addict."

The multi-millionaire chef waited while everybody muttered the usual hellos. Before Nick had chimed in, she was off like a horse out of the gate, giving them all a blow-by-blow of her recent divorce and its triggering effect. He felt Donelan's eyes on him again and had the uncomfortable sensation that the priest knew he wasn't paying attention.

At the end of her allotted time, Donelan nudged her to wrap up her story but she went on talking another five minutes before she came to an abrupt halt and said, "Done."

Nick drifted through a chorus of members thanking her for sharing and waited to see who'd go next, his thoughts reverting to his phone call with Dalton. *Brendon Thompson*. He was sure it was a fake name so why did it bother him so much? He couldn't shake the idea he'd heard that name before, though for the life of him he couldn't remember where. Not during an investigation. Not socially.

He had the feeling the connection was there somewhere in the back of his head. He knew it was. But he couldn't remember.

Nick realized with a start that all eyes were on him.

"Callie was just pointing out," Donelan said with only a trace of disapproval, "that you're the only one in this group who hasn't shared since you've been here. She thought you might want to go next."

He fought the impulse to lunge across the circle and strangle the woman. What the hell had he done to her? Nick cast around the circle for a friendly face, or at least somebody who looked as if they'd be willing to take his place. He knew it was a lost cause. They were all waiting patiently for him to spill his guts.

"Go ahead, Nick," Donelan said encouragingly. "We're all friends here."

Yeah, sure. "I, uh, wouldn't want to take anybody's turn."

Donelan raised a hand off his knee in a magnanimous gesture of good faith. "Does anybody else want to share?"

Silence.

"Looks like you've got the floor."

Nick swallowed. To his embarrassment, a sheen of sweat broke out across his forehead. He couldn't get out of it. He had to give them something.

Justin laid a hand on his shoulder. "Hi, Nick. Glad you're here."

"Hi Nick," Nargeeta echoed.

The chorus of hellos traveled from one end of the group to the other until it stopped at him. He swallowed again. "Hi, I'm Nick—"

What the hell was wrong with his voice?

Jesus.

If Callie pointed out that he was doing it ass backwards, he'd kill her. But she said nothing, just watched him with those deep brown eyes. No one else spoke either.

He took a depth breath. "Hi, I'm Nick and I'm an alcoholic."

A few people nodded encouragingly.

He took another deep breath. "My dad was an alcoholic too. His job was, uh, kind of stressful and he got in the habit of pouring himself a scotch every night after he got home from work. Pretty soon it was two scotches, then three, then the whole bottle. I don't remember how old I was when it started but by the time I was in high school it got bad enough that he couldn't do his job anymore. They fired him. Twenty-five years busting his ass for the Bureau and they called him upstairs one morning and told him he was done. Escorted him out of the building. He never even got to go back to his office for his briefcase."

Nick stopped, afraid to meet the gazes of the people in the circle. Strange how the facts didn't begin to capture what it had been like, growing up with a man who harbored so much bitterness. So much anger. So much hurt.

"Relates."

He looked up at the sound of Donelan's voice. He didn't know the priest's backstory—Donelan seldom shared personal information. Nick knew he'd been an alcoholic at some point in the distant past but that was it.

"Relates." Callie flashed him a smile.

Would wonders never cease?

"After that it got worse," Nick said. "A lot worse. My mom had to go back to work because we didn't have any money and my dad was supposed to look after us kids. 'Course he couldn't even look after himself, never mind the five of us. I was a junior in high school by then and I could drive, so I used to do most of the shopping and stuff like that. My dad never said anything but I think he resented it. Hated me for it. I thought it would be better after I went to college but it wasn't." Nick plunged on before he could change his mind about sharing. "Somebody called DSS. The two youngest—the twins—got placed in foster homes. The older two got the hell out of there before DSS placed them too."

Nick broke off. What was the point in going into the rest? It was a familiar story, the stuff of HBO specials. The parents who blamed each other and were never the same. The violence that always followed the arguments. The day Nick was inducted into the FBI was the day his father turned up dead, found in a car driven off the road not far from the bar where he'd spent the night downing shots.

"I told myself I'd never be like my father. For most of my life I believed I was different," he said. "Then my wife got cancer. When she died—no, before she died—I started drinking. It was the only way I could think of to kill the pain. But I don't want to be my father."

"What happened to the twins?"

The voice had come from behind him. Nick turned to see Mia standing in the corner of the room. Her hair was loose instead of pulled up in the usual bun and she wore jeans that accentuated her long legs. How long had she been there?

"Hey," Callie protested. "She's not supposed to be here." She half rose out of her chair, looking as if she was ready to deck Mia. "This is a *private* meeting. *Patients only*."

A few of the other patients mumbled in agreement.

Mia took a step backward toward the door. "I didn't mean to intrude."

"Well, you did," said Callie, unwilling to let the violation drop.

"It's okay," Nick said. "I don't mind. Mia's a friend of mine." He wasn't sure if either statement was true but another few minutes and she was going to be lynched by a mob of recovering alcoholics.

"Friend or foe," Donelan said, the brogue in his accent coming out, "Ms. Jackson's right. I'm sorry but you'll have to leave, Miss Ward."

"It's Lindgren," Mia said stiffly.

Not helping, Mia. How could somebody as smart as Mia have so little clue when it came to social situations?

"I just wondered if I might have a word with Mia," Nick said quickly, rising out of his chair and striding over to her. "It won't take long."

"About what?" Mia asked.

"We can discuss it out in the hallway."

A cacophony of voices reached him before he reached her. "Thanks, Nick." "Thanks for sharing." "TFS!" they called out. Callie's voice rang out loudest of all.

It felt oddly comforting to have shared his story after so many years of holding it inside him. He hadn't intended to do it but now that it was over he was glad he had. He would never be friends with the people in the room—his job made that impossible—but he felt connected to them in a way he hadn't before. To Mia too, for all her intrusiveness. He wouldn't have said what he had if he'd known she was listening. But now that she knew he felt relieved. She knew the worst. Whatever happened—or didn't—between them it wouldn't be because he'd misled her about who he was.

When the two of them reached the door, Mia turned and tried for a smile. "I'll bring him right back," she said brightly. "I promise."

The ice queen was really making an effort to win them over, he had to give her that. He watched her fidgeting in the silence and knew the only thing he wanted at that moment was to be alone with her.

Unfortunately, nobody else appeared to feel the same way.

The members of the group had come to a silent consensus that the best solution would be to ignore her existence. Mia had definitely taken his place as the most hated person in the room.

"Come on," Nick said under his breath. "Looks like you've been voted off the island."

Chapter 8

Mia trailed behind Nick as they left the session. As soon as they were out of earshot, she turned back toward him. "I didn't mean to eavesdrop."

"I know."

"What you said in there—about your dad—"

He shrugged. "Ancient history. Everybody tells their story and I finally got cornered."

She wanted to ask about his brothers and sisters. And his wife. But something in his expression held her back. "So what did you find out about the autopsy?" she asked finally, to break the silence.

"In due time." He put a finger to his lips. "Follow me."

They hurried down the corridor, which was mostly empty aside from an elderly woman using a walker and one of the counselors he remembered from check in. When they reached the lobby he walked over the door and held it open for her. "This way."

She wondered if he planned on leaving the premises again, but he headed in the opposite direction of the parking lot. As she followed him down a path lined with roses, she took in the beauty of the grounds. *Not a bad place to recover.*

It was so peaceful.

It had still been light out when she arrived to visit her mother, but now the moon had come up over the bay and the stars were out. She slid onto the bench where Nick had sat down, being sure to keep a safe distance between them.

"I don't bite."

"I know, I just—"

"Are you afraid I might kiss you?"

"No!" She tried to laugh it off and failed.

"The reason I dragged you out here is that this is the only place I can be sure nobody's going to listen in on our conversation. But if I've got to shout that kind of defeats the purpose."

"Fine." She inched toward him until their legs touched. "Happy now?"

"Ecstatic." He turned to face her. "Now what did you want to talk to me about? Or were you checking to see if I heard back about the autopsy?"

"Did you?"

He nodded.

"So was he murdered?"

"I don't know."

"What do you mean you don't know? Shouldn't the coroner have been able to figure that out?"

"It's not as straightforward as that. Mike—the body—did show extensive abrasions and there was substantial bruising."

"That seems pretty clear then."

"Not necessarily. I guess that kind of thing's common when the person drowns."

"Isn't there some way to tell if the bruises were pre- or post-mortem?"

"Apparently not. The body had been in the water almost twenty-four hours before it washed ashore. That makes things difficult. At least that's what my buddy told me."

In the moonlight, Nick's eyes shone. How could she be feeling romantic when they were talking about her friend's dead body? She felt like a monster. "But it's possible he got those bruises before he fell into the water."

"There was also a wound on the back of the head."

"So somebody attacked him—"

"The coroner thinks he fell."

She shook her head. "If anybody knew his way around a sailboat it was Mike."

"He was drunk. Even somebody who knows his way around a boat can fall if he's downed a bottle of vodka."

Mia started to protest but stopped before the words were out. The night before Mike had died she'd made it clear she'd never think of him as anything but a friend. Even worse, she'd pulled away at his touch. Winced. That might be the reason he'd gotten drunk.

His death would be her fault then.

Just like her sister's.

"Are you okay?"

"I'm okay."

"Well, you don't look it," he said. "Don't tell me Mike had a drinking problem too."

"No." Her throat was so dry she could hardly get the words out. "He went out a lot with friends on the weekends. But he never had a problem. And he never drank alone. At least I'm pretty sure he didn't."

Nick turned his gaze toward the ocean. The moon had risen higher in the sky, casting a wide swath of ghostly light across the water. For several seconds he didn't speak. "He must've had a pretty good reason then. Is that what you're thinking?"

She laughed. "That's what I'm thinking."

Nick kept his eyes on the scene before them. "You wouldn't have something to do with his inebriated state, would you?"

"He was in love with me." The words were out before she could take them back.

"Well, that doesn't come as a total surprise." He turned back toward her, an unasked question in his eyes. "Probably inevitable, seeing how much time you two spent together."

Mia was suddenly painfully aware of his thigh against hers. Fighting the impulse to move away from him, she met his gaze. "If he was drunk it was my fault. My fault he died."

She'd spent so much time creating a story about his death. Now it seemed preposterous. Even worse, she'd dragged Nick into it when he should be spending his time at Seahaven. She'd disrupted his group meeting, for God's sake. Why not add another notch to the tally of people she'd destroyed.

"Don't let your guilt cloud your ability to think rationally, Mia. You think he was murdered and so do I."

Somehow his faith in her theory helped. She still felt guilty but at least she didn't feel quite so alone. And he was right about the guilt clouding her judgment. "You do?"

"You were right when you said it didn't make sense. Maybe the guy got decimated by fish, but considering what you found in the lab, along with the articles we took from his condo, it seems more likely that he got involved in something dangerous—

dangerous enough for somebody to beat him senseless and dump the body."

"Somebody else is gone. Chien Lu. The guy I was supposed to start working with. Only he disappeared."

His brow furrowed. "When?"

"He never went home last night. Didn't show up for work this morning. They've got video of him leaving the Institute but there's no trace of him after that. At least that's what Trask told me."

"Trask? That's your boss, right?"

"He's head of our unit."

Nick nodded. "Chien and Mike—what was their relationship? Were they friends? Did they ever work together?"

She tried to remember a time she'd seen the two men together and came up blank. "The only time they saw each other was at staff meetings. And they definitely weren't friends."

"They didn't get along?"

"No, it wasn't that. They just didn't have a lot in common," she said. "Chien was very private. He never talked about his life. Mike was the complete opposite. He was always going on about his boat or his family or his old Harvard friends. There wouldn't be any reason for them to hang out. And they were assigned to different pathogens."

"You're talking about him in the past tense."

"Oh, God. I—it was just a stupid mistake. I don't think—"

"If he doesn't turn up tomorrow, I want you to call me. Has his wife reported him missing?"

"Not yet."

Mia shivered. The day had been blazing hot but

now it was cool, even a little chilly. But she wasn't sure that was the reason she felt cold. "You don't think Chien could've killed Mike, do you?"

"I don't know," he said, putting his arm around her. "It's possible."

"Anything's possible." Her first instinct at the unexpected gesture had been to pull away and she wondered if he sensed that. If he did, he didn't say anything. They sat like that a few minutes in silence, watching the distant water. Behind them, Seahaven was ablaze with light.

If her mother looked outside, she might see the two of them. Mia dismissed the idea. They were too far from the complex. Even in the moonlight, it would be impossible to know it was them. For some reason she didn't want her mother to know she and Nick were out there. When she'd seen her mother earlier that evening, Angela had seemed happy—almost too happy. Mia knew her well enough to know she'd been acting, putting on a show for her benefit. When she'd prodded her mother, Angela admitted she still hadn't heard from her stepfather. Under her mother's casual tone, there was a kind of desperation. Maybe Seahaven had been a last-ditch effort to save her marriage.

If Angela Ward's marriage did fail she knew it wouldn't be long before her mother found someone new. She understood her mother's need to be in a relationship but she didn't want to be like that. She didn't want to depend on anybody for anything. Especially not happiness.

She brushed a speck of imaginary dust off her jeans and stood up. "It's getting late," she said carefully. "I'd better get going."

Nick stood up too. His face was inches from hers, so close she could feel his breath on her skin. "Don't pull away from me, Mia."

"I'm—not—I—"

Before she could finish her sentence his lips were on hers. He buried his hands in her hair and pulled her toward him, pressing his body to hers. She felt enveloped in warmth, a warmth that made it impossible not to kiss him back. He opened her mouth and his tongue twined with hers until the heat radiated through every part of her. She wrapped her arms around his neck and kissed him harder, her heart fluttering in her chest.

She didn't want it to end. But she couldn't let it go on—couldn't allow him to gain such a hold on her emotions. Mia pressed her palms against Nick's chest. "Stop—I—can't."

He pulled back and stared down at her, his eyes unreadable in the darkness.

"I'm sorry," she said.

"Don't be," he said in a clipped voice. "I shouldn't have kissed you. You came here to visit your mother, not me. I said I'd help you figure out what happened to your friend and I will. As for anything else, I have no expectations. I overstepped my bounds. It won't happen again. I'd walk you to your car but I get the sense you don't want the company."

He turned and strode up the path before she could protest.

She fought the impulse to call out to him.

Even if she did he wouldn't be back. Nick Doyle wasn't the kind of guy who'd chase a woman. She'd told him she didn't want him and he'd respect that.

Even if it wasn't what she wanted. Even if she did want him. Desperately.

Mia didn't make many mistakes. She'd been a perfectionist all her life and had always been careful not to undertake anything she'd fail at. She'd made a mistake once with Holly and the consequences had been irreparable.

Now she'd made another. One it was too late to fix.

****

She felt almost normal.

Mia waved at the guard as the gate lifted and she pulled into the Institute parking lot. Sure, she was an hour late but she wouldn't have been any good to anybody if she'd shown up on time. She'd woken early and taken Dante for a long run, then driven by Nailini's place on her way in so she could feed Hera and Zeus. Her friend wasn't due back until the following week and not for the first time Mia wished she hadn't promised to take care of the parrots. Nailini's ramshackle farmhouse was twenty-five minutes away from her place and it hadn't been easy finding the time to get there on a regular basis.

The smart thing to do would be to move the birds to her place. But that would raise even more issues. If her husky couldn't keep away from her throw pillows, how would he react to a couple of birds? But she'd have to figure out a better solution—sooner rather than later.

She glanced at her watch. 10:07 a.m. Sixty-seven minutes after the time she should've been there.

After the previous night's fiasco, she hadn't slept well. She'd finally caved and taken a sleeping pill, something she rarely did. When she woke she'd resolutely banished any thought of Nick from her mind. It was over between them and there was nothing she could do about it. Better to accept it and move on. So she'd pulled on her running shoes and grabbed Dante's leash, ignoring the time. Running always calmed her. Afterward, she'd headed to Nailini's to check in on the birds, not realizing how late she already was. Still, what could it matter?

But maybe she should've called in. Especially with everything going on.

Too late now.

She maneuvered her Subaru into her spot and killed the ignition, shoving the keys into her purse and slamming the door. As she squeezed through the narrow space between her car and an enormous SUV, she glanced up at her office window.

Trask stood at its center, staring down at her.

He didn't look pleased.

A surge of indignation rose up within her. He didn't have any right to be angry at her. It wasn't as if she made it a habit to play hooky. She'd hadn't come in late in two years. Not once.

And what the hell was he doing in her office, anyway?

She slid her ID card through the slot next to the main entrance and pushed through the double doors, her resentment building. By the time she emerged from the elevator she was angry too.

Then she saw the officers outside Chien's office.

One of them glanced up, his stare intense enough to make her uncomfortable. She gave him what she hoped was a friendly smile.

He didn't smile back.

When she entered her office, Trask wasn't smiling either.

"Where the hell have you been?"

"I overslept," she lied. If she told him what she'd really been doing, he'd be furious.

"Don't you ever answer your cell?"

Mia set down her purse on the desk. "It was turned off."

Trask folded his arms across his chest. "I don't know whether to believe you or not. But feel free to delete the six messages I left."

He looked so pissed she almost forgot her own anger. "It won't happen again," she said. "What are you doing in my office, anyway?"

"In case you haven't noticed, one member of our team turned up dead several days ago. And another's missing. Forgive me for thinking something might have happened to you too."

Mia almost laughed aloud. Trask was usually the definition of grace under pressure. Nothing got to him. "You were *worried*?"

"Yes," he said through gritted teeth. "I was."

He picked up a sticky note off the middle of the desk and handed it to her. "I also left you a note, when you didn't answer your phone or respond to the emails I sent you. Mrs. Lu brought in the police this morning. They're going to want to talk to you."

"Me?"

"It's standard procedure. They already interviewed me this morning and one of them is talking to Caleb right now. Shouldn't take long."

Mia glanced down at the note, not sure it explained his presence in her office. "Do they have any leads?"

"I don't know. They're not very big on sharing."
He walked around the desk so that he stood a few feet
from the door. "There isn't anything you're not telling
me?"

"Of course not." *Not if you don't count searching
Mike's place and working with an FBI agent on
mandatory leave.*

"Chien never said anything to you—or Mike? I
know you two were close." He placed a bit more
emphasis on the word close than was necessary.

So he thought they'd been involved too, just like
Nick had. And it sounded as if he wasn't buying into
the drowning theory either.

She shook her head. "No. Nothing. Not a word. If I
knew anything, I would've told you already." *Methinks
the lady doth protest too much.*

His dark eyes bored into her. Almost as she were
one of his specimens, something to be studied and
labeled. "There's something else."

Her stomach tightened. She wasn't sure she wanted
to hear what he had to say.

"I need you and Caleb to autopsy a monkey."

She'd expected him to say more but he seemed to
be waiting for something. Mia had done more than her
share of autopsies, though she much preferred working
with slides. Cutting up an ordinary corpse was bad
enough. But examining one riddled with one of the
hottest viruses known to man was an ugly business. It
always scared the hell out of her to look down and see
her gloved hands awash in infected blood, no matter
how many times she'd done it. "Okay."

"As soon as you finish with the cops, I want you
both to suit up and open him up. Write up whatever you

find and drop it off at my office before you leave."

Mia tried to hide her surprise. Her boss had never asked her to write something up and drop it off at his office. She usually spent several days analyzing a sample, not hours.

"Why's there such a rush?" She doubted he'd tell her—it was policy to keep things confidential—but she couldn't keep quiet.

He laid a hand on the doorknob and studied her a few seconds before answering. Almost as if he were debating how much to tell her. "Two weeks ago a woman in Aniak, Alaska bled out. Eighty-two years old, extensive bleeding from the nose. Red eyes, dilated pupils, mask-like face. Twenty-four hours later, her daughter dies. Then a couple of days later her doctor dies. Another day goes by and the nurse and the attending die. All of them had the same symptoms the old woman did."

"If it's a virus, that's a pretty fast incubation period," Mia said. "Around twenty-four to forty-eight hours?"

Trask held up a hand. "Early this morning, a clerk at the grocery store the old woman used bled out. Aniak's under quarantine and the authorities are trying to keep it from hitting the news but it's only a matter of time. The CDC has their people on it but they want us to have a look as well. Yesterday we injected one of the monkeys in Ward 3 with a sample of the virus. This morning he bled out in his cage."

"Same symptoms?"

"Same symptoms." Trask smiled grimly. "They all had them."

"What?"

"The monkeys in Ward 3. All of them were dead."

Mia had always made it a point to distance herself from her work. If she got too involved she wouldn't be effective. But Trask's story unnerved her. "I don't get it. How could the virus have spread so quickly?"

"That's what I'm hoping you two can figure out."

"Is it Ebola?" It couldn't be Ebola, not if it were transmitted that rapidly. Still, the symptoms matched.

"Like I said, that's what you're going to tell me."

She hoped she could. Her mind was already sorting through symptoms, looking for clues. It did sound like Ebola—and yet there were differences. For one thing, Ebola patients didn't die right away. The incubation period was days, not hours. And Ebola was fairly difficult to contract, for all the panic it generated. To become sick, a person had to come into contact with the bodily fluids of someone infected with the disease. The old woman might have done that with her daughter and the hospital staff. But a grocery store clerk? And what about the monkeys? They were in close proximity so it was possible monkeys in nearby cages had been sprayed with blood. And the old woman could have had bodily contact with the clerk. Still, this virus seemed like something else.

A uniformed police officer appeared behind Trask. "Dr. Lindgren?"

She nodded. "Yes?"

"Can you follow me please?"

Why did she suddenly feel as if she were in trouble?

Chapter 9

Nick opened his eyes and stared at the ceiling. It had to be late.

He sat up and squinted at the clock next to the bed. When he saw the hour, he groaned aloud. Another fifteen minutes and he'd miss breakfast.

He pulled on a pair of jeans and a t-shirt then stumbled into the bathroom. He looked into the mirror but it was Mia's face he saw.

"Christ," he said, opening the tap and splashing some water onto his face. "You hardly know her."

The water didn't do much. The memory of Mia's lips on his was enough to give him the beginnings of an erection. Not what he wanted. He grabbed the brush off the counter and ran it through his hair. Morning stubble darkened the lower part of his face but he didn't have time to shave. He needed coffee. Lots of it.

It wasn't until he'd locked the door behind him that he realized he'd left his cell in the room. He thought about going back then changed his mind. Somehow he didn't think Mia would be sending him any cute text messages. Earlier he'd checked to see if she sent anything about Chien but his message folder was empty. And Dalton had made it clear he didn't want to hear from him in the near future. There wasn't anybody else who'd call him, not when he was on leave.

He hadn't realized until he'd checked in to

Seahaven how much worked dominated his existence. Now it was tough to avoid the lack of real friendships in his life. He'd never been into social media and until Rosa's death most of his free time had been spent with her.

Maybe it was time to make a few changes. If he went back to the Bureau and threw himself into work, he was setting himself up for the same problems. He'd meant what he said at last night's session. He didn't want to become his father.

He would though, if he didn't start forging a new life. He'd never forget Rosa and a part of him would always love her. But he had to begin to think about moving forward.

He had to let go of the past.

Only that wasn't going so well. The previous night came back to him in excruciating detail. The moonlit night, the physical contact with Mia as they'd sat side by side, the scent of her perfume.

Maybe it hadn't been Mia he'd reacted to. Maybe he'd just gotten caught up in the moment. Or he'd wanted to fill the empty space inside him so badly he'd ignored the signals she'd been sending him since day one.

She didn't want him.

She didn't want anybody. He remembered what she'd said about Mike being in love with her. He'd assumed the two of them had been involved but he believed her denial. He'd never met a woman who didn't seem to need anybody else. Until he met Mia.

What made her push everyone away?

Whatever the case, she'd made her feelings—or lack of them—very clear. He had to accept that and continue on. Which didn't mean he intended to hop into bed with the first woman he met. No way was he ready for that kind of intimacy. But it wouldn't kill him to catch a game with the guys after work or to have dinner with Dalton and Laura once in a while. Hell, they asked him enough.

When he'd gotten back to his room last night he'd expected to want a drink. The funny thing was he hadn't. For the past year, liquor had been a way to stay in the past. He'd spent nearly every night since Rosa's death drowning in memories.

Like a fly in amber. Or a brain preserved in formaldehyde.

For the past few days he hadn't felt that way anymore. As much as Mia's rejection stung, the pain wasn't wholly unpleasant. At least he knew he could still feel things. That was better than going through life like some kind of zombie.

Several people waved when he reached the cafeteria. Angela was there as well, though she didn't turn in his direction. Her admirer from the other night sat next to her, obviously as infatuated as he had been at the meeting. Justin raised a hand in greeting on his way out, still deep in conversation with Nargeeta.

More romance.

Didn't matter. Romance didn't concern him.

Nick gave him a nod and lifted a tray off the pile. He was almost at the end of the line when Father Donelan came up behind him and laid a hand on his shoulder.

"How's our friend?"

Nick set his coffee mug onto the tray. "Friend?"

"That pretty woman who seemed so interested in

your story last night," he said slyly. "Angela's daughter."

He smiled at the priest's all-too-obvious hint. Funny, Donelan didn't strike him as the matchmaker type. And Mia was the last thing he wanted to discuss. "She's fine."

The priest fell into step with Nick as he headed toward a vacant table. "Mind if I join you?"

He wasn't at all sure he wanted to eat breakfast under Donelan's watchful eye but he couldn't exactly say no. Father Donelan hadn't brought up his absence the other night and Nick wanted to keep it that way.

"Sure," Nick said. "Though I'm not very good company until I've downed at least two cups of coffee."

"A benign addiction." Donelan sat down across from Nick and smiled. "At least that's what I tell myself."

Nick bit into a cinnamon roll. "Better caffeine than booze."

"Quite right."

The cafeteria was thinning out. Most of the patients were on their way to the morning's sessions or heading toward the fitness center. A few of the parents were trickling toward the children's dormitory. Donelan believed families should eat together but kept children apart from the adults for most of the day. Too much contact would interfere with recovery. Or so he said.

"And what about you?" Donelan asked, his gaze sharper than usual. "Do you feel you're making progress here?"

He took another bite of his roll and set it on the plate. "Actually, I think I am. This place is a lot better than I expected."

Donelan chuckled. "I appreciate your candor."

"I'm usually a little more subtle."

"Most of you are." He paused. "Subtle."

The conversation skipped a beat.

"Most of the patients, you mean?"

The priest waved to Angela when she and her companion rose to leave. "No," he said, his voice low and musical. "Patients can be subtle or direct, depending on their personalities. But you government types, especially the ones who've spent time in the military, tend to be pretty closed mouthed. Been working with Uncle Sam close to two decades now and there's never much variation."

Nick sipped his coffee. He'd heard of other agents being sent to Seahaven before and there certainly was no shortage of veterans on the premises. It surprised him though, to hear the priest would admit such a connection so openly. At a few of the sessions, he'd sensed one or two of the patients might still be working for the government. But what Donelan had just said implied a more formalized relationship.

"So there are a lot of us—here?" he asked casually.

"There are a lot of broken warriors in the world." The priest leaned back in his chair. "Luckily for this country, most of them can be fixed."

"Maybe." Nick wasn't so sure. Before he signed on with the FBI he'd spent a few years in combat overseas. In his travels he'd come across more than a few warriors who were well past fixing. Men whose legs and arms had been blown off, who'd lost their hearing or their sight. Or their souls. He'd seen plenty of that.

Donelan opened his mouth to speak but Nick unintentionally cut him off. "Oh, hell." He set down his coffee onto the table so hard some of the brown liquid sloshed over the sides of his mug.

The priest stared at him in surprise. "I didn't mean to offend you."

"You didn't." Nick wiped up the spill with his napkin. "It's not that."

"You hadn't realized our connection with the Bureau?"

Nick crumpled the dirty napkin into a ball and deposited it on the tray. "I didn't. But that's not what I was thinking about. It's nothing you said. Well, I suppose it was, in a way. The other day somebody mentioned a name to me. It sounded familiar but for the life of me I couldn't figure out why."

"And you just made the connection?"

Nick nodded. "Brendon Thompson. We fought together in Afghanistan right after 9/11. Same platoon. He died over there. Twenty years old."

Donelan's eyes darkened. "May he rest in peace," he said quickly. "Terrible thing, to die so young. But he gave his life for a noble cause. There's no greater sacrifice than dying for one's country."

Nick couldn't argue with him but over the years he'd had his doubts about what it meant to die for one's country. He'd even thought about saying to hell with the Bureau and starting fresh somewhere as far away from Washington as he could get. In the end, he never did. The U.S. government could play dirty, no doubt about it. But there were plenty of groups out there that made America look squeaky clean by comparison.

He drained his cup and took hold of his tray. It was a weird coincidence, that the man who'd rented the car had used that name. Nick hadn't been close with

Thompson but everybody had liked the guy. His death had hit them all pretty hard, especially because he'd died on what they thought was a routine mission that was intercepted by a splinter terrorist group now known as the New World Army. Back in October 2001, they hadn't called themselves that—hadn't been organized enough to call themselves anything. It had taken the Taliban's hospitality and some training from Al Qaeda to transform them into the international threat they eventually became. Of course, even back then they'd been organized enough to kill Thompson. The body had been beaten and tortured so badly it was nearly unidentifiable when they got it back.

When he stood up, Donelan remained where he was. "You said that name came up the other day," the priest remarked, meeting his eyes. "Would you mind telling me in what context you heard it?"

Nick hesitated. "You didn't know him, did you?"

"No. Can't say that I ever met anyone by that name."

An unasked question hung in the air between them. After a few moments, the priest rose from the table as well.

"Sorry, I didn't mean to pry," Nick said. "You seemed to react quite strongly when you realized the connection."

Donelan shrugged. "Did I? I suppose it was the boy's death that troubled me. Such a tragedy."

The priest was lying, no doubt about it. The question was why. If Donelan had known Thompson before he died, why not just say so? Before he could figure out a way to get the priest to tell him what he knew, Callie Jackson appeared at Donelan's side and

143

whisked him off in the direction of the group session room.

"You're coming, Nick, right?" she called over her shoulder.

Donelan called out to him too but when he made an excuse about getting a second cup of coffee, the priest didn't argue. If his smile was any indication, the guy was downright relieved.

You're not off the hook yet, Father.

Nick dumped his tray and headed back to the coffee area. Before he'd poured cream into his second cup, he knew what he needed to do.

****

Mia stood inside Biolevel-2, blue light bathing her face. She'd already showered and put on the clean white socks. Two levels to go.

She willed herself to remain calm.

It didn't work. She hadn't been calm all morning, not since she'd parked and seen Trask glaring down at her from her office. From there, things had gotten even worse. She'd spent the past two hours being questioned by not one but two police officers. Apparently they were questioning Mike's drowning now too. And they seemed to be looking for a connection between Chien's disappearance and Mike's death. A connection that involved her. *What was her relationship to the deceased? When had she last spoken to Chien? When was the last time she'd been to the Lu residence? To Mike's condo?*

The last question had her especially rattled. She'd worn gloves the night she searched his place but she knew there was no way she hadn't left traces of her presence. A strand of pale hair, an imprint of her shoe.

She'd almost confessed her nocturnal adventure but had thought better of it. Even if they did find evidence she'd been there, she could brush it off as a sign that she'd spent time with Mike.

In his bedroom closet.

She could only hope they hadn't searched the place very thoroughly. Somehow she didn't think she could count on that. Why did she get the impression that they believed she could tell them something? If she didn't know any better, she'd think they considered her a suspect.

So much for feeling almost normal.

Mia thought she heard movement on the other side of the door to Biolevel 1, though she knew that wasn't possible. Caleb wouldn't have started the autopsy on his own. Nobody—not even Mia—was crazy enough to undertake something like that without help.

It had to be Caleb though.

She felt a stab of annoyance.

He could have at least waited in the outer room for her. She and Mike always checked each other's suits before they entered BL-4, just to be on the safe side. Caleb seemed all too intent on identifying the pathogen that killed the old woman and her daughter in Aniak. Or maybe he was careless. Or just plain inexperienced. Trask had told her as much that morning.

Not good.

She wondered who else had been exposed to the virus up in Alaska. Were more people in Aniak already infected? Had it spread beyond the town?

Mia sighed and pushed through the door to BL-3. Hanging around in stocking feet wasn't going to get her the answers she needed. When she passed into the room, the first thing she did was grab a pair of latex gloves. She lifted the shaker of baby powder off the counter and shook it onto her hands before pulling on the gloves. It took her longer than usual to tape the cuffs of her gloves to the sleeves of her scrub shirt and attach her socks to her pants.

Her hands, she realized, were shaking.

Great. So much for the karate lessons Trask had talked her into. Despite hours of martial arts training her hands were as unsteady as ever. She held out her hands before her and waited until they grew still.

That's more like it.

Now if only she could keep them that way.

She grabbed her space suit off its hook and laid it out across the floor, checking it carefully for holes. The heavy blue plastic looked perfect. She stepped into the suit and put her arms through the sleeves. Her hands slid easily into the rubber gloves.

She pulled her helmet over her head. Reaching for the air hose, she slowed her movements. It didn't matter if she was a few minutes late. Or a few hours, if she counted the time with the police.

What mattered was that she did everything exactly the way she was supposed to.

No more mistakes.

The suit ballooned up and she waddled toward the stainless steel door that led to BL-4. She'd seen the biohazard symbol and warning so many times, she normally didn't notice it.

This time she did.

Just get it over with.

The sooner she started the autopsy the sooner she could get her report to Trask. And go home.

Normally, she hated leaving the Institute. But the idea of hanging out on the couch with Dante at her feet seemed a lot more appealing than what she was about to do.

Trask needed answers. The people of Aniak needed them too.

She had the inexplicable urge to cross herself.

Instead she unplugged the air hose and opened the steel door. She walked quickly through the air lock and entered BL-4.

The monkey lay flat on a stainless steel table at the center of the room. Even from a distance she could see that his skin was covered with red blotches where his fur had fallen out.

She'd been right about Caleb waiting to start the autopsy. He stood in his Hazmat suit, a few feet away from the table. The autopsy tools lay on a tray at the head of the table, untouched.

She wanted to ask him why he'd suited up without her but talking in BL-4 was too difficult to make it worth the effort. Anyway, it didn't matter. What's done was done.

Caleb crossed toward her as she was picking up a pair of latex gloves. She held up her hands so he could pull them over the rubber gloves. Maybe it was overly cautious to don a third pair of gloves but Mia didn't care. Better safe than sorry.

After Caleb finished helping her, she did the same for him.

"Ready?' he mouthed through the helmet.

"Ready."

The dissection tools were laid out in a row on the tray. Caleb chose a pair of blunt-ended scissors and began opening the monkey. Mia stood on the other side of the table and watched him work, ready to assist. The monkey's eyes stared at the ceiling, the whites stained a brilliant red. The area beneath the nostrils was covered with blood as well.

Caleb's skill with the scissors surprised her. She would've expected him to be less confident. He was only a couple of years younger than she was but he could pass for a kid in high school. It would definitely take some getting used to, being partners with somebody she thought of as a younger brother.

After handing him another dull tool, Mia admitted she was glad he was the one doing the cutting, not her. She'd gotten the shaking under control but wasn't sure she'd be able to keep it that way.

She lifted a small sponge off the table and mopped up some of the excess blood. The hemorrhaging was extensive, much more so than Mia would have expected to see, even with Ebola, if that's what they were dealing with. The liver was swollen and the lungs were enlarged as well. Mia tied off some of the blood vessels and clamped an artery that was leaking blood.

There was so much blood.

She reached for another sponge and mopped it up. It didn't do much good.

Caleb set down the scissors. "Looks like Ebola," he said, his voice muffled by the helmet.

Mia shook her head. "I don't think so."

A look of confusion flickered across his features. "Same symptoms," he mouthed.

He was right. The symptoms—most of them, anyway—were the same. But something about the corpse struck her as exceptional. She tried to understand what she was seeing. "Look at the lungs," she mouthed.

"I am." Apparently Caleb didn't see anything out of the ordinary.

He held out the scissors toward her. "Do you want to take a sample?"

She grasped the scissors by the handle and leaned forward, deliberately avoiding the bloodshot eyes. She carefully began cutting into the lung, removing one in its entirety and dropping it into a jar of preservative. If they were looking at Ebola, it was unusual to see lungs of that size. The color was odd as well. A neon shade of red, so bright it seemed to glow under the lights that hung overhead.

She'd started cutting slices from the right lung when Caleb reached across the table and grabbed her arm. The scissors flew out her hand and landed halfway across the room.

"What the hell do you think you're doing!" Mia pulled her arm out of his grasp and glared at him.

Caleb didn't answer her. He was pointing at her right hand, his face deathly white.

She followed his gaze. At first all she saw was blood. The outermost glove was covered with it, as was the arm of her blue suit.

When she saw the tear she fought down the screams rising within her. She couldn't panic. There wasn't enough time.

She tore the damaged glove off and rinsed the rubber glove beneath it in disinfectant. The glove looked clean, slick with disinfectant. But no blood. She unplugged her suit from the air hose and moved toward the exit.

Then she felt it. A wet sensation in between the rubber glove and the latex one underneath it. The infected blood.

Her throat felt like it was closing up inside the space suit.

She couldn't breathe.

Fighting for air, she sank to the floor, her entire body shaking. *Don't panic don't panic don't panic.* She kept repeating the phrase over and over, as if it were a prayer.

As if it could save her.

Caleb rushed toward her and knelt by her side. She flailed at his arms, pushing him away. Inside the suit, sweat covered her body and she felt her face growing hot.

She was suffocating.

Caleb grabbed her arm and held it steady with both hands. He was stronger than she was, too strong to fight. He turned toward her and pointed. "Crack!"She looked down. A small dark line ran across the place where the glove met the space suit. Whatever had killed that monkey had seeped inside her suit through the crack.

Which was when she remembered the cut from the bagel knife. Covered by a Band-Aid. If the blood penetrated the final glove she'd be dead in less than a day.

Caleb slid his arm behind her and tried to lift her off the floor. "We've got to get you out of here!"

She clawed at the helmet, desperate to get it off. Her breath came in jagged gasps.

"What the hell are you doing!" Caleb shouted.

She fumbled to pull down the suit's zipper but

couldn't grasp it. She needed to get the suit off her body. She needed to breathe.

Caleb collapsed onto the floor next to her. In the suit, she was too heavy for him to lift. He too seemed to be struggling to catch his breath.

"Mia, Listen to me. You're not thinking clearly. You've got to work with me. We've got to get you out of here."

Air. She had to have air.

"Do you understand?"

Was the blood already seeping through the latex glove? Had it penetrated the skin yet?

"Get up, Mia."

Caleb's voice reached her from a great distance. She let her helmet touch the floor and closed her eyes. She was so tired. The glass on the helmet had fogged over, making the room a blur of stainless steel and cement.

"Get up, dammit!"

She wanted to tell him to calm down. She was just taking a nap. Nothing to get worked up about. Up above, the fluorescent lights shone down on her.

So bright. So terribly bright. In the corner of the room, the security camera's red eye stared down at her.

All of it on video.

Her final mistake.

"Do you want to die?"

She closed her eyes.

Caleb's arm wedged itself under her again just as the door opened. A figure in a spacesuit rushed toward her, pulling her to her feet. Her helmet was so foggy she couldn't tell who it was.

The two men dragged her into BL-3 and slammed

the door shut behind them.

Someone pulled the chain that hung from the ceiling.

The decon jets sprayed her suit with chemicals while her mysterious savior held her up from behind. Clear fluid streamed down her helmet as she waited for the chemicals to wash her suit clean of blood.

How long did the shower last?

Six minutes? Seven?

It didn't matter, not really.

If the blood had reached her cut, it was already too late.

Chapter 10

"I thought I told you *not* to call."

Nick grinned. "Sorry, buddy, I meant to leave you alone."

On the other end of the line, Dalton sighed. "Don't you have a therapy session you need to get to?"

"Not at the moment."

"Let me guess," Dalton said. "You need me to check on another license plate for you."

"Not a license plate a name. Brendon Thompson."

"You haven't been drinking again, have you? Because I already ran that name when I ran the plate number for you. And in case it's slipped your mind, nothing came up in our database."

"I don't want you to run the name through the criminal database. I want you to run it through our database."

"What do you mean, *our database*?"

He glanced up the path and saw Angela heading his way. As usual, she was dressed to kill in a fitted sundress, strappy sandals and oversized sunglasses. From the rapidity of her strides and the fact that she was alone, he guessed she was on a mission. A mission he wasn't sure he wanted to be a part of.

It served him right. He hadn't needed to return to the same bench he and Mia had sat at. He could just as easily have called Dalton from his room.

"There's a slight possibility Brendon Thompson may have worked for us at some point," Nick said. "Either as an agent or as a consultant. Or maybe for one of the other agencies. I also think it's possible the guy may have been a patient here at Seahaven."

"And what makes you think that?"

He hesitated. Would it help his cause or hurt it if he explained his theory that his former platoon buddy might not have been killed in Afghanistan? Thompson's body had been badly damaged when they found it. What if it hadn't been Thompson they came across after the mission—what if he'd escaped the Taliban somehow and turned up in the States later?

If Thompson had made it out, it was possible he would have ended up working for the government in some capacity. A lot of Nick's platoon buddies had gone that route. And if Thompson had worked for the government then it was possible he'd ended up at Seahaven. That's the only thing Nick could come up with that would explain the priest's odd reaction to the name.

Because Donelan had known somebody by that name, somebody in the military, Nick would bet his life on it. Even if it was a different Brendon Thompson the name should still come up in a database search.

Still, there were a lot of ifs.

Talk about a long shot.

But if he could figure out who Thompson was he could start to piece together what the guy was doing visiting Mike's condo in a rental car. Without some clue as to who Thompson was, he was at a dead end as far as Mike's death went.

Nick didn't like keeping things from Dalton. But if

he explained, he wouldn't get what he needed. "Just a hunch," he said finally.

"A hunch."

"You believe in those, don't you, buddy?" Nick knew he was pushing his friend's buttons but he also had a point. Laura's premonitions had saved Dalton's life more than once.

"Don't bait me, Doyle."

Angela was closing in. Another sixty seconds and she'd be within earshot. "Just run the check for me, okay? Can you do that?"

Dalton swore. "As for our databases, sure. I can run that for you. But you know we can't access the personnel databases of other bureaus. And we definitely can't access the names of agents who went to rehab. That stuff's off limits."

"And we both know someone who can get around those limits."

Nick didn't need to elaborate. Elijah Todorev might be a hacker but he'd saved both of their asses more than once. The last time Nick had seen the computer genius he'd been at National Airport, suited up for a Dr. Who convention. The ex-NSA agent had seemed out of place outside his dimly lit basement apartment, like a fish out of water. Strange, that a guy who was the equivalent of a fourteen-year-old boy could find a way to break into pretty much any database in the world. Or maybe it wasn't so strange, after all. Hacking was never work for Eli, only play. Another game.

"I'm not sure he'd be interested," Dalton said.

"He'd be interested."

Silence.

"You do realize you're on leave, right? *Mandatory* leave."

"Yep."

Another sigh. "Okay, okay."

"Thanks. How soon do you think you can get me something?"

"It's not like I've got anything else on my plate. Terrorists planning to blow stuff up, kidnapping people, infiltrating the U.N. Minor stuff like that. As for our friend, I can't make any promises. Who knows what cosplays are on this week?"

"But you'll talk to him?"

"Yeah, I'll talk to him."

"Like I said before I owe you."

There was a pause on Dalton's end. "Just do me a favor and get better, okay? We need you back here. And stay put. Calling in for info's bad enough. But don't do what you usually do and play the hero. "

"Sure thing." Nick was tempted to ask him again about Laura's dream but decided against it. Better not to know. And it wouldn't change his mind about anything anyways.

He disconnected the call just as Angela reached him.

"That wasn't my daughter you were speaking to by any chance, was it?"

Angela's worry lines looked deeper than usual. Either that or she'd gone a little lighter on the make-up. He wondered what sort of answer she wanted to hear. Normally he would have said Mia's mother didn't want him anywhere near her daughter. But something in her tone was off.

"No," he said. "Just a friend."

Her lips curled into a feline-like smile. "I see."

But she didn't. She didn't know the first thing about him. Or his relationship with her daughter. Or lack of one.

Which was enough reason not to tell Angela he'd been on the phone with a guy from work. That might raise its own set of prying questions. "Is there something I can do for you, Mrs. Ward?"

She plopped down on the bench and crossed her legs at the ankles. "This may come as a surprise but I actually hoped it was Mia on the phone just now. I haven't been able to reach her all day."

It occurred to him that her daughter might be deliberately ignoring Angela's messages. The woman was high maintenance as a fellow patient, and he doubted she'd be any different as a mother. Definitely a handful, that was for sure.

"If you don't mind my asking," Angela said, "when was the last time you spoke with her?"

As a matter of fact, he did mind. "I saw her last night when she was here visiting you."

"I know." There was a sly jibe in her answer. If he didn't know better, he'd suspect her of spying on them. If she'd witnessed the little scene at the bench she'd sound just like that.

Hell, maybe she had. So what if she did. It wasn't like he'd see the woman after his time at Seahaven was finished. Or her daughter.

"Look, Angela, I'm not sure what you want out of me, but I'm not planning on getting involved with Mia. I offered to help her get some information about something, which I did. End of story."

All the energy seemed to go out of her. She pushed

her sunglasses on top of her head and stared up at him. "I've been texting her all day. And you may think so but I'm not a complete idiot. I realize my daughter ignores me from time to time. And yes, I'm well aware she's got an important job. But she usually responds at some point."

"I'm sure you'll hear from her soon." Though now part of him was worried too. "She's probably caught up in something at work. But—if you don't—come and find me."

So much for staying out of Mia's life. Anyway, she'd probably be in touch soon enough. If not with him then at least with her mother. He'd been paranoid about Rosa too, even before she'd gotten sick.

Of course Mia's best friend had just turned up dead. And her new partner was missing.

He pressed his lips together. "Why don't you try her again?"

"She won't answer," Angela said. "Trust me."

"Humor me."

She pulled down her sunglasses and stared at the phone in her lap. After a few seconds, she tapped the screen and hit speaker. Both of them waited in silence as the called went through.

When it kicked over to voice mail, Angela ended the call. "Maybe you should try her. You might have better luck."

"I doubt it."

Nick couldn't see her eyes behind the dark glasses but he got the impression they'd narrowed, ever so slightly. "She didn't tell you, did she?"

"Tell me what."

"What happened to her. To *us*."

"I don't know what you're talking about."

Angela tucked her cell phone into her dress pocket and looked away from him. "When she was younger— she'd just turned thirteen—her sister was kidnapped when they were at a park. A few days later they found a body. My child's body. Not too long afterward my husband left me. And by left I mean took off. Out of state, out of the country for all I know."

"I'm sorry," he said. "Mia never mentioned it. Did they ever catch the man who did it?"

"I didn't really think she would have." She pulled out a Kleenex and dabbed at her eyes. "And no, they never caught the man. Mia had nightmares for years. We both did."

Nick sat down next to her and reached for her hand. He decided not to risk saying anything that would upset her even more.

Angela took a few deep breaths. When she spoke again she seemed calmer. "Somebody took my Holly," she said flatly. "Mia's all I have left. I can't lose her."

"Nobody said anything about you losing her."

"I know, I know. But I can feel it. Like that feeling in the air before a storm. I'm going to lose her." When she looked up, her eyes were glassy. "I am going to lose my daughter."

He wondered fleetingly if she'd been drinking. But her breath smelled of mint and aside from the tears, she seemed aware of what was going on around her. Nick cast his eyes around in hopes of seeing one of the counselors or even Father Donelan. Hell, even another patient. The kinds of people who could deal with this kind of thing.

Not him. Anybody but him. He had no idea what to

say.

"Angela, you're letting your fears get the best of you. I understand why you'd jump to conclusions but you're basing your worries on nothing."

"On nothing."

Wrong phrase. Definitely the wrong phrase. "I'm sure she's fine, Angela."

"*Like her friend?*" she shot back at him.

"Or that other scientist, the Asian man. It's all over the news, you know. Even living under a rock like this place, there are people talking about it. Do you think I have no idea what's going on—that I don't know my daughter well enough to know she's been looking into Mike's death?"

He was the one who felt as if he had no idea what was going on. So he hadn't turned up. Not that he'd expected him to. "Dr. Lu's disappearance—it's on the news?"

"So you did know about it." Smug. Angry.

"Yes." He couldn't blame her for being upset.

"CNN ran a story about an hour ago. I got an alert on my phone when I was trying to call Mia. Ordinarily I don't read anything like that—I keep meaning to shut the damn alerts off because it makes me crazy, worrying about her—but I recognized the name of the Institute and clicked on the link." Angela reached into her pocket and pulled up the story on the phone. "Here. See for yourself."

He held his hand over the screen and squinted at the headline. *Eminent Infectious Disease Researcher Missing.* In the bright sunlight it was tough to make out the rest of the story, especially without sunglasses. He cursed himself for leaving his pair in the room. From what he could tell there weren't any new developments in the case. He wasn't sure if that was good or bad but at least police hadn't found a body.

He was about to close out the news app when the phone buzzed. He stared down at the second alert. *Alaskan Village Under Quarantine. Seven confirmed Dead, Dozens Stricken Ill.*

Angela peered over his shoulder. "What is it? Is there something else?"

Nick didn't answer. He scanned the story quickly, tilting the phone toward him so that it faced away from the sunlight.

"The writing's too small." Angela leaned closer to the screen. "I don't have my reading glasses. What does it say?"

"There's an outbreak somewhere in Alaska. Looks like it could be some kind of infectious disease, though the CDC hasn't issued a formal statement. The place is under quarantine."

"Is the Institute involved?"

He scanned the article a second time. "It doesn't say one way or another. But they very well could be. Though there isn't much to go on. They're not giving out much information."

Nick handed the phone back to Angela. Neither of them spoke. The sense of uneasiness Angela had set off inside him was getting worse by the second. From the firm set of her mouth he got the impression Mia's mother wasn't feeling all that great either.

"That second story," Angela said tentatively. "It could be completely unrelated to what's happening at the Institute, right?"

"Right."

"But you don't think so."

"To be honest, I'm not sure what to think. Alaska's a long way from Maryland."

"Don't tell me things you don't believe, Nick. It's a plane ride away."

She was right, of course. And if there was an unidentified pathogen on the loose anywhere in the U.S. it was a good bet that the Institute was involved in some way. "Neither of us has enough information to make any kind of rational judgment. But if the Institute is working with the CDC, then your daughter's probably pretty busy right now. That could explain why you haven't heard from her."

Angela sniffed. He had a point and she knew it.

"Just let me know if you hear from her, okay? That's all I'm asking."

She stood up and smoothed back her hair. With a dismissive nod, she headed in the direction of the main building. A couple of counselors passed her on their way to the parking lot.

Five o'clock.

Just about the time most people got off work.

Luckily he wasn't most people.

****

Mia pushed up from the couch and looked around. The break room was empty, aside from an unfamiliar guy in a lab coat who stood before the vending machine. He bent down to grab a candy bar and hurried back into the corridor, avoiding her gaze.

It took her several seconds to remember what had happened. She looked down at her hand. The Band-Aid had been replaced but other than that it was unharmed.

Trask walked in when she was rising to her feet.

162

"Sit down, Mia."

She sat back on the couch. From the grim set of his mouth, she knew it would be pointless to argue. "I thought I'd be in biocontainment."

Mia had never been inside the biocontainment area but she'd heard horror stories about it. Anybody exposed to a biological agent got sent there, to be treated by doctors and nurses wearing Hazmat suits. Some didn't stay very long. They went straight to the morgue, which was down the hall from biocontainment.

Convenient.

Trask pulled a chair out from one of the round tables at the center of the room and set it down before her. He sat down and folded his arms across his chest. "The inner glove was dry. No blood got through to the skin," he said. "You got lucky."

She nodded. "Were you the one who—"

"No. I was still in with the police when it happened."

"Then who was it? I want to thank him."

"One of the guards saw it on the feed. He called one of the doctors in biocontainment. Lev Anderson."

She searched for a face to put to the name. "I don't know him."

"Neither did I. Until today."

Mia touched the new Band-Aid. "And you're sure nothing got through."

"Do you think you'd be here lying on the break room couch if that weren't the case?" he asked in a clipped voice.

She couldn't blame him for being abrupt. "I panicked."

He didn't answer.

"It won't happen again."

"It won't."

Why did such simple words sound so ominous? Mia fought the impulse to get up and sprint out of the room. Anything to stop what was coming. "Is that supposed to mean something?"

"You know it is."

Outside in the corridor, she heard laughter. A pair of off-duty nurses walked in and quickly turned to go. It didn't take much to sense the storm that was coming. She remembered the tear in her outer glove. Maybe the crack on the rubber suit could be explained but what about the tear? "I think somebody made a hole in my glove."

"Caleb says you may have nicked it with the scissors."

"What?" Mia fought to remember what had happened back in that lab. So much of the time before she'd passed out was a blur. "No. That didn't happen."

He sighed. "Well, that's what he told me. And what it says in the accident report."

Accident report. Mia controlled her temper. It was protocol to fill out a report when anything went wrong in the lab but she hadn't expected it to be done before she even had the chance to talk to her partner. "How long was I sleeping?"

"Maybe an hour."

"Where's Caleb? I want to talk to him."

"He left early. He was pretty shaken up."

Fine for *Caleb* to be shaken up. Fine for *him* to take off early. If she reacted after being exposed to whatever the hell killed that monkey it was a major incident.

She wanted to chalk her boss's reaction up to sexism, but she knew it wasn't true. There was no excuse for her behavior in that lab room.

Still, she hadn't cut her own glove. She was sure of it. "Those scissors—they're not even sharp."

"They're sharp enough to cut open a dead monkey."

"I didn't cut that glove. It was already like that," she protested. "I'm sure of it."

"Then why didn't you notice the tear before you started the autopsy?"

She resisted the urge to bite her lip. She refused to play the distraught woman.

Stay calm. You can still salvage this.

"You're right. I should have noticed it. But Caleb was already inside, waiting to start cutting. I guess I must've rushed. But the tear must have been there."

"And you missed the crack in the suit's glove as well."

"I made a mistake."

Trask's gaze fixed on the window behind her. In the distance, the sun had dipped below the horizon. The light fell across his features, accentuating the deep lines on either side of his mouth. When he looked back at her, there was sadness in his eyes. Or maybe it was regret, Mia wasn't sure.

"In this business we can't afford mistakes," he said. "You of all people should know that."

She stared at him. "Are you firing me?"

He shook his head. "No. I wouldn't do that."

"Then what are you saying?"

"I'm taking you off the unit. You'll start work for Colin Simmon's unit sometime next week, as soon as I send the paperwork through. You'll be working exclusively in Biolevel 1 from now on." Trask said. "In the interim, I want you to take some time off."

BL-1, home of baby viruses like the strains of flu that laid people up in bed for a couple days every winter. After what she'd been through, she should be happy to work in such a low-key environment. "No."

"That's not your call, Mia. I'm sorry but I can't have somebody up here that I can't rely on."

She leaned forward on the couch, her hands clasped in front of her. Almost as if she were praying. "You can rely on me."

"You missed two perforations in your suit. You nicked your glove during a procedure. And you panicked, not only putting your own life in jeopardy but placing your colleague in danger as well. Consider yourself lucky Caleb chose not to file a formal complaint against you."

"And did you suggest that," she asked, her anger rising to the surface, "filing a formal complaint?"

He didn't answer.

"You fucking bastard."

Trask ran a hand over his buzz cut. "I've never been sure of you, Mia. You've never had steady hands. I thought the martial arts might help, which was why I suggested it. But apparently it didn't. You act like I'm out to get you but I've got an entire unit to think of. Not to mention the rest of the goddamn world. In case you've forgotten, there's an unidentified hot agent killing off the residents of an Alaskan village. The story broke today so on top of everything else, I've got the press to deal with."

She fought back tears. So many mistakes. Her

career ruined in less than fifteen minutes. Maybe she *had* nicked the glove. She hadn't noticed the tear, so maybe she hadn't seen the slip up with the scissors either. The worst part wasn't that her carelessness had cost her position. It was that she'd delayed the autopsy. Every delay in identifying the virus meant more time for the disease to spread. "Are more people dead?"

"Half the village. And most of the rest of them are already sick."

"What did the autopsy show?"

His brows shot up in surprise. "The autopsy? The autopsy didn't happen."

She stared at him. "Please tell me you're joking."

He laughed but there was no humor in it. "I wish I were. The lab's a mess. Contaminated blood all over the place. Caleb's nerves were shot to hell. And in case it's slipped your mind, Mike's dead, Chien's AWOL, the floor's crawling with cops—would you mind telling me who the hell I was supposed to get to finish up what you screwed up?"

His words cut into her. Trask had never been one to pull his punches. Neither had she. *"People are dying."*

"People are always dying, Mia. Every day. In Africa, thousands have died of Ebola. A few dozen people die in Alaska and you think it's a national crisis," he said. "The autopsy can wait until tomorrow."

Her cheeks burned. "You're twisting my words. You make me seem like some kind of monster. You know as well as I do that I give a damn about what's going on in Africa. I risk my life every day because I give a damn. How many people can say that?"

"Are you really doing it for them? Or for yourself—to placate your own demons?" he asked wearily. "Don't play the saint, Mia. It doesn't suit you."

For the first time in the years that they'd worked together it struck her that she didn't really know her boss very well. She'd always thought the tough exterior masked a compassionate man. Now he just seemed brutal.

Had Caleb really said she'd nicked herself? Or had he succumbed to the power of suggestion? For all she knew, maybe he hadn't written any such thing. If Trask wanted her out badly enough, why not tell her that just to get her out of the unit?

"I want to see that report," she said.

"You can see it when you get back."

"No. I want to see it now."

The conversation skipped a beat.

She'd crossed a line and they both knew it.

"You're not thinking clearly, Mia."

It was the second time someone had told her that today. If she knew what was good for her, she'd shut her mouth and go along with what Trask told her. But that wasn't going to help the people who were dying in Alaska.

"No, *Dan.* You're the one who's not thinking clearly. Somebody sabotaged my suit. Somebody didn't want to me to do that autopsy."

Trask stood up. "Go home, Mia. As a friend—and I do consider you a friend—I'm telling you to let this go. I don't think you realize how paranoid you sound right now. It's one thing to talk this way to me, but don't think you can get away with saying this stuff to anybody else."

She stood up as well. "Is that advice—or a threat?"

"Take it however you want. But if you don't start

thinking a little more rationally you're going to regret it. Enough with the conspiracy theories. You're a scientist, for Christ's sake, not an escaped mental patient. You might just start acting like one."

Her hand flew up from her side before she could stop it. When her palm made contact with his cheek, he winced but recovered quickly.

"You're going to regret that."

She brushed past him in her hurry to get out of the room. When she reached the doorway, she turned. In the distance the sun glowed orange, setting the sky on the other side of the windows ablaze. It seemed fitting somehow, now that her entire world had gone up in flames.

"I already do."

Chapter 11

Mia turned the key in the lock and stepped into the dim interior of her house. All was quiet, a welcome relief after her shouting match with Trask. She hung her purse on the hook next to the door and took a few steps into the kitchen.

Usually Dante was waiting on the other side of the door to greet her but he was nowhere in sight. She started to call out to him but stopped. Moving forward a few more steps, she peered into the living room and waited for her eyes to adjust to the gloom. Nothing looked out of place, thought it was tough to tell without turning on a light.

Something told her that wouldn't be a good idea.

It was too quiet. Too still. Unless Trask had been right about her paranoia.

She didn't think so.

Mia backtracked to the entryway and picked up the baseball bat she always kept next to the door. Holding it with both hands, she moved quietly through the lower rooms. For the first time in her life, she wished she owned a gun.

Nobody in the kitchen.

Nobody in the living room. Or the downstairs bathroom.

From somewhere above her, something moaned. Or someone.

She stood perfectly still at the center of the living room. Listening. Waiting.

The second time there was no question. The sound was coming from an animal. An animal in pain.

Dante.

Her stomach clenched. Tightening her grip on the bat she stole toward the staircase and began the climb to the second floor, one step at a time. The back of her mouth began to water but she willed herself not to throw up. If somebody upstairs was holding her husky captive, she was going to get him back. She didn't have time to get sick.

This time she wasn't going to panic.

When she reached the landing she saw that the bathroom door had been shut. It hadn't been shut that morning. She stood motionless for a full ten seconds, listening for sounds of somebody on the other side of the door.

Another moan.

Definitely Dante.

She lunged toward the closed door, pulling it open. With her right hand, she reached for the light switch and turned it on. Fluorescent light flooded the small room.

When she saw the husky sprawled out across the tiles she fell to her knees. He tried to raise his head toward her but gave up after a few seconds. His eyelids fluttered but didn't open.

Aside from the dog, the bathroom was empty.

Don't die on me.

She didn't care about losing her job. If she'd ruined her career, she could live with that. But she couldn't lose her dog. She couldn't lose the one being that truly loved her.

Swiping at the tears on her cheeks, she felt for a pulse and found one. It was slow but steady. She cradled his head in her lap, cursing when she realized her phone was in her purse. She had to go downstairs and get it so she could call the vet. But she didn't want to leave Dante.

She smoothed back his fur and gently laid his head back onto the tiles. "I'll be right back," she whispered fiercely. "Don't worry."

The dog didn't move. Mia rushed to the stairs and hurried down the steps, not bothering to conceal the sound of her movements. If whoever had done this to her dog was still in the house, they already knew she was there. And she didn't much care if she ran into the attacker. She almost wanted to see the person who'd done it. She could do a lot of damage with a bat. And she had her buddy Trask to thank for her brown belt in martial arts.

She could do some damage with that too.

When she reached the entryway, she pulled her phone out of her bag and powered it up. She'd turned it off during her interview with the police and hadn't looked at it since. The message light blinked green but she ignored it. Whatever it was, it could wait.

If only Nailini wasn't still out of the country. Her friend would have been there in minutes. It would probably take her three times as long to get Dante to an animal hospital. She pulled up the number for Nailini's practice and dialed it. She couldn't remember who was filling in for her friend but supposed it didn't matter. All that mattered was that somebody there could help her.

It was after five, so the answering service picked up. After leaving a message she took the stairs two at a time and jogged toward the bathroom. She could see Dante's chest rising so she knew he was still alive.

"Stay with me, okay?" she said, sliding down next to him again. "We're going to go for a ride soon."

She felt for his pulse again. Still slow. Still steady. How long until the vet called her back?

Five minutes later the phone rang. After a quick conversation, she arranged to meet the on-call veterinarian at an animal hospital not far from where she lived. Mia didn't recognize the name of the place, but that didn't matter. It was a hospital and that was good enough for her.

Mia had gathered the dog into her arms and was stumbling toward the landing when the doorbell rang. Leaning against the wall for support, she debated what to do.

She'd need to put down the dog to answer the door.

No way was she doing that. No time.

The doorbell rang a second time.

Her mother was still at Seahaven and so was Nick, not that he wanted anything to do with her anyway. Nailini was in Bolivia, Ashley up at school. And God knows her stepfather had no interest in her. Trask would never show up at her home—and he didn't want to see her anyway. Which left...no one.

Maybe it was one of the Jehovah's Witnesses who always seemed to turn up her door. What better time to try to convert her than when her world had just been turned upside down?

She was breathing hard, doing her best not to lose her hold on Dante. He had to weigh close to a hundred pounds. His legs hung motionless and his head kept slipping off her shoulder, his entire body a deadweight. She didn't want to think about how she was going to get him into the Subaru.

The doorbell rang twice in quick succession.

Whoever it was, they were getting impatient.

Let them. She had enough to deal with.

"Go away," she mumbled as she made her way down the stairs, one shoulder leaning against the wall. She was breathing hard and her heart was hammering in her chest. Another few minutes and she'd probably have a heart attack herself.

At the bottom of the stairs, she collapsed onto the floor with her back against the wall. Dante rested against her while she took great gasps of air.

The doorbell rang. Whoever it was, they were certainly persistent.

She pushed a sweaty strand of hair behind her ear and maneuvered her body out from under the dog. "This had better be important." She strode into the kitchen and yanked the door open.

Caleb stood on the uppermost step, his fingertip poised over the buzzer. The usual bowtie was missing and his curly hair was even wilder than it usually was.

"Caleb?" She hoped he hadn't picked up on the disappointment in her voice. Of course it wouldn't be Nick. He wasn't even speaking to her.

"Sorry to bother you," he said, a spot of crimson appearing in each cheek. "I tried to call you a few times but you weren't picking up. When you didn't answer I got worried. I just wanted to make sure you were okay—after what, uh, happened in the lab today."

"I'm fine."

"Like I said—"

"You were worried. Right. I got it. But as you can see, I'm fine. So if you don't mind I need to go."

She knew she sounded like a complete bitch. Still, it was his report that had gotten her pulled off the unit. On the drive home she'd remembered more of what happened. And she'd swear on a stack of Bibles she hadn't torn that glove. Which meant either Caleb had misremembered events or he'd lied, maybe to secure his spot in the unit.

Whatever the case, she didn't have time to pursue it now.

"Sorry to bother you," he said, a trace of irritation in his voice. "I didn't intend to stay."

She hesitated, her hand on the door. "Look, my dog's sick, okay? I've got to get him to the vet."

"Do you need any help?"

"No." Behind him, she could see her Subaru parked in the driveway. A good twenty feet from her front door. "I can handle it."

"Well, I guess I'll be going then. I'm glad you're okay."

He turned and started walking down the path to the street where his car was parked. At the end of the block, a streetlamp blinked on.

Another hour and it would be completely dark. Her car was too old for GPS and she didn't know her way to the animal hospital.

"Wait," she called after him. He may have screwed her over in his report but he could help lift a dog. She couldn't afford to blow him off. She'd never get Dante into her car on her own. Or if she did, it would take her far too long.

He stopped walking and turned back toward her.

"Actually, I could use your help," she said. "If you wouldn't mind. My dog's pretty heavy."

"Sure." If he hesitated it was only for a second. "I'd be happy to."

****

Nick pulled into Mia's driveway and stared at the darkened house. Her car was gone too.

Dammit.

He should've left earlier. Not that he was certain anything was wrong. He hadn't fully bought into Angela's intuition that something was off. But the fact that she wasn't home didn't do much to reassure him.

He killed the lights and got out of his car, not sure what he planned on doing. He didn't have a key to her place and even if he did he wouldn't use it. Worried or not, he didn't have the right to enter her house without her permission. She wasn't a suspect in one of his cases.

He strode toward the front door and stood before it, trying to catch a glimpse of the house through the windows. It was too dark inside to see anything.

Strange, that the dog hadn't barked. Huskies weren't big as watch dogs—they were more likely to lick a burglar than bite him—but he'd gotten the impression Dante mostly hung out downstairs. And most dogs would at least go the window when a stranger showed up at the front door.

Well, maybe she took him for a run. She'd told him she ran with the dog.

Not at this time of night.

Mia wasn't foolish enough to risk going out alone after dark, especially not with everything that had been

176

happening. And she hadn't struck him as the type who'd go out on a weeknight.

So where was she?

And where was the dog?

He laid his hand onto the doorknob and turned it. It wasn't locked.

A muscle in his jaw worked. What the hell was going on?

He pushed the door open a few inches and called into the darkness. No answer came but he hadn't expected one. The place was empty.

He stepped inside and turned on the kitchen lights. With his luck, somebody would call the police but he'd left his flashlight in the car. And he didn't want to waste time. If Mia showed up with the dog and gave him hell, he'd deal with it.

Somebody besides Mia had been there.

The place hadn't been trashed but the signs of a search were easy to spot. Nick had developed the habit of memorizing things long before he'd joined the bureau. His father had been the same way, so he supposed he'd picked it up from him. He'd only been in Mia's house once but he was sure objects had been moved, ever so slightly.

Whoever had been there had been looking for something. It hadn't been a common thief either. The intruder hadn't taken any of the things burglars usually went for. From what he could tell, the searcher hadn't taken anything at all. Or at least nothing obvious. His mind flicked back to the planner and the articles he and Mia had found at Mike's condo. He'd never thought to ask what Mia had done with them.

A surge of panic coursed through him. Maybe

Angela had been right after all. No, he thought, moving through the living room toward the stairs. If the intruder had taken Mia there would have been signs of a struggle. There were no overturned tables. No broken picture frames. Even the couch pillows were undisturbed.

The second floor was no different than the first. He'd never been upstairs so he had no point of comparison but the place felt *off* somehow. The light to the bathroom was on, though whether that meant something was anybody's guess.

He strode to the end of the corridor and stood in the doorway.

A wet spot on the tiles caught his attention. He knelt and lifted a few stray dog hairs off the tiles. Dante had been there, lying down. The wet spot was where the drool had pooled while he was on his side.

Dante had been lying on the bathroom floor.

He straightened and shut the door. Several long lines ran down the lower half and the paint had chipped here and there. Somebody had locked Dante in. Whatever had knocked him out must have taken long enough for him to scratch the wood.

It made sense. Whoever had searched the place took his time. The guy wouldn't have wanted a barking husky interfering.

So why not just kill him?

If whoever had searched Mia's place was behind Mike's death and Chien's disappearance, he wasn't exactly Mr. Nice Guy.

So why leave the dog alive?

It didn't make sense.

Nick's phone vibrated in his jeans pocket. He

pulled it out, hoping to see Mia's number light up the screen.

Dalton.

It was better than nothing. Maybe he'd located the mysterious Brendon Thompson. He clicked on the call. "Got something for me?"

"Nice chatting with you too." Beneath the sarcasm, Dalton sounded tense. "As a matter of fact, I don't. Our mutual friend ran the name through our database, as well as the databases of a few other agencies I thought might interest you. Went back twenty years. Even looked at consultants. But as far as I can tell, no Brendon Thompson ever worked for us. Or for the NSA. Or the agency."

Nick walked back out into the hallway. He'd been sure there had been a connection. Donelan's face had given him away. He'd known Nick's story about Brendon Thompson before he'd told it, he was sure of it. "Well, thanks for trying. I know you've got other things to spend your time on."

"You always were a royal pain in the ass."

"Right back at you."

"Truth be told, it's good to talk to you."

"Bad day?"

"Thanks for asking, honey," Dalton joked. "As a matter of fact, yeah. It sucked. As bad days go, it was the mother of all bad days."

"Well, if it's any consolation, my day hasn't been stellar either."

"I don't know which is worse, you being stuck in therapy or me dealing with the same bullshit day after day."

Nick got the impression Dalton wasn't saying

everything he wanted to. "Something going on?"

"Something's always going on. But this thing's worse than usual. Can't get my head around it."

Nick took a wild guess. He hadn't seen much news but there was one story that had caught everybody's attention. "You wouldn't be working on anything connected with that village up in Alaska, would you?"

There was a silence on the line

"Gotcha," Nick said. Even if they weren't on an unsecured line, Dalton couldn't get into details. Nick had hired him but now Dalton ran his own unit, one that worked exclusively on the New World Army. Aside from killing Brendon Thompson back in '01, that had been the terrorist group responsible for setting off an explosive on Capitol Hill a couple of years ago. It wouldn't surprise him if the NWA was involved in what was going up in Aniak. Over the past year the NWA had claimed responsibility for more than a few terrorist attacks, both in the United States and overseas. They weren't quite on the level of ISIS in terms of numbers but they were gaining support every day. Suppose the NWA had changed tactics. Suppose they'd traded their explosives for a smaller weapon. A lot smaller.

Questions raced through his mind, but he pushed them aside. Later, when he had more time, he would consider the case from a new angle—one that took NWA into account. But for the time being he had to figure out what had happened to Mia and her dog.

"I tell you one thing," Dalton said. "I sure as hell wish you were dealing with this instead of me."

Now Nick was the one who didn't answer.

"You know I meant that hypothetically, right?"

"Right."

"Because you're kinda giving me the impression that the dead sailor you wanted that autopsy on—the one who just happened to work with deadly viruses—might have something to do with what's going on up there in Alaska. In which case, maybe we do need to talk."

"I don't know. That's what I'm trying to figure out. You know as much about those autopsy results as I do. If I had anything concrete, I'd tell you. But I don't."

"Don't hold out on me."

"I'm not."

"Okay. But you find something out, you let me know."

"I will." Nick grinned. Was his friend giving him tacit permission to keep looking into what was happening at the Institute? Whatever the case, he'd all but forgotten about Nick's group therapy sessions. Which was fine by him. "There is one last thing I want you to do for me though."

"Of course there is."

"Tom Ray, Enji Chan, Ken Goodman, Sam Brown, Cormac—"

"Whoa there," Dalton interrupted. "Am I supposed to be writing these down?"

"No, just thinking aloud. I'll send you the names. I want you to have our mutual friend run those through the databases too."

"Mind if I ask why?'

"Just a hunch."

"Right."

"Whose names are they? Can I at least know that?"

"They were the guys in my platoon over in

Afghanistan."

"Uh-huh."

The skepticism was hard to miss. "Tom, Liam and Enji were the ones who were closest to him. What if one of them—or somebody else in the platoon—never got over Brendon's death? Or the war in general. Christ, it was a mess over there. It wouldn't be all that surprising if he chose the name Thompson to use as an alias, especially if he went rogue. Sort of a way of keeping him alive."

"That's a little too much pop psychology for me."

"Maybe. But now that I think of it, why would Thompson use his own name to rent a car if he were working on something? Why go to the trouble of renting a car and paying cash then use your own name? Doesn't make sense."

"In other words, you were wrong."

Nick laughed. "It looks that way. But say Thompson really did die—and say one of Thompson's buddies ended up working for the government and ended up in rehab at some point? Then there's a damn good chance he would've ended up at Seahaven. He might have talked about Thompson in group therapy or maybe just to Donelan. I know it sounds a little crazy, but it's all I've got right now."

"A little crazy?" Dalton asked doubtfully

"Yeah, I know," Nick agreed. "But that doesn't mean I'm wrong."

"You were wrong the first time around."

"Ouch."

Neither of them spoke.

"You think this is related to Aniak?" Dalton asked finally.

"Maybe, maybe not. I'm not sure yet. I'm not sure of anything. It could—or it could be another dead end."

"Fair enough," Dalton said. "I'll put our buddy on it. That probably makes me as crazy as you, but our friend's been bored lately."

"No Dr. Who conventions going on?"

"Apparently not."

Nick disconnected the call and sent Dalton a text with the names. There were ten in all and he'd ranked them according to their relationship with Thompson. Close friends at the top, acquaintances and enemies at the bottom. None of them had been his enemy— Thompson hadn't had enemies—and none of them had really been acquaintances. It was impossible to spend that much time together and not feel some kind of bond. Especially under those circumstances.

It was fully dark in the house, except for the lone light that shone in the bathroom. He dialed Mia's number but, as expected, she didn't pick up.

The message on the other end of line told him to leave a message but he hung up. No point in leaving yet another plea for her to call him. He half contemplated calling again just to hear her voice then changed his mind.

It wasn't so much that he needed to hear her voice. He did, but it was the casual tone of the message that he wanted. Anything to help convince himself that everything was okay. That she was okay. It was a trick of the mind and he knew it but that didn't make it any easier to resist.

Nick turned off the bathroom light and went downstairs. He sat down on the couch and closed his eyes. At Seahaven, they'd be in the middle of a group therapy session. He could imagine Callie filling everybody in on her latest marriage difficulties, or making sly remarks about his absence.

Had one of his platoon buddies done the same thing before him? Or was he really nuts for thinking it in the first place? Most of them had been pretty messed up after they'd gotten back to the States. Everybody who saw combat had scars—inside and out—but Nick had to believe what they'd dealt with over there had been worse. He didn't like to remember, which he supposed was one reason he'd never kept in contact with any of them afterward.

Tom Ray, Enji Chan, Ken Goodman, Sam Brown, Cormac Sanderson, Liam Gallagher.

Ray, Gallagher and Chan had been closest to Thompson. The three of them had been devastated by his death but none had seemed unhinged by it. Goodman? Nick had the vague sense the guy had gone on to work for the CIA, but from what he'd heard the guy was married with a bunch of kids. Didn't fit the profile of a rogue agent. Brown and Sanderson had ended up working for the government as well, a lot of the guys had. He couldn't remember which agency though. Neither of them had been particularly close to Thompson. Who else?

Patterson? Hadn't heard from him since they flew out of Bagram.

Massie? Nick was pretty sure he'd died in combat, somewhere in Iraq.

Which left…nobody.

Maybe he was wrong.

So why couldn't he let it go?

Nick pinched the bridge of his nose. He needed to

talk to Donelan again. Not on the phone though. If the priest was going to tell him what he knew, he'd have to get it out of him in person. There had to be some kind of confidentiality agreement that forbid him from discussing former patients. Nick would have convince him to break that.

****

Caleb glanced up from the magazine he'd been reading when Mia walked into the waiting room. The animal clinic had closed at seven p.m., so he was the only person there. A lone lamp shone on the table next to the rather uncomfortable looking chair he'd spent the past four hours in.

She hadn't expected him to be there. "You didn't have to stay, you know."

"I know." Behind his glasses, his eyes were hooded, as if he were about to fall asleep. "How's your husky?"

"Sleeping. The vet's keeping him overnight for observation but he says I should be able to pick him up tomorrow at the end of the day. Apparently whoever broke into my place gave him a dinosaur-sized dose of sleeping pills. It could have killed him, though the vet seems to think it wasn't deliberate. I mean, whoever drugged him did it on purpose, probably to get him out of the way so he could search the place. But the vet said if the intruder meant to kill him there would have been better ways to go about it."

Mia debated whether she should go sit next to him and decided against it. He'd gone above and beyond the call of duty, as far as helping her get Dante to the vet. If he hadn't showed up when he did, Dante would be much worse off.

185

But he'd still screwed her over in that report.

Caleb closed the magazine and set it on the coffee table. "It's still a pretty nasty thing to do," he said. "Have you called the police yet?"

"Not yet. I'll do it in the morning. It's not like I've got anything else on the agenda."

He stood up and walked over to her. "Do you want me to follow you home? It might not be safe to go back to your place. Whoever did this to your dog might decide to try again."

"I doubt it. And if he does, I'll kick his ass." She managed a weary smile. "I am a brown belt, you know."

He smiled back and reached up to lay a hand on her shoulder.

The door was only a foot or so away but she had the impulse to bolt. Of course, everybody made her feel that way.

Except Nick. Yet she'd pushed him away anyway. She hadn't been able to get past all the fear.

When she'd finally gotten around to checking her messages, she had been surprised to see several voicemails from Nick interspersed with the dozen or so calls from her mother. She hadn't expected to hear from him. She hadn't wanted to leave Dante alone and it didn't seem like a good idea to play them with Dr. Cooke standing six inches away.

She wasn't sure why he'd called her, but that hadn't stopped the rush of feeling that warmed her when she'd seen his messages.

Caleb, on the other hand, definitely did not give her butterflies.

Her new partner left his hand where it was,

oblivious to the fact that he was making her uncomfortable. "You're sure? It's no problem."

"I'm sure," she said firmly, taking a step back so that his arm fell to his side. "All I want to do is sleep. And I really don't think whoever it was is coming back. Either they found what they wanted or they didn't. They knew my schedule and picked a time when they knew I wouldn't be home. I doubt they'd risk breaking in a second time at night. And they can't know I haven't called the police."

"Yeah, I guess you're right," he agreed.

Mia pushed through the door with Caleb following close behind.

When they reached their cars, he slipped his keys out of his pocket and deactivated his alarm. His beat-up SUV looked about as old as her Subaru. "So what do you think they were looking for, anyway?"

She pulled her keys out of her purse and stopped a few feet from her car. "I don't know."

The conversation skipped a beat.

Mia got the impression he was waiting for her to change her mind about him following her home. The parking lot was almost completely dark. The only light came from the back room of the hospital, where Dante lay sleeping it off between a couple of overweight cats. Aside from Dr. Cooke and the overnight attendant, the place was deserted. Suddenly the idea of a long drive home wasn't all that appealing.

Either way, she wasn't going to change her mind.

"Thanks again for all your help. With everything. And good luck with the autopsy tomorrow." Yes, it was a dismissal. Even geeky Caleb couldn't miss that hint.

"Don't worry about calling in tomorrow," he said.

"I'll let Trask know first thing that you're taking the day off."

Mia stared at him. "Are you telling me you don't know?"

"Know what?"

She fought to keep her composure. Losing her position was almost too painful to talk about, especially with the person who was at least partially responsible. "I'm out of the unit. Starting tomorrow. Trask's forcing me to take time off and when I get back I'll be working on the common cold for the indefinite future."

"I know he said you wouldn't be in on the autopsy because you, uh, kind of panicked in there. But removing you from the unit seems a bit over the top." Caleb made no move to unlock his car, as if he were frozen in place by the news. "Can't you try to talk to him?"

He really did seem as if he meant what he said. Maybe she'd misjudged him all along. The only thing he'd ever done was try to help her.

And lie in a report.

Unless he believes you did slice the glove.

That might make him wrong but it didn't make him an asshole.

She walked over to her car and slid the key into the lock on the driver's side. "I already did. It didn't go well."

Caleb remained where he was, keys in hand. "I could talk to him."

She pulled the door open and stood with her hand on the metal. "Thanks, but you've already done enough."

His face fell. Mia winced when she saw the effect

her words had on him. She hadn't intended to sound so bitter. "I'm sorry. I know you only wrote what you thought was the truth. I didn't cut the glove—I'm sure of it—but I can see how you might think that."

His face was blank. "What are you talking about?"

"The report. You wrote in the report that I was the one who made the tear in the glove. When I was cutting out the lung."

He shook his head. "I don't know what you mean."

"What?"

"I didn't write that," he said quietly.

She slammed the door shut and strode over to him. "What do you mean, you didn't write it? Are you telling me Trask made that up? Why would he do that?"

She wasn't sure who she was asking.

Caleb's shoulders slumped. "That's not what I'm saying," he said, clearly distraught. "Maybe he misunderstood what he read."

"Trask misunderstood what he read." She looked at him in disbelief. "When has Trask ever misunderstood anything?"

"I don't know him as well as you do," he hedged.

"Let's get this straight. You're telling me—you're—" She broke off. "Caleb, listen. I need you to tell me what you wrote in that report. Right now."

"I—can't—remember."

"Don't give me that."

"I really don't think this is time. You've been through a lot. If you call me in the morning I promise—"

Mia took hold of his shoulders and shook him. *"Tell me what's in the goddamn report!"*

She knew she shouldn't have grabbed him as soon

189

as she'd done it. She felt as if her endurance was stretched to the breaking point. Too much was happening all at once.

Thank God Trask couldn't see her. Or would Caleb inform him about that as well?

She let go of his shoulders. "I'm so sorry. I shouldn't have done that. I'm—not myself."

"You've been through a lot." He adjusted his shirt and smiled tentatively.

She wanted to make him answer her, but she couldn't. She'd already gone too far as it was. Unless Caleb was an idiot, he wasn't going to contradict Trask. If Trask said the report mentioned her cutting the glove he wasn't going to buck it. It was Mia's job, not his, on the line.

But she couldn't sort it all out. Was Caleb lying so she wouldn't be mad at him? Or had Trask tampered with the report? Or just plain lied to her about its contents? When she'd asked to see it, he'd stalled. Still, there could be more than one explanation for his reluctance to let her look at it. Legitimate explanations.

"Actually," Caleb said, "I have a question for you."

"Ask away." She had no idea what he wanted to know and she didn't care. Maybe she could use it as some kind of bargaining chip.

"You and Mike were—close."

For a second she thought he was going to ask if they'd been lovers. How strange it would be if Caleb's interest in her was purely romantic.

She nodded. "We were."

"I didn't know the guy all that well but I got the impression something was, well, off the last week or so before he, uh, drowned. And now with Chien gone, I got to thinking—I mean it all seems pretty weird—the two of them being out of the unit. And now—" He stopped.

Touchy subject.

"And now I'm off the unit too," Mia finished for him.

He breathed a sigh of relief. "Yeah. Well, it just seems kind of—odd—you know, and I started wondering if maybe Mike might've said something to you before he died."

"Like what?" she asked warily.

He shrugged. "I don't know. Maybe something he was working on. Or something he'd seen. One day he was coming out of the break room. And he was talking with Chien. It was probably nothing but—I don't know—something about the way he looked made me wonder."

"The way Mike looked?"

"Both of them, actually."

"How did they look?"

He paused. "Guilty?"

"Guilty," she repeated. Mia thought about the slides she'd found in Mike's desk in BL-4. The cells in two of the slides obliterated. And now people in Alaska were dying of some mysterious illness. Chien missing, Mike dead. Mike with a bunch of articles about deadly viruses at his condo. *What went wrong?* Mike's notation came back to her. If the two of them were working together on something, was what was going on in Aniak somehow connected with it? She made a mental note to google Aniak the moment she got home.

A shock of curly hair fell across Caleb's face, making him look about fourteen. "I mean, do you think something was going on with them?"

"No," she said resolutely. "I'm sure it was nothing. Now that Mike's dead and Chien's gone, it's easy to read into every little thing that happened."

"I'm sure you're right." He laughed. "Hard not to get a little paranoid these days."

Paranoid. Trask's words came back to her. Was it paranoia—or was something truly dangerous going on at the Institute? Either way, she wasn't about to share what she knew with Caleb. Mike had been her friend and she wasn't about to start throwing around theories she couldn't prove.

"I'd better get going."

"Be careful, okay?"

"You too."

She remembered something she'd forgotten from earlier that day. The lungs of the monkey, the concentration of blood there. "There's something you should look at when you finish the autopsy tomorrow. The lungs—the amount of blood—suggests the infection could have started there. You need to look at the samples we took. Because if I'm right, the infection might be transmitted through the air, not through bodily fluids."

"I thought you said it looked like Ebola."

"It does," she said. "And that's what scares me. If the virus is some sort of mutation of a strain of Ebola—though God knows how it surfaced in Alaska—then it's a thousand times more dangerous than any virus we've ever dealt with before. Luckily the village is under quarantine and is remote enough that the possibility of containing it's pretty high. But if an airborne mutation of Ebola reached a suburban area, the consequences would be devastating."

Caleb pushed back the shock of hair, only to have it fall back into his face. "Jesus. And you really think it might be airborne?"

"I never got the chance to finish the autopsy."

She didn't need to tell Caleb how dangerous an airborne version of Ebola would be. Even the average citizen was well aware of that nightmare scenario. She just hoped he had the skill to learn everything he could from the dead monkey. He hadn't seemed to pay much attention to the lungs at all.

Maybe her replacement would be more observant. "Who did Trask assign to assist?"

"Trask."

"I don't understand."

A look of dismay settled over his features. "He wants to finish it himself."

Chapter 12

It was close to midnight by the time Mia pulled into her driveway. She was too tired to react to Nick's car parked out front. Not to mention too confused. First, the phone calls. Now his car. She wasn't sure if the knot in her stomach was due to anxiety or euphoria.

The house was dark when she walked in but she sensed his presence immediately. "Nick?"

No sign of him in the kitchen.

She walked into the living room and saw him sprawled out on her couch, his arms wrapped around one of the throw pillows. His hair had fallen to one side and he was snoring lightly. Funny, that a guy as tough as Nick could look so vulnerable.

He was vulnerable. But he went out of his way never to let anybody know it.

Which, she supposed, could be why he'd ended up at Seahaven. She remembered the story he'd shared the previous night. The way his voice had gone hoarse when he talked about his father's drinking. And his wife's death. It wouldn't surprise her if that was the first time he'd talked about either of those things. What would it be like to go through life always keeping things hidden away from the rest of the world?

It didn't take much imagination to figure that one out. She'd done the same thing for almost sixteen years. The only difference was that Mia didn't even trust herself. If she drank she couldn't be sure she'd be able to keep her thoughts from the person she feared most.

Herself.

At least Nick had experienced pain. Sure, he'd self-medicated when the memories got too intense. But at least he'd felt something. At least he'd grieved for his father. And his wife.

She'd never mourned her sister. In all these years, she'd never allowed herself to relive the events of that day at the park. She hadn't even permitted herself to remember Holly at all. Her house had no photographs of her sister and none of her father. Another loss, albeit a different kind of loss. She didn't know where he was and hadn't allowed herself to care. For all she knew he could be dead. He probably was. It had been nearly two decades since she'd gotten his final postcard. It hadn't been any different than the others and now she wondered if he'd meant it to be the last.

Not that it mattered. She'd long since thrown it away, along with most of the others he'd sent her. Day by day, the images of her father—and her sister—were fading. Maybe someday they'd be gone forever.

That's what you wanted. To forget them.

True. Even her relationship with her mother was ruled by Mia's desire to put the past behind her. It was she, not her mother, who was responsible for the distance between them.

Mia hadn't wanted a family at all. It was easier that way.

But it wasn't really living and she knew it. Her existence was as devoid of life as one of the sterile rooms at the Institute. Aside from Dante and Nailini, she had no one. Even her friendship with Nailini was mostly one of proximity. They talked about Mia's work, or Nailini's work at the animal clinic or her latest relationship. But never about Mia.

That had always been fine with her.

She sat down on the couch next to Nick and lowered her hand, holding it a few inches above his hair. Of all the times to finally have steady hands it had to be now. When it didn't matter at all. She wanted to touch him. But she couldn't let down her guard, even when he was sleeping, even when he'd never know she'd done it.

Pathetic.

Nick's hand closed around her wrist before she realized he'd woken. He opened his eyes and gazed up at her. His hand on her skin felt warm, even hot.

They stayed there like, neither of them speaking. Neither of them moving.

"What happened to the dog?" Nick asked.

"Somebody gave him sleeping pills. He's okay now. They're keeping him overnight at the hospital." She tried to pull her arm out of his grasp.

"Don't." He grabbed her other wrist then pushed her onto her back until she was beneath him, her face inches away from his.

"You're wasting your time on me," she said hoarsely. "I don't care about you."

"I know." Beneath his jeans, he was hard as a rock.

She closed her fists and used all her strength to wrench her arms free. But there was no way she could get away, not if he didn't want her to. He wasn't gripping her that hard but his hands felt like steel just the same. "Let go."

"I want you to tell me one thing."

She lay beneath him, perfectly still. "You should find someone else. Someone who can be the person you want me to be."

"Is that a deal?" His eyes locked onto hers.

"I can't be her," she whispered, looking away. "I can't heal you."

"One question." His voice was low and controlled, but his heart was beating so hard she could feel it against her chest.

"What gives you the right to make me answer you?"

He searched her face for something and seemed not to find it. "Nothing," he said at last. "Nothing at all."

He released his hold on her wrists and sat up on the couch, turning away from her. She immediately sat up as well, pulling her arms to her side.

She waited for him to say something but he didn't. He stayed where he was, facing the wall.

"Okay, fine. What do you want to know?" she blurted out.

He didn't turn around.

"Are you going to stay like that forever?" Tears pricked at the backs of her eyes.

Without speaking, Nick got up off the couch and sat down before her on the carpet. As gently as possible, he lifted one of her arms off her lap and stared down at it.

"There's no mark," she said. "If that's what you're looking for."

"That's not what I was looking for."

"You weren't holding me that tightly."

"I know," he said quietly.

"Then what—"

With the tip of his finger, he touched the spot where his hand had grasped her left wrist. "I was looking for the scars."

"Scars?"

He brushed his finger along the inside of her wrist, making it tingle. "But those are on the inside, aren't they?"

So many feelings were fighting their way to the surface. If she gave in now, what would happen? She tried not to think about the sensation of his hand against her skin. "I don't know."

"Do you care about anybody at all, Mia?"

"I—don't—know—"

From where he sat on the floor, he leaned forward and took her face between his hands. "Maybe this will help you make up your mind."

The kiss was different than the first. There was no gentleness in it, only need. Mia realized she was kissing him back just as furiously, her need as great as his. With both arms, she pulled him up until he lay beside her, her hand fumbling at his belt.

He helped her undo it, stepping out of his jeans and returning to her arms. His shaft jutted upward, tenting his boxers, and when she reached inside and closed her hand around it, he groaned aloud. She couldn't do anything to prevent what she knew she'd wanted from the moment she met him.

Nick's hands were in her hair, on her breasts, her stomach. His kisses grew frantic as he unbuttoned her blouse and struggled to unlatch her bra. When he'd gotten the clasp undone, she reached up and pulled her shirt over her head. She removed her bra as well and lay back before him.

"God, you're beautiful," he breathed.

With his thumbs, he circled her nipples with exquisite slowness until they grew hard. He lowered his head and sucked, gently at first and then with increasing ferocity. When he switched to the other breast she arched toward him.

"Don't stop," she whispered, running her hands down his muscled back until they reached the rim of his boxers. With both hands she grasped the elastic and pulled them down over his buttocks, reveling in the sensation of her palms on his rough skin.

"You next," he said, releasing her breast and bending down to remove his boxers.

She slid her panties down over her hips and tossed them onto the floor. She was wet deep inside, desperate to feel him inside her.

He touched his lips to her shoulder and traced kisses along her collarbone. He lowered his mouth to her breasts again but didn't linger, moving downward toward her stomach. His tongue flicked across her abdomen, and she writhed beneath him, opening her legs wide enough for him to cover her with his mouth.

The stubble on his chin rubbed against her wetness. He moved his lips even lower, sucking and licking. She lifted her mound toward him, feeling the tension building within her. His tongue probed her depths, to be replaced by his fingers, moving in and out of her so expertly she knew she wouldn't be able to hold off much longer. Just when she reached the edge of pleasure, he removed his fingers and stood over her, letting the cool night air wash over them.

"Are you sure?"

She reached up and tried to pull him closer. "I'm

sure."

He lowered himself onto her and pushed slowly into her opening until he was fully sheathed inside her. She moved beneath him and he thrust forward, then back, as the tension built within her. When he came inside her, she couldn't stop the waves of pleasure that washed over her.

Afterward, they lay in each other's arms. The light she'd left on in the kitchen cast a pale shadow across the carpet.

Nick ran his finger along her shoulder and leaned down to kiss her. "Now that wasn't so bad, was it?"

"It wasn't," she agreed. "But I think I need to try it again to really be sure."

Mia stood and pulled him up off the couch. When she'd walked in the door all she'd wanted to do was fall into bed and sleep. Now she wanted to fall into bed, but sleep wasn't what she had in mind.

Strange that she didn't feel self-conscious in front of Nick. She didn't have a stitch of clothing on and yet it seemed unnecessary to cover up. He rose to his feet and stood across from her, his shaft already growing hard again.

"Come on," she said over her shoulder on her way toward the staircase. She could feel his eyes on her body without having to look. By the time she reached the first step, he'd caught up with her.

He circled his arms around her waist and nuzzled her ear. "Are we going where I think we're going?"

She took his hand and climbed another step. "I guess you'll just have to wait and find out."

****

Nick had been awake for an hour when Mia opened

her eyes and turned toward him, pulling the sheet across her chest. "Oh, so now you're modest?"

"It's morning. I don't do mornings."

He reached for the sheet and pulled it away from her. "That's too bad. Because I do."

She jumped off the bed, dragging the sheet after her, before he could catch her. "You're too damn quick," he said. "I don't know if I can keep up with you."

Mia wrapped the sheet around her and glanced down at his jutting shaft. "Something tells me that's not going to be a problem."

He grinned. The first time he'd seen her he'd thought of her as some kind of goddess. Now that he knew her better, he saw the real woman. But as she stood there draped in white with the morning sunlight firing her pale hair, it was hard not to revert to his earlier theory. "Being around beautiful women tends to have that effect on me."

She raised an eyebrow. "Women?"

"Make that woman." He leaned back against the headboard. "Singular."

When he caught her staring at his body, she blushed.

"That's more like it," she said, keeping her eyes on his face. "I've never been very good at sharing."

"Neither am I."

She crossed to the hamper and stuffed the sheet inside. Grabbing a bathrobe off a hook in the closet, she slid into it and turned back toward him. "I'm taking a shower."

The thought of warm water running over Mia's body was enough to revive his erection. "Want me to join you?"

"Absolutely not." She tied the robe around her waist. "My entire body is sore. I feel muscles I forgot I had."

"Guess you'll need to start working out then. Get back into shape."

"Hey!"

"You know what I mean."

A smile played across her lips. "Thank you," she said a little uncertainly. "For what you did for me."

"I wasn't doing you any favors."

"I know." She pulled her hair up off her neck and knotted it in a messy bun. "I got demoted yesterday. I can't even go into the office until next week. I—needed—to forget about all that for a while."

"Glad to be of service," he said drily.

Under ordinary circumstances, he would have been offended. He wasn't used to being the means for women to forget their troubles. If anything, it had been the other way around. But with Mia it was different.

"It's been a long time since I've, uh, been with anybody. Or even opened up to another person. Sometimes I think I've spent my whole life pushing people away."

"Because of what happened to your sister." He knew he was treading on dangerous ground but if Mia was going to ever come to terms with the past she couldn't keep pretending it didn't exist.

She looked a bit taken aback. "How do you know about Holly?"

"Your mom told me."

"My mom?"

"Yeah."

She didn't say anything.

"She was worried about you yesterday. When you weren't returning her calls. She thought something happened. The conversation kind of went from there."

"Uh-huh."

He fought to remember what Angela had told him about the girl's death. Something about a park. "I don't know all the details—maybe sometime you'll share them with me—but I am certain of one thing. It wasn't your fault."

Mia didn't answer.

"You were, what, in high school when she disappeared?"

"I was thirteen."

"Too young to shoulder the blame for what some perverted bastard did to your sister."

He knew as soon as he said it he'd screwed up. A look of pain flickered across her features but she quickly controlled it."

"Like you said, we can talk about it another time."

"Sure," he said quickly. "Whenever you're ready. Or if you want, we don't have to talk about it all."

He waited for her to leave the room but she stayed where she was. Part of him was surprised she'd even told him what she had. He wanted to ask her more—and to find out what had happened at the Institute—but thought better of it. She didn't look as if she was ready to talk about it. And something told him it was going to be a long conversation.

"Go take your shower," he said. "We can talk when you get out."

"Okay." She walked over to him and planted a quick kiss on his lips. Before he could react, she whirled away and disappeared into the hallway.

A minute later he heard the shower turn on. He wanted to get up off the bed and take her again, to force the sadness out of her eyes. But he held back.

Give her space.

He still wasn't sure if they were just playing house or if the previous night's sex had meant something more. The night before Mia had told him she was unsure of her feelings for him. The sex between them said something else. And now this morning she seemed affectionate, even warm.

That was one word he'd never thought would apply to her. She was smart, beautiful, dedicated. Despite her cool demeanor, she could be passionate. She'd proved that to him last night, more than once. But there was a sadness inside her he couldn't reach—an empty space he couldn't touch—even at the height of their lovemaking. And that sadness created a breach between them he wasn't sure he'd ever be able to mend.

He was pretending too, in a way. No, not pretending. His feelings for Mia were real. But he was deliberately choosing not to think about anything beyond those four walls. To his surprise, he didn't feel guilty. Mia was the first woman he'd been with since Rosa but it didn't feel like a betrayal. The night before, Mia had said she wasn't "her," which he supposed referred to his former wife.

He didn't want Mia to be a replacement. He'd never thought of her that way. He just wanted Mia. Or at least to take a shot at having a relationship with her. If she'd have him—which was open to debate.

Now that was a topic he definitely didn't want to think about.

He also didn't want to think about what Father Donelan would say when he drove back to Seahaven to retrieve the rest of his things. He hadn't finished the program and Donelan wasn't going to change his mind about that. No way was he leaving Mia alone in her house another night. Not with two of her colleagues dead or missing and an intruder who'd drugged her dog.

He knew his superiors at the Bureau wouldn't be happy about him going AWOL. Never mind Dalton and Laura. Even if he told them it was for a case it wouldn't do much good.

He was on leave.

Mandatory leave.

And it wasn't a case, it was—well, he wasn't sure what the hell he was dealing with.

One of the cell phones on the nightstand vibrated. He couldn't tell which one but grabbed his in case the call was for him.

So much for shutting out the world.

No new messages or missed calls. Not his phone.

He set it back down next to Mia's and ignored the second buzz. It would be easy to take a look at her screen to see who was trying to get in touch with her. He could justify the intrusion in a hundred ways but he didn't want to take that route. He'd never pried into Rosa's life and didn't plan on starting with Mia either.

He had to trust her.

Nick pulled on his boxers and padded across the room to the TV. He grabbed the remote off the dresser and clicked it on. Fortunately he didn't have to waste time channel surfing. The screen went straight to CNN. A reporter stood on a very rustic looking Main Street, interviewing somebody who did not look at all as if he lived there. He didn't recognize the name of the Alaskan town at the top of screen but he guessed it wasn't too far from Aniak.

Hopefully it wasn't all that close either. He wasn't sure how much information had been released but the press had to know how dangerous the situation was. Which, he supposed, would only make the media even more determined to get as close as possible to the scene of disaster.

He turned up the volume until he could make out what the reporter was saying. From what he could tell, events had taken a turn for the better. Or at least they hadn't gotten worse. Most of the residents of Aniak were infected and more than half hadn't made it. One hundred and twelve dead with three times as many in critical condition.

The good news was that it looked as if the quarantine was working. The previous day a woman in a neighboring town had fallen ill but other than that, no new cases had been reported.

Nick sat down on the edge of the bed and listened as the CDC official ticked off the list of symptoms. Bloodshot eyes, mask-like face, the mind turned to jelly. The changes began almost immediately after exposure and ended in death. So far there were no survivors. Every last damn person in Aniak had been infected and so far nobody had managed to hang on more than twenty-four hours. The average time between contact and death was between eight and forty-eight hours.

He swore under his breath. It sounded like one of the horror movies he'd watched as a kid. The zombie apocalypse. Only this one was real.

Or almost was, he amended. If the press accounts were true, then it looked as if the apocalypse had been averted. Just barely. According to the official, the disease was transmitted via bodily fluids and though the symptoms were similar to Ebola, it was not believed that the infection was, in fact, Ebola.

Smart too, to turn the town into a hospital instead of treating residents at nearby medical facilities. Better to fly in medicine and supplies than risk letting the virus spread. For once, he agreed with the government's approach to the crisis. For once, everybody seemed to be on the same page.

Even so, there was something odd about the whole thing. But he couldn't pinpoint what it was that bothered him about it.

Something didn't feel right. He didn't know what and he didn't know if it was the government's unified response or something else entirely that bothered him. There were a lot of unanswered questions, that much was certain. The disease was so similar to Ebola and yet it had surfaced in such an isolated area, one that was literally on the other side of the world from the country where the Ebola outbreak originated.

Then there was the similarity between Aniak and the village in Siberia where everyone had died a year earlier. The children had survived that virus but this time nobody had beat it. Yet other than that, the circumstances were remarkably similar.

And Mike Chandler had that clipping in his condo the day he died. Suppose that had been what the intruder had been looking for in Mia's apartment.

It seemed a bit far-fetched. There were other ways to get hold of a news clipping. But Nick knew in his gut the events were connected. He just couldn't figure out how.

Yet.

Mia walked back in the room in her robe, a towel wrapped around her head. She disappeared into the walk-in closet and reemerged a few minutes later wearing jeans and a Fall Out Boy t-shirt. Her wet hair fell long over the towel she'd wrapped around her shoulders.

"Feel better?" He glanced at the shirt. "Don't tell me you're a fan," he said doubtfully. "I thought you said you only liked classical."

"And the Beatles," she reminded him. "You forgot about the Beatles."

"The Beatles and Fall Out Boy don't have a whole hell of a lot in common. At least I don't think they do." He'd more or less memorized the entire Beatles discography but wasn't sure he could name a song by the punk rock group.

Mia sat down next to him on the bed. "Actually, I don't think I've ever listened to them—at least not intentionally. The shirt was a present from my stepsister," she said. "She's seventeen."

"That explains a lot."

"She used to get upset with me because I friend-zoned Mike."

"Friend-zoned?"

"Use your imagination." The light went out of her face. "I wish I hadn't."

Nick fought down the ugly surge of jealousy that shot through his entire body. Mia had said Mike was in love with her but she'd never told him how she felt. "Did you—have feelings for him?"

"Don't tell me you're jealous."

"I'm not jealous," he said. "But I'm also lying."

Her eyes darkened.

He pointed a finger at her. "Don't. Start."

"I won't."

"I mean it."

She turned her gaze toward the TV. The newscaster and the CDC official had been replaced by the President, who was commenting about the latest sex scandal. "What's going on in Alaska? Has it spread?"

"Actually, it looks as if they've got it under control. No new cases. They've sealed the place off from the rest of the world. Kind of reminds me of the way they used to lock people inside their houses to die during the Bubonic plague. Though I can't say that I blame them."

"I think it's airborne. If I'd gotten the chance to finish the autopsy, I'd have been able to say that with more certainty. But it looked as if the lungs were the source of the infection."

"You autopsied one of the people from Aniak?"

"No, sorry. I forgot I still haven't told you what happened yesterday. The Institute has samples of the virus. Some of the test monkeys received injections, some didn't. The next morning all of them were dead."

He pressed his lips together. "Sounds familiar."

"The monkey we examined hadn't been injected. It's possible he contracted it when one of the other monkeys bled out—you'd be surprised how far blood can travel. But based on what I was seeing in the lungs…"

"Why didn't you get to finish?"

"There was a tear in the outer glove. And in the

glove underneath it."

"Jesus. Are you okay?" Nick's stomach clenched. The thought of almost losing Mia was hard to take. Hell, he'd just found her. He pushed the images from that morning's news broadcast out of his head. Thinking of Mia's body desecrated in such a way was enough to make him physically ill.

"In case you're worried about last night, I'm not harboring any deadly pathogens."

"Very funny," he said. "I assume it's occurred to you that those tears didn't get there by accident."

She nodded. "Trask says my new partner—the guy who was performing the autopsy with me—claims I nicked myself when I was cutting. Caleb denies it. To be honest, I don't know what to believe. But I'm pretty sure I didn't cut myself. I would've felt that. And I wouldn't forget it, even if I did pass out afterward."

He furrowed his brow. "You passed out?"

"Total wimp. Which is another reason I've been demoted to the common cold." She smiled wanly.

He didn't smile back. Mia might be able to make light of what had happened but he wasn't as willing to let it go. Somebody at the Institute had either wanted her dead—or they'd intended to scare the hell out of her. Either way he didn't like it. He didn't like it all. "You're lucky to be alive."

"Thank God the monkey blood didn't penetrate the final layer."

He didn't know her boss but it seemed pretty harsh to punish her for getting upset as a result of her suit being sabotaged. Not to mention the fact that the guy didn't seem to be doing a damn thing about investigating the situation. The guy wasn't FBI but any idiot could see something was up.

Nick wanted to tell her what he thought of the guy but he wasn't sure how she'd react if he started trashing him.

"Anybody would've panicked," he said neutrally.

She shook her head. "No, not everybody. I'm a trained scientist. It's my job to stay cool in situations like that and if I can't, then I shouldn't be there. Especially not when it involves something as important as a virus like the one killing people in Alaska. Trask was right to be upset. If Caleb and the doctor hadn't gotten me out of that lab I could have suffocated. Trask can't risk endangering the other staff members. If I'd reacted differently maybe we could've finished the autopsy. Then we'd be one step closer to figuring out how to stop people from getting infected."

Apparently Trask can risk endangering you, Nick thought. "If your boss is such a great guy, why did he lie about the report?"

"We don't know that."

"So you think the other guy, the new partner—Caleb—is the one lying."

"He says it's all a misunderstanding."

"Misunderstanding my ass. Torn safety gloves in a biohazard zone—that's one hell of a misunderstanding, if you ask me."

Mia glanced at the TV, as if she were waiting for something, before turning back toward him. "Why would Trask make that up? Or Caleb? What could either of them possibly have to gain by lying?"

What indeed. But he didn't know enough about either of them—or about the Institute—to even make a guess about their characters. Or their motives. "It seems to me you're the one who can answer that question."

"I just don't know." Her eyes met his. "Ever since Caleb helped me get Dante to the vet, I've been trying to figure him out. He seems like a decent guy and he was the one who tried to save me in that lab. On the other hand, Trask has been rock solid. The kind of guy who's always got your back. Until yesterday, I would've trusted him with my life. Then I think maybe it was all some kind of crazy mix-up. Then I remember that Mike's dead and Chien's missing. And that somebody broke into this place yesterday. My mind keeps going in circles."

"Trust me," he said. "I know how you feel."

"I should probably call the police," she said. "To report what happened last night."

"Maybe not."

"Why not? What if whoever it was comes back?"

"I went through the place pretty carefully last night. Your intruder knew what he was doing. A professional isn't going to leave much evidence behind. I'm not sure the police are going to find anything. Is anything missing?"

"No. Nothing."

"What about the stuff we took from Mike's place?" he asked. "I didn't see it last night. Though I'm guessing you hid it pretty well."

"Very well."

He waited for her to say more but she remained silent. Maybe she still didn't trust him one hundred percent. Well, he couldn't blame her. Everybody around her seemed to be turning out to be someone else.

She turned back to the TV and scanned the

newsfeed at the bottom of the screen. He wondered if she were looking for something about Chien or simply searching for a way to change the subject. Strange, that nothing about him had come up yet. He would've expected it to follow the story about Aniak. Then again, the media's interest in anything never lasted very long. Maybe Chien was already old news.

Before she could answer, her cell buzzed.

"Shit," Nick said. "It was doing that before and I forgot to tell you."

She got up and grabbed the phone off the table. "They hung up."

"Did they leave a message?"

"I don't know. Number unknown," she said slowly. "But there are about a dozen messages from you. And my mother. Looks like the vet called too."

"You should call your mother," Nick said. "She seemed really worried about you."

Mia didn't seem to be paying attention. Instead she tapped her screen and held the phone to her ear. "They want to keep Dante another night," she said a few seconds later. "The vet says it's only for observation."

"Then it's only for observation."

"It feels so strange without him here," she said, glancing around the bedroom. "I wish Nailini was back. She's always taken care of Dante."

"That's the friend with the parrots? She's a vet?"

"She's the one who pawned Dante off on me. Somebody abandoned him and she'd been keeping him at her house. I have no idea how she did it, but she convinced me to take him. She said she thought it would be good for me to have a pet. Of course, I was thinking more along the lines of a cat. Or maybe fish."

"Well, that explains one thing anyway. The woman seems to have a fondness for classical literature, at least when it comes to naming animals."

She was only half listening to him. "You don't think the animal hospital would keep anything from me, do you?"

"No. I don't. Not everybody's as secretive as you are."

He'd expected her to laugh but she seemed to barely hear what he'd said. Clearly, her mind was elsewhere. He couldn't blame her though. She'd been through a hell of a lot.

He got up and crossed to the window. Below them the street was quiet, empty. Farther off, a woman stood outside watering the roses that lined her walk. Across the way, a man was mowing his lawn.

Just another ordinary morning in suburbia. It suddenly struck him as odd that Mia would have chosen to live in a neighborhood like that. No, not odd. She seemed to try very hard to keep her life as organized as possible. The manicured lawns and neat houses were probably a part of that effort. But there was another side of her, one that was far more complex. Far more interesting. The part that bought the only eyesore on the block, a dilapidated Victorian fixer-upper. He'd glimpsed it last night and had seen it surface when she was with her husky. Maybe that was the real Mia.

He realized he didn't know her well enough to say one way or another.

"What did my mother say?" Mia asked absently. Her hair was still damp and she'd pushed it behind both ears. She wore no makeup and the band t-shirt gave made her seem younger than she was. Almost innocent.

Except for the eyes.

The eyes would always be old. He wondered if they'd been like that since she was thirteen years old. Since her sister disappeared.

"She had a feeling something was wrong." Nick let the curtain he'd pulled back drop back into place. "She's the reason I ended up on your couch."

That at least got her attention. "So you're saying my mother's the reason we had sex?"

"I'd rather you didn't put it that way."

She laughed. There was a kind of musicality to it and he realized he hadn't heard her laugh like that before. "I'm in total agreement with you on that one."

"Funny though, that her intuition was right. I've never felt all that connected with my mother."

"Maybe you should give her a chance."

"Maybe." She sounded thoughtful. "Maybe I should visit her again. It's not like I don't have the time."

"Why don't we head out there together? I want to talk to Donelan about something. And I need to get the rest of my things."

She shifted her position on the edge of the bed so that she faced him directly. "You're not checking out. I can take care of myself."

"This isn't negotiable, Mia. I can sleep on the couch, if you want."

"I don't care where you sleep. But I'm not going to let you mess up your situation with the FBI. I've already ruined one career this week, I'm not about to destroy another one."

"Let me worry about the FBI."

"That's exactly my point. You need to focus on

getting back into your old position, not protecting me."

"I wasted a lot of years putting my job first. Probably my whole life. Maybe I might not be following doctor's orders, but protecting you is the thing that's going to heal me. That has healed me."

Nick walked over and sat down next to her. He wasn't sure what to expect. For all he knew, she'd tell him to get the hell out of her house. Out of her life. He'd meant to take things slow, but here he was spilling his guts to her and forcing his presence on her. A mellow disposition wasn't something he understood. He'd never been laid back and he supposed he wasn't going to start now.

"All right," she said. "You can stay. On one condition."

"What's that?"

"That you take the right side of the bed. Left side's mine. That's non-negotiable."

"Done."

"And you know this is just temporary?"

"Got it."

Mia stood up and handed him her towel. "We'd better get going. As it so happens I've got the day off. But first you need a shower."

"Sure you don't want to get naked again?"

She laid her palms against his chest and pushed him toward the door. "Move."

"We've got a quick detour to make."

"Detour?"

"Time we paid a visit to Mrs. Lu."

Chapter 13

The FOR SALE sign on the lawn of the sleek contemporary home was nearly hidden behind a news van parked out front. Aside from the two guys drinking iced coffees in the van, the media was conspicuously absent. The police weren't on scene either.

Chien had been gone since last Friday and he was already old news.

Until somebody finds the body.

The sunlight streamed through the trees, illuminating the home's many windows but that didn't make her feel any better. There was no reason to think her colleague was dead. Nothing she'd read or heard so far pointed in that direction. For all she knew, he'd turn up before nightfall.

But she didn't think so.

Nick pulled up in front of the van, eliciting minimal attention from the two men inside. No doubt there'd been plenty of people coming and going. And from their bored expressions, Mia guessed they'd been on their stake-out for a long time.

Nick killed the ignition. "Ready?"

"I'm not sure she'll talk to us. It's not like Chien and I were close or anything. I've never even been to his house.

"Looks like you were missing out."

"It is pretty impressive." Mia peered through the

passenger side window and wondered what the listing price was. The place had to be worth at least a million dollars, though it wasn't the sort of house everybody would want to live in. The rectangular shape and floor-to-ceiling windows were beautiful, but she couldn't shake the impression it would be like living in a glass house. Someone—Mrs. Lu? The police?—had drawn the curtains but she guessed that wasn't the normal state of affairs. She couldn't imagine people whose lives were that open.

Granted, the house was set far back from the street and they were practically in the middle of nowhere. Picasso Avenue was sparsely dotted with homes, all of them equally modern and probably just as pricey. The Lu's home was at the very end of the street. Behind the house, woods stretched out indefinitely.

Nick was waiting for her on the street. She took a deep breath. Why didn't she want to meet Chien Lu's wife? She knew the answer but didn't want to think about it. Another disappearance. Another grieving wife. Just like before.

"Okay," she said. "No more stalling."

She eased out of the seat and shut the door. The two guys in the van were staring hard at her and she half expected them to descend upon her before she reached the front door. But they stayed where they were, though she could feel their eyes on her as she walked up the long driveway.

In one of the upper windows, a curtain flickered and fell back into place. Someone knew they were there.

When they reached the front door, Nick pressed the doorbell. Chimes echoed through the house but no one answered. After a few minutes passed he pressed it a second time. The chimes rang out again, filling the house with their ghostly melody.

A chill ran down her spine. "I think we should go."

Nick's finger was poised over the doorbell. He lowered it to his side and studied her face. "If that's what you want."

"We shouldn't be here," she said. "It's not our business."

"What if we can help Mrs. Lu find her husband?"

"What can we do that the police can't?" But that wasn't why she didn't want to stay. She didn't want to stay because she couldn't shake the conviction that Chien Lu wasn't ever coming back. And she didn't want to have to face his wife.

"I can't answer that until we talk to her," Nick said.

"I want to leave."

He nodded. "Okay."

They'd already turned away when the door swung open. A small Asian woman stood in the entryway, her dark hair neatly combed and her lips painted a deep shade of red. She looked beautiful and ageless, like a painting in a museum. On her left hand, an enormous diamond glinted in the light.

"I remember you," she said to Mia. "You work with my husband."

"Yes," Mia said, holding out her hand. "I'm Mia. Mia Lindgren."

Mrs. Lu took Mia's hand and held it between both of her own. "Thank you for coming. He thought very highly of you. He often spoke of your work with the greatest respect. Not many of his friends have been in contact. I suppose they don't want to intrude."

Mia fumbled for something to say. It surprised her to hear Chien had spoken of her at all, never mind in such glowing terms. She'd known next to nothing about him and his life outside the Institute was a mystery to her. The few times she had spoken to him, he'd asked about her research. His questions had always been intelligent, even brilliant at times. More than once he'd set her inquiries in a completely new direction. Of all the members of the unit, he'd been the most gifted. He'd also spent long hours in the lab. She'd lost count of the nights she walked past his office door and seen a crack of light beneath it.

Mrs. Lu's glance fell on Nick. "I don't think I know you."

"This is my friend Nick Doyle," Mia said hurriedly. "He's, uh, been helping me with a few things. We wondered if we might speak with you. It shouldn't take very long."

Cindy Lu hesitated, but only for a moment. "Please come in."

They followed her into a white room that overlooked the woods behind the house. Even in the middle of the day, the trees were awash in shadows. The lawn hadn't been mowed for quite some time and overgrown grass added an air of neglect. A sense of gloom seemed to hang over the yard.

Not exactly a selling point for prospective buyers, Mia thought, relieved that the interior wasn't nearly as depressing. The place was spotless and elegant, with few of the usual distractions. Overhead, a ceiling fan whirred quietly. There was no TV and no toys were visible. The walls were mostly bare but the room didn't seem sparse or cold, only spacious. By comparison, even Mia's neat house seemed cluttered.

Mrs. Lu sat down in a Swedish chair and gestured for them to sit on the leather couch across from her. "So what can I do for you?" she asked. "I take it your visit isn't solely to express your concern for my husband."

Nick leaned forward. "You still haven't heard from him, Mrs. Lu?"

"No." She pushed a shiny strand of hair behind her ear. "And please—call me Cindy."

It surprised Mia to see the woman so composed. When Holly had gone missing, her mother had been hysterical for days. If it weren't for some heavy duty sedatives, she wouldn't have gotten through that time. Maybe it was different with a child. Though her mother hadn't reacted too well when her father took off either. Either Cindy Lu was very skilled at hiding her emotions or she wasn't all that upset by Chien's departure.

"Do the police have any leads?" Mia asked.

"I'm afraid not."

"And you haven't heard from him?" she continued. "Nothing at all?"

"Nothing at all."

A lull fell over the conversation. Clearly, Cindy Lu was waiting for them to tell her why they were there. Mia had intended to share her misgivings about Mike's death but something about Cindy Lu's reserved demeanor made her hold back.

Mia's gaze fell onto a pen-and-ink sketch that hung over the mantel. The young girl in the picture seemed to stare back at her, her dark eyes beautiful and serene. She couldn't have been more than seven or eight but there was a certain wisdom in the girl's face.

"What a beautiful portrait," she said.

Cindy Lu followed Mia's gaze. "Yes, it is well done. The artist who drew it is quite good."

"Is that you as a child?" Mia asked.

"No," Cindy corrected her. "My daughter."

"She's lovely," Mia said, hoping her surprise wasn't too obvious. There were none of the usual signs of a child in the house. No toys scattered across the floor, no drawings on the walls, and most importantly, no child in sight. "The resemblance is quite strong."

A look of pain crossed Cindy's face but she quickly controlled it. "Thank you."

Another silence descended upon them.

Mia struggled to think of a way to get Cindy to reveal more information. Mia was sure Mrs. Lu knew more than she was telling. And though she had deliberately avoided making eye contact with Nick, she had little doubt he was thinking the same thing.

Beside her, Nick shifted his weight on the couch. "If you don't mind my asking, do you think your husband was taken?" he asked. "Or is it possible there's some other explanation. Something less...sinister? Maybe your husband simply wanted a break. The Institute isn't exactly a stress-free environment."

He was fishing and he wasn't making much of an effort to hide that fact. Well, maybe a more direct approach was what they needed. Mia's attempt to draw her out certainly hadn't accomplished anything.

Cindy Lu turned her attention toward him. After a few seconds had passed, she said, "I don't think he was taken, no."

"So you think he may have simply wanted some kind of break?" he probed.

"It is possible. As you said, his job carried a lot of

responsibility. Chien wasn't one to take his work lightly."

"Is that what the police think?" Mia cut in.

Cindy smiled politely. "I wouldn't attempt to guess their thoughts on this."

"What about your husband's vehicle," Nick said. "Has that been located?"

"Not yet."

Not yet. So Cindy Lu believed it would be. At least that's what her statement implied. Almost as if she knew where her husband was. Or that he meant to return. That would explain her composure, as well as her lack of curiosity about the case. Mia had expected Cindy to bombard them with questions about Chien's behavior before he disappeared but so far she hadn't posed a single question beyond her inquiry about the nature of their visit.

Maybe that explained the lack of police presence. If Cindy had acted the same way with the detectives assigned to the case they may well have decided it was simply a lover's quarrel. Or that Chien had run off with a mistress. Whatever the case, the lack of a body and a car suggested something along those lines.

"What about his credit cards? Has he used them at all since he disappeared?"

"No," she said, a trace of impatience creeping into her voice. "He hasn't used them. And to answer your question before you ask it, he didn't withdraw any large sums of money from our accounts on the day he vanished. But I've already told this to the police. I thought you said you were here for something else."

Mia tried for what she hoped was a winning smile. "You're aware that one of our colleagues—Mike

223

Chandler—drowned recently."

"Yes. Chien attended his funeral. Were you close to him?"

"He was my partner." Despite her best efforts, Mia's voice wavered.

For the first time since their arrival, Cindy's face softened. "I'm sorry."

Mia nodded. "So am I."

She felt Nick's hand clasp hers. Cindy's eyes darted downward then returned to her face. Was Nick trying to convince her they were involved? Or was it a genuine sign of affection? She turned toward him, ever so slightly, but his eyes were on Cindy Lu.

"I'm not sure if you're aware of this, but Mike— my partner—was an excellent sailor."

Cindy Lu waited for her to go on, hands folded neatly in her lap.

"According to the autopsy, he may have been beaten before he died." She might be overstating it, but she was getting tired of skirting the issue. "There was a blow to the back of the head and his body was covered with scratches and bruises."

"Do you think someone killed your friend?"

"I think it's possible. I find it hard to believe Mike would have fallen off his boat and drowned. Besides being an expert sailor, he was a strong swimmer. In college he competed nationally."

"Not all strong swimmers can survive if the conditions are inhospitable," she remarked. "And there are many skilled sailors who don't return to shore. Life can be…unpredictable. Things don't always turn out the way we plan."

Mia's gaze flicked to the sketch over the mantel.

Had something happened to their daughter? Perhaps she had died too? She wanted to ask but knew that would be the end of their meeting. Still, she was willing to let Cindy Lu off the hook, at least not completely.

"It was far from inhospitable the night he died," Mia said a little tartly. "A mutual friend told me last night that he spotted your husband and Mike one day as they were leaving the break room. He said they looked...odd."

She arched a perfectly shaped brow. "Odd? I'm not sure I know what you mean."

"I'm not sure I do either. But he got the idea that they may have been arguing about something. That whatever your husband said to my friend disturbed him greatly. Do you have any idea what that might have been? You were right when you said your husband and Mike were colleagues. But they very rarely spent time together. Chien's work and ours—mine and Mike's—were quite different."

"And yet my husband told me the two of you might be working together."

"That's true. But that was because of Mike's death. Otherwise, that wouldn't have happened." She'd never thought of it from that perspective. Could Mike's disappearance have something to do with Chien's desire to work in her section?

No, that didn't make sense. Chien could never have been certain of taking Mike's place. Another thought occurred to her. Had Chien been vying for her spot the day he'd been seen talking to Mike? Was that why Mike had appeared to be angry? Certainly, Mike wouldn't have reacted amicably if Chien had been trying to usurp her spot as his partner.

But it still didn't explain his disappearance. If Chien's goal had been to work on Ebola, then why had he bolted?

Maybe Cindy Lu's assumption was wrong. Maybe somebody had taken him. Why though? She always came back to that question. Why would somebody kidnap Chien Lu? Or kill Mike?

Cindy pressed her lips together. "My husband never mentioned anything about an argument with your friend. As you pointed out, the two weren't close. Until Chien informed me of his death, I don't believe my husband ever mentioned him at all. Perhaps your friend—the one who saw my husband and Mike together—was mistaken about what he saw."

Mia felt a twinge of worry. That made two times that Caleb's statements were being called into question. But she came back to the same question she'd had the night before when he'd contradicted Trask's statements. Why would Caleb lie about seeing Mike and Chien together? Or was it truly unintentional—maybe he just wasn't very good at reading people. He wouldn't be the first scientist to bungle that kind thing. A good portion of the Institute staff were more at ease analyzing deadly pathogens than chatting with other people in the break room. Caleb definitely fit into that category.

"Maybe he was mistaken. But you must admit your husband's disappearance so shortly after the death of a colleague seems unusual."

"Do you mean suspicious?" she asked, placing a bit too much emphasis on the final word.

"I wouldn't put it that way," Mia said quickly.

"But that's what you're implying."

"I'm not implying anything."

Cindy glared at her. The friendly mask had fallen away completely. "My husband didn't have anything to do with your friend's accident. He didn't know him well but he was saddened by his death."

A sound in the corner of the room caught Mia's attention. A girl moved out of the shadows and stumbled toward them. It took Mia several seconds to realize it was the girl from the picture. She was completely bald and so thin her bones jutted through her loose nightgown. Without the dark hair, she looked younger not older. And unlike the girl in the sketch, there were hollows below the cheekbones and the eyes seemed enormous in her thin face.

Cindy stood up. "Ming, what you are doing out of bed?"

"I heard voices." The girl reached out a spindly arm and grabbed onto one of the chairs. Her legs were even frailer. She couldn't have weighed more than sixty pounds.

Her mother crossed to where she stood and knelt before her. "You shouldn't have gotten up."

"I'm bored, mommy."

Cindy turned toward them. "Thank you for expressing your concern about my husband. Please excuse me while I return my daughter to her room. I trust you can find your way out."

Nick stood up and took a few steps toward them. "Need any help?"

"Thank you for offering," she said coldly, glancing over her shoulder. She slid both arms under her daughter's and lifted her over her shoulders. "But I don't require your assistance."

"I can walk, mommy."

"I know, sweetie," she said. "I just like to carry you."

"I'm not a baby."

"Of course you aren't."

The girl's eyes fixed on them as her mother carried her out of the room. "Who are those people?"

"No one, honey," Cindy murmured, placing her hand on her daughter's scalp. "Just some friends." Her voice caught on the word friends.

"Did they find Daddy yet?"

"Not yet."

When they disappeared from view, Nick released his breath all at once. "That is one very sick little girl."

"Chien never mentioned anything about his daughter having cancer," she said. "Or whatever's making her so sick. I didn't even know he *had* a daughter."

"Maybe he didn't want people's pity."

"Could be." She tried to remember a time when he'd talked about his home life and came up blank. Not that she'd been any more forthright about her own life. Even Mike didn't know about her sister. Maybe Nick was right.

She got up off the couch and went to stand beside him. "We should go."

Nick nodded. "After you."

It wasn't until she reached the main entrance that she realized he wasn't behind her anymore. She stopped and listened. The place was dead silent. She knew Ming and her mother had to be somewhere upstairs but where was Nick? How long had it been since he'd been behind her?

If she called out to him that might alert Cindy Lu.

She remembered the way the upstairs curtain had flickered as they were approaching the house. Ming's bedroom probably.

Something told Mia she was there now, in the same spot. Waiting to see them walk away from the house and drive off.

"Nick," she called out quietly.

No answer.

Well, she wasn't about to leave him behind. On the other hand she couldn't just hang out in the entryway. If Cindy Lu didn't see them on the walk soon she'd come downstairs to investigate. Mia didn't want to be there when she did.

"Nick!" She whispered a little louder this time, praying Cindy Lu wasn't already making her way toward her. "I don't know what you're doing, but you'd better hurry up."

She'd made up her mind to return to the living room when he emerged out of a side hallway. *"Where were you?"* she asked under her breath.

He held a finger to his lips. "Not now."

Moving ahead of her, he crossed the entryway and pulled the door open. When she emerged into the daylight, she felt as if she'd escaped from prison. The place might be beautiful but she was glad to get out of there.

Nick caught up to her when she reached the driveway. He shot her a warning look and she nodded. They walked the remainder of the distance to the car in silence.

By the time they reached the car, the men in the van had already lost interest. Mia turned around in her seat and strained to see the house. Cindy Lu stood in one of the upstairs windows, one hand holding back the curtain Mia had seen flicker when they had arrived.

The press, such as it was, had lost interest.

But Cindy Lu hadn't.

Neither of them spoke until the house was almost out of sight. When they turned onto the road that led back to the highway, Mia couldn't hold back any longer.

"Where the hell were you?"

Nick pressed on the gas and waited while the car picked up speed. "I took a detour."

"Another five minutes and she would have come back down. Do you know what would have happened if she ran into you on your little detour? She could have called the police. Do you have any idea how risky that was?"

"It was a risk," Nick said. "But a calculated one. Cindy Lu won't be calling the police, at least I don't think she will. She's already played that card. She did what she was supposed to do and now she's just got to sit tight."

"What do you mean?"

"I'm not sure, exactly. But if the bills on the kitchen table are any indication, she's hoping one of two things. Either she wants him dead so she can collect on the insurance. Or the two of them worked out some kind of debt erasure plan that's on the wrong side of the law."

"You looked at their bills?"

"They'd already been opened. No doubt she would have gotten rid of them if she'd had more time. But our arrival didn't give her the chance. They've got medical bills that run to triple digits. And I only saw the morning mail. My guess is—"

Mia remembered the For Sale sign on the lawn. "The house—"

"Right," he agreed. "Tough to pay a mortgage on a place like that when you're in debt up to your eyeballs. Especially when mommy quit her job two years ago to care for your dying kid."

She felt a surge of sympathy for the Chien and his wife. Bad enough to have a child dying of cancer. Even worse not to have the money to get her the help she so desperately needed. "Wouldn't insurance have covered most of that stuff?"

"It would have covered ordinary treatments, sure. But if the insurance company eventually denied treatment based on her prognosis the Lus might not have been willing to accept that. Or maybe they were pursuing an alternative approach—or seeking treatment from another doctor, one not covered by their plan. Whatever the specifics were, they've obviously expended their resources."

"How do you know she quit her job?"

"I don't. But that picture was at least a few years old. She was healthy then but from the dates on the bills she's been sick for a while. It would make sense for Mrs. Lu to quit her job."

"You don't even know she had a job."

"Her Ph.D. was hanging next to his in the study on the way to the kitchen. They attended different universities. My guess is she and Chien probably met when they worked together. Somebody who goes to the trouble of getting an advanced degree in microbiology isn't going to give all that up just to play mommy."

"Hey—"

"Are you telling me after all the trouble you've gone to with your career, you'd give it up to stay home with an infant?"

She'd never thought about it. She'd never considered children at all. Which, she supposed, proved his point. On the other hand, if she did have a child maybe she'd want to see it grow. To know what it felt like to be somebody's mother.

"Yes," she said slowly. "I might. If I ever do have kids, I wouldn't want to miss out on anything. I'd guess I'd like to think I could find a way to be a mom and a scientist. But if my child was sick—really sick—I'd stop being a scientist without giving it a second thought."

He looked at her as if he weren't sure if he believed her. She supposed she could understand his skepticism. She knew she didn't exactly come across as the nurturing type. Until that moment, she'd never even considered having a family even though she was coming up on thirty. Maybe that was another part of her she'd buried along with Holly.

"Either way, she's not working now. No way she could work and take care of her daughter. And whatever's going on, that woman loves her child."

"Funny she didn't mention her though. When I asked about the picture. She acted like Ming was already dead."

"She's protecting her. The question is how far would she and her husband be willing to go to save their child?"

Chapter 14

Angela was waiting for them in the lobby.

Nick cast a sideways glance at Mia and saw that she was as surprised as he was. No suitors were in attendance and for the first time since he'd met her, Angela Ward looked tired. It took him a few seconds to realize she'd foregone makeup. In place of the usual matching ensemble, she wore a plain blouse and tan slacks. Her hair was pulled back into a ponytail.

Nick held the door open for Mia. "Looks like somebody misses you."

Mia shot him a look. "I doubt it."

Angela rose from her chair and waved. She stood where she was, as if she were unsure whether to approach them. "I wasn't sure if you were still coming."

He took hold of her elbow and guided them toward the sitting area. When they stood across from Angela, he planted a quick kiss on Mia's cheek. "See you back here in an hour."

If the kiss surprised Angela, she didn't say so. Instead she took her daughter by the hand and leaned forward to plant her own kiss on the other cheek.

Mia looked about as uncomfortable as he felt. "You'd better get going," she said quickly, taking a step back from both of them. "See you in an hour."

Nick headed toward the elevators. He resisted the

impulse to look over his shoulder. On the drive down he'd encouraged Mia to talk to her mother about the events that had driven them apart so many years ago. Whether she would follow through on his advice was anybody's guess. He did believe Angela loved her daughter—and he was convinced Mia needed to realize that before she could open up to anybody. But he hadn't considered how competitive the woman was with her daughter.

No, it wasn't that. Angela didn't want him or any other man Mia was interested in. What she wanted was her daughter's affection, so long withheld from her. If he did get involved with Mia, would she make it a competition between them? Or would the two of them be able to reach some kind of truce?

In a way, he supposed it didn't matter. As long as Mia and her mother could reach their own truce. With her sister dead and her father gone for so long, Angela was the only family Mia had. He knew what it was like, to feel abandoned by the people who were supposed to love you the most. That was at least part of the reason he'd ended up at Seahaven.

He'd half expected to see Donelan waiting for him as well, but the priest was nowhere in sight. When he'd called to schedule an appointment with the priest, the secretary had put him on hold for a solid ten minutes. Her voice on the other end of the line had been pleasant and efficient but that didn't make her words any less ominous. "He's been trying to locate you," she said when she picked up the call again. "You're to report to his office immediately upon arrival."

It felt a lot like being called to the principal's office.

Nick pressed the button for the elevator. The compartment opened immediately and he stepped inside, only to find himself staring across at Callie Jackson. He groaned inwardly and prepared for a barrage of reprimands.

He gave her a perfunctory nod and stared forward at nothing in particular. Another sixty seconds or so and he'd be on his way.

"We missed you at last night's meeting," she said archly. "And this morning's."

"I've been busy," he said. "I trust things went smoothly without me."

Their eyes met in the mirrored glass that lined the elevator. Wherever he looked, there she was. The elevator rang at the second floor and the third. No one else got on.

Thirty seconds.

"You're not going to get better, if you spend all your time holed up in your room."

"Thanks for the advice but I've got things under control."

"Is that how you ended up here?"

The bell rang. Third Floor.

The doors opened.

All he had to do was step out of the damn elevator and walk down the hall to Donelan's office.

He stepped over the threshold.

"I'd say 'See you tonight' but I doubt you'll be there."

He turned around.

Callie Jackson stood on the other side of the doors, smiling smugly.

He reached out and laid a hand on one of the doors,

preventing them from closing.

The smile faltered.

"It's none of your business, but I haven't been spending my time here holed up in my room. I know it may not occur to you that some of us have a life outside these walls but I do. And that just happened to get in the way. And yeah, it's going to get in the way again tonight. Correct me if I'm wrong, but isn't the whole point of being to get our heads together so we can go back to those lives? So if it's all right with you, I'm going to do just that. I trust you'll make my apologies to everyone tonight."

To his surprise, she laughed. "You're so full of shit. You with all your talk about having a life. I heard you."

He was gripping the side of the elevator so hard his hand was starting to ache. "What do you mean you heard me?"

"Last night. I heard you. In your room."

"Well you heard wrong," he said. "I wasn't in my room."

"Please." Her voice dripped with condescension.

"What, are you stalking me or something?'

"I've got better things to do than stalk you."

He wasn't so sure about that. Granted, he hadn't expected a multi-million dollar chef to take any interest in him. Surely the woman had better things to do than press her ear to his door.

Some of the bravado went out of Callie's voice. "Nargeeta, Justin and I were walking back to our rooms last night when he heard you pacing around in your room. Or maybe throwing something. You were pretty loud. If you don't believe me, ask one of them. Oh, and by the way, I'd bet my right arm you were drunk as a skunk. So don't pull this *I've got a life outside these walls* shit with me. Believe it or not, I was trying to help you. After what you said in group the other night, I felt sorry for you. I almost knocked on your door but Nargeeta said we'd better leave you alone. You sounded like you might hurt somebody."

Nick stared at her. That she was telling the truth, he had no doubt. "What was the time?"

"Can't you remember?"

He counted to three and exhaled. "Callie, I know you don't particularly like me. I get it. I've blown off a lot of meetings and I haven't exactly been all that friendly toward you. But I really need to you to try to remember what time you passed by my room last night."

Something in his tone seemed to soften her resolve to insult him. "I'm not sure."

"Try to remember," he said, reining in his impatience. "It's important."

She opened her mouth then shut it. After a minute, she pursed her lips together. "Well, it was after group. We went over—maybe by about fifteen minutes—and then some of us hung around afterward."

"So how long do you think you stayed?"

"Not longer than twenty minutes. So it was maybe 10:45. Not later than eleven. I remember checking my phone when I got back to the room. It was just after eleven by then."

He released his hand from the elevator door. "Thanks."

He turned on his heel and headed in the opposite direction of Donelan's office. Toward the staircase that led downstairs to his room.

The doors opened and Callie Jackson stepped out into the hallway just as he pulled the stairwell door open and rushed to the stairs.

"Why do you want to know?" he heard her calling as the door swung shut. "What's so important?"

Downstairs, his room was locked. Not that it meant anything. Easy enough to relock a door. Nick turned the key in the lock and stepped inside the room.

If he hadn't run into Callie he never would have known anybody had been inside.

Everything was exactly the way he'd left it. Suitcases in the closet, bedspread undisturbed, cheap thriller lying half-finished on the nightstand.

Who had been there? Donelan? The same person who'd searched Mia's place? And was that the same person who had been at Mike Chandler's condominium? Chien? One of the other researchers in Mia's unit? Brendon Thompson or whatever name he was using at the moment?

Who the hell was it? And why would somebody need to search his room? What were they looking for?

Possibilities flashed through his brain. He stared at his neatly arranged belongings. His mind felt like it was set to warp speed.

Only he wasn't getting any closer to figuring out the answers.

Slow it down. Think. Stop spinning your wheels.

Nick sat down on the bed and closed his eyes. On the other side of the door he could hear a few of the patients talking as they passed by. No question Callie would have been able to hear what was going on inside. She'd said he'd sounded angry. But nothing was amiss.

Whoever it was must have cleaned up. And something had made him angry.

Nick opened his eyes and scanned the room. There was no sign of violence. The desk chair was pushed up against the mission-style desk. The bed made. The hardwood floor free of scuff marks.

He walked over to the bathroom and flicked on the light. His shaving kit rested on the edge of the sink and the towel he'd used the day before lay drying on the rack next to the door.

He caught his reflection in the mirror and studied it a few seconds. There was gray at his temples and the beginnings of lines around his mouth. He was older than Mia by at least seven or eight years. He wondered if that would bother Mia.

He hoped not. He'd never stop loving Rosa but he'd felt things with Mia that he hadn't experienced with any other woman. If she did let him get close to her, it wouldn't be easy. She wasn't the type to go for a whirlwind courtship. As for marriage and kids, he wasn't sure that stuff was even on her agenda. It was one thing to say she'd quit her job to care for a sick child another thing to pursue a real relationship.

One step at a time.

He'd always been intense, always wanted to jump the gun. It was about time he started living for the moment.

Or maybe not just yet. First he needed to figure out what the hell was going on.

He opened the medicine cabinet. It was just as empty as it had been the day before. Nothing out of place.

Maybe Callie had imagined it. Or said what she

had out of spite.

No. She'd been telling the truth. He was sure of it. Most likely whoever had been at Mia's had been at Seahaven too. And at Mike's condo. Beyond that, he couldn't draw any conclusions.

Nick closed the cabinet. To the right side of the mirror there was a dent. It was unmistakable. He'd made the kind of dent before on his own walls in the blurred weeks after Rosa's death.

Somebody had punched the wall.

What was there in that bathroom that would upset a man enough to punch a wall?

He stared at the indent and then back at his reflection.

The reflection.

Whoever had been in his room had looked into that mirror and hadn't liked what he'd seen. Had hated what he'd seen enough to smash his fist in the wall right next to it.

Almost as good as smashing the mirror.

Almost as good as destroying the face itself.

But not quite.

He grabbed the shaving kit and returned to the bedroom. Aside from a few shirts hanging in the closet, there wasn't much else to pack. He zipped the suitcase closed and carried it out into the hallway, locking the door behind him. The hallway was empty.

When he reached Donelan's office suite, he set down the suitcase and walked over to the secretary's desk. He laid the key onto the blotter. It wasn't the usual procedure, but checking out early wasn't the usual procedure either. The vast majority of patients made it the entire thirty days.

"I'm Nick Doyle," he said. "I'm here to see Father Donelan."

The secretary lifted the key and deposited it into an envelope. "You can go right in," she said, a trace of disapproval in her voice. "He's been expecting you."

The cell phone in his pocket buzzed and he pulled it out of his pocket. Dalton. Well, he'd have to wait. Nick needed to do this now. If he took the call he'd have to leave the suite and who knows where the priest would be by the time he returned. He sent the call to voicemail and shoved his phone back into his pocket.

He picked up his suitcase and set it down at the back of the waiting room. The phone buzzed with a message as he walked through the entrance to Donelan's office. He ignored it, shutting the heavy wooden door behind him.

The priest sat behind an ornately carved antique desk, one that looked as if it belong at the Vatican. "I take it you've decided you're no longer in need of our services."

Nick sat down in one of the chairs in front of the desk. "I would have stayed."

Donelan raised a shaggy brow. "What's stopping you?"

"I think you know," Nick said. "Or at least have some idea."

"Is it this business about the friend of the pretty blonde woman, the scientist who died?"

Nick fixed his eyes on Donelan. "Someone was in my room last night."

The priest gazed back at him, his blue eyes untroubled.

Nick wasn't sure what he'd expected but Donelan's

serenity unnerved him a bit. "Was it you?"

"No." Donelan sighed. "Not me."

"But you know who it was?"

Donelan didn't answer right away. "I don't presume to know such things."

Whatever he wasn't telling, he wasn't going to share it. Nick decided to try another tack. "The other day when we spoke at breakfast, you said you've dealt with a lot of guys…like me."

Another sigh. "That I have."

"And when I mentioned the name Brendon Thompson, and told you the story about what happened to him, you seemed to react. As if you already knew it. That wasn't just my imagination, was it?"

"No." Donelan looked weary. There was a tiredness in his voice too.

He waited for the priest to offer more information but he seemed to have forgotten Nick's presence in the room. Donelan turned his gaze to the enormous windows that looked out on the grounds. Outside, the sky was overcast.

Nick leaned forward in his chair. "I need you to tell me why you knew that story. The other night somebody searched the condo that belonged to Mike Chandler. Somebody whose car was registered under that very name—Brendon Thompson. Now maybe that's just a damn coincidence. But the man who drowned washed ashore with multiple lacerations and a nasty blow to the back of the head."

Donelan turned away from the window. "You think he was murdered?"

"The coroner says the injuries can be explained by the time the body spent in the water."

"And what do you say?"

"I think he was beaten. And at the end of it I think whoever it was who beat him dumped his body into the Chesapeake Bay."

Donelan nodded, ever so slightly.

"Who told you about Brendon Thompson's death?"

"You know as well as I do that I can't share that information with you."

"I'm asking you a favor."

"A favor." He chuckled. "And if someone, say another patient here at Seahaven, came to me and asked me to reveal information about you, how would you feel about that?"

"If I'd killed somebody, then hell, yeah, I'd want you to share that information."

"But that's the million-dollar question, isn't it? On the one hand, you have a car registered under the name of someone you fought alongside decades ago. A fairly common name, I might add. Add to that your misgivings about the manner of death of a man who worked in a fairly dangerous field. And your possible misreading of my facial expressions a few days later when you mentioned the name. It's not very much to go on, is it?"

"No. It's not." He hated to admit it but the priest was right. He'd worked as an agent so many years, he'd gotten used to relying on instinct. It wasn't supernatural—certainly not the extrasensory perception Dalton's wife Laura claimed to have—but it wasn't hard logic either. He was reaching, no doubt about it. But he was also damn sure he was reaching in the right direction.

"And based upon this—shall we call it a whim?—

you want me not only to break the confidentiality agreement that applies to all patients who've been treated here, but my vows as well."

Vows. The word sent a ripple of certainty through Nick. Because the only vow that came to mind was the vow of secrecy. Had the man Donelan was protecting confessed to the priest? And what exactly had he confessed to—something in the past? Or was his confession more recent?

"You left the priesthood. You're not bound by the seal of the confessional. And even patient confidentiality doesn't extend to protecting a murderer. You know that as well as I do."

"I made my vows not to the Vatican but to God," he said quietly. "Those vows are eternal. If someone comes to me seeking forgiveness, I have an obligation to hear their confession. And that confession is bound by the laws of God, not man. There is a salvation on earth and another waiting for us in heaven."

"Did this man confess something to you?" Nick laid his hands on the desk and rose out of his chair. "Has he been to see you recently? Is that why you barely blinked when I said someone had been in my room?"

"As I've made clear, I can't share any information with you."

"Can't—or won't."

"I think I've made that clear as well."

Nick wanted to shake the old man. But that would get him nowhere.

He removed his hands from the desk and stood all the way up. "I assume you also know another man's gone missing. Chien Lu, a colleague of Mike Chandler.

His life may depend on what you say—or don't say—Father. And in case you don't follow the news, there's a village of people up in Alaska dying because of an unidentified virus that I'd bet my badge has something to do with Chandler's little mishap on the boat. Do you really think God would want you to keep a promise if it means another man may die? Other men—and women and children? If this virus gets into the wrong hands we might just be looking at Armageddon, Father."

Donelan raised his eyes to him. There was a kind of pleading in them, almost as if he were asking Nick's forgiveness. "I don't presume to understand the mind of God."

"Well, I sure as hell doubt He would approve of you protecting a murderer," Nick said in a low voice. "Or doing nothing to stop Armageddon. And if He does, then I may have to start looking for another religion."

The old priest gripped the sides of his chair and rose to his feet. "I'm a great believer not only in the Almighty but in Fate. In submitting ourselves to ends beyond what we can see or understand. To try to do more is nothing but vanity. I suppose my thinking on this isn't so dissimilar to the Greeks, pagans though they were. Oedipus sought to avoid killing his father and in doing so created the very circumstances that brought about Laius's death. Interference may well be the mother of all tragedy. The only way to find peace is to admit our own powerlessness and place ourselves into the hands of one greater than ourselves."

"Thanks for the lecture, but I'm not ready to do that just yet. I'm all for interfering if it saves lives."

A ghost of a smile crossed Donelan's face. "We all

follow our own destinies. My path is to heal and to offer absolution to those who seek it."

"And my path?"

Donelan eased out from behind the desk and crossed to the door. "Your path is to catch a murderer. And perhaps to stop Armageddon," he said, pulling it open with surprising strength. "As time is of the essence, I suggest you do so without further delay."

Chapter 15

Nick hit the accelerator and merged onto the highway that led back to Mia's town. It wasn't rush hour yet, but the traffic was already heavy. The sky ahead of them was an angry gray. They were driving straight into a storm.

"So how did it go with your mother?" He glanced at her then returned his eyes to the road.

"Not bad." Which was true. For the first time in years, her mother seemed *focused*. As if someone had drawn back a curtain and she were seeing Mia as she was in the present, not years ago. Mia shouldn't have been thrown off by it but she was. As a drunk, her mother had been easy to avoid, easy to fool. The new Angela was startlingly insightful.

She was also caring. Or at least she gave a good impression of it. Mia still couldn't trust it though. After so many years spent listening to slurred phone conversations, she wasn't ready to let her mother back into her life—never mind her heart.

Her mother had made progress, there was no denying it. Where that would lead was anybody's guess. She wasn't even sure she wanted to know the answer to that question.

Apparently Nick had decided to let her choose whether she wanted to talk about it.

She didn't. Too much, too soon. "How did it go

with Donelan?"

"Not good."

"He didn't tell you what you wanted to know."

"Nope."

"Well, maybe he'll change his mind."

He laughed. "I don't see that happening."

"You never know."

"You're right about that. I don't know. I'd bet my life that the guy's covering for somebody but it could be anybody. It might be somebody I've never even met. Either way, if Donelan's not talking and Eli's coming up short, we're at point zero."

"Eli?"

"You might call him a friend of mine. More like a hacker. World class. Used to work for NSA but got bored. He was, for lack of a better word, accessing the government databases trying to look for a connection. I thought maybe one of the guys in my platoon might have used Brendon Thompson's name. Thought maybe there was a connection that might help us figure out who killed Mike."

"But there wasn't?"

"Grasping at straws. I thought I was following my gut but apparently my gut was wrong. Dalton left a message while I was in with Donelan. Eli's still coming up blank and that's something Eli doesn't usually do. We've got nothing. Nothing on Thompson or anybody in my old platoon. Nothing on Chien's disappearance, other than the fact that the guy was in debt up to his eyeballs. Nothing on Mike besides a few articles and some nasty virus slides and a strange note at the bottom of a news clipping. Nothing on whoever searched his place—or your place, for that matter. Meanwhile people in Aniak are dying in a manner identical to the way they did in Siberia a year ago, other than the fact that this time kids are dying too. Which by the way was described in the article we found in your friend's condo. But whether that's got anything to do with any of this is totally unclear."

Mia didn't blame Nick for being frustrated. She was too. Deadly viruses she could handle. Real life, not so much. "Maybe none of it's related."

"It's related. Trust me, it's related. I just can't see how."

"Not yet."

"Not yet," he said. "According to Father Donelan, it's my destiny to figure it all out. Stop Armageddon."

She bit her lip. "At least he's not asking too much of you."

"Of course, his preordained role is to stay out of it," he said drily. "Seal of the confessional and all that. I knew there was a reason my faith lapsed."

"Wait a minute. You're saying he told you whoever killed Mike *confessed*? That whoever it was used to be a patient at Seahaven?"

"No. But a lot of agents go there. Apparently there's a virtual feeder system Seahaven's got going with Uncle Sam. And somebody—one of us, that is— told him *something*. Beyond that, I have no clue. But I think he knows who's behind Mike's death. And Chien's disappearance. When I mentioned somebody had been in my room he barely reacted."

"What?"

"There was a dent beside my bathroom mirror. Somebody punched a wall."

"Are you sure? Maybe it was there before." That

249

certainly seemed more likely than somebody breaking in and doing battle with a bathroom wall. On the other hand, the idea of somebody drugging her dog would have seemed pretty outlandish—if it hadn't actually happened.

Nick hit the directional and maneuvered the car into the left lane. "One of the other patients heard whoever it was the night before."

"What do you think he was looking for?"

"Your guess is as good as mine."

Mia hadn't been inside Nick's room but she couldn't imagine he would have left anything of importance there. From what he said, the intruder had been there the night before. Which would place him at Seahaven a few hours after the break-in at her place. "Wait."

"What?"

"Mike's planner. I looked through it that first night and didn't find anything but maybe we missed something. Maybe that's what they want. Say the intruder figured out we took it from Mike's place. So he waits for the right opportunity, searches my place and comes up empty. If he's been watching us, he'd know you've been helping me. He knows you're with me and not at Seahaven so he drives out there and figures out a way into your room. He thinks maybe I gave you the planner. But he doesn't find it, so he gets angry and punches the wall."

Up ahead, the exit for Route 95 loomed. Nick slowed down and changed lanes. "Maybe," he said slowly. "But remember I went through that planner too—pretty carefully. There wasn't much there, certainly nothing obvious."

Mia grew thoughtful. "How do we know the killer, if it is the killer, even knows the planner exists?"

A muscle moved in Nick's jaw. "We don't."

"Maybe whoever it is thinks there's something else. Something besides the planner, I mean. Maybe there was something else we were supposed to find that night. At the condo. What if we go back?"

He pressed his lips together. "I don't know. We searched the place pretty thoroughly. And remember the police have been through there too."

"But it doesn't make sense. Let's say whoever it was was a patient at Seahaven at some point. A former agent, maybe a friend of Brendon Thompson. There's got to be a reason behind the break-ins. And there's got to be a link between the break-ins and Mike's death. But why would he want to kill Mike? Or Chien?"

Nick turned off the highway. The traffic thinned out and slowed down, but he didn't lessen their speed. "We don't know Chien's dead."

"I'm hoping he's not. But let's say somebody took him. Or forget about Chien, but let's say you're right about this guy being one of your former buddies in Afghanistan. Why would some veteran and/or government agent you used to know want to kill Mike?"

"I don't know. But let's say for argument's sake it does have something to do with those news clippings. The virus in Siberia. The genetically engineered one in Wisconsin or wherever the hell it was. Let's say for argument's sake that our guy believes Mike has information. Or maybe he believes Mike's involved in something—that he's selling this stuff to terrorists."

"So he decides to kill Mike," Mia said tentatively.

"To stop it from happening. The sale."

"Maybe he's the one who thinks he's stopping Armageddon."

"He would be," she agreed. "But Mike wouldn't do that. He would never deal with terrorists."

"It takes a lot of money to own a boat. Live that sort of lifestyle."

"It doesn't take a billion dollars. And Mike was rich. He didn't need money. He didn't even care about it, as long as he had enough to keep his sailboat."

"What about Chien?"

"Chien wouldn't do that either. You don't know them. Chien might be in debt but he wouldn't agree to destroy the entire human race!"

"Who said anything about the entire human race?"

"You're the one who keeps bringing up Armageddon. And much as I hate to admit, you just might be right—about that part, anyway. Whatever killed those people up in Aniak, whatever killed those monkeys at the Institute, is airborne. And it kills within hours. And there's no antidote. It's like some kind of virus on steroids. If anything like that ever made it to a major city—"

Nick whistled. "Goodbye, civilization."

"Exactly."

Neither of them spoke. What Nick was suggesting was unfathomable. Sure, she'd considered it before. How could she not, working at the Institute? But as deadly as the viruses she dealt with were, there was usually some small saving grace. The strains of Ebola she'd seen weren't airborne. Other viruses didn't affect all segments of the population. Or they surfaced in remote areas and died out before they became pandemics. Even swine flu and bird flu had been contained. But this new virus—whatever it was—didn't have any obvious flaws. It was almost perfect.

Almost as if it had been created in a lab. Created by someone with Armageddon in mind.

The possibility floored her. Was it possible someone at the Institute had actually tried to create a virus of such magnitude? Mia remembered finding Mike's notes in the laboratory the day after he disappeared. The slides with the obliterated cells. And there had been the articles in his home—articles about genetically engineered viruses and obliterated cities.

Were the Siberian village and Aniak test runs for something larger?

If so, what was going to happen? And when?

The idea that Mike could be behind something so evil seemed impossible. And yet, how well had she really known her partner? He'd never mentioned he'd been working on a new virus. If he hadn't died, she probably would never have found those slides. Or the articles.

And Caleb had seen him talking to Chien.

Had the two of them been in on it together?

Had Chien killed Mike and gone into hiding? If the two of them had been working together, it might make sense.

Mia closed her eyes. She felt like a mad woman. Trask's words in the break room came back to her. Was she acting like a lunatic and not a scientist? Was it all some whim—a figment of her imagination? Like forcing a pattern out of random dots. Creating her own zodiac of paranoia?

"You've been quiet for far too long."

"I—

She never got the chance to finish. Nick's cell phone vibrated and he grabbed it off the seat. "Doyle."

She couldn't hear what the voice on the other end was saying but from the expression on Nick's face, she knew it couldn't be good. After a few terse questions, he pulled out of traffic and parked on the side of the road. He got out of the car and walked away, keeping his back to her. She couldn't hear what he was saying but from the way he was pacing she knew he didn't like what he was hearing. A few minutes later he turned and strode back to the car.

His expression made her stomach clench.

Nick opened the door and climbed inside. Before she could form a question, he reached over and grabbed a pen out of the glove compartment. He scribbled an address and ended the call.

"What was that all about?"

"Liam Gallagher."

"Was he one of the guys in your platoon?"

"He was." Nick folded the paper and slipped it into his shirt pocket.

"And he's—" she searched for a word and couldn't come up with one that fit. "Involved?"

There was no triumph in his eyes, only sadness. "It looks that way."

Mia laid her hand on his. She wasn't used to expressing emotion and it felt strange to her, not quite right. "What did you find out—can you tell me?"

Nick squeezed her hand and released it. "I'll tell you everything I know. But first we need to get you home."

"Get me home?"

He turned away and started the car. "Dalton's had a team watching his place for the past three hours. There's been no movement inside the house but the radar sensors indicate at least one person is inside. I'm heading over there now. When it's over, I'll call you. In the meantime I want you to lock yourself in and stay there."

"I want to go with you."

"No. There's nothing you can do. If Gallagher's inside I'm sorry, Mia, but you're better off at your own place. I promise I will tell you everything I know as soon as we take him into custody."

"Can you at least tell me how you know it's him?"

"Eli hacked into the CIA's database of active and inactive consultants, as they're called. Liam's name never came up. It's not listed in the agents database either."

"I don't get it. How—"

"Hang on a minute. After two days of nothing, Eli finally got creative."

"What do you mean?"

"He hacked into *Seahaven's* database. Well, actually, not just their database. He hacked into their patient files."

"Can he do that?"

"No. Absolutely not. But he did it anyway because he's Eli and he doesn't give a damn. Luckily, he doesn't work for us and we have no known relationship with him."

"What did he find?"

"Liam Gallagher was a patient at Seahaven twice. Once back in 2005, not too long after he started working for the agency. And once about eleven months ago. Right after the agency nixed him. No idea how he paid for it—sure as hell wasn't the agency. According to the file of his therapy sessions, he started working as an agent not too long after we got back from Afghanistan. About five years back, he got transferred from the States to the one of the black sites in the Middle East, then in Romania. He spent a lot of time assisting our foreign counterparts with questioning suspected terrorists."

"Assisting—as in torturing?" Mia didn't know a lot about the black sites, but she'd heard enough to know the Agency had taken a lot of heat for what went on there.

"As in torturing," Nick said. "Otherwise known as enhanced interrogation techniques."

"Like waterboarding?" Mia remembered reading about that in the newspapers.

"Like waterboarding. And a few other things I'm not going to get into."

Mia nodded. She wasn't sure she wanted to know. She was all for stopping terrorists but wasn't sure how she felt about the means the agency had used to obtain information. Didn't that kind of thing make the "good guys" a little too similar to the bad ones? Or was she being naïve? "Why did the agency get rid of him?"

"I'm not sure what went wrong but something did. A few of the terrorists Liam interrogated died. One of them turned out to be innocent. Apparently it was somebody related to the royal family in Saudi Arabia. Big mistake."

"What happened?"

"The CIA hushed it up but somebody in the press got wind of it and wrote a series of articles about the agency's unorthodox methods. Gallagher was officially out of the agency but apparently they still used him quite a lot. A year ago he was questioning Chudnovksy, a low-level mafia boss from the Ukraine, about a certain virus that killed a bunch of people in Siberia."

Mia sucked in her breath. "The article—

"Right," he said. "The article."

"The files are, shall we say, a bit sketchy but from what Eli could tell something went wrong. Guy died of a heart attack. CIA finally cut Gallagher loose for good—too much of a loose cannon. That would explain why his name doesn't show up in the CIA databases. They wiped it after what happened in Romania. Or maybe sooner, who knows."

"You're sure he really did work for the agency? That he wasn't just making it all up to impress Donelan or something?"

"I'm sure. In the report there's a reference to Gallagher's claim that Chudnovsky told him the virus was some kind of demonstration. That the seller made it to order, so to speak."

Mia felt slightly nauseous. "What do you mean, demonstration?"

"Gallagher claimed the New World Army was the buyer. That the village was meant to show the NWA what Virus X could do. Only it didn't convince them."

"Convince them of what? Everybody died. If the NWA wants a biological weapon, that seems pretty convincing."

"Not everybody died. Remember that the kids survived."

She could barely form the words. *"Why didn't it kill the kids?"*

"Apparently the NWA doesn't consider a virus that leaves potential survivors enough of a threat. Apparently they're looking for something a little more potent."

"Aniak."

"Aniak."

"Jesus Christ."

"Father Donelan might not approve of your word choice. But I think he'd agree with the sentiment."

"And you think that somebody at the Institute," Mia said, "that Mike—

"After Gallagher got out of rehab, he rented a cabin on the outskirts of Somersville under an assumed name—not Thompson, by the way—and got a job flipping burgers. And he started looking into things at the IRID. Maybe it was coincidence. He was already in the area and maybe he decided to start with the Institute. Maybe he got lucky. Or maybe he knew something already and that's why he chose Seahaven to rehab in, because of its proximity to the Institute. That way if anybody from the agency bothered to check up on him, which believe me, does happen, it would look like he was doing his damnedest to get better. Put the past behind him, start a new life, all that jazz. Hell, maybe he even initiated contact and fed that spiel to them so they'd leave him alone. But all the while Gallagher's not doing his damnedest to heal, he's investigating the Siberian incident on his own. And apparently he found something."

"You think he found out Mike was the seller. That Mike was the one who wanted to give the virus to the NWA."

"Gallagher apparently thought so. Or at least it

looks that way. Dalton says there's a waitress who saw Gallagher and Mike at a local diner about a week before he was killed. Hopefully we'll know more once we take him into custody."

"Do you think he's got Chien?" she asked. "That he took him because he's involved in this?

"It's definitely a possibility. If Chien was involved and he didn't bolt when Mike turned up dead, then, yeah, I'd say there's a pretty good chance Gallagher went after him too."

"I just can't believe Mike—or even Chien—"

"I know," Nick said. "But people aren't always what they seem. Let's see what Gallagher has to say."

He pressed on the gas and they picked up speed. She didn't want to look at the speedometer to see how fast they were going but that didn't stop her from shaking. Trees and houses blurred by and the cars receded behind them. He careened past an SUV and swerved around a corner. To her relief, the car shot out onto an open stretch of road. In the distance, the sky flashed silver.

Mia gripped the armrest and stared straight ahead. "Can I ask you something?"

"Sorry. I know I'm driving too fast."

"I was going to ask you if you can go any faster."

****

If he hadn't known better, Nick would have said the place was beautiful. It was, in the way old things could be both picturesque and ugly at the same time. It stood in quiet disarray at the center of a copse of trees, the leaves burning green in the sunlight. The tin roof had rusted long ago and the wooden beams were gray with age. Most of the windows were boarded up, though from the color of the wood, somebody had done it recently. A stone chimney rose on one side of the cabin and an uneven porch ran along the front. He wondered who had lived there once, what their lives had been.

Nick shivered. He'd never believed in ghosts but something about the place gave him the creeps. Like someone walking over his grave. He remembered Laura's dream, the one that had spurred her to convince her husband he needed to get Nick into rehab. Dalton hadn't wanted to give him the address and Nick wondered if that was the reason. Maybe the place was his fate.

How would the former owners feel if they'd known a killer would one day take up residence in their happy home?

If all went well, Liam Gallagher wouldn't be there much longer. Nick pulled his Glock out of its holster and made his way toward the cabin.

He scanned the surrounding woods for signs of human activity. It didn't take him long to find what he was looking for. The rustic scene shifted before him, became something else. Two snipers had climbed nearby trees and lay in wait, their rifles trained on the front door. Other agents were scattered across the area, crouching just out of sight. Dalton stood behind an elm in what passed for a front yard, a handheld radar device aimed at the cabin.

"What the hell are you doing here," Dalton said when he came up behind him. "I told you we didn't need you."

"You gave me the address."

"Yeah, well, my mistake. Go back to your truck

260

and get your butt back to rehab."

"You never did tell me about Laura's latest dream."

Dalton gave him an exasperated look. "I don't think this is the time, okay, buddy."

Nick grinned. "Neither do I. But don't try and protect me."

"Who's protecting you?"

"Nobody but me. Glad we got that straightened out." Nick glanced down at the radar. "You sure he's in there?"

"No. I'm not. But somebody is and this is the address he's been using," he said. "You got your vest on?"

"It's on. I haven't been out of the field that long," Nick said. "And did you mean one somebody—or two?"

"Not sure. We're picking up on one person for sure. There's been some movement, though not much. Haven't seen any signs of a second person. Could be a body in there though. Or somebody badly wounded. Radar wouldn't pick up on that."

"If there's a chance Chien's in there, shouldn't we already be inside? Or at least have alerted Gallagher to the fact that we're here?"

"If he's in there, he knows we're here."

Dalton was right. Maybe an ordinary killer might not have picked up the activity outside, but a former agent wouldn't miss it. "What about a negotiator?"

"We're working on it. We want everything in place first. I could be wrong but my guess is he's got the place rigged with explosives. Or at the very least, he's heavily armed. We want Chien alive, we want

Gallagher alive and we want what's inside. I'm not willing to rush things and jeopardize any of that. And my guess is Gallagher's not gonna want to talk."

It made sense. In a way, the contents of the house were even more important than apprehending Gallagher. If Gallagher had discovered a link between Mike and the NWA, then they needed that information. "How long are we going to wait?"

On the radar monitor, a red dot moved across the screen. "Not long."

Dalton stashed the radar detector in his belt and picked up his radio. "What you got for me, Jonesy?"

Nick couldn't hear what the sniper said but Dalton's nod didn't reassure him. "Okay," he said quietly. "Show time."

A man Nick recognized but didn't know stepped out into the clearing and raised a bullhorn to his lips. "We've got the place surrounded. Step out of the building with your hands raised over your head, Liam."

No response. The only sound was the wind through the trees.

Dalton laid his hand on Nick's shoulder. "Jonesy thinks he caught a slight movement toward the back of the cabin. Somebody else might be inside. Whoever it is may still be alive but just barely. We need to move. Soon."

Nick nodded. Moving as quickly as possible, he positioned himself behind an oak about ten yards from the house. He cocked his gun and glanced over at Dalton, who was speaking into his radio.

The negotiator began speaking again, raising his voice to be heard over the wind. Nick felt a drop of rain hit his face, and another. Another few minutes and the sky would open.

What the hell was Dalton waiting for?

But it wasn't his operation, it was Dalton's. Dalton was calling the shots this time and Nick had to go along with it. Sure, he might have run things a little differently. But Dalton was a good agent and he knew what he was doing.

"...if you don't show yourself, you leave us no choice but to come in and take you by force. Do you understand that?" the negotiator concluded, with a worried glance at the dark clouds massing overhead.

Nick held his breath. Gallagher wasn't coming out. He was sure of it. Nick just hoped Dalton was wrong about him rigging the place. Even if Mike was dead, that didn't mean he hadn't already provided the NWA with biological weapons. Were there other "demonstrations" planned? Or, even worse, was the NWA ready to launch the real thing—the kind of catastrophic event Father Donelan had alluded to. If that were the case, maybe Gallagher had names, dates.

They needed those names. Those dates.

In the distance, a clap of thunder split the sky.

What the hell was he waiting for?

The wind had picked up. Great gusts tore across the clearing, lifting fallen leaves off the ground and whirling them into the air. The drops were coming faster now, the sound filling the air until their *tap, tap, tap* was all Nick could hear. *Tap, tap, tap.* Krasnoyarsk, Chudnovsky, Aniak. *Tap, tap, tap.* Krasnoyarsk, Mike Chandler, Aniak. *Tap, tap, tap.* Aniak, Chien, New York.

The name of the city constricted his chest until he couldn't breathe.

What if this time the NWA was satisfied with the demonstration in Aniak? After all, this time no one had survived. An unqualified success—at least in the minds of the terrorists who couldn't think beyond destroying the western world.

Maybe the final purchase had already happened.

They had to get inside, had to find out what Gallagher knew.

Nick counted to ten. *Don't think. Don't think. Don't think.*

The sky opened just as Dalton raised his arm and pointed toward the cabin. *"GO!"* he shouted but the sound was lost in the screams of the wind.

He sprinted across the overgrown yard, his Glock held out in front of him. Other agents appeared beside him, all of them running full speed through the deluge. Someone beside him slipped, someone else fell. Up ahead, several agents had already reached the porch and were scrambling toward the door. There were so many of them he couldn't see who finally kicked open the door, only watched as they streamed into house.

Dalton leapt onto the front steps just ahead of him and disappeared into the darkness. Nick slipped but recovered, jumping onto the rotting boards and making his way toward the empty square where the door had been.

He was seconds behind Dalton, seconds from finding a man he would have given up his life to save a decade earlier. A man he'd gotten drunk with and shared stories with and fought beside. A man who had been part of the family their platoon had fashioned itself into during that year spent fighting in the ditches outside of Kabul. He'd respected Gallagher for his no-holds-barred brand of courage, even revered him at times.

Now that man was the enemy.

Nick pressed his body against the entryway wall and moved toward the back of the cabin. The place was crawling with agents but Gallagher was nowhere in sight. The rain poured down the roof, leaking through in several places. The place seemed strangely quiet compared to the racket outside.

At the end of hallway, Dalton stood against the wall. Someone had pulled the door to the next room shut. From the other side came the sound of labored breathing.

Dalton held a finger to his lips. His other hand cradled an AK-47 against his ribcage.

Nick nodded. He knew what they had to do.

"Ready?" Dalton mouthed the words and removed his finger from his lips.

"Ready."

Using his gun to push in the door, Dalton exploded into the room. Nick was right behind him, his Glock raised and ready to fire. Several agents filed in behind them and positioned themselves around the room. Nick could hear agents in the rooms behind them, shouting back and forth to one another. Looking for Chien.

Or his body.

Gallagher stood with his back to a stone fireplace, an AK-47 aimed at Dalton's head. A chipped wooden table stood between him and the agents. "Drop your gun."

Dalton didn't move. "I'd say you're outnumbered. So I'm gonna repeat what you said, only you're gonna be the one who puts down his weapon."

"I might be outnumbered, but I don't think your buddies want to see their leader get hurt. Even if one of them is stupid enough to get off a shot, you'll be dead before I hit the floor. *If* I hit the floor. In which case you'd have died for nothing."

Gallagher wasn't lying. The guy had on a bullet-proof vest and then some. He was rigged to the gills with explosives. No way a couple of bullets were going to do accomplish anything.

Other than to blow them all to hell.

"You were one of us not that long ago," Dalton said. "How about you start acting like it? There are more important things than playing the desperado. Tell us what you know, Gallagher. It's not too late to do the right thing."

"Too bad you're wrong. On all counts. But I'll give you bonus points for trying." He seemed almost cocky. He was smart enough to know they wanted him alive. Smart enough to know nobody was going to risk trying to kill him.

Would he try to take out Dalton?

Nick didn't doubt it. But for now Gallagher was enjoying the game of cat and mouse.

Good.

Better that than the alternative.

Nick took a step forward, his gun steady on Gallagher's face. "Have you forgotten what the NWA did to Brendon Thompson back '01? Because if you don't shut up your goddamn ego and tell us what the hell's going on they're going to win, Liam. Just like they did back in Afghanistan. Is that how you're going to honor your dead friend's memory? By letting them get hold of the most dangerous weapon since the nuclear bomb?"

When his gaze fell on Nick a flicker of recognition crossed his face. "Jesus. Doyle?"

"Been a while," Nick said.

Gallagher didn't answer.

"Where's Chien Lu?"

"I don't know where that crazy fuck is."

"Bullshit," Nick said. "And if anybody's a crazy fuck, it's you. What the hell have you been doing?"

"You don't know what you're talkin' about. I'm the only one in the agency who's not crazy."

"You're not in the agency anymore. They fired you. Remember?"

Gallagher's shoulder twitched but he kept the gun steady. "Yeah, I remember. I remember I tried to tell them what the fuck was going on and they wouldn't listen. Wouldn't do a damn thing about what I said. Thought I was some fucked up drug addict with PTSD."

"Aren't you?" Nick asked. "Isn't that why they sent you to rehab?"

"Takes one to know one, eh, Doyle? Took a little tour of your room the other night. Looks like I'm not the only one with a substance abuse problem. Guess it runs in the family. In the genes and all that. Tough to avoid."

Nick held the gun steady, its barrel aimed squarely at Gallagher's head. "Yeah, well, I've been avoiding it pretty well lately. And I don't hate myself enough to want to smash the mirror that holds my reflection."

"You will." Gallagher chuckled softly. "You will."

Nick reined in his temper. Anger wasn't going to help him find Chien Lu. Or learn what Gallagher knew about Mike Chandler. "What's that supposed to mean?"

"You'll find out. All in good time."

"Where's Chien?" Nick repeated.

"I already told you I don't have a fuckin' clue where he is."

"Is he here? In this cabin?" Nick took another step toward him. "Or did you kill him and stash the body somewhere else?"

"You don't remember, do you?"

"Remember what?"

"What they did to him. To Brendon."

"I remember."

"But you didn't see him. I did. I saw him after they got through with him and left his body out in the open to rot like a piece of meat. Beaten so badly I couldn't even tell if he had clothes on or not. His spine was snapped. He'd been bleeding out of his ass and both arms had been pulled out of their sockets. They raped him—"

His voice broke.

Nick fought down a wave of nausea. He hadn't thought about Thompson for a decade. Probably a lucky thing or maybe he would've gone the same way Gallagher had. But he did remember. Coming across Thompson's body that day on their way to the next village.

A warning. That's what it had been, really. The NWA training camps were nearby and Thompson was their way of telling them to mind their own business. They were there to shut down the training camps the Taliban had allowed Al Qaeda to set up outside of Kandahar, that was their mission. The NWA wasn't the focus. Everybody—the NWA, the Taliban, even their superiors—had told them to leave the New World Army alone. They weren't enough of a threat. And nobody wanted to hear about another terrorist group, not when half of America was terrified enough as it was. People wanted Al Qaeda's camps shut down and that was that. Keep it simple.

At least that's what they'd been told.

So for all intents and purposes Thompson's body didn't exist. His death didn't count. It was something to be forgotten.

Only they hadn't forgotten. Some of them had dreamt of Thompson's carcass for weeks, even months. Nick had. Maybe Gallagher was stilling dreaming it.

"Is that why you used his name when you rented the car?" Nick asked quietly. "To honor his memory? Or maybe just to remember?"

Gallagher snickered but the tears brimming in his eyes gave him away. "A stupid slip up. Amateur hour from start to finish. I didn't want to use my assumed name because somebody could trace it back to me. Couldn't use my real name because Liam Gallagher had dropped off the face of the world. It was the first name that came to mind, if you really want to know. Didn't think twice about anybody making a connection. I should've been more careful."

Behind him, Nick could feel the agents tensed, ready to spring. Waiting for the gun to waver, even for a second so they could tackle him. If they shot at his head Gallagher could still get off a round or two before he hit the ground. A guy with his training wasn't going to miss. Not when his intended targets were only feet away. And Gallagher's hands were steady. He might still grieve for his friend but he wasn't about to break.

"What happened to him wasn't anybody's fault," Nick said. "It was theirs. The terrorists. We're still on the same side, Liam."

Gallagher shook his head. "I was supposed to go. That's the funny fuckin' thing. Everybody always thought I was the one with the balls. It was him. I did it for him—didn't want him to think I was the scared-shitless kid I really was. But that day, I don't know. I had a bad feeling or something. Backed out at the last second. Brendon said he'd go in my place. And he did. He died in my place. I'm the one who should be dead."

"Where's Chien Lu." It wasn't a question. More like an order.

"I don't have any fuckin' idea."

"Jesus, Liam. For Christ's sake, tell me where he is." Nick felt his self-control slipping. "Did you kill him? Did you kill him like you killed Mike Chandler? Was he working with them? Is that why you took him?"

"I didn't take him," Gallagher spat out the words. "I'm not saying I wouldn't have if I'd had the chance. I knew what he was, fucking traitor, I don't give a damn about his dying kid. But he never showed. Gone. Maybe he bolted. Maybe he's on some island in the south Pacific, complete with new identity and a Swiss bank account. Jesus, Nick, I don't know."

"And Chandler?"

"I beat him. Jesus, I beat him to a bloody goddamn pulp. I'd made contact with him around ten months ago, told him I was CIA. Hell, how would he know I wasn't? At first I thought I could cultivate him as a contact within the Institute. You want to know the funniest thing of all?

"Sure," Nick said.

"When I first got back to the states I went to Seahaven to get better. Told myself I needed to get my head together before I started hunting the NWA. I'd been there before, had enough money saved to pay for the treatment. I was doing pretty good, too, until I came across another agent in a therapy meeting. Got kinda friendly with the guy. Pretty soon he tells me something funny was going on at the Institute, something dangerous. Mentions the NWA. But he got pulled before he could pursue it. The agency forces him into rehab. Puts him on leave. Sound familiar?"

Unfortunately, it did. Nick didn't like where Gallagher's story was headed. "And you believed him?"

"Yeah, I believed him. When the guy fell off the face of the earth without a trace a week later, I found that pretty convincing. Left Seahaven the next day and started looking into things. As for Chandler, he was an easy mark. I'd read about him in the papers. He was always winning some race in that damn boat of his. Extroverted as hell, always at the marina bar buying everybody drinks. Not so hard, to strike up an acquaintance with him."

Nick didn't dare look at Dalton. Gallagher's gun was still aimed straight at Dalton's head and the more he looked at it, the more he was sure the vest was the real thing. Gallagher wasn't the type that bluffed. *Keep him talking.* "So you thought Chandler was involved with the NWA? That's why you made contact?"

"Hell, no. I just wanted somebody inside, somebody who could feed me information. Knew the guy worked on Ebola and thought I could maybe figure out a connection with the NWA. That was the extent of it. In the beginning."

"In the beginning?"

"At first Chandler tells me there's nothing going on at the Institute—that I had it all wrong. Didn't want anything to do with me or informing on his colleagues. So I gave him my card and that was that. Never heard from him again. I'm talking months and months. I was onto somebody else from the CDC when one night out of the blue he calls me up and tells me he has something for me, something important. Wants to meet ASAP on the boat. So when I get there and tell him to show me what he has—he says he has to take me somewhere then suddenly changes his mind. Says no, he's made a mistake. That he doesn't have shit. Thank you and goodbye."

Nick was careful not to react. If Mike Chandler had really found something, he very well could have called Gallagher. But suppose Chandler was savvy enough to figure out sometime during their little sail that Gallagher had been lying to him about working for the agency. It would make sense that he'd back out. He would've wanted to take what he had to the real thing.

"What the fuck was I supposed to think?" Gallagher went on. "That he'd gotten cold feet? Either that or he was the one working with the NWA and he'd lured me out there so he could kill me. Whatever it was, I wasn't having any of that shit. So I turned the tables."

His voice was loud now, too loud for such a small space. Now that he was talking, he didn't want to stop. He'd probably kept everything bottled up for too damn long. Thompson's death had festered inside him until it destroyed everything good left in him.

"How'd you do that?" Nick asked.

Gallagher snickered. "You still think you're gonna have a chance to investigate all this, don't you?"

A ripple of panic ran through Nick. What if he was wrong about Gallagher's need to tell his story? What if he pulled the strap on his vest and destroyed them all before they could reach him? "How'd you turn the tables?" he asked, ignoring Gallagher's attempt to bait him.

Gallagher smiled. It was a slow, sly smile, neither friendly nor unfriendly. A mask of a smile. What was underneath it was anybody's guess. "I started asking him questions, wanted to find out what he knew. But by then he'd made up his mind to keep his mouth shut. Even when I started pulling fingernails. Wouldn't talk."

"So he never told you anything."

Gallagher's eyes blazed. "Nothing. Not a goddamn thing."

Nick took another step forward. "Is that why you killed him? Because he wouldn't give you what you wanted?"

"Stay where you are."

"He's right, Nick." Dalton's voice, from somewhere behind him.

Another step.

"One more step and your buddy dies. We *all* die."

Nick stood his ground. "You don't want to do this."

"Hell, yeah, I do. I'm sick of the bullshit, sick of being the only one who gives a damn about stopping the NWA. You say you want to but you still want to play by the rules. Well, I got news for you, cowboy, you can't play by the rules when the other guy doesn't even understand what rules are. You won't win a war that way."

"If we don't play by the rules, then that makes us as bad as they are. Then what the hell are we fighting for? This country's got to stand for something. Otherwise none of it matters."

"It matters when we're talking about the end of the goddamn world."

"Is that what we're talking about?"

"That's what I've been telling you ever since you dropped in," he said in a low voice on the verge of hysteria. "I needed Chandler alive. And he *was* alive when I left him. I don't know how the hell he could've made it upstairs and into the water. Couldn't stand up, never mind climb up a ladder. But he was breathing. He was awake. He knew what was going on, kept asking for a doctor. I brought the boat back into port and went to get some supplies. I wasn't done with him, not by a long shot."

"You killed him. You just can't face it. But we all have to face up to our mistakes, Liam. Time you faced up to yours."

"No!" Gallagher roared, kicking a chair over with his foot. "When I got back, the boat was gone. I don't know what happened. But I swear to God I didn't kill him."

The clatter of the chair echoed across the room. Outside, the storm raged on.

"You're lying." Nick's stomach tightened but he stayed where he was. Gallagher was a literal powder keg, ready to explode. One wrong move and they were all dead.

"I am not lying."

If Liam was telling the truth and he had left him

alive, then what had happened? Was it possible Mike Chandler had been faking it—making himself seem worse off than he was so Gallagher would let down his guard? When he did, Chandler took his chance and escaped. Only he was in bad shape, such bad shape he stumbled off the boat while he was trying to get away.

It was possible. But that didn't explain what happened to Chien Lu. He knew by now that the scientist wasn't in the cabin. Had he hooked up with the NWA? Run somewhere else he thought nobody would ever find him?

Also possible.

But there was another alternative, one he liked a lot less.

"Why did you search Chandler's apartment?"

"Can't you guess?"

"You were looking for what he found out. You believed he was telling the truth when he told you he was innocent. You wanted the evidence that would link the Institute with what happened in Siberia."

Gallagher said nothing.

"But you didn't find it," Nick continued. "So you figured maybe his ex-partner had it. Or maybe the FBI agent she'd started hanging out with. So you searched our rooms. And came up with nothing."

Gallagher's eyes were glassy but his muscles were tensed. He hadn't let down his guard and Nick's questions hadn't distracted him. It made sense. After all, the guy had been trained to deal with this kind of interrogation. Hell, maybe none of what he'd said was true and it was all some paranoid tale. Ex-Veteran Goes On Rampage. "I just have one question."

"Only one?"

"Why did you drug the dog? Why not just kill it?" The guy hadn't killed Gallagher but that was only because he'd wanted more information. Otherwise he had no problems inflicting pain on anybody or anything that got in his way.

"I didn't."

"You didn't."

"Mutt was out like a light when I got there."

Mia. The one word cut through him. Somebody had been there first. Somebody who was out there right now.

From somewhere behind him, a shot rang out. Nick lunged forward and launched his body into the air at the moment Gallagher's weapon flashed fire. His hand went to the string on the vest as Nick landed on top of him.

The room exploded into chaos.

Behind him, Dalton cried out. And someone else.

He heard his own voice.

He looked down at his hand and was surprised to see blood. Whose was it? Then the world spun out of focus and he felt Gallagher on top of him. He fought the weight of arms and shoulders pressing against his face, dragging him down into darkness.

Chapter 16

Mia stood in Nailini's kitchen, leaning back against the counter. Across from her, Hera and Zeus squawked in hungry solidarity. Their constant chatter was more than annoying but they were beautiful to look at. Zeus's feathers were deep aqua, with a splash of yellow near his beak. Hera was scarlet with black and white stripes around her face that made her look both wise and exotic. Mia couldn't understand how her friend put up with the parrots' banter, but she wouldn't mind waking up to such colors every day.

"Sorry, guys," she said, filling their cages with seeds. "Or maybe I should say gods."

She'd promised Nick to stay home but that was before she remembered she hadn't fed her friend's parrots yet that day. It was the first time Nailini had asked her to house sit and she wasn't sure how long parrots could go without food but she didn't want to take any chances.

Anyway, it wasn't as if she were in danger. If anybody's life was on the line it was Nick's.

She fought the urge to sink to the floor.

Stop being so melodramatic. He'll be fine. They've got an entire SWAT team out there. That's a thirty-to-one ratio. Do the math. You're a scientist, for God's sake.

The line was wearing thin.

She didn't feel rational. She wasn't thinking at all, actually. It had been so long since she'd felt any sort of emotion that she couldn't identify what she was experiencing. It couldn't be love. She hadn't known him long enough.

Not possible.

It was still afternoon but she'd turned on the kitchen lights because of the storm. Outside, the rain fell in silver sheets. Even running the short distance from the driveway to Nailini's door had been enough to soak through her clothes.

She stood shivering before the twin cages, her wet hair pulled back. Apparently Hera and Zeus couldn't live together. Parrots weren't all that different from people, she supposed. Or at least fifty percent of the population, anyway.

She was soaked to the bone.

Nailini's closet was stuffed with outfits and she knew her friend wouldn't mind if she changed. Mia was six inches taller than her friend, but there had to be something that would work.

With a nod to the parrots, she jogged upstairs and entered the bedroom. Unlike Mia's bedroom, which was hospital ward neat, Nailini's was a cluttered mess. Knick-knacks covered every inch of table space and colorful weavings hung from the walls. The walk-in closet was just as full, with no apparent pattern to the racks of dresses and skirts and blouses that hung inside.

Mia stepped inside and ran her hands over the rack to her left. She normally wasn't the type to wear gauzy dresses but there didn't seem to be a pair of jeans in sight and she'd be too tall for them, anyway. With a resigned sigh, she squirmed out of her wet clothes and reached for a flowered Maxi dress with spaghetti straps.

She slid the dress over her head and stared into the mirror that hung on the back of the bedroom door. Surprisingly, it fit, though it was a bit on the short side for a Maxi dress. Mia stood in bare feet and turned in a slow circle until she stood facing her reflection. She raised her hand to her hair and pulled out the elastic, watching the damp blonde strands fall over her shoulders.

Who was she, really?

The woman staring back at her didn't look familiar. The Mia she knew was disciplined, logical, obsessively organized.

Distant.

Elitist.

Lonely.

The woman who stared back at her seemed more like a long-lost twin than a part of herself. Would her sister have looked like this, had she survived? Holly had always been the kinder of the two of them, the girly one who begged her to play Barbies and dress up. Mia had been the risk-taker, the one who climbed trees and disappeared for hours in search of new "specimens," the one who cajoled her mother into buying them a lizard instead of a kitten.

She was still that girl. After all, how many people worked with deadly pathogens? But she'd stopped taking other kinds of risks. She'd shut her life up inside a lab, pushed anybody who wanted to get close to her away.

She didn't want to be that person anymore. She didn't want to live inside such a small box for the rest of her life. She didn't want to push Nick away. And she didn't want to go on being afraid all the time.

Mia slipped on a pair of sandals and grabbed her wet clothes. She pushed open the bathroom door and draped her jeans and t-shirt over the shower rail. The rain was still coming down hard and when she walked back into the kitchen, a clap of thunder sent the parrots into a frenzy.

"Pretty bird, pretty bird."

"Oh, shut up, shut up, shut up."

"Gimme kiss, gimme kiss, gimme kiss."

"No, no, no, no."

The parrots continued their agitated squawking. Mia wondered if her friend had purposely trained the two of them to sound as if they were fighting, like their Greek namesakes. A quick glance at her cell phone told her there were no new messages from Nick.

Well, it hadn't been that long.

He was bound to call or text soon.

"Pretty bird, pretty bird."

"Shut up, shut up, shut up."

Another clap of thunder, another round of mad dialogue. Luckily the two birds were caged, otherwise they just might tear each other's throats out. Mia walked over to the stove and put the kettle on to boil. Now that she was here there wasn't any point in going out until the storm eased up. She searched through the cupboards and grabbed a mug, along with a teabag, saucer and a spoon.

She was pushing one of the cabinets shut when she saw it. Mike's planner and the articles she'd stashed out of sight in Nailini's kitchen. Pushed all the way back in the corner. She still found it hard to believe the planner contained anything of importance. On the other hand, there had to be a reason somebody had searched her house.

Mia set the cup and the tea things onto the counter and stood on tiptoe to retrieve the planner. She pulled it down and walked over to the kitchen table, removing the three articles and setting them beside it in a neat pile. She opened the planner to the first page, which was almost a year earlier.

September first through eighth. There were only a few entries, scrawled in Mike's familiar handwriting. *Lunch with Mia.*

She turned to the second week. It didn't look much different than the first week, other than the absence of her name.

The kettle on the stove whined, followed by another clap of thunder crashing down.

"Watch out! Watch out!"

"What did you say to me!"

"Watch out! Watch out!"

If she didn't know better, she could almost believe they were trying to warn her. Shaking off her fears, she got up from the table and poured the boiling water into her mug. She tugged at the tea bag a few times and carried it back to the table, setting it down several inches away from the planner.

Week three. Mom and Dad in for the weekend. Staff meeting. Sailing with Mia.

Et cetera.

She forced herself to focus. The entries might seem mundane but there had to be something she was missing.

Race with Jeff. Dinner with Toni. Sailing.

Toni. Another woman? Mia wasn't jealous but a

part of her still didn't like it.

She read on. Every now and then one of her colleagues' names popped up. Drinks with Trask. Sailing with Caleb. Dinner with Chien.

Chien.

So apparently the two of them had known each other socially. She didn't know why she was so surprised. After all, it would make sense that she wasn't the only co-worker Mike hung out with outside of work. Strange though, that Mike had never mentioned any of those meetings to her. If he'd been hanging out with them—and obviously he was—then how had it never come up?

It was odd. Definitely odd. She turned another page.

"Watch out! Watch out!"

"Oh, shut up, shut up, shut up!"

She squeezed out the teabag and set it into the saucer. When she took a sip the tea was lukewarm. Served her right for letting it sit so long. She set down the cup and looked back at the page before her.

It wasn't until she'd made her way through the first eight months that she began to notice a pattern. When she'd gone through the planner the first time, she hadn't paid much attention to the notations about Mike's time on the boat. He'd sailed for as long as she'd known him, so the trips penciled in every weekend hadn't caught her attention. But after going through the entire year, she realized the number of times he'd written in the letters "BI" next to his sailing times had increased. Not excessively. There were still plenty of weekends when he wrote in an actual destination—one of the marinas they'd visited together or one of the hundreds of islands that dotted the bay.

But the closer she got to the present, the more "BI" showed up.

What was BI? Or who?

Was "BI" Brendon Thompson? Maybe the second letter wasn't an "I" but a "T."

It certainly seemed possible. If Nick's platoon buddy Liam Gallagher had used the name once as a cover, he may well have done it again. He could have met Mike and introduced himself as Brendon. And if Mike really was involved in selling a genetically engineered virus to terrorists, Gallagher would have taken his time about investigating it.

Still, something about that scenario didn't work.

She was no expert in psychology—it was the one science she diligently avoided—but Mike was pretty methodical. He would have seen through Gallagher's ruse.

He was, after all, a scientist. Slow. Careful. Skeptical.

Suppose she'd been right at the beginning. Suppose Mike hadn't been working with the terrorists. If he'd suspected Chien or somebody else at the Institute of creating a super virus, he wouldn't have moved right away. He would have watched, waited, then watched some more.

What if Mike was looking at the Siberian incident not from his own point of view, but from the perspective of the terrorists? Or of the scientist at the Institute who was working with them? That would explain the odd notation at the bottom of the Siberian clipping.

If Mike did suspect somebody at the Institute of

working with the NWA, he wouldn't have moved right away. He would have been slow and cautious and skeptical.

And careful. He would have been very, very careful.

Maybe that explained his meetings with Chien and Caleb and Trask. Mike had never spent any time with them before, yet he'd befriended all of them over the past year. He'd always wanted to get away from work, that's why he loved the boat so much. Yet he'd spent his free time with people he had little in common with. And with BI. Or BT. Except the second letter didn't look like a T. Not at all. She knew her partner's handwriting.

Mia tried to remember everyone at the Institute whose first or last name began with the letter B or I. There were dozens of people who might fit that description. And then there was the possibility it was a code—or even a nickname.

Another thought struck her. What if B wasn't a person but a place?

With shaking fingers she flipped through the book in reverse order, searching for a reference to a place that began with B. On October 7, nearly ten months earlier, she found it.

Bloodsworth Island.

The name was jotted in pencil, in his barely legible scrawl. She scanned the rest of the planner for a second reference and found none.

Mia grabbed her phone off the counter and typed the name into google. Within seconds, the search produced a Wikipedia entry, along with several other links. She skipped the Wikipedia entry and went to the second result, a pdf document issued by the state of Maryland.

USN Bloodsworth Island

Dorchester County, Maryland

The USN Bloodsworth Island (BWI) is located in Dorchester County near the convergence of Fishing Bay, the Nanticoke River and the Honga River. This island covers an area of approximately twenty-five square miles. BWI, along with South Marsh Island and Smith Island, form the boundary for the Tangier Sound near the mouth of the Chesapeake Bay. Site History Bloodsworth Island was purchased by the United States Navy in 1942 and immediately put to use as a training ground for both surface forces and aircraft. Most of the island was designated as an impact zone for naval and aircraft bombardment. Between the years of 1942 and 1967, it is estimated that 230,000 rounds were fired at the island from surface ships alone. Training activities on BWI reached their peak during the early 1970s, in support of the Vietnam conflict. Through the late 1980s, BWI was also used for Naval gunfire support exercises involving simulation of shore bombardments in support of amphibious landings. Until October 1995, the Air Force and Air National Guard used BWI for air to ground training (ordnance included: machine gun ammunition, explosive bombs, smoke bombs and rockets). At the end of 1995, all bombing activity ceased and the island was abandoned by the U.S. Navy.

Due to extensive contamination by unexploded ordnance, the entire island is off limits to the public.

Mia scanned the entry and then reread it. BI had to be Bloodsworth Island. She was sure of it. But even if all the BI's did stand for Bloodsworth Island, why would Mike sail to an island that was contaminated— and off limits to the public? Was he looking for something on the island? If so, what? What could possibly be on an island that had been deserted for decades?

Her head was starting to hurt. "I don't understand, Mike," she said aloud. "What are you trying to tell me?"

"I don't understand Mike!"

"What are you trying to tell me!"

"I don't understand Mike!"

"What are you trying to tell me!"

"Stop it!" she yelled, turning toward the parrots.

"Stop it, stop it, stop it, stop it!

"Be quiet!"

"Be quiet, be quiet be quiet!"

She wanted to scream. She could only imagine how that would end. Two parrots named after Greek gods screaming bloody murder. It was as if she were caught in the slapstick version of a Hitchcock film.

Why did Mike go to Bloodsworth Island?

She kept coming back to that question.

Well, there was only one way to find out the answer.

She needed to go there.

You mean you and Nick need to go there. The FBI needs to go there.

Her internal radar was right. Though she wanted to drop everything and race out to the marina, rent a boat and head out there, she knew it would be madness.

She'd wait until Nick got back. Then she'd tell him her theory and try to convince him there was something to it. Even if he didn't believe her, he'd have to at least check it out.

Feeling better, she grabbed her cup and dumped the remains of her tea into the sink. She took a sponge and turned on the tap. Outside, the rain was finally abating. The storm was moving off.

A stray black cat stole across the lawn and disappeared into the mountain laurels that ringed the yard. A dark shadow among shadows.

Her spine tingled.

Oh, stop it, she thought. *Next thing you'll be avoiding the cracks in the sidewalk.*

She finished washing the cup and saucer, then cleaned the spoon. She set everything into the dishrack next to the sink. There was no sign of the black cat.

She'd grabbed the planner and the articles off the table when she heard it.

The sound of a car in the driveway.

She stood frozen. Nailini wasn't due back for another week. Maybe it was a neighbor. Or maybe not. Or maybe she was being paranoid.

A door slammed and Mia waited, unable to move.

At the sound of footsteps on the walk, she sprang into action. She shoved the planner and the articles back into the cupboard and grabbed her cell off the counter.

The cell clattered to the floor and fell under the kitchen table.

She picked it up but her hand was shaking so badly she dropped it again. She was bending to retrieve it a second time when the doorbell rang.

A sense of Déjà vu rippled through her.

The doorbell rang again. She straightened and made her way toward the living room, praying the parrots would stay quiet for once. The curtains were drawn and the room was almost completely dark. As quietly as possible, she crossed to the window and peered through a crack between the panels.

A man in a windbreaker stood at the door, his finger on the doorbell buzzer.

The hood had been drawn up over his head, making it impossible to tell who it was. But she knew anyway. No reason for him to be here. No reason except for her.

She let the curtain drop into place and stole back into the kitchen, grabbing a knife from the wooden block on the counter. If she could make it to the back door, she'd have a decent shot at reaching her car before he spotted her.

Bring the planner or leave it?

Leave it. She had what she needed.

The hand holding the knife was shaking so badly she thought she'd drop that too but she managed to hold onto it.

A knock on the door, loud enough to rattle the windows.

"I know you're in there!" he shouted. "Open the goddamn door!"

Hera and Zeus were off again.

"I know you're in there!"

"Open the goddamn door!"

It was worse than being trapped in an echo chamber. So much for making it to the car undetected. Mia sprinted toward the back of the house, toward the door that led to the mud room.

He was already there when she reached it, leering at her through the window at the top of the door.

She held the knife out in front of her with both

hands. "Come into this house and I'll kill you!" she shouted through the door.

He laughed softly and backed away from the door. A few seconds later a gunshot echoed through the house and pierced the door.

He'd shot through the lock.

Mia turned and ran. She didn't know where she was going, didn't think about anything at all. Adrenaline had taken control of her body.

She was a few feet from the front door when he caught her. His boot cut into her back as he shoved her face against the floor. The knife skittered across the linoleum and stopped just below the parrots' cages.

"Fight me and I'll blow your brains out."

"Go ahead." She tried to push herself up but the boot held her down. The coppery taste of blood filled her mouth.

Caleb Hastings knelt over her and pressed the gun to her temple. "Don't tempt me."

Mia closed her eyes, bracing for the impact of the shot. It didn't come.

"Fear suits you." He caressed her hair with the hand that held the gun. "You've never looked as beautiful as you do right now."

"Go to hell."

He tucked the gun into his belt and pulled her arms behind her. Reaching into his windbreaker, he pulled out a roll of duct tape and wrapped it around her hands quickly and securely. He was stronger than she expected. Rougher.

Minus the bow-tie and the glasses, Caleb looked as threatening as he really was. The endearing smile was gone, as were the baggy clothes that disguised his bulk.

He was thin but now that he wasn't wearing an ill-fitting lab coat, the sinews in his arms were shockingly obvious. Even the top of his wild hair had been pulled back into a short ponytail. As if his entire personality had been a ruse.

Which, she supposed, it had been.

"Who are you really?"

From her behind her, she heard him snicker. "Are you expecting the evil twin? Good ol' Caleb wouldn't ever do anything like this, right? Just like Chien wouldn't—or your buddy, Mike? All of us just *too good* to sell out."

"You're nothing like Mike. He was a good man."

"Unfortunately, you happen to be right about that. If he hadn't gotten suspicious and started looking into things, I'd already be on a beach in Bali and half the country would be dead. As it is, he's delayed my delivery to the NWA by more than a few days."

He was, she realized, utterly mad. "So you are…actually a scientist?"

"I *was* a scientist. The ultimate geek, the nerdy guy who couldn't get laid unless he paid for it. Not that I didn't enjoy working with pathogens on a daily basis, but I'd much prefer the life of an anonymous billionaire."

"How can you not realize what you're planning on doing—even aside from the ethics of killing the entire U.S. population, the virus you've developed could wipe out the entire species. I'd expect that kind of idiocy from terrorists, but if you really are a scientist—"

"Now who's being an idiot. That always was one thing that amused me about you. You always thought of scientists as some kind of twenty-first century riff on

290

priests. But we're not holy—hell, most of us aren't even all that ethical. If we're not interested in it for the baser motives, then the extent of our interest in what we do is purely intellectual. Oppenheimer, the A-bomb, Los Alamos. Any of that ring a bell?"

Or maybe he wasn't mad, at least not in the usual sense of the word. Maybe he simply lacked a conscience. Unlike the man who invented the nuclear bomb to stop Hitler, Caleb couldn't care less what forces he unleashed upon the world. "Oppenheimer spent the rest of his life trying to undo what he set loose."

"Well, maybe there's hope for me yet. Maybe when I'm sunning myself on that beach in Bali, I'll have a change of heart too."

"You won't be sunning yourself on any beach. You'll be dead, along with the rest of the species."

"Oh, come, come, Mia, don't be so dire. I'm sure some bright young man will develop an antidote before the virus migrates to Southeast Asia. I'd say woman, but they can be so emotional—not sure one of 'em could handle that kind of pressure."

He finished binding her hands and started on her feet. The tape was so tight her hands and feet were numb.

"Too tight," she whispered, "Can't. Feel. Anything."

He rolled her over and stood looking down at her. "I would've thought you'd like that, Mia."

Hera and Zeus, who had been watching silently, burst into chatter.

"Like that, Mia."

"Like that, Mia."

"SHUT THE FUCK UP!"

"Shut up, shut up, shut up!"

"Shut up, shut up, shut up!"

It was the first time anything seemed to bother him. He lashed a hand out at Hera's cage and knocked it onto its side. She hit the side of the cage and fell silent.

Mia wondered if he'd killed the parrot. Just like he was going to kill her. He hadn't done it yet, but she had no doubt he would. The only question was when. Maybe he didn't want to do it in the house. Too much evidence.

Whether Zeus fell silent out of a sense of self-preservation or grief for his mate, Mia didn't know. He sat perched on his bar, his black eyes fixed on the intruder.

She suddenly had an almost overwhelming urge to laugh. Father Donelan had told Nick you couldn't avoid fate and she guessed it was true. After all she'd done to stay safe, here she was about to die under the watchful eye of none of other than Zeus himself. Tragedy at its best.

A life for a life.

Hers for her dead sister's.

What she'd always known she deserved. Her fate. Cosmic retribution at last.

A snicker escaped from her lips but she managed to quell it. But the dam had burst. Once it started, she couldn't stop. She collapsed into a fit of giggling.

His hand made contact with the side of her face. "Pull yourself together," he said. "I'm not in the mood to deal with a hysterical bitch."

Tears leaked out of the corners of her eyes. It was more shock than fear or sadness that was making them water. "Why just not kill me now and get it over with? Then you won't have to hear it."

"Luckily for you, I need you alive a little while longer." A slow smile lit his face. "Or maybe you're not so lucky after all. Depends on how you look at."

"What's that supposed to mean?"

He pulled her off the floor and shoved her back against the cupboards. "It means you're going to tell me where it's hidden. And then you're going to tell me what you found."

"I think you've vastly overestimated your powers of persuasion."

He had the knife in his hand before she realized he'd picked it up. With a swift motion, he slit a line across her collarbone. She felt the blood trickling onto the fabric at her neck. Irrationally, her first regret was that she'd ruined Nailini's dress.

"Where is it?"

"Where's what?"

"Whatever it was that is going to tell me where Mike was going all those months when he was spying on us. Don't lie to me, Mia. I know you found it. I saw you going through it that first night after you searched his place."

She stared at him through glassy eyes. "You watched me."

He pressed the tip of the knife against her skin. "Of course I've been watching you. I've been watching you for weeks, thinking eventually your buddy would get tired of you and leave you to yourself so I could get hold of whatever you found at Mike's condo. Not to mention that excuse for an agent with a God complex. He's been watching you too. Been watching everybody at the Institute ever since Mike turned up dead. Which has been a bit inconvenient."

"If Gallagher has a God complex, what does that make you?"

"I don't have any such pretensions. I'm a simple man at heart. A man who happens to love money more than he loves the human race. Not that it takes much. Human beings are pretty pathetic. Most animals are far better company."

Mia remembered finding her husky passed out across the floor. Some animal lover. "Is that why you didn't kill the dog when you searched my place? Because of your supposed love for animals?"

He stood across from her, breathing hard, with the knife in his hand. He was sweating so much Mia could smell it. She forced herself to breathe through her nose.

"It wasn't necessary," he said casually. "I only do what I need to."

He wanted her to think he was in control. But his own body was giving him away. He might not have a conscience but he was nervous.

Bloodsworth Island.

The name seared itself into her mind. What if her instinct had been right? What if Mike had picked a place where he could be sure nobody would find the evidence he'd been gathering against Caleb and the NWA? What better spot than an off-limits ex-military island.

No need to worry about deadly pathogens there. The entire place was a minefield of old explosives.

She sucked in her breath as a new thought struck her. What if Mike had stashed more there than evidence? What if he'd gotten hold of the virus somehow?

That would explain Caleb's desperation to get hold of what she'd taken from his condo. No virus, no NWA.

And no billion dollar payoff.

She wasn't sure what the idea did for her, but she felt she'd somehow gained an advantage over Caleb. He might be pressing a knife to her throat but he wouldn't kill her. Couldn't kill her. He hadn't been lying about that. All he was doing now was posturing.

"So selling a bunch of terrorists a virus that could wipe out the entire planet is something you need to do?" she asked. "In case you haven't realized it, a lot of animals are going to die too, when the NWA sets that virus loose on the population."

"The NWA wanted a product. I found a means to supply them with said product. If they choose to use it, that's their choice."

"That's like saying Victor Frankenstein wasn't responsible for the people his monster killed. Or that the scientists who invented the bomb bear no responsibility for Hiroshima."

"A lot of people don't think they do."

"I thought you didn't care what other people think."

"Oh, I don't. I most certainly don't."

Another thought struck her. *Us.* When he'd said Mike was spying he'd spoken as if there were others working with him. "Who really created the virus?"

He dragged the knife along the top of her neck, lightly enough so that the pain didn't even register. "Ah, now you're on the right track. You're finally setting aside all that pretty emotion and thinking."

"Chien." It wasn't really a question. She'd wanted to believe in his innocence, but had always known deep down that he was involved. *What would you do to save a child?* Nick's question came back to her, only now she had the answer.

"He was always the real brains at the Institute. The only one capable of this kind of work. I don't know what I would've done if his kid hadn't gotten cancer."

"Where is he?"

The slow smirk again.

"Did you kill Chien? And Mike, did you kill him too?"

"Now why would I do that?"

"Now why would I do that? Now why would I do that?"

Zeus. Apparently the fall hadn't damaged him too much. Hera, on the other hand, remained silent.

Caleb whirled toward the bird's fallen cage and kicked it. "Shut up!"

No answer.

Mia didn't blame the parrot. He was annoying, no doubt about it, but she'd much rather listen to Zeus than Caleb. At least all he did was repeat the stupid things other people said. Better that than to come up with original material the way Caleb did.

Her neck felt slick, warm. How deeply had he cut her? "You are evil personified. A monster. That's why you'd kill Chien."

He lowered his face to hers. His breath was warm against her skin. "Earlier you compared me to a mad scientist. Accuracy, Mia," he whispered, almost as if they were lovers. "Which is it—am I the madman or the monster?"

She turned her face away from him. "Both."

"But that still doesn't explain things to your satisfaction, I hope. After all, you must have some brains in that pretty little head of yours."

She hated him in a way she'd never hated anyone. She wanted to kill him. To get hold of the knife and thrust it in between his ribs. To see him bleed out until the life was completely drained away.

He touched her chin and forced her to face him. He glanced at her through hooded eyes. "This is around the time you tell me I'll never get away with it."

She felt nauseous, dizzy. "You'll never get away with it."

"Bravo!" he shouted. "If I weren't holding a knife to your neck I'd applaud."

"You don't have it. You can't destroy the world—or get your precious money—without it."

"By it I'm guessing it you mean the virus. No, I don't have it. But I will. Because you're going to help me find where your friend hid it after he stole it from me."

She looked straight at him. "I'd rather die than help you. Anyway, I'm sure you've got some of the virus stashed away somewhere. Up in Aniak maybe?"

He dragged the knife across her collarbone, making a new cut. "Too bad you're wrong about that. I only brought enough to Alaska to do another little demonstration—just enough to satisfy the NWA that this time the stuff would work a bit more thoroughly than it did a year ago. To carry more would have been stupid—too easy for the NWA to kill me and use one of their own to create a larger dose."

The blood on her skin felt warm. He'd gone deeper

this time, deep enough that she couldn't completely block out the pain. He wasn't going to kill her, but he was having fun scaring the hell out of her. "What makes you think that's not exactly what they're planning?"

"Oh, I'm sure they've thought of it. But once the exchange is made I'll be long gone. With a new identity. A new untraceable identity."

"Don't you feel any remorse at all? For the people in Siberia who died—or in Aniak?"

He stroked her chin with his free hand. "Not really. All in all it was quite satisfying, this time around. As a scientist, I can't take human suffering into account. It's the bigger picture that matters. The final, wonderful end to all my hard work."

It was almost unbearable to hear him talk. His ego was colossal. "Don't you mean Chien's hard work?"

"I have no problem taking credit. I was the one who first approached the NWA."

"You approached them?"

"Of course. In case you haven't noticed I'm a twenty-something nerd. Not exactly at the top of their most wanted list."

He was right. A terrorist organization like the NWA wouldn't want to waste time on a kid just out of grad school. But they would want one of the top scientists in the field. "You got them Chien."

"I got them Chien."

She ignored the blood dripping onto the floor. Her blood. "When's it going to happen?"

He pretended to pout. "Now I have a bit of a problem with our conversation. There needs to be a bit more give and take. You're the one asking all the questions and that just doesn't seem fair. So now it's my turn."

She stayed silent.

He pressed the knife against her throat at the jugular. So far he'd avoided her arteries, content to cut her in places that didn't put her life in any real danger. Clearly, he'd decided to change tactics.

"If you don't give me what I want, there won't be any reason to keep you alive. I believe I asked you about your dead friend's belongings."

"They're not here."

"Oh, I think they are."

"You're wrong."

"I've been very patient with you, Mia. Do you know how easy it would have been for me to kill you the other night? How tempting it was, standing inches away from you in that parking lot?"

"If you want to kill me, then do it. You already tried once, back in the lab. Though I've got to admit, you almost had me convinced it was Trask and not you who lied about that accident report. But it was you who cut the glove—wasn't it?"

"Of course I cut it, but believe it or not I wasn't trying to kill you. I needed you alive. But you're too smart for your own good. It was only a matter of time until you figured out the virus was airborne—and that it had been genetically engineered. I had to get you out of there before you saw too much."

"I don't remember you cutting me."

"I made the incision before you got there. To be honest, I never knew about the crack in the inner glove—you've got your own carelessness to blame for that. My only intention was to delay the autopsy before you got too deep into it and then lie about you making the tear yourself with the scissors. I was going to go to Trask and complain about your infamous shaky hands. Say I didn't think you were psychologically ready to be on BL-4 after Mike's death. If I could get you out of the unit for a while, I wouldn't need to worry about you screwing things up for me."

"But you tried to save me."

"I didn't want you dead, I just wanted you off the autopsy. I needed you alive—you were the only person who might be able to tell me where Mike had been working all those months. I figured he must've told you something relevant, even if you didn't realize what it meant. And we were on camera, remember?"

She shook her head. "Mike never told me anything."

"Seems your friend was planning on turning my little virus—and everything else he'd found over the past year—over to the authorities. But he made one mistake. He trusted the wrong man."

"Gallagher."

"Thought he was the real thing. CIA. Never suspected the guy'd been cut loose. Never suspected he was flying solo. Or that he was mad as a hatter."

She realized what must have happened that Sunday. "Mike arranged a meeting. To tell him what he knew. And give him the virus."

"You bet he did."

The thought of Mike dying for trying to do the right thing was hard to think about. Had Gallagher killed him? Or had Caleb done that too?

"What happened?" she asked dully. Suddenly she was so tired. So tired of it all.

"Mike wasn't the brightest bulb on the tree but I'll give him this: he figured it out. Better late than never, as they say. Wasn't gonna give his precious hard work to a crazy man who'd lied to him about being connected with the agency. So he tried to back out, lie his way out of it, until he could find somebody legit. Only our crazy man Gallagher wasn't having any of it. Needs a little anger management, that one."

"Did he kill Mike?" She had to force the words out. She wasn't sure how much longer she could go on listening to him. It was one thing to study monsters under a microscope, another to encounter one close up in real life.

Caleb, on the other, seemed to be getting more excited as their conversation went on. He loved talking about himself, loved playing the villain. As if it were all some kind of game. "Hell no. Gallagher needed him alive, if for no other reason than to draw out his pleasure. Torture can be quite sexual, you know."

She ignored his remarks and her tiredness. He was trying to get a reaction and she wasn't going to give him one. "So it was you."

He didn't reply.

"I don't get it. Why would you kill the one person who could give you what you wanted?"

For the first time since they'd been talking, Caleb looked unsettled. "I didn't. Funny thing is, the coroner was right. It wasn't murder. Gallagher beat him to a pulp but didn't come close to killing the guy. When I got to the boat, Mike was still alive and kicking—trust me on that one. The plan was to force him to tell me where the virus was and get him to take me there on the boat. But Mike had other ideas."

Mia tried to concentrate. Something wasn't right. She was so tired. "You really had no clue who he was, did you? Mike would never do that."

"Yeah, unfortunately you're right. Even offered him money, not that the bastard deserved it. But he wouldn't budge."

"So you killed him?" she finally managed to say. Her tongue felt thick, full of cotton.

He was watching her closely. "No. I didn't. I don't know how he did it, but he got free of the ropes. Ran on deck and jumped into the water before I could stop him. God knows how he thought he'd make it to shore but maybe that's not what he was going for. I tried to pull him back in, but he was already under the water when I reached him."

Mia turned over what he'd told her but she felt as if her mind were working in slow motion. Why was she so tired?

Focus, Mia.

She blinked several times. The room seemed brighter, a little blurred around the edges.

Focus.

Mike knew every knot known to mankind. And if he did get free, he would've tried to get off the boat. He'd been a champion swimmer back in college. Maybe he'd thought he could reach shore. Or maybe he'd wanted to die. To make sure Caleb would never learn where he'd hidden the virus. For the first time since Mike's death, she felt the urge to cry. All this time she'd doubted him. But he'd been a hero. Tears rolled down her cheeks and the room spun round. She felt drunk.

"Even if Mike hadn't died that night he never

would've told you where he'd hidden the information." Her words sounded far away. Not like her own.

His eyes darted from her face to her neck to her breasts and back again. "You might be right about that. But since he's dead we'll never know."

"IssssthatwhyyoukilledChien?" What was wrong with her voice?

"Now what did I tell you about proper abduction etiquette? Too many questions, Mia. Tsk, tsk. Now where is it?"

Suddenly the room was spinning, reeling. She was so tired. She didn't want to fight, she wanted to sleep. To sleep forever.

"Where is it?"

Her head fell to one side. The knife pressed harder, its blade cool. She was so tired.

"You want to sleep, sleep." He shoved her against the cupboards. "We're not in any rush. By the time your buddy and his friends figure out Gallagher's not the killer, we'll be long gone."

"He'll be here." Nick. Where was he? Some kind of stake-out?

"Sleep tight, Mia." Caleb touched his lips to her face. "Sweet dreams."

He released her and her body slid to the floor. Underneath her cheek, the linoleum was cool, slick. The sounds of him rifling through the cabinets reached her as if from a great distance. Every now and then, Zeus squawked and blurted out a phrase, but the parrot's outbursts didn't seem to faze Caleb anymore. He was too intent on finding the planner.

He'd drugged her. Even in her hazy state of mind, she could realize that. With what? She was too tired to think about it. Her eyes closed.

"Ah, here we are," he murmured several minutes later.

She opened her eyes. *Don't fall asleep.* At the other end of the kitchen,

Caleb stood rifling through the planner as the articles she'd tucked inside fluttered to the floor.

From the silence that followed, she guessed he hadn't found what he was looking for. He continued flipping pages for another few minutes, then strode back over to her and knelt, the planner dangling from one hand. "Feeling a little more talkative yet?"

The knife. He'd put something on the blade. "Youdruggedme."

"Only a little."

"Whatdidyougiveme?" Her words echoed strangely.

"Just something to make you a little more, er, compliant. And to loosen that tongue."

"Youdisgustme."

"What's in the book, Mia? Where was he going? Or did he tell you? He must have told you something, after all. You were his partner, his best friend, the love of his love, his confidant."

"Henevertoldmeanything."

"Bullshit."

"Nevertoldme." Her words were garbled but her will was still strong. She wasn't going to give in to him, no matter what he did to her. If Mike could die a hero, so could she. And Nick—Nick would come. He had to.

He pushed her away in disgust. "Do me a favor and shut up if you're going to keep repeating yourself, okay? You're worse than the goddamn parrots."

She was so tired. The floor was a different color than before. Red. The floor was red. Everything was red. Nick would come for her. No. Nick was somewhere else, she couldn't remember where. He couldn't come for her.

Wake up, Mia.

The voice wouldn't leave her alone. Why wouldn't it leave her alone? It was in her head now. Loud, too loud.

Wake up!

The voice of a child. A child yelling. Her sister's voice.

She opened her eyes. "Holly—"

No one there. The drug. It had to be the drug. What had he given her?

"Now that's touching." Caleb's eyes crinkled around the corners. "The dead sister appearing in the nick of time to save the day. After all those years!"

"Shut up!" The room came into focus. She looked down and saw the dress speckled with blood, the floor covered with blood.

He thrust the planner before her. "Tell me where he was going or I swear to God I'll finish this right now."

"You keep saying that," she murmured, "but you haven't kept your promise."

The gun. Get the gun!

She turned her head toward the counter and saw the gun perched on the edge. So far away. How could she reach it? Her hands were bound behind her. Could she knock it off somehow?

"No, you don't."

Caleb followed her gaze and walked over to the gun. He tucked it into his belt again and went back to the planner. A few seconds later he hurled it to the floor.

"Jesus Christ."

"Jesus Christ, Jesus Christ, Jesus Christ!"

"Shut up!"

The second cage hit the floor. Zeus flapped his wings but stayed quiet.

Mia watched him bend to retrieve the book from the floor. Her cell phone lay under the kitchen table, a foot or so away. Her cell phone with the pdf document of Bloodsworth Island.

He grabbed the book. Stopped. Looked.

"Well, well, well, what have we here?"

He reached under the table and picked up the cell phone. She hadn't logged out. Her automatic lock timer was set for thirty minutes. It hadn't been thirty minutes.

He straightened and held out the phone before him, a smile curling his lips. "Let's see what we find." He clicked on the power button. "Hmmm….."

"Theresnothingthere."

"Bloodsworth Island," he said, staring down at the screen. "Former weapons testing facility. Off limits for safety reasons. Sounds lovely. I think I'd like to make a visit, what do you think? Weather's clearing up, should be a nice little boat ride. Care to join?"

"Go to hell."

"That's exactly what we're going to do." He tucked the phone into his windbreaker and smiled down at her. "What we're all going to do."

"Go to hell! Go to hell! Go to hell!

This time Caleb didn't bother with the bird. Or maybe this time he didn't mind hearing what Zeus had to say.

Chapter 17

It took Nick a minute to realize he was still alive.

The explosives hadn't gone off. He'd tackled Liam in time to prevent him from pulling the detonator. Gallagher lay across him, his face slack and his body a dead weight.

Using all his strength, Nick heaved the ex-agent off him and opened the vest then knelt to feel for a pulse.

There was one. It was thready but if they were lucky he'd pull through and give them the information they needed. He stared down at the rigged vest.

He decided to leave it alone. Gallagher didn't seem cognizant enough to pull the detonator and Nick didn't want to accidentally set the thing off when he removed it.

He didn't feel great about the decision, but the alternative seemed worse.

Blood seeped from a wound in Gallagher's thigh. Whoever had shot him had pierced an artery. Nick glanced around for something to stop the flow.

Gallagher's gun lay at his side. Nick kicked it away. No way he'd be using it but at least he could eliminate that possibility fairly easily.

"Stay back, everybody!" a voice yelled. "We need him alive."

Not Dalton's.

It should have been Dalton's.

Nick looked around the cabin but couldn't see his friend. There was too much movement, too many people between him and the place Ross had been. He knew Gallagher had discharged his weapon but thought the shot had gone wild.

"Dalton!"

No answer.

"Where's Ross?" he shouted but nobody paid attention.

He glanced down at Gallagher again. The top half of his pants leg was soaked through.

He ripped a strip from his shirt and used it to make a tourniquet. He used another to stanch the blood flow. Within seconds, the strip turned crimson. "Somebody call for a helicopter. We need to get him out of here."

No answer.

"This man needs help! Somebody needs to call the paramedics!"

Nick ripped another strip from his shirt and pressed it over the first strip. Maybe he hadn't made the tourniquet tight enough. He reached down to retie the knot.

Gallagher's eyelids flickered open. "Don't waste your time."

"Shut up, Liam."

"I'm a dead man and you know it."

"The paramedics are on their way. You just have to hold on till they get here."

"I don't want to hold on."

"That's too damn bad. We need you, Liam. We need to know what you know."

"I just want it to be over."

"Yeah, well, that's not gonna happen."

"Please—"

Nick stared down at Gallagher. He understood. And part of him wished he could give Liam the peace he wanted so badly. But he couldn't.

"I can't let you go," Nick said brusquely. "I'm sorry. We need to know what you know."

"It's all there."

"All where?"

"There," he said, his forehead bathed in sweat. "Home."

The color had drained out of Gallagher's face. His green eyes were glazing over, taking on an unearthly sheen. "Stay with me, buddy."

"Forgive me."

Behind him, men were running in and out of the room. Someone groaned. Overhead, he heard helicopters mixed in with the sound of the rain. They must have already called. Or maybe they'd been waiting.

"There's nothing to forgive," Nick said. "You made a mistake."

He wasn't sure if he believed it or not. Gallagher had killed and tortured innocent people. But he'd done it out of love for his country. To save his country, when nobody else had been paying much attention. He'd crossed a line but Nick couldn't find it in his heart to blame him, not while he lay dying before him.

He'd seen Brendon Thompson's body, just like Liam had. He knew what those kinds of images could do to the mind. And the heart. What if he'd been Thompson's best friend instead of Liam? He couldn't be sure what he would have done, how he might have turned out.

And Gallagher hadn't figured out how to torture suspects on his own. He'd had help. From both sides.

If Gallagher was to blame, then so were others. On both sides.

"Don't let it happen." Gallagher's breath came in shallow bursts. "Find them."

"Find who, buddy? Chien Lu?"

"Both of them."

"Who else, Liam? Tell me who else."

"Don't. Know." Gallagher's whole lower body was covered in blood. So was Nick's. "Don't. Let. It. Happen.

"Let what happen?"

"Armageddon."

Gallagher's eyes stared at something Nick couldn't see. He could feel Liam slipping away even as he held him.

"I won't."

Gallagher lay still.

He was gone.

Nick closed Liam's eyes. "I won't."

He lay the body down on the floor next to him. A shimmer of metal caught his eye. Gallagher's dog tags, worn around his neck. He lifted the tags off the body and held them in his palm.

Gallagher
Liam
034-52-8721
A positive
Catholic

~*~

Thompson
Brendon

062-33-9922
Rh positive
No preference

Brothers to the last, in death and life.

Let the dead bury the dead.

Nick got up. Several agents stood toward the back of the room, blocking the doorway. Nick pushed through until he stood before a man laid out on the floor.

"Oh, Jesus, oh, no."

Dalton opened his eyes and tried to grin. "Now that's sweet."

"Shut up," Nick said. "You okay?"

"Aside from the blood gushing out of my shoulder, I'm fine."

Nick turned to one of the agents beside him. He looked familiar but he couldn't put a name to the face. "What happened?"

"Shoulder wound," the agent said, stating the obvious. "Bullet went straight through. Better that way. In and out."

"He'll be all right," another said. "Tough bastard."

Dalton called up to him from where he lay. "Gallagher?"

"Dead," Nick said.

Dalton swore. "I didn't want that."

Had Dalton been the one to kill him? Or had it been someone else? For that matter, who shot first? Gallagher? Dalton? Another agent? Nick fought the impulse to ask questions. Dalton didn't need to deal with that now. And in the end it didn't matter.

"Serves him right," the agent next to Nick said.

"Crazy bastard," the other agreed.

Nick realized he was still holding Gallagher and Thompson's dog tags. He shoved them into his pocket. "No crazier than the rest of us."

"Speak for yourself."

"Clear the way," somebody shouted. "Paramedics are here."

Several men carrying a stretcher appeared in the doorway. The agents cleared a path for them as they moved toward the spot where Dalton lay. A dark stain radiated from his right shoulder but other than that, he looked unharmed.

Gallagher probably hadn't been shooting to kill. Nick tried to call up a memory of what had happened but it was already a blur.

One of the paramedics glanced over at Gallagher but Nick motioned him away. They could come back for the body later. Better to focus on getting Dalton out of there.

After several minutes, they strapped Dalton to the stretcher and backed out. "Is this really necessary?" he asked as they were wheeling him out. "I've got a case I need to close."

Nick laughed. Only Ross could want to keep working after being shot. No, not only Ross. Any of them would have said the same thing. Even Gallagher. All of them had the same desire, the same passion. To bring down the enemy.

Only that hadn't happened. Not yet.

He remembered his promise to Gallagher. Where was Chien Lu? Gallagher hadn't known. And he'd said there was more than one person at the Institute. Who else? That asshole Trask? Mia's partner? Someone else? Gallagher hadn't mentioned a timetable. If there was a super virus, had it already changed hands? Or was the exchange slated to happen sometime down the road?

He sure as hell hoped it hadn't happened. But he couldn't be certain. He needed to figure out what Gallagher had meant when he said the information he'd found was at home. Surely he hadn't meant the cabin. His hometown, the house where he grew up? It was worth checking into. Where else?

His mind ran through the possibilities. He'd need to make a list, start going through it one by one. He just hoped there was time for that.

Home.

Mia.

Funny how the two words went together. He hardly knew her and yet, when he was with her, he felt that way—as if he'd come home. He grabbed his cell and scanned it for messages.

Nothing.

He pulled up Mia's number and hit send. The call wouldn't go through. He glanced at the top of his phone and saw a single bar. No reception.

Well, at least that might explain why he hadn't heard from her.

He should've expected it. God only knew how far the nearest cell phone tower was. As soon as he got back onto the main road, he'd call her. And she'd probably sent him a text. He'd promised to let her know what was going on, and she wasn't the type to wait around.

She wasn't the type to wait around.

The statement niggled at his brain.

No. Mia hadn't been all that happy about letting

313

him go after Gallagher without her, but she wouldn't do anything foolish. She'd told him she would go home and stay there, and he believed her.

Anyway, he'd be back at her place within a couple of hours. There was nothing more for him to do here. Gallagher was dead. The other agents would spend the next several hours going over the cabin inch by inch. Even if they did find something, Nick's presence wasn't going to make much difference. He was going to catch hell for being there in the first place.

And he had his own line of inquiry to pursue. But first he needed to talk to Mia. Needed to be sure she was okay. He glanced again at the single bar, as if by staring at it he could force it to change.

No such luck.

He shoved the phone into his pocket and walked over to the cabin door. Several agents carrying equipment pushed past him as he stepped onto the porch and watched as the paramedics lifted Dalton into the helicopter. They climbed in after him, and the chopper rose into the sky until it disappeared beyond the clouds. It was still raining steadily, but the worst of the storm was over.

So why did he get the feeling it was only just starting?

****

Waves slapped at the sides of the powerboat, sloshing over the edges and pushing the boat off course. Mia gripped the sides and prayed that the next wave wouldn't be the one to capsize them.

Maybe somebody would see them. Maybe the guy who'd rented them the boat would think better of it and call the harbor master. He hadn't bothered to hide his shock when Caleb told him he wanted to rent the runabout. He'd even tried his best to talk them out of it.

Maybe the Coast Guard would come to their rescue.

Not likely. The way her luck had been going, she'd have to rely on her own wits. Which weren't in great shape at the moment. Whatever Caleb had given her was wearing off, though not fast enough to make her much of a threat. And on top of it all, she was seasick. Her head ached and her entire body was sore, as if she'd gone out drinking earlier. Or at least that's how she thought she'd feel—if she ever had gone out drinking.

Why hadn't she ever done that? Happy hour with friends, a night out with a boyfriend, even a glass of wine sipped on her back porch after a long day—she'd never even tried any of it. Never had children. Never gotten married. Never fallen in love.

At least she might have had a shot at that last one—if she weren't on her way to a deserted island with a madman who intended on killing her. She wished she'd had some way to leave a sign for Nick. Something to tell him how she felt about him, to say what she'd told him with her body but never said aloud.

Nick would probably dismiss their one night together as a fling. Pure sex, with no emotional ties. He'd said he thought of her as an ice queen at first. That he'd realized his mistake after they made love. But he'd been talking about passion, not love.

She didn't love him. She barely knew him, after all. But what she felt for him was more than lust—much more. She'd opened up to him in a way she hadn't opened up to anyone. Ever. But she'd never get the chance to find out where things between them might lead. Or even to tell him how much he'd helped her.

She had to tell him. She couldn't die without doing that.

Think.

Caleb had her cell in his pocket. She needed to get hold of it somehow.

Not possible. For one thing, there was no reception. For another, he'd easily fend her off. She was still weak from the drug he'd given her and her sense of balance was off. And he was far stronger than she was.

Then there was the fact that he had a gun.

And that she was still bound hand and foot.

She could push him out of the boat. If the sea got rough enough. He might lose his balance and she could lunge at him.

Yeah, right.

Even if by some miracle she did manage to knock him out of the boat, she wouldn't be able to save herself. The boat would drift until the waves tipped it on its side and she'd drown.

She'd have to wait until they got to the island. Though her prospects didn't seem much better. She'd still be bound and he'd still have his gun.

"Trying to think of a way out?" he called back over his shoulder. "Or are you saying a few last minute prayers. You know what they say, there are no atheists in foxholes. I guess the same thing's true for boats."

He was shouting but the wind made it almost impossible to hear him. "Are you saying we're going to die?" she shouted back.

"Only you."

"Well, I won't miss the company."

"I see you're feeling better."

"A little too much better," she called out. "I prefer you a bit blurry around the edges."

"That can be arranged." He turned back toward the horizon.

Up ahead, an island loomed up before them and faded away in the fog. Mia wondered if it was Bloodsworth or another island, one of the dozens not far from their destination. From what she could remember, Bloodsworth was set apart from the others, several miles beyond it to the east.

Bloodsworth was the ideal place for a virus but she wondered why he hadn't simply destroyed whatever samples he'd stolen from Caleb and Chien. It seemed risky not to, even if he did store the virus on a deserted testing site.

Maybe he'd planned to destroy it. Only he never got the chance. On the other hand, if Caleb and Chien lived there was no reason they couldn't create more samples.

Or maybe he'd planned to take Gallagher there. That was why he'd insisted on meeting on the boat. When he realized Gallagher had been cut loose, he must have realized he couldn't let the ex-agent anywhere near Bloodsworth Island.

And he'd paid for that change of heart with his life.

What would have happened if Mike had trusted the ex-agent? Would Gallagher have done the right thing and turned the evidence over to the authorities? Or would he have tried to go on playing the hero—the rogue agent who would wipe out the NWA single-handedly and destroy anybody who worked with them?

Something told her the second option was the one

he would have gone for. The only problem was it was hard to take on a group like the NWA. They'd become too powerful, with too many members in too many countries. Eliminating them was the equivalent of wiping out a virus that had spread all through the body. A lethal entity somehow independent of the individuals that comprised it. A kind of no man's land where concepts like conscience and compassion didn't carry any weight. And it was growing stronger every day.

Only in this case the body it would ultimately destroy didn't belong to an individual or even a specific country. The planet itself would die.

It seemed beyond belief that the NWA would unleash a virus without first having an antidote. But then again, the NWA's actions had always been beyond belief. They defied logic, defied every definition of goodness.

Caleb slowed the engine and steered toward the cove that appeared before them out of the fog. With its sparse shrubbery and deserted beach, Bloodsworth Island looked as bleak as the name suggested. A perfect setting for bomb testing.

How many bombs lay just below the surface, ready to explode? She prayed they wouldn't venture beyond the beach. What were they even looking for? A shelter of some sort, most likely. Some place Mike could store a lethal virus and be sure no one would find it.

Nobody was going to find it there, not by accident, that much was certain. Nobody in their right mind would set foot on the place, not even the military.

Caleb cut the engine as they reached shallow waters. The beach faded away again, lost in the ghostly whiteness. Everything seemed dream-like, unreal, as if the whole place were nothing more than a mirage.

More like a nightmare, Mia amended. She shivered at the thought of the unexploded bombs scattered across the island's interior. Neither of them knew the layout of the island or even which direction to head in to find Mike's hiding spot.

Maybe he'd leave her in the boat. At least on the beach she'd have a chance of being rescued.

As if in answer to her question, Caleb made his way toward her and cut her free. He ripped off the tape and tossed it onto the floor of the boat. "Get up," he said sharply. "You're going to need to pull the boat the rest of the way."

She tried to ignore the way her skin stung. "Pull it yourself."

"Would you rather I tied you back up?" He pulled the gun out of his jacket and jerked the barrel toward the water. "Move. And if you try anything—anything at all—I shoot you in the back of the head."

Her feet and hands tingled as the blood flowed back into them. She stumbled against the side of the boat as she tried to walk. She was free, that's all that mattered. She had the use of her arms and legs again. She could run. Hide. Get the gun. Something. Anything.

She gripped the sides of the boat and hoisted her body over the edge. The shock of the water and the sting of the salt on her wounds chased away the rest of the drowsiness she'd felt on the trip over. Slowly, she fought her way toward the prow and grabbed onto the tip, pulling it into shore.

When she'd gotten the boat onto the beach, she collapsed on the sand and lay motionless. Her breath came in gasps and the fog closed in around her, filling her lungs with moisture.

Caleb climbed out of the boat and stood over her. "Get up."

She pushed up on her elbows and looked around. At the edge of the beach, a border of pines floated out of the fog. Their dark forms twisted toward them, stunted branches reaching out to the water, as if they too wanted to escape.

She got up. "Where are we going?"

He clamped his hand around her upper arm and shoved her in front of him. Before she could wrench her arm free, he'd bound her wrists with duct tape again. "To explore the island."

Her heart sank. "This place is full of unexploded bombs," she said over her shoulder. "One wrong step and we're dead. You know that, right?"

He prodded her with the tip of his gun. "That's why you're going first."

Chapter 18

Nick stared at the note on the table and swore. No wonder Mia hadn't texted. She'd known he wouldn't be happy to learn she'd done the very thing he'd warned her not to do. Not that he could blame her. After all, she was only going to her friend's house to feed the parrots with the weird names.

Nothing dangerous about that.

So why hadn't she responded to his calls or come back to the house?

It didn't take four hours to feed a couple of birds.

Something had gone wrong. He didn't need one of Laura's dreams to tell him that.

Nailini. Mia had written out her friend's first name but he had no idea what her last name was. She hadn't mentioned it, or if she had he didn't remember.

Nailini was a vet, that much he did remember. She'd been the one to foist the husky off on Mia. He tried to remember the name of the clinic and came up blank. Somewhere local. Not the place Dante was at. Someplace else.

He hit voice record and spoke Nailini's name into his iPhone, then added veterinarian and Maryland. "Don't hold out on me, Siri."

The familiar female voice told him to "hang on."

He hung on, reluctantly.

"Hurry up, Siri."

"Okay, here's what I found," the voice said. "Nailini Krishnan, veterinarian, Keep 'Em Healthy Animal Clinic, 3221 Plainsville Road, Rockville, Maryland."

Krishnan. "What is Nailini Krishnan's home address?"

"Checking on that."

Seconds later, Siri rattled off an address in Rockville, not far from where the clinic was located. Nick was out the door and down the steps before she'd finished speaking.

Maybe he was jumping to conclusions. Maybe Mia was just hanging out there, watching Netflix on her friend's couch.

But he didn't think so.

Nailini Krishnan's home stood at the end of the longest driveway in the world. Or at least the entire state of Maryland. The old colonial looked far too large for one person, but based on the woman's occupation, Nick guessed she'd had her share of house guests of the furry and feathered variety.

The place was shrouded in darkness. No lights shone in the house, though Mia's car stood in the driveway. Up above, the sky had cleared and a few stars shone through the breaks in the clouds.

He cut the engine and got out of the car, gun in hand. For the second time that day he wondered if he'd need to use it. The place was quiet, too quiet, but that didn't mean it was empty.

He made his way along the porch and tried the door.

It was unlocked.

He pushed open the door and stepped inside.

"Shut up, shut up, shut up!"

The parrot's voice cut through the silence and Nick jumped. "Jesus," he said. "You scared the hell out of me!"

"You scared the hell out of me! You scared the hell out of me! You scared the—"

He hit the light switch next to the door and took in the disarray. Broken crockery lay across the floor and most of the cupboards stood open. The parrots' cages lay sideways across the linoleum, bird seeds trailing out of the gaps between the bars.

It didn't take much to figure out what had happened.

Wherever Mia was, she wasn't there. Whoever had trashed the place had taken her with him.

Nick stepped around the broken dishes and righted the two cages. One of the birds lay motionless but the other seemed unharmed, aside from a few lost feathers.

"What the hell happened, Hera?" he asked aloud, half expecting the bird to answer him. "Or are you Zeus?"

"What the hell happened, Hera, what the hell happened, Hera!"

"Well, you're no help at all." Nick wasn't sure what type of parrots they were, but he seemed to remember that they could only mimic what others said. They didn't understand any of it, and their conversations were only replays of things they'd heard before. In the same way some birds picked up shiny objects, parrots gathered words and phrases.

"No help at all," the parrot replied.

Nick pushed past the birds and made his way toward the counter. He wasn't sure what he was looking for. He studied the chaos for a sign she might have left him and found none.

At the far end of the kitchen, a dark smear of crimson stained the floor. Nick walked to the spot and knelt.

Too much blood.

Was it Mia's? His jaw tightened. What had happened here? Who had hurt her and why?

Whoever had been inside Mia's place before Gallagher got there.

The person Mike had been investigating.

The one who'd deliberately cut her glove.

One person. Somebody who wanted her dead.

Somebody at the Institute. Had to be.

Not Chien. He'd already gone missing when the accident and the break-in happened. Even if he was involved somehow, he wasn't the person who had Mia now.

Her boss? Maybe.

Her new partner? What was the guy's name? Caleb? Also a possibility.

Anyway, he wasn't sure any of it mattered at the moment. It wasn't going to help him find Mia.

Where had the killer taken her? Why trash the kitchen?

He'd been looking for something.

The planner? The articles? Whatever he thought Mia had found the night she searched Mike's condo.

Mia must have hidden them at Nailini's. It would make sense. She wouldn't risk keeping it at her house or the lab. But Nailini's place would be perfect. No one knew she was watching the place, as far as he knew. No one would have any reason to go there.

Unless they were following her.

So the killer had followed her. If the blood was any indication, she hadn't volunteered much information. But he'd found what he wanted. Otherwise they'd still be there.

He'd looked through that planner. And read the articles. More than once. What had he missed? What had Mia missed?

"If you want to kill me, then do it!"

Nick turned back toward the bird. Its eyes fixed on his. Zeus. It had to be, Father of the gods, overseer of mortal fates. Father Donelan's words about following his destiny came back to him. "Where did they go, Zeus?"

"If you want to kill me, then do it. If you want to kill—"

He walked back to the bird and stood before its cage. "Where did they go?"

"Monster, monster, monster, monster!"

"Where did they go?"

"Shut up, shut up, shut up, shut up!"

Nick ran an agitated hand through his hair. He wanted to take hold of the damn bird's cage and shake it until he got what he needed. He was losing his damn mind. Using his foot to kick the broken shards out of the way, he crossed to the table and fell back into one of the chairs.

Zeus lifted his wings and rose off the bar before settling back onto it. "If you want to kill me then do it! If you want to kill me then do it! If you—"

"You have no idea, how much I'd like to take you up on that offer."

"Gimme kiss, gimme kiss, gimme kiss!"

In spite of everything, he laughed. "Not on your life."

"Bloodsworth Island."

Nick stopped laughing. "What did you say?"

The bird blinked. Its beady black eyes fixed on him.

He didn't move.

"Bloodsworth Island."

Didn't speak.

"Bloodsworth Island, Bloodsworth Island, Bloodsworth Island."

"You know what, Zeus. I take it back. I could kiss you."

"Gimme kiss, gimme kiss, gimme kiss."

"Sorry, but you're gonna have to take a rain check on that."

He reached for his cell and typed in the name. Bloodsworth Island. Twenty-five square miles, located in the Chesapeake Bay. Off limits to the public. Not all that far from the marina where Mike Chandler kept his sailboat.

Why would the killer take Mia to Bloodsworth Island?

Had Chandler left something there? Evidence? Something—something important enough and dangerous enough for Chandler to risk leaving it there.

He looked up at the parrot.

"You'd better know what you're talking about."

"Know what you're talking about."

"That's not reassuring."

"Not reassuring."

He pulled up Dalton's number and hit send. Should he even be calling him? Whether his friend would answer—whether he was even awake—was another question altogether.

"Ross." The voice on the other end of the line sounded groggy. Heavily medicated.

"I need you to do something for me."

"You do realize I was shot maybe three hours ago."

"All you have to do is make a call."

"...that I'm in the hospital."

"One call."

Nick heard murmuring but couldn't make out what was being said.

"Tell me what you need." He'd expected Dalton's voice but it was Laura on the line.

"Hi, Laura."

"Hi yourself."

"How is he?"

"He'll live. Now tell me why you're calling."

Funny, that Dalton was the FBI agent and it was Laura who was the tougher of the two of them. Not that Ross wasn't tough. But Laura was tough in a different way. She was a survivor and had the strength that came from enduring true pain. She also happened to be psychic, not that he believed in any of that stuff.

"I need Dalton to call his boss-our bosses-and send his team to Bloodsworth Island by helicopter. I also need to be a part of that team. And I need it to happen now."

There was a pause on the other end of the line.

"Can you tell me why?

"A parrot told me."

Another pause.

"Nick?"

He sighed. He knew what was coming. "Yeah?"

"Can I ask you a question without you getting mad at me?"

"No, Laura, I haven't been drinking."

"Are you sure?" she asked. "Because that's definitely the strangest thing you've ever said to me."

"No, I haven't been drinking and yes, I really do need a team sent out to Bloodsworth. And yes, I'm basing my decision on a parrot."

Pause.

"Okay."

"If I'm remembering correctly, I believe you based at least one pretty big decision on a dream."

"Touché."

"I need you to trust me on this, Laura. No way will they send a team if I ask, even if I've been at the agency fifteen years. Especially if I can't give them a reason."

"Yeah, I wouldn't mention the parrot."

"Thanks for the advice."

"Can I count on you? Will you do this for me?"

Another pause.

"Okay. I'll try. That's all I can promise. Dalton's in charge of his team but I don't know if his superiors are going to listen to him, not in his current state of mind."

"But you'll give it a shot?"

"Yes."

"Dalton said you had one of your dreams. About me."

"I'll tell you about it later, okay? Right now I've got to get him focused enough to make a call to his boss."

"Thanks, Laura."

"No problem," she said. "And Nick—"

"I know. Be careful."

"That's not what I was going to say. Though of course I do want to you to be careful. But there's something you should know."

"What?"

"Dalton got a call right before you called. The police down in Hampstead found a body that matches the description of Chien. Shot through the head, execution style. No ID on him but based on the photos, they're pretty confident it's a match."

"Did they run the prints?"

"They couldn't."

"Why not?"

"The hands were, uh, missing."

"What the hell was he doing in Hampstead?"

"That's the funny thing. No ID or cell in the car, like I said. Car was a rental so nothing came up with the registration."

"Don't tell me a guy named Brendon Thompson rented it?

"Nope. They haven't traced a name yet. But here's the funny thing—"

He waited.

"When they pulled up the GPS history on the car, the directions that came up were to the CDC."

"Chien was driving to the CDC?"

"Apparently."

"Did they find anything else?"

"No. That was it."

"Okay, thanks, Laura. I'll be in touch. Give my love to the husband."

In the background, Nick heard loud protestations. Dalton wanted to know what was happening. Well, he'd find out soon enough. There were few people on the planet he trusted more than he trusted Laura Drake.

He hung up the phone and stood up. So Chien had been on his way to the CDC. It looked as if the scientist had a change of heart. Had he planned to tell the authorities there what he knew about the virus up in Aniak? Was that why he'd been killed? And who'd gotten to him—the man who had Mia or the NWA?

"Sorry to leave you in such a mess," he said to Zeus. "But I've got to fulfill my fate."

"Fulfill your fate, fulfill your fate, fulfill your fate."

He intended to. He just hoped the gods were really on his side. Because he was going to need all the help he could get.

****

They'd been walking an hour, maybe more. Caleb's headlamp flashlight lit the path before them, but not by much. Nailini's borrowed dress clung to Mia's body, soaked through with seawater, sweat and blood. The rain had stopped but the fog still hung over them, keeping visibility low. She couldn't see much beyond the arc of the flashlight, though it was so dark the fog didn't make much difference. She wasn't sure if she wanted to find the place or not.

She knew she couldn't keep going much longer.

She also knew nobody was coming to rescue her.

Too much time had passed. Nobody realized she was gone, nobody knew where they were. Even if Nick saw her note and went to Nailini's place, there was no way for him to find out where she was. Caleb hadn't given her the chance to leave anything behind to lead him to her.

"Hurry up," Caleb said from behind her. "We'll be out here all night at this rate."

She stumbled forward and fell onto the ground.

Waited.

Nothing exploded.

Another reprieve.

How many times had she fallen since they'd left the beach? Five times? Six? She'd lost count. All she wanted to do was stop.

That was what she wanted now. For everything to stop.

"Get up!" Caleb's gun slammed up against her back. She lay in the glare of his headlamp and closed her eyes. She didn't want to move.

"I said get up!"

He reached down and yanked her hair back. Her head jerked up from the ground, a few pine needles stuck to her face. He didn't stop pulling until she was bent so far back she thought her spine would snap.

"Let go of me," she whispered. The skin around her neck hurt where he'd cut her. Her arms hurt from being pulled behind her back. Her face hurt where he'd hit her. Everything hurt.

"Then get up off your knees and keep going. I'm surprised you haven't gotten both of us killed by now. I probably would be better off on my own."

"By all means, don't let me hold you up." She laughed brokenly when she got up and stumbled forward. "It's not like you have the faintest idea where you're going."

"Shut up."

"We could be out here for hours."

"Shut up or that will be the last thing you say."

She snickered. The side of the gun connected with the back of her head. She stumbled forward. Fell again.

Darkness surrounded her this time. He stood behind her, gazing into the woods. The ground beneath her was damp, cold.

"Get off the ground!"

She tried to use her shoulder to get up onto her knees, but she didn't have the strength to do it. Tears stung her eyes from the impact of the blow.

Run!

The voice again. Her sister's voice.

An auditory hallucination. It had to be. She'd learned about them in psychology classes. A common side effect of intense stress and psychotropic drugs.

Caleb walked over to her and pulled her to her feet again. The beam from his headlamp swung crazily from tree to tree. "Go."

She started walking, more slowly this time, so she wouldn't fall.

Run!

Another step. A few more. They were descending again, the path before them winding down toward another cove. She wondered vaguely how big the island was. She couldn't remember what the document she'd downloaded onto her phone had said, but she knew it was fairly large. What would happen if they didn't find shelter soon? Would they camp for the night? Go back?

No way they were going back.

How far was the boat?

Three miles away? Four?

They'd stayed on the path the entire time. It veered off at multiple points, but Mia had been paying close attention. She was sure she could find her way back to the boat on her own. She was sure he'd left the key in the ignition.

Careless. Or just overconfident. As usual.

Which was a lucky thing for her.

A few more steps.

A few more.

She tripped over a tree root, managed not to fall. Held her breath and waited for a blow that didn't come. Below her, she could hear the ocean even though the fog hid it from view. The waves crashed to shore, echoing across the silence. No birds, no animals lived on the island. Aside from the scattered pines and shrubs, the place was barren. If she could break free, the sound of the waves would muffle her footsteps and the fog would hide her from view. All she had to do was find the strength to sprint away from him.

Run!

A few more steps.

Run!

A few more.

Run!

Her heart was hammering in her chest when she jumped off the path and started running through the brush. Now that she was off the path, the terrain was even worse than it had been. Tree roots jutted up and threatened to send her flying headlong into the dirt again. Branches clawed at her face as she stumbled through the darkness.

"Mia!" He was after her in seconds. She could hear him behind her, thrashing through the brush

Don't look back!

He was gaining on her. She was panting hard, fighting her exhaustion, ignoring the pain. Gravity was in her favor. If she could make it to the bottom of the cove she could hide out of sight and make her way back to the boat. The surf would be too loud for him to detect her. Another twenty yards and she'd be at the border where the beach met the pines.

Ten yards.

Eight.

Behind her all was dark. No beam of light, no sign of him. She couldn't hear him either but didn't dare look back.

Had she lost him?

No. He was still behind her. She could hear the rustle of the pine needles as he forced his way through the brush. A stray beam of light flashed to her right.

She stumbled forward, frantic to put more distance between them. The branches tore at her dress, scratched her arms.

Six yards.

If she ran out onto the beach, he'd see her. She couldn't turn back. All she could do was skirt the edge of the trees until she found a hiding place. Hopefully he'd go in the opposite direction but if he didn't she just needed to keep out of sight.

A tree root thrust itself up before her, almost as if it had a will of its own. Her feet flew out from under her and she sailed through the air. When she landed, something inside her snapped and she cried out. A rib, she realized dazedly. She'd broken her rib. Or maybe more than one.

He was on her in seconds, his body heavy against her back, the gun pressed to her temple, the beam of light falling around her head. "Not a good idea, Mia."

Her ribs ached too much for her to talk. The weight of his body was excruciating but she refused to give him the satisfaction of hearing her scream.

"Holy shit." He rose while she lay coughing on the ground, her body shaking from the pain and the cold. "Well, looks like you did us both a favor, after all. Nice work, Mia."

He jerked her to her feet. An abandoned cinderblock structure stood before them. Squat and small, but large enough to hold several men. Or enough of virus X to end the world.

"Come on," Caleb said, grabbing hold of her arm and dragging her toward the building. "I've got a feeling you found what we're looking for."

It was pitch black inside. Caleb pushed her onto the floor and turned in a slow circle. "Ah, here we go." He walked over to a corner of the room behind Mia and knelt before what she guessed was a generator.

He picked up one of the gas cans lined up next to the machine and poured it into the opening on the side. A few seconds later the hum of a motor broke the silence. Suspended rows of fluorescent lights blinked on, bathing the interior of the building in a cool, almost unearthly glare.

The first thing she noticed was the bulletin boards. There were four in all, lined up side by side across one of the walls. Each of them covered with photos, maps, news articles. There were dozens of photos, most of them taken from news articles, pinned to the maps with colored tacks. A few of the pictures were actual photos. She recognized the Institute and several were of Chien and Caleb. There were a few of other faces she didn't recognize. NWA operatives perhaps. Or other scientists they'd worked with.

A chalkboard hung on the opposite wall, nearly filling it. She recognized Mike's handwriting immediately. There were dozens of equations, DNA sequences, diagrams of cells. She squinted at the board in hopes of making sense of it but what he'd written was beyond anything she'd done. It would take weeks to understand it, months even.

Toward the end of the room, lab tables filled with equipment gleamed in eerie light. Vials and microscopes, books left half open, uniforms that looked a lot like the ones they used at the Institute.

Clearly, Mike had been stealing equipment from the Institute. Because there was no way anybody would authorize him to use it, not outside of Somersville. He'd made the abandoned building into a makeshift lab and located it in a place that nobody would dare visit. It was, she realized, the only place besides the Institute that he would have felt safe doing those kind of experiments.

He hadn't just been investigating Caleb and Chien. He must have been trying to create an antidote—or possibly a vaccine. Something to counteract the evil the NWA planned to unleash on the world. Destroying the virus wouldn't be enough, Mia realized. Mike couldn't be sure there weren't other vials out there, couldn't be sure the "demonstrations" in Siberia and Aniak had been completely contained.

Caleb turned his back to her and studied the maps and photographs. She inched toward the wall and propped her body up against the cement. Her rib cage throbbed and she groaned aloud. Even breathing hurt.

She half expected him to stop what he was doing but he seemed to have forgotten her. He leaned forward and ripped one of the photos off one of the bulletin boards. Whirling around to face her, he held it up and mimicked the startled expression in the photo. From the blue background in the photo, Mia guessed that Mike must have taken the shot when the Caleb was on the boat.

"What do you think?" he asked. "Do you see a resemblance?"

"I see two assholes," she said through gritted teeth. "Is that what you mean?"

He pinned the photo back into place. "You know, Mia, I'm glad we've had this time together. I never realized you had such a wonderful sense of humor."

"I'll never forget it."

"Oh, I think you will." His lips curved into a half smile.

She said nothing.

He returned his gaze to the photo. "Funny thing is, I remember exactly when he took this. It was the first time I really began to suspect him. I mean, sure, I thought it was pretty weird already—that somebody like Mike Chandler III would want to spend time with me. The golden boy with his money and his sailboat and his Ivy League pedigree. And so honorable too, the kind of boy who actually believes in the Harvard Code of Conduct and all that bullshit. I suppose deep down I always knew what he was after. But I let it go on—far longer than I should have—because I wanted to understand."

"Understand what?"

"What it felt like. To be what he was." He leaned back against the counter and stared down at her. "You were the only thing he couldn't have. Probably the first woman in his life that turned him down. Which is why he wanted you so badly."

Gwenan Haines

Mia hated hearing Mike's name on Caleb's lips. She hated the way he'd put her rejection of him under a spotlight, as if it pleased him. "I cared about Mike. How many people would say the same about you?"

"No one." He crossed to the chalkboard and ran a finger down its center, smearing several equations. "Too bad he didn't have the brains to accomplish what he wanted. He was trying so hard to come up with a vaccine. All those months when he was supposed to be out on his beloved boat, spent here, in this excuse for a lab. All the research, all the time, all the materials stolen from the Institute. All for nothing, in the end. He just wasn't smart enough. That's really what it comes down to."

Mia remembered the samples she'd analyzed after Mike's death. The third slide with the virus—and the healthy cells. Maybe her partner had succeeded after all. She laughed and instantly regretted it. The pain sliced through her. "He had the brains to figure out what you were up to. And to get the virus away from you before you could sell it."

"As I said, a stupid mistake. I shouldn't have stored the stuff at the Institute. I mistakenly thought the place would be secure but I miscalculated your partner's dedication to saving the world. But as they say hindsight is twenty-twenty. And in the end, it didn't make any difference. Mike couldn't save himself. Or stop what's going to happen."

He picked up the metal briefcase lying on the table in front of the chalkboard and clicked it open. Lifting one of the vials from its padding, he turned toward her and held it out. "Care for a sample?"

"Is that meant to scare me?"

He set the sample back in place. "Your voice always gives you away. You try so hard to seem like the ice princess but your heart's in your voice. But don't worry, I have no intention of opening any of these here. They're needed elsewhere. And I don't plan on falling ill myself."

She smiled, willing him to drop the vial. How would he feel about the virus if he were the one dealing with its effects? "Better be careful."

"Oh, I will be." He inspected the contents a few more seconds then snapped the briefcase shut. "There's enough of the virus in here to wipe out the entire country. Which is exactly the plan. New York. Chicago. Boston. Houston. Los Angeles. One vial for every major city, to be released simultaneously."

A sense of despair settled over her. "When?"

He shrugged. "I don't know. My only role is to make the exchange. After that, it's out of my hands. As I believe I mentioned, I've got a one-way ticket to paradise."

"And everybody else can go to hell."

He picked up the briefcase and walked toward her. "Is it really going to be that much of a loss? Maybe a hundred years ago, or even fifty, this country was something to be proud of. But now? Shootings every day, kids who don't ever look up from their phones, people glued to their TVs twenty-four/seven. Nobody really cares about anybody more. Look around you, Mia."

"There will always be good in the world. And it won't stop in America. There are planes leaving those cities every hour of every day. How long do you think it'll be before the virus spreads beyond the U.S.? A day? An hour? What you're planning is insanity."

"True. I almost wish your friend had come up with a vaccine. I could have sold that as well. So I suppose it's unfortunate your friend was a bit of an idiot."

She turned her head away from him. Bad enough to have to listen to his mad spiel. Even worse to sit there and watch him gloat. "Why didn't you invent one yourself, seeing as it would have been so lucrative?"

"I was, actually. Well, we were, the two of us. We were getting close before your friend decided to go all Secret Agent on us. Ironic, isn't it—if it hadn't been for Mike, we might very well have invented a cure. Chien was so sure his vaccine might work he had a change of heart and decided to bring what he had to the CDC. Such a shame he never made it there."

"So you killed him too." The sense of impending doom she felt deepened with every secret Caleb told her. What Chien had done was horrific, but at least he'd tried to do the right thing in the end. If he'd made it to Georgia at least there would have been a chance to contain the virus. Without his work, the epidemic would ravage the country in a matter of weeks. Long before researchers could come up with a way to stop it.

To her surprise, Caleb didn't answer directly. "It doesn't matter who pulled the trigger. He's dead. And the sample vaccine he was planning on delivering mysteriously disappeared, along with the flash drive that laid out his research on it step by step. Though perhaps it might reappear at some point, who can say? Not that the NWA will use a vaccine for Americans. But the price would have been right. And somebody will invent a cure, of that I have no doubt. And they'll make a hell of a lot of money off it, too."

She turned back toward him, ignoring the pain it caused her. "Even if you're right—which you may not be—how many millions will have already died by the time it's put on the market?"

"Probably no more than died in the influenza epidemic. Definitely not more than died in the bubonic plague," he said. "Like most people, you can't see the larger picture. Individuals don't matter, Mia. Plagues happen for a reason—has that ever occurred to you? It's nature's way of cleaning up. Clearing out the old to make way for the new. If we wipe out all the corruption in this country, then we leave things open for a new kind of civilization."

"You're mad." There was no anger in her words. She'd passed rage. What she was feeling now was something else, something far worse. She could feel the resignation. She was giving up on herself, on everything.

His tone matched hers. "I believe you've already pointed that out. And if I am mad, then so is God. Ever heard the story of the flood? There was a boat in that story, too."

Caleb set the briefcase down just inside the door and walked back over to her. "Much as I've enjoyed our conversation, it's time for me to go. But I do so appreciate your help. Sure you won't change your mind and join the dark side? I hear Bali's wonderful at this time of year."

"I'd rather die."

He knelt and clamped his hand around her chin, pressing his lips to hers and forcing his tongue into her mouth. She flailed at his body with her bound arms but she was too weak to fight him off.

When he released her, she spit at his face. "Get away from me."

He wiped his cheek with the back of his hand. "Oh, I intend to. I wouldn't have taken you with me anyway, but I hoped to see you beg. Though I must say your defiance is even more exciting. Unfortunately, I've got a sale to make."

His voice was controlled but his eyes glittered with anger.

She didn't say anything. The sooner he left the better. She couldn't stop him, couldn't change his mind, couldn't call for help.

When it became clear she wasn't going to respond, he stood up and crossed to the generator. He picked up one of the gas cans and unscrewed the top. She watched him douse the bulletin boards, the tables, the chairs with gasoline. When he'd finished, he pulled out the files and scattered them across the floor, sprinkling the remains of the can onto them until the entire room reeked of gasoline.

She heard the flare of a match and looked up in time to see him hurl it onto the pile of manila at the center of the room. He lit another and walked over the bulletin board he'd pinned his photo onto. He held the match to the corner of the photo and watched as it caught. By the time he stepped back, the entire board was engulfed in flames. Smoke billowed across the room in dark waves and she struggled to free her wrists.

"Oh, that's right," he said as he backed away from the fire. "I almost forgot. How careless of me."

He strode across the room and quickly bound her feet. "Not that you're going anywhere. But I don't like to leave any *loose ends*."

Still smiling at his pun, he picked up his briefcase and crossed to the door.

With his hand on the knob, he pushed it open and stepped over the threshold.

"Bye bye, Mia."

****

The island lay below them, less than a mile away. Nick scanned its contours but they were still too far off for him to see anything besides an ever-shifting outline that seemed to dissolve in ghostly shadows. He raised his eyes and studied the horizon but saw no sign of the chopper that had taken off a few minutes before them.

Two agents sat behind him, armed and clad in bullet proof vests. He didn't need to tell them guns and vests wouldn't do much good if they stepped on an undetonated bomb. They knew it as well as he did.

"How long till we land?" he asked the pilot, raising his voice over the whirring of the blades.

"Five minutes, maybe six." The pilot took them down ten feet or so. The storm had passed but the air was still rough. Nick's stomach flip-flopped. He'd never liked flying much.

"Radar pick up anything yet?" Nick asked.

"Not yet."

He leaned forward and peered into the fog. If only willing them to land would make it happen sooner. The skepticism in the pilot's voice had been muted, but it had been there all the same. He knew there'd been talk at the bureau about him. He didn't want to know the specifics but he had a pretty good idea what people were saying.

Had Dalton used his name when he requested the teams be sent to Bloodsworth? Surely, he must have,

343

though he was certain his friend hadn't mentioned Nick's reason for picking that island.

A damn parrot. Maybe he was as nuts as the rumors claimed he was.

Well, they'd find out soon enough.

A light appeared before them. The first chopper. He watched as it began its descent toward the beach below. They were close enough now for him to see the contours of the island. Shrub pines and brush appeared and disappeared into the fog that shrouded the abandoned military facility.

What if he was wrong?

What if Mia was halfway around the world? Or in another abandoned location? Or already dead.

The idea clutched at his heart. He couldn't lose her, not when he'd just found her. Couldn't imagine a world of empty days again. Before they'd taken off, Mia's boss had phoned to let the FBI know Caleb Hastings had apparently gone missing. A search of Hastings' place confirmed that his passport and other documents were not on the premises. And according to Eli, Hastings' bank account—which was strangely bloated—had been cleaned out the week before.

There was no indication of where Mia's colleague intended to go. Not even a hint of a destination. And no trace of any contacts with the NWA.

He'd been careful. But not careful enough.

Whatever was on Bloodsworth Island, Hastings needed to get hold of it before he left the country. And he'd brought Mia along for the ride. At least that's what Nick was hoping.

"Is that a boat?" Nick pointed toward a dark shape on the beach.

"Forget the boat," the pilot said. "Take a look to your left."

At the tip of the island, smoke billowed from a squat building not far from shore.

"How close can you get?" Nick asked.

"Close enough."

He gripped the sides of his seat as they plummeted toward the flames. They were about to land beside a burning building on an island full of unexploded bombs. Nick just hoped that for once luck was on his side.

****

Mia lay with her back against the wall as smoke filled the room. Above her, row after row of fluorescent lamps exploded, the pieces raining onto her. Flames licked at the bulletin boards, blackening the photos and maps Mike had so painstakingly put together over the past ten months.

Another few minutes and the entire contents of the room would be engulfed in flames. All that would remain would be a blackened cement building, an empty shell that may or may not be discovered.

Not that it would matter.

How long until Caleb made his sale? She wondered idly if the NWA would kill him too or if they'd honor their agreement and pay him the millions they'd promised.

Once they had the virus, they'd use it. Mia was sure of that. She tried to imagine the future but the scope of the plan defied imagination. City after city sickening and descending into chaos, millions dead, the country a skeleton of what it had been.

She was glad she wouldn't be alive to see it. Glad

to die there, alone and afraid, just like she'd always been. No goodbyes, no words, only darkness. Darkness at last.

The smoke burned her lungs, setting off a fit of coughing. Her eyes smarted as the beakers on the far side of the lab burst and sent their fumes into the air. All around her, tables and chairs were catching fire.

Her skin felt hot, so hot. Her whole body was covered in sweat, the inside of her throat burning up. She closed her eyes.

How long until it was over?

Not long now. It won't be long.

Her sister's voice was close, a whisper in her ear, nothing more. High and light and free from worry, the voice of a child.

"Holly." Mia's own voice was a rasp, the name painful to say.

Don't try to talk. Lay your head on the floor. It's cooler.

Mia collapsed onto her side and lay with her cheek pressed against the cement. Her hair fell across her face but it didn't matter. Nothing mattered.

Holly was with her. At last.

"I'm…sorry."

Shhhhh. The voice was so beautiful. Just like Holly. She felt a hand on her cheek, against her hair. So cool, so cool, the slender fingers. *We'll be together again. I'll watch over you.*

"I—was—the—one—" She couldn't finish her sentence, her thought. *My fault.* She tried to form the words but another fit of coughing stopped her.

Shhhh. Not long now.

She lay still on her side, the cool hand stroking her

hair, taking away all the pain. Behind her eyelids, colors flared and faded, forming patterns that flowed together like a watercolor painting. She was thirteen again and they were walking to the park, Holly sprinting ahead with her hair flying out behind her. Sunlight all around them, around her, as she ran ahead, not looking back, never looking back.

"Holly!" she cried after her retreating form.

Holly didn't look back. The light on her hair brightening, everything brightening, so bright it blinded her.

Wait. Wait.

Smaller and smaller.

Don't go! Don't leave me!

Mia felt her body being lifted, rising through the heat and the smoke. Strong arms carrying her through the flames into darkness, cool air. Warm hands pushing her hair away, warm lips against hers, warm air filling her lungs.

When she opened her eyes, Nick was bent over her, his hands balled in a fist on her chest. She coughed once, twice. Tried to rise onto her elbows.

"Hurts," she said, still coughing.

"Sorry about the ribs. I didn't have a choice."

He leaned down toward her and slid his arm around her so that she was sitting up with her head against his chest. She realized her arms and legs were free and wondered when he'd cut the tape. How long had she been unconscious?

Twenty yards away, flames escaped through broken windows of the building that had been Mike's lab. The air smelt of smoke and chemicals, blotting out the clean scent of the salty ocean air. She'd expected to die there.

Holly. Holly had been there with her. Protecting her. She'd heard her, felt her.

Mia pushed the thought away. Too much pain. Too soon. "Caleb. He's got the virus. You have to—"

"Not for long." In the distance she could see dark forms sprinting toward the trees, fading into the fog.

"If it breaks—the men—" She tried to find the words to explain the danger and failed. Her mind wasn't working right, everything was happening in slow motion.

"We can't worry about that right now. We need to get out of here. God only knows what's underneath this place. Do you think you can walk?"

"No."

"Okay." He lifted her into his arms and cradled her body against him. They'd reached the end of the path when shouting echoed toward them from the woods. Mia looked up in time to see a pillar of fire shoot upward into the night. The ground shook and the sound of an explosion split the silence. Nick threw his body over her as they fell, shielding her from the rain of debris that covered them.

The shaking stopped. Mia opened her eyes. Nick was speaking to her—she knew that because his lips were moving—but she couldn't hear him.

"What happened?" she asked but no sound came out of her mouth.

Stumbling to his feet, he lifted her into his arms and touched his lips to her forehead. He mouthed something to her but she couldn't understand him.

Epilogue

Mia stepped into Seahaven's lobby and searched for her mother without finding her. Morning light fell through the windows, making the place look more like a posh hotel than a rehabilitation facility. It was Sunday and several patients stood with their families, exchanging hugs and goodbyes.

She'd only walked from the parking lot, but it took her a few minutes to catch her breath. Beneath the medical tape, her ribs ached. She knew she should have sent somebody else to pick up her mother but not one of Angela's many friends had been available. And Mia couldn't stand to think of her mother riding home alone.

She wondered who had brought her mother a month ago. Somehow Mia couldn't picture her stepfather exchanging farewell hugs with Angela. But then again, she couldn't fault him when she hadn't even bothered to call her mother to wish her luck. She'd been to see her mother twice over the past week but that was the first time she'd made an effort in years.

Her mother had made it through the thirty-day program without falling off the wagon. It wasn't much, but Angela's time at Seahaven was the longest Mia could remember her mother going without a drink. The question, she supposed, was whether or not her mother could stay off the booze in the real world.

The doors pushed open and she smiled at Nick as

he crossed the lobby toward her. Several of the women cast curious glances in his direction, perhaps wondering which category he fell into: patient or visitor.

At his own insistence, he'd gone back after the events at Bloodsworth Island and made up for the time he'd missed.

The FBI had been willing to let him off the hook. Apparently the fact that he'd saved the world convinced them he was ready to return to work. But to her surprise, he'd put that off too. He would go back—she had no doubt about that—but not until the full two months had expired. She couldn't imagine what he planned to do with himself but she liked that about him. She could predict the behavior of most specimens she studied but Nick Doyle defied expectation.

No, not defied it. Surpassed it. At her insistence, he'd returned to rehab immediately, even though it meant he hadn't been able to visit her at the hospital. He hadn't been happy about that, but she'd finally convinced him that her injuries weren't all that serious. Which they weren't. Aside from a few broken ribs, some minor burns and badly singed hair, she'd escaped the fire unscathed. She'd gotten lucky—in more ways than one.

She hoped things between her and Nick wouldn't change now that they were both back in the "real world." She'd gotten far too used to him being a part of her life. She'd thought losing her position on Trask's unit was the end of her world—because her job had been her world. Aside from Dante, it was all she had.

Funny, now that the truth about Caleb had come out and Trask had reinstated her, the job didn't seem quite as important. She would always love her work.

Research was a passion she wouldn't willingly part with. But the past few weeks had helped her realize she was more than a scientist.

When Nick reached her, he wrapped her in his arms but was careful not to hold her too tightly. He pushed a strand of her newly shorn hair behind her ear. The affection still felt a little unsettling—how many years had she spent pushing people away—but she was getting used to it.

She smiled up at him. "Need a ride?"

"As a matter of fact, I do." He planted a kiss on the tip of her nose. "Know anybody who can help me out?"

"I'm here for somebody else, but I've got an extra seat. As long as you don't want to ride shotgun."

"I guess I'll have to settle."

She stood on tiptoe and touched her lips to his just at the moment her mother appeared in the entry way, two overstuffed suitcases on either side of her. Her hair had been pulled into a chignon and her sleeveless dress hung loosely on her. Even apart from the weight loss, she looked good. Happy. The word came as a bit of a shock to Mia. Her mother always looked beautiful but how long had it been since her smile had seemed genuine?

Funny too, that both Nick and Angela were scheduled for departure on the same day. And that both of them seemed to be getting along better than she could have imagined.

"Sweetheart," Angela hurried toward her and planted a sticky lipstick kiss on both cheeks. "So wonderful to see you."

"I seem to be pretty popular all of a sudden." Mia stepped back and felt Nick's arm encircle her.

Her mother eyed Mia's mid-section doubtfully. "How are you feeling? Do you want me to drive?"

Strange too, to hear her mother asking about her health. "I'm okay."

"I still think I should drive," Angela said briskly. "I insist."

"All right. If you insist." Mia didn't have the energy to resist. She still hadn't quite caught her breath. And she was working on suppressing her need to control everything. Just a little.

"Need any help with that, Angie?" Nick asked.

Angie. That was new. In thirty years, Mia had never once heard her mother referred to as Angie. Or even thought of her as Angie. Well, leave it to Nick to bring out the casual side to her.

"I sure do." Angela linked arms with Nick and gave him a wink, much to the dismay of her newfound companion. "C'mon, let's get the hell out of this place!"

Mia suppressed a smile. Next thing she knew her mother would be drinking beer instead of Chianti. Or not drinking at all.

She hoped so. She hoped Seahaven would do what all the years of therapy and AA groups hadn't. It seemed hard to believe that a month could work that kind of miracle. But after her escape from Bloodsworth Island, she'd started to rethink her ideas about the miraculous.

"I'd love to take you up on that offer," Nick said. "But there are a few people I need to say goodbye to first."

The group of them stood in a ragged circle at the other end of the lobby. To her surprise, Callie Jackson was the first to step forward and wrap Nick in a bear hug. When she finally released him, Justin Sands held out his hand and gave hers a firm shake. Nargeeta was close behind him, as were a few of the others. Mia recognized a mother and her daughter who'd been staying there, as well as an elderly man leaning on a cane. Some faces were new, others missing. Mia wondered if they'd finished the program or had dropped out.

She felt a hand on her shoulder and turned to see Father Donelan at her side. His wild auburn hair was combed neatly back, making him seem more subdued than usual. But his blue eyes shone when he looked around the lobby.

"Thank you," she said to him.

"For your mother? Or Nick?"

"Both."

"It's them you should thank. They're the ones who did the work."

She nodded. He was right, of course. "But you gave them a place to heal."

"I'm not the only one who's helped with the healing process." To her surprise, he winked. "Hopefully the two of you will have a lot more time now to…heal."

"I hope so too," she said, her cheeks suddenly hot.

"What are you two talking about?" Nick asked, appearing at her side. "You're not propositioning her, are you?"

"Quite the opposite," Angela said. "He was giving you two his blessing."

Nick turned to Donelan and held out his hand. "I can't thank you enough."

When the priest released his hand, he said, "I hope this won't be the last I see of you."

"You're not saying you expect me back?"

Donelan laughed. "Only as a guest speaker. If you'd consider it."

Nick hesitated. "I don't know. I'm still feeling my way through all this. But down the road, why not?"

"I'm sorry I couldn't give you what you needed when you came to me that day. I hope you understand."

"I do. I'm not sure if I buy into what you said about all of us fulfilling our destinies but I respect your devotion to the patients—you did your best to protect Liam. And you stayed true to yourself and your beliefs. That's the best any of us can do."

"Well, you certainly fulfilled your destiny. Thank the Lord for that." As if to emphasize his point, Donelan made the sign of the cross.

"Amen," said Angela. Though most of the incident had been kept out of the news, several versions of the story had leaked out into the press anyway. Mia wondered if she would ever tell her mother the whole story.

"Mia had something to do with it, too," Nick said.

"Yes, yes, of course," Donelan agreed. "We all had our part to play."

Mia stayed silent. She would be forever grateful to Donelan for Seahaven, but she still hadn't quite forgiven him for withholding what he knew about Liam Gallagher from Nick and the police. Several witnesses had corroborated Callie Jackson's story about someone being in Nick's room and others had seen Donelan walking the grounds with an unfamiliar man later that night.

Had it been Gallagher, seeking the priest's counsel after he searched Nick's room? If so, how much had the former CIA agent told Donelan?

They would probably never know for sure. Because Donelan wasn't talking. The only thing he'd admitted to was enrolling Gallagher as a rehab patient back in 2005 and again a year earlier, shortly after the incident in Siberia.

Nick had his own theory about that late-night meeting between Donelan and Gallagher—and about his own conversations with the former priest. He was convinced that it was Donelan, with his remarks about Seahaven being allied with the military, who had intentionally directed him to search for a link between the men in Brendon Thompson's platoon and Seahaven. He was sure Gallagher had opened up to the former priest about Thompson's horrific death at the hands of the NWA and about his "work" for the CIA. Not only that, Nick believed Gallagher had even told Donelan his suspicions about the Institute. The priest couldn't break his vow of silence, but he could drop enough hints to set Nick off on the right track. He also believed Donelan didn't bring in the authorities because he knew that Gallagher—though his methods were reprehensible—was working to prevent a catastrophe.

That was Nick's theory, anyway. Mia wasn't sure what to believe.

She would probably never know the full story about Donelan and she had to accept that. And she had to be grateful to him for what Seahaven had accomplished with Nick and her mother. Anything beyond that was unsupportable—mere conjecture.

What had happened was in the past. What mattered

was the present. And the future. What mattered was that she was alive and the virus had been destroyed that night on the island when Caleb stumbled onto an undetonated bomb and incinerated himself along with the briefcase he'd been carrying. According to the CDC, there was no way any type of virus, no matter how resistant, could have survived an explosion of that magnitude.

No more cases of the virus had surfaced after Aniak and the documents they'd found in Liam's mother's home, along with the contents of Caleb's place and CIA files Eli had hacked into, suggested that Caleb had been telling Mia the truth. Both Siberia and Aniak had been demonstrations. Caleb's passport bore stamps that coincided with the Siberian outbreak and Mia had little doubt the current investigation would put him somewhere in Alaska shortly before the Aniak outbreak.

If her guess was right, no one at the NWA had access to the virus at any point. It would have been too much of a risk for Caleb; if they could reproduce the sample, he'd never get his money. The contents of Mike's makeshift lab on Bloodsworth Island, however, had been totally destroyed the night of the fire. All those months of work gone. Mia tried not to think of it. She still hadn't processed Mike's death, hadn't fully accepted her partner was gone. Maybe one day she would.

In the meantime, she'd start working on a new Ebola vaccine. All she had to guide her were the three samples Mike had brought to the lab, samples she now realized had to contain the airborne strain of Ebola from Siberia. Two with cells blown apart by the virus and the third undamaged slide where the virus had been immobilized. She'd torn the lab at IRID apart in search of the vaccine she suspected Mike had been working on but come up with nothing. No more samples, no notes and certainly no vaccine. Whatever Mike had succeeded in creating had probably burned along with everything else in the lab on Bloodsworth. But that didn't mean she couldn't keep trying. More than 28,000 people had died in the most recent outbreak of the non-engineered strain of Ebola. Surely, the third slide could help her begin to find a remedy.

Whenever she got a new partner, that is. For once Trask was letting make the decision. But that was another thing she wasn't ready to think about yet.

She wouldn't ever fully understand what had happened to her in those final moments before she blacked out on Bloodsworth Island. Had Holly really been there, watching over her? Or was it all some kind of fantasy, a side effect of the fumes that had filled the room? Even the voice she'd heard at Nailini's place could be explained away. Sleep deprivation and intense stress often result in auditory hallucinations. There was nothing unusual about it all, if she looked at the situation as a scientist.

But she couldn't look at it solely as a scientist. She was a sister too. Holly might be dead but the connection between them was unbreakable, whether her sister existed in spirit form or not. Maybe someday she would find out. But for once she was content to let the moments with Holly simply be.

For once, she wasn't going to put her experience under a microscope.

Maybe that was the best way to live, anyway. To

accept that life wasn't something you could ever understand, at least not fully.

With a start, Mia realized her mother had just asked her a question.

"Sure," she said firmly. "Absolutely." Whatever she'd agreed to, she hoped it wouldn't be too unpleasant.

"Great then. It's a date. Next Tuesday at nine sharp."

From the bemused look on Nick's face, she knew whatever she'd gotten roped into was going to be terribly unpleasant.

"It's time you do something with that hair. If you want to grow it out, fine, but that doesn't mean you need to spend the next six months looking like an escaped prisoner. You'd look gorgeous in a pixie cut, and my stylist would kill to expose those features. Now that I'm on the wagon, I've got to find something to fill my days."

Mia bit back a reply. Her mother meant well. That was the main thing. Anyway, it served her right for not paying attention. "Actually, uh, I'll need to check my calendar."

Angela smirked. Mia would have to wait to find out if her mother had been teasing her. Unless she could come up with an excuse before then. Like a new super virus to analyze.

Nick raised a hand to Mia's choppy, slightly singed hair. "I think she's beautiful the way she is."

"And that's why I like you." Her mother made a *tsking* sound with her mouth and stepped forward with her bags. "All right, enough sentiment. I've never liked goodbyes. Nick? Is your offer still good?"

He leaned down and picked both of the overstuffed bags up off the linoleum. "You're right," he said, turning to Mia. "It's been what—six minutes?"

"Seven, actually," she corrected him.

She might be more affectionate, but she was still the same Mia. Obsessive, hyper-organized, logical to a fault. The only difference was she now had a guy in her life that she hadn't friend-zoned.

Which, she thought, wasn't bad. Wasn't bad at all.

With a final nod to Father Donelan, Nick headed for the lobby doors, flanked by her mother and two very large suitcases. Mia watched them go but didn't follow. On the other side of the glass windows, the sun shone across the landscaped grounds. She couldn't help thinking that, once she left the lobby, her life would never be the same. Mia took a deep breath and tried to ignore the dull ache beneath the bandages. True to form, her mother sped across the lobby and burst out into the summer heat without looking behind her.

Finally free.

When he reached the revolving doors, Nick stopped and turned back toward the lobby. He flashed her a crooked smile as he stood with an overstuffed suitcase in each hand. The light fell across his rugged features, erasing the lines around his eyes and mouth. "You're not going to abandon me now, are you?"

"Not a chance." She shoved a strand of singed hair behind her ear, then hurried to catch up with him.

Author's Notes

Collateral Risk is the risk of loss arising from errors in the nature, quantity, pricing, or characteristics of collateral.

Bloodsworth Island is an actual island located in the Chesapeake Bay. As Mia's search reveals, it is off limits to the public. I took some liberties with the terrain but the description of its use for military purposes, as well as the dangers of unexploded ordnance, is taken verbatim from the Maryland State's description of the site.

Yoshihiro Kawaoka is a scientist at the University of Wisconsin. The particulars of the story referred to in this novel are accurate. In 2014, Kawaoka and others used genetic engineering in a college campus facility to create a virus that is only three percent different than the Spanish influenza virus. There is no known antidote to the genetically engineered virus.

I'm much indebted to the many authors who have written on this subject, especially Richard Preston, whose excellent books *The Hot Zone* and *Panic in Level IV* discuss deadly pathogens and give detailed descriptions of the scientists who work with them. Mia's incident with the Band-Aid is loosely based on an incident with a real scientist Preston interviewed in *The Hot Zone*.

A word about the author…

Gwenan Haines lives in New England with her daughter and a Siberian husky born on Halloween. She loves to travel and has visited Italy, Sweden, Pakistan, Germany, Russia, Greece and other countries. She collects old books, colored glass, and complicated recipes she can't actually make. You can follow her on Facebook or visit her blog at
http://gwenanhaines.blogspot.com.